To Don and Pat

I hope you

story. May it draw you

Closer to God and inspire

you to pray bold prayers

Alan W Harris

(I corinthians 15:58)

TALES OF LARKIN

HAWTHORN'S DISCOVERY

TALES OF LARKIN

HAWTHORN'S DISCOVERY

WRITTEN AND ILLUSTRATED
BY

ALAN W. HARRIS

[signature: Alan W. Harris]

---⊕---

Fruitful Tree Publishing
Lexington, South Carolina 29072

This book is published by:

Fruitful Tree Publishing
509 Aspen Glade Court
Lexington, South Carolina 29072
www.talesoflarkin.com

ISBN-13: 978-0-9773633-08
ISBN-10: 0-9773633-0-9

Library of Congress Catalog Card Number: 2005934330

Jacket cover illustration by Alan Harris
Enhanced by Mike Rudy and Deb Tremper

Jacket designed by Deb Tremper of Six-Penny Graphics

This book is lovingly dedicated to my wonderful wife, Valerie,
and
to the greatest fan club a man could ever have; my children:
Lisa,
Clint,
Natalie,
Mitch,
Juliana,
and Alec.

CONTENTS

List of illustrations

PREFACE:

The Story Behind the Story

My wife, Valerie, and I moved to Auburn, Alabama, shortly after we were married in August of 1975. She began working on her master's degree in clinical psychology, and I began taking a few needed courses to apply to veterinary school. In the fall of 1977, I entered Auburn University School of Veterinary Medicine. At that time the freshmen and sophomores in the vet school got their summers off, and I managed to get summer employment.

Whenever I had a little time to spare, I would spend it exploring the forest behind where we lived. Far back in the woods I found a creek with a small, three-step waterfall, the tallest of which was not over a foot in height. I could see a crack in the rock behind the uppermost fall, and I remember wishing that I could be one inch tall so that I could go explore that tiny opening in the rock behind that small waterfall. As my creative juices began to flow, the one-inch-tall race of people known as Larkin were born. I really was fascinated with the idea and spent the next two to three weeks using most of my spare time thinking about a story. We were just barely making ends meet at the time, so I couldn't afford to waste notebook paper. I began handwriting my story on the backs of my wife's old Psychology 101 exam sheets that she had kept from the class she was teaching. I was inspired, and in a few days I had written fifty pages of my tale.

At this point two things happened. First, my last two years of veterinary medical school started, which was to dominate and command every waking moment (and some non-waking ones) for the next two years of my life. The second thing that happened was that I discovered, in my zeal to tell a good story, that after writing fifty pages, I was still only at the beginning of this evolving saga. My little story was starting to take on epic proportions. Seeing how far I had to go to finish it and being overwhelmed with academic demands on my time, I bid a fond farewell to my literary endeavor. I stuffed all of my writing and notes in an old manila envelope that I pulled out of the waste can at work and filed them away.

It was at least five or six years later that I pulled the notes out again and tried to read it to my daughter, Lisa, and my son, Clint, when they were very young. They were quickly bored with it and asked if they could go play. I filed it away again.

Over ten years later, when Lisa was sixteen years old, Clint was thirteen, my daughter Natalie was ten, my son Mitch was two, and my next two children, Juliana and Alec, hadn't even been thought of yet, we were all sitting around in the den one night telling stories. We were having a great time, really connecting and enjoying one another. At one point we ran out of stories to tell, but we weren't ready to quit. That's when Lisa remembered my Larkin story.

"Whatever happened to that story you wrote, Daddy?" Lisa asked.

"Yeah," added Clint, jerking up from where he had been lying on the floor, "I remember that. It was about those little men."

"What story?! What story?!" Natalie wanted to know. "I've never heard about this!"

"But you and Clint didn't like it," I said.

"We were just kids then," responded Lisa.

"We'll like it now, Dad!" Clint said with enthusiasm. "We promise!"

"PLEASE READ IT, DADDY!!!"

So out it came again, the pages yellowing and the edges worn, and I began to read. As I did, the old excitement began to creep back over me. Without realizing it, I began doing voice characterizations for the different people in the story. The kids were very disappointed when it was bedtime and we had to stop. They made me promise to read some more to them the next night. We read Larkin every night for several days. When I read to the end of my fifty pages, I thought I was going to have a riot on my hands. The children were in a panic to find out what happened next. So, with that intense public demand, I pulled out the old pen and paper and started writing again. It was 1994.

The reason that I hand-wrote the story is because I started it in 1978, before the invention of the affordable personal computer, and since I didn't type very well, it was easier to just write by hand.

When I began to work on the story again, I was very busy being the sole practitioner and owner of a veterinary clinic that I was trying to grow, as well as being a husband and a father to my growing family. In addition I had a lot of church obligations and responsibilities. I had very little time to write, but I managed to work on it a little bit here and there. I went back and added fifty more pages to the middle of what I had already written and then took up the story again.

As I would finish writing a chapter, which would take several weeks or even several months from the last reading, we would stage a big family celebration. On the soonest possible weekend evening, we would have a special meal, and after cleaning up the dishes, the family would settle in the den where we would review what had happened the last time we read. When we were all together on the story, then I would read the new chapter. The children were so enthusiastic and encouraging that I had to keep writing. We kept this up for seven years--even after Lisa and Clint went away to college. Whenever we would talk with them on the phone, at some point they would always ask how "Larkin" was coming along. When I finally did finish a chapter, I was forbidden to read it to anyone until Lisa and Clint could come home for the whole family "premier" reading. Those were such fun evenings! Our family was really bonded together by these exclusively "Harris" events.

On one of her breaks from school, Lisa said that I needed more "girl heroes" in the story.

"What do you suggest?" I asked.

"Hmmm . . . I don't know," she responded, thinking hard. Finally, with a silly giggle, she offered, "How about Wanda, the Vine Woman?"

A short time later, I was able to finish another chapter and called another celebration. I had my story notes spread out on my desk as I was finishing it, and I noticed that Lisa had been messing with them, but I didn't think much about it. However, as I was reading the chapter to the family, I came to a particularly exciting part and read the penciled-in phrase ". . . and then Wanda swung in." Everyone jerked up and looked at me like I was crazy. I looked at Lisa, and she just put her hands over her mouth and started giggling. We still talk fondly of Wanda, the Vine Woman, although she hasn't made it into the official story yet.

I didn't want my story to be predictable and I did want it to be somewhat believable (for a tale about one inch tall people), so I decided that occasionally through the course of the narrative a selected character would meet a tragic end. I remember as I was reading to the kids, the first time in the story that one of the popular characters met his untimely demise that my

vii

kids got mad at me. In fact, they got so mad at me that they wouldn't speak to me for a couple of days. It took a lot of talking and "repenting" to get myself out of that hole.

Natalie was one of the most demanding of my "public". She constantly encouraged me to write, begged for the next chapter, discussed possible actions of the various characters, etc. Whenever she would get suspicious that I might be thinking of "bumping off" a character in the story that she liked, she would begin this intense lobbying campaign to save his life. If you talk to her, she will take credit for saving the lives of several of them. Had it not been for her insistence and persistence, the story probably would not have progressed as it did.

It took seven years of writing to finally complete the story, which took place at eleven p.m., March 12th, 2002. It was enormously satisfying to finally finish it, but it was also a little sad to know that all of those family "chapter celebrations" would come to an end.

At this point I began the enormous task—for me—of typing five hundred hand-written pages into the computer. As before, I only had small bits of time to work on it. By November of 2002, I had about half of it typed in. Lisa, Clint, Natalie, and Valerie all volunteered to type in a certain number of chapters each, which they did for me as an early Christmas present. With their help it was all typed in quickly. Then began the next huge task of corrections and editing.

Because of her love for me and her intense commitment to helping me be successful in anything that I have set my hand to do, my wonderful wife, Valerie, volunteered to edit the manuscript. After thirteen years of home schooling our children and grading countless English papers, reports, and essays, I figured that she was amply qualified. She labored over this story for hours and hours and hours and . . . Well, you get the idea. I can not thank her enough for the tremendous amount of work she did turning my story into something much more readable, as well as keeping me from looking like an ignorant savage with all my spelling and punctuation errors.

"Thank you, Sweetheart. You are wonderful!"

Obviously, all of my family has had a big influence over the writing of this story. I would never have finished it if it had not been for the enthusiastic support and encouragement of my children.

It is my sincere hope and prayer that not only many others enjoy the story, but also that each reader and hearer be drawn closer to the Lord Jesus Christ. I hope that as you read this tale that you will receive a vision of what your life, your family, and your community could be like if you trusted Jesus enough to be the controlling influence of every aspect of that life. I hope that your prayers become much more frequent and much more fervent, and that you spend more time faithfully waiting on God's answers to those prayers rather than taking charge and working it out yourself.

May God raise up an army of believers who will faithfully submit to the leading of King Jesus in everything, so that the uncovered glory of the Son of God will be clearly seen on this earth through the lives of those who let Him live through them.

Alan W. Harris
Lexington, South Carolina
June 5, 2005

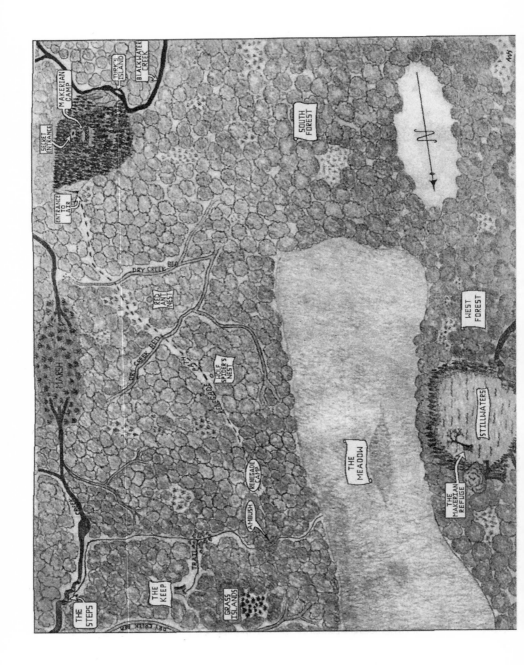

CHAPTER ONE

THE KEEP

Slowly, ever so slowly, the impenetrable blackness began to lighten. The secret, hidden things of the night began to retreat with the darkness. At first it always seemed as if his eyes were playing tricks on him, but within a moment or two his mind was reassured, as darkness merged with dimness and dimness cleared, that indeed another glorious morning had come. It was this way each time he stood the third watch. Viewing the birth of a new day never failed to stir his heart. Wondering how many of the seven others on watch were sharing his feelings, he guessed that their thoughts were probably all lost in the anticipation of a hot meal. His stomach was growling too, but right now his eyes were feasting on the glories that the Maker had placed here for all to see.

Such were the thoughts of Hawthorn, son of Savin and Rose of the Third Clan of Larkin. He was a member of a race of people whose existence was unknown to humans. There were several good reasons why man was not aware of these people, one being that they lived their lives in the deep woods and glades where few men ever walked. They were also a people who were masters of wood lore, and when they desired not to be seen, heard, or smelled, they were not—at least not by the dulled senses of humans. But the primary reason that the Larkin remained undiscovered was their size. By man's measure, the largest of these people were not over one inch tall.

They called themselves *Larkin* as man would call himself *man*. Their name came from a great leader in their past. He, Larkin, was literally the father of this people. Larkin had had seven sons, and the descendants of his sons made of this people. Larkin had had seven sons, and the descendants of his sons made up the clans of Larkin. Hawthorn was a member of the Third Clan, which meant that he was descended from Larkin's third son.

There were presently four hundred thirty-six Larkin in the Third Clan, only seventy-three of whom were seasoned hunters. But there was a good crop of young Larkin coming along, and soon the number of capable hunters for the clan would increase.

If man were present viewing the scene as Hawthorn saw it, he would see the golden light of the sun sending its searching rays through a broad expanse of oak, hickory, sweet gum, and poplar trees. Interspersed among these was an occasional pine or cedar. Below the trees could be seen sparse thickets of huckleberries, myrtles, saw briers, and wild grapes. Below these were the grasses, sages, mosses, and lichens. In the midst of all this natural beauty protruded a large cedar stump that was nearly four feet tall and three feet in diameter at the base. It was from the top of this stump that Hawthorn and his seven companions watched as the new day unfolded before them, for this was the Keep, the home and fortress of the Third Clan of Larkin.

As Hawthorn stood on the watch deck of the Keep, leaning on his lance and watching the rising sun, he was startled by a sudden booming noise coming up from underneath the deck on which he stood. He realized that old Charlock, who was in charge of the last watch, had descended the steps from the watch deck to the next level and was slowly pounding on a large, wooden drum, sending its deep tones vibrating into the lower levels of the Keep. This was to awaken the rest of the clan, letting them know that morning had arrived. As those below began to stir from their sleep, they listened intently to the deep, booming sounds for the message they contained. By the way in which Charlock pounded the long, hollowed log, each one who heard knew not only that the sun was climbing into the sky, but also that the morning was clear and that there was no threat of bad weather—at least not for the present.

As the noise below his feet ceased, Hawthorn continued to watch the east. The sun was clear of the earth now, though still partially obscured by the tall trees. Hawthorn's gaze left the sunrise, and he began to scan the forest and thickets around the Keep. The living things of the day started to move from under rocks and patches of grass. The birds commenced their beautiful, morning songs. The flying insects also lent their own hums and buzzing to the scene, seeming occasionally to add harmony to the choruses of the birds. Hawthorn felt like joining the birds in their morning songs, and he might even have done so were it not for the presence of the others around him.

2

"Hawthorn!" barked a raspy voice from the opposite side of the watch deck. "Present yourself!"

"Yes, sir!" returned Hawthorn as he hastened over to see what Charlock wanted to say to him.

Charlock was standing near the cedar wall on the northwest side of the fortress, and beside him stood a young Larkin of about sixteen seasons. This youth was dressed very much like Hawthorn. He wore a long sleeved, light brown tunic of tanned animal hide which came to the middle of his thighs. He also wore leggings made of the same material. These leggings disappeared into a pair of dark brown leather boots that extended up his legs and were cuffed back down to just below his knees. At his waist was a dark brown leather belt. Draped across his shoulders was a green, hooded hunting cloak that was held in place by a pair of thongs tied around his neck. On his head was a helmet made from an acorn cap which was carved and sized to fit him. He leaned against a tall lance, the wooden shaft of which extended well above his head and ended in a large, narrowly tapered, shiny black lance head that had been made from the largest of the thorns of the black locust tree. This young Larkin was named Poke. He and Hawthorn had grown up together and were good friends.

As Hawthorn approached Charlock and Poke, he couldn't help comparing the smooth, youthful face of his friend with the heavily bearded and deeply creased features of old Charlock. Charlock was almost a legend to Hawthorn. He wondered how many great acts of bravery this old warrior had accomplished. Hawthorn was sure that there were many that no one would ever hear about, because Charlock never spoke of his own deeds.

"Hawthorn to serve you," he said as he respectfully stood before the watch master. Charlock began to speak to them in short, gruff phrases, emphasizing the seriousness and importance of standing the watch.

"While on watch you must never forget your duties . . ." Poke and Hawthorn had heard this lecture several times before in the past twenty days that they had been on watch duty, but out of respect for the old warrior, they would listen again.

After reaching the age of sixteen seasons and having gone through much instruction under the direction of the clan wise ones called Shaman, the young Larkin were allowed tours of duty in the various activities of protecting and providing for the clan. This training gave the young Larkin opportunity for growing in responsibility, maturity, and experience.

"I have spoken to the Shaman about both of you," Charlock continued. Poke and Hawthorn both stiffened in apprehension of what might be coming next. "I told them that you both were doing very well in your work, that you

3

CHARLOCK AND POKE

were taking on more responsibility with each watch, and that I was proud of both of you."

Hawthorn and his friend looked at each other in amazement. Charlock had never said anything like this to them before. The kind words were so unlike the rough exterior that Charlock always presented.

"They have agreed with me," Charlock continued, "that it is time for you to learn the ways of the Larkin hunter. To do this, you must first learn to make and use the weapons of a hunter. Your instruction begins this afternoon. I will be at the gate right after midday. You will both meet me there at that time, and you will bring your cutting flints. Is all that clear?"

Both of the young Larkin nodded their heads, their eyes wide and their mouths slightly open in an expression of complete surprise. They could not believe their ears. Not only had Charlock praised them, but they were actually going to become hunters!

"The Larkin are arriving to take the day watch," Charlock was saying. "Your duty is finished here. Why don't you two go and get something to eat, and I'm sure you both have chores to do before midday."

"Y-y-yes, sir. Of course, sir . . . uh, thank you, sir!" The two youths tried to swallow the excitement that was charging through them. Standing tall and proud and trying to appear confident, both inclined their heads respectfully to the watch master. Then they turned and, with measured steps, walked over to the opening in the floor and descended the steps that led to the level below.

Charlock watched his two apprentices as they descended into the darkness below with their chests stuck out and heads thrown back. His cheeks rose slightly, and a low chuckle came from the depths of his thick gray beard. A few moments later, a shriek of delighted excitement and youthful laughter exploded from the level below. At this sound, all of those on the watch deck looked at each other and joined in the laughter. Old Charlock rolled his eyes and shook his head. Everyone on the watch knew that this was, indeed, a great day for these two young Larkin. All of them had, at one time, shared in the same excitement.

The level below the watch deck was one large room and was called the watch chamber. Against the walls, placed neatly in stands or hanging on pegs, was a large collection of weapons for use in defending the Keep. There were lances, throwing spears, bows, quivers of arrows, shields, and the long, piercing swords made from prickly pear thorns that the Larkin called stings. In the center of the floor stood the long, hollowed drum by which messages were sent through the Keep. It was beside the great drum that Hawthorn and Poke stood laughing and slapping each other on the back.

"What do you think Charlock will teach us first, Thorn," Poke asked, "throwing spear, bow and arrow, or sting and shield?"

"I don't know," Hawthorn returned, "but I think I'd like to learn the sting and shield first."

"So would I," Poke agreed.

As they discussed what might be involved in their training, they began to move toward the west side of the large chamber to the opening which led into the carved, slanting passageway that twisted and spiraled its way into the heart of the Keep. On entering this passage, the smell of cedar became stronger, emanating from the walls which were close on either side. The two friends paused for a few moments to let their eyes adjust to the darkness. They made their way down the winding passageway at a reasonably moderate pace for two excited young Larkin. The passage was lit by an occasional box lantern made of thin, transparent sheets of mica. Inside the mica box was a small lamp that burned plant oils and resins for fuel. As Hawthorn and Poke made their way further down the passage, they ritualistically looked at each lantern that they passed. From their childhood all Larkin were taught to respect what fire could do, both to the Keep and to the world around them. Every Larkin, young or old, was taught to examine each flame that they passed in order to prevent a disaster, especially within the confines of the wooden Keep.

Descending further into the maze of passages and chambers, they began to smell the aromas of various foods being prepared and to hear the sounds of people moving through the Keep to do their morning chores. Drawing up next to a side passage that led into the sixth level living chambers, Hawthorn turned to Poke. They both stood there for a moment just grinning at each other, then Poke reached out a hand and laid it on Hawthorn's shoulder. "Remember, Thorn, midday at the gate!"

"I'll see you then," returned Hawthorn, "and don't forget your flint!"

"Right!" grinned Poke as he turned and made his way quickly down the passage to the lower levels.

Hawthorn watched his friend disappear down the dark passageway, then he turned and darted into the side passage leading to his family's living chambers. He had very exciting news to share!

There was only one entrance to the Keep. The gate was located on the southern side of the great cedar stump and was formed by two large, carved oak doors which could be quickly drawn closed and bolted securely at the first sign of danger. There had been many times in the past few seasons that the only things that stood between the inhabitants of the Keep and certain death were the stout oak doors and the defenders on the walls. But today there was no threat of danger, and the gate was open. Posted by each of the two doors was a Larkin guard armed with sting and shield. A short distance beyond these guards were four more guards armed with lances and posted to protect the gate path that led between the outstretched roots of the big cedar stump.

Just inside the gate were two large, sealed casks made of wood, each of which was filled with a thick, black, foul smelling fluid. This fluid was an extract of a number of different plants and berries and, when spread on the ground in front of the gate, was a deadly poison to many of the insects that might attack the Larkin fortress

In the shadows next to one of these casks sat two forms. Hawthorn and Poke had both been sitting there for quite some time, Hawthorn having finished his chores in record time. Since he had nothing else to do, he decided to go on down to the gate and wait for midday to arrive. When he got there, he found Poke waiting for him. It wasn't long before they were discussing the skills that they would soon develop as Larkin hunters. Each time someone approached, they would stop mid sentence to see who was coming. They greeted each one who came by respectfully, but then, not seeing their teacher, the two boys would continue their discussion. For the ninth time the two friends gazed into the shadows toward the sound of approaching footfalls. This time they saw the bearded figure of Charlock materialize out of the darkness of the inner passageway, and both boys quickly jumped to their feet.

The old warrior walked over to them, his stern eyes gazing at them beneath thick, bushy brows. "Do you have your flints?" he rasped.

Both answered, "Yes, sir!"

His eyes seemed to soften and a rough sort of pleasantness spread across his features. "Well, come on. If I'm to make hunters out of you two, we'd best begin."

Hawthorn and Poke smiled at each other as they followed Charlock through the gate and out into the sunlight. Charlock nodded a greeting to each of the guards that they passed. As the three reached the end of the gate path, Charlock walked over to one of the older-looking warriors who was obviously the watch master in charge of this particular company of guards. After talking with him for a few moments, Charlock returned to his two students.

"I have just spoken with Hickory, the watch master. There has been no sign of enemies today, and it looks as though this good weather the Maker has given us will hold. I have also told the watch master where we will be going and when we intend to return. If we have not returned by that time, scouts will be sent to find us. You will both, from this day forward, always check with the watch master at the gate when leaving and entering the Keep."

They both nodded understandingly. Charlock then turned and led them off to the west.

They had quite a busy afternoon. As the three of them made their way through thickets, grasses, and leaves, Charlock would lapse into a lecture on the lore of weaponry. The old warrior's two younger companions hung on every word he spoke. Twice Poke fell flat on his face due to paying more attention to what was said rather than where he put his feet.

Charlock halted his lecture and the procession before a small patch of prickly pear cactus. With his right hand, Charlock drew the long, tapered sting from its sheath at his waist. He held it before him so that Poke and Hawthorn could examine the long, slender weapon. "You both will become proficient with all the Larkin weapons, but, more than anything else, your life and the safety of the clan will depend on your skill with a sting."

Charlock spoke briefly on the advantages of using the long thorns of the prickly pear rather than those of other thorny plants like the black locust or wild pear. He also warned them about the small, insignificant-looking spines located at the base of each of the rapier like thorns. The selection of a thorn with the proper length and weight was worthy of careful thought. Once the decision was made and the coveted thorn carefully removed, there remained the work of carving a handgrip and pommel on the base. This last work had to be done slowly so as not to ruin the natural balance of the thorn. Finally the handgrip was wrapped with a heavy leather strip to provide a good gripping surface and a bit more weight at the base of the sting.

There was only opportunity for a little practical instruction before it was time for them to return to the Keep, but in the days that followed, there were many hours of teaching and much diligent practice by the two young Larkin. They were both eager to learn, and Charlock taught them much. Within a few weeks their ability with a sting was deadly. To improve their skill Charlock had his two students stand with their stings ready. Then he took small, green huckleberries about the size of his fist and tossed these at Poke and Hawthorn. They protected themselves by quickly spearing these small berries as they came flying at them. Occasionally one of the projectiles would get through, thudding solidly against the chest or head of a slightly humbled young Larkin. But as the days passed, fewer and fewer of the small berries got past the points of those two stings.

Charlock also taught them to make bows of hickory wood and bow strings from the silken threads of cocoons. Arrows were made by using willow splints for the shafts. Thorns from the saw brier were then fire-hardened to make arrowheads. They also learned to make throwing spears.

Although they practiced diligently with each of these weapons, Charlock did not let a day go by without working on their skill with the sting.

One warm summer day, a little before midday, Poke and Hawthorn were sitting just inside the gate in their usual place, waiting for Charlock.

"Did you hear about Burdock?" Poke was saying.

"I heard about that a few days ago," Hawthorn answered.

"What did you hear?" Poke asked slyly.

"Well, I heard that he was out with a food-gathering party near the meadow. Before they could make it back to the Keep that big storm blew up. Burdock slipped, falling into one of the streams, and was washed away."

"Is that all?!" Poke asked in amazement.

"I did hear some of the grownups say that if he didn't drown, then between the ants, the serpents, and the Renegades, he would never make it."

"Thunder and sky fire, Hawthorn!" Poke exclaimed. "You must live with your head in the ground! Haven't you heard?!"

"Heard what?" said Hawthorn as he began to get irritated with his companion.

"Burdock is alive, Thorn! He came back this morning."

Hawthorn instantly forgot Poke's chiding remarks and sat up, eagerly anticipating the telling of an exciting rescue. "That's great news! Where did they find him?"

"That's just it! Nobody found him. He walked right up to the gate this morning like someone who had just finished a nice stroll through the woods. Ha! I'll wager those guards dropped a jaw and bugged an eye when Burdock showed up right there at the gate of the Keep all by himself!"

"How did he survive?" Hawthorn asked thoughtfully. "He's only one season older than we are."

Poke dropped his gaze a little and shook his head slowly. "Don't know," he answered. "I did hear that he mentioned something about Renegades. You don't suppose he had to fight some of them, do you?"

Hawthorn was deep in his own thoughts and didn't hear the question. "You know, Poke, with all the search parties and Larkin scouts that have been out looking for him the past few days and nights, I can't understand how he could walk all that way through the woods right up to the very gate of the Keep without any Larkin seeing him."

"That is sort of hard to believe, isn't it?" mused Poke.

"Where is Burdock?" Hawthorn asked.

"Well, let's see . . ." Poke paused to reflect on what he had heard. "He was to spend the morning getting cleaned up, getting something to eat, and resting. At midday he was to report to the Shaman—HEY! Where are you going?"

"I'm leaving," Hawthorn said over his shoulder as he walked back into the Keep.

"Leaving? Charlock's gonna' be mad if you aren't here."

Hawthorn stopped and turned to face his confused companion. "Charlock is Burdock's uncle and has served as his guardian since Burdock's father died two seasons ago. It's midday now, so if Burdock is meeting with the Shaman, then Charlock has to be there, too, to represent the head of Burdock's family." A smile began to spread across Hawthorn's face as he said, "Poke, you must live with your head in the ground!"

Poke jumped up and laughingly chased Hawthorn down the dark hallway leading to the inner reaches of the Keep's first level. Hawthorn stopped suddenly and turned on Poke in the dark hallway. They began to wrestle with each other, but that soon deteriorated as they both fell, sprawling on the floor, laughing ridiculously.

"I know exactly what I want to do," Poke said after finally gaining control of himself. "I'm going to finish working on the sheath for my sting. Come on, Thorn, I'll show you what it looks like." Poke jumped to his feet and beckoned to his friend to follow.

"I've got some things I need to do," Hawthorn said absently. Then quickly fixing his attention on Poke, he smiled and said, "I'll let you show it off for me when you get it finished."

"Oh, all right. Don't let the ants get you!" Poke jokingly exclaimed as he headed off down the dimly-lit passageway.

Hawthorn was still contemplating the mystery of it all as he made his way up the long, sloping passage that led to the Council Hall. There were many tales of heroic deeds done by young Larkin. It was even told that Charlock himself had had quite a few adventures as a youngster. But every way he looked at it, he kept coming up with the same questions. How could one young Larkin, essentially as young and inexperienced as himself, survive being swept away by a raging creek, pull himself out, and wander four days and nights in woods full of ants, serpents, dragons, spiders, shrews, Renegades—he had almost forgotten about the Renegades. There was no way that he could have fought off even a small band of those murdering cutthroats!

As Hawthorn reached the side passage which led to the Council Hall, he slowed his pace. He wasn't really sure what he was doing there, and he didn't want to have to try to explain it to the Shaman. Hawthorn carefully peered around the corner. The passage before him was illuminated by four lamps hanging on the walls, two on each side, right across from each other. Between the two on the right hand side was a highly polished, carved walnut bench which was used as a place of waiting for those summoned to meet with the Shaman. Between the two lamps on the left side were the large walnut doors which led to the Council Hall itself.

Since the passage was empty, Hawthorn pulled his head back around the corner and settled down in the shadows to think. He would have given a whole quiver full of arrows to know what was being said on the other side of those walnut doors right then. As it turned out, Hawthorn got to keep his arrows. At that moment the doors opened, and two figures walked out into the passageway. As Hawthorn again silently peered around the corner, he saw the slender form of Burdock slump exhaustedly onto the walnut bench. The other Larkin standing beside the tired young Larkin had his back to Hawthorn, but there was no mistaking that burly frame. Even at his age, Charlock was still quite powerfully built.

"Uncle, I don't understand!" Burdock was saying. "I've done nothing wrong, yet the Shaman treat me as if I'm on trial! Why do they ask me so many questions?!"

"You are young, my son," rasped Charlock. The husky voice seemed gentler than Hawthorn had ever heard it. "The Shaman only desire to know if you were harmed by the Renegades."

"But I told them what happened three times, and they still didn't seem to believe me!"

"Well, you have to admit, young one, that was a rather fantastic story you told."

Burdock looked up quickly at his uncle. "Then you don't believe me either?"

"Of course I believe you!" Charlock returned. "It just doesn't make sense. Ever since the first evildoer was banished from a Larkin clan and became a Renegade, they have been attacking and robbing our people. As you well know, it was a large band of Renegades who ambushed the Sixth Clan of Larkin eight seasons ago while they were traveling to the Steps for the Great Gathering. The Renegades killed many of our people that day. There have been five different times that I myself have had to fight the Renegades, barely escaping with my life on two occasions. So you see, Burdock, when you tell us that not only did the Renegades save you, but that they also fed you, cared for you, brought you safely to the very gate of the Keep, and then turned you loose—these things are very difficult for us to understand!"

"I don't understand it either, Uncle. But I also don't understand why the Shaman keep twisting my story around to make my rescuers look evil!"

"If they weren't evil, then they wouldn't be Renegades!" roared Charlock in a sudden burst of frustration.

There was silence in the hallway for a moment, then Charlock began to speak again, his voice low and gentle, "I'm sorry, Burdock. I'm not being a very good uncle to you. It's just that . . . well . . . it doesn't look like the Shaman are going to believe you, and I don't know how to help you."

Hawthorn was looking at Burdock while Charlock was talking. He seemed so tired as he sat slumped down on the bench. His chin rested on his chest, and he seemed to be staring at the floor. Hawthorn's gaze now went to the bulky figure of Charlock, who was pacing back and forth.

"I just can't understand it!" Charlock was saying more to himself than to Burdock. "For generations the Renegades have done nothing but great evil to our people."

"They may be evil, but they only showed me kindness," Burdock said, still staring at the floor.

After this there was another long period of silence. Then suddenly, as though he had just thought of something, Burdock raised his head, sat up, and said, "What if they weren't Renegades, Uncle?"

"What are you talking about, Burdock?" Charlock growled as his frustration began to build again.

"Listen. These people were different from us. Their clothing was different, their weapons were made differently, and they acted differently from any Larkin I've ever met. But they were also totally different from all that I've ever heard about the Renegades. I've always heard that Renegades wear horrible masks."

"That they do," added Charlock. "It's to put fear into those whom they are attacking."

"That's just it," continued Burdock. "None of my rescuers had any masks. I thought they were Larkin at first. Then they told me that they used to be Larkin but were not anymore. That was when I figured that they must be Renegades. But now I don't think so.

12

"They smiled and laughed a lot, but it wasn't an evil laugh. It was the kind of laugh that you hear from someone who is just happy. One of them always wanted to sing, but the others wouldn't let him because they might be discovered.

"The one who was obviously the leader seemed to be about your age, Uncle. He personally took care of me after two of the younger ones pulled me from the stream. He saw this large cut that I have on my arm, and I told him that it happened when I fell into the stream. He washed the wound and rubbed a thick salve on it, and the pain stopped almost immediately. I asked him what the salve was, and he said it was one of the Maker's secrets. It was this leader who told me that they used to be Larkin. He asked me what clan I was from, so I told him. When he found out I was from the Third Clan, he got excited and asked me about three or four different Larkin that he knew from this clan. One of them was you, Uncle."

"What?!" Charlock stiffened, his eyes getting wide under his thick, bushy brows.

"Yes," Burdock continued. "He wouldn't tell me his name, but he asked me a lot about the Second Clan of Larkin, so I figured that was his clan."

"Tell me, Burdock, what did he look like?"

Burdock thought for a moment. "He was tall and rather thin, with a short, gray beard; and he had a long scar running from between his eyes, down his nose, and out across his right cheek. That scar made him look frightful to me at first."

Charlock was slowly shaking his head. "That scar! That sounds like Lavar of the Second Clan! But he's dead!" Charlock was lost in thought for a few moments.

"SKY FIRE!!" Charlock finally exploded. "This doesn't make a bit of sense!

"Fifteen or sixteen seasons ago, Lavar was out with a hunting party. They were attacked by red ants. Three of the hunters escaped. They said that they got separated from the others and managed to jump into a creek before the ants could reach them. The last they saw of Lavar and the others was when they were in a small clearing surrounded by thirty or more red soldier ants, with more fast approaching. A rescue party was sent out, but all they found were some broken weapons, torn pieces of clothing, a few dead ants that hadn't been dragged off, and some blood. After that, nobody ever really considered the idea that any of them might have survived. But from what you say, he and some of the others must be alive. Did he say anything about how they survived and why they never came back?"

"No, he never spoke of his past. But he and the others did some strange things that I didn't understand," Burdock responded thoughtfully. "Looking back on it now, Uncle, I really don't believe they were in their right minds. At daybreak each morning and just before they set the watch each night, they would get together in a group and do something. I never was close enough to hear. They also seemed to know a lot about the Maker. From the way they spoke about Him, it was almost as though they had actually met Him.

"Oh! There was something the one with the scar told me this morning as they left me a short distance from the Keep. I guess he was trying to give me some sort of advice, but it sounds rather foolish. He said for me to always remember that to be truly happy, I must first weep, and to really live, I must first die."

Burdock sat looking at his uncle, who was apparently deep in thought as he stood absently scratching his beard. Finally Charlock spoke, "It is as you say, Nephew. Lavar must have paid for his bravery with his mind. They should all be brought back to their people. Even though many seasons have passed, we might yet be able to help them. It would be . . ."

At that moment, the large walnut doors behind Charlock opened. A tall, straight figure clothed in a long, dark robe appeared in the doorway. Hawthorn recognized this figure at once as one of the Shaman. The robed figure motioned with his hand, indicating that Burdock and his uncle were wanted inside.

"Come, Nephew. You must tell the Shaman everything you've just told me."

When they had entered, the heavy doors closed again, leaving the hallway exactly as Hawthorn had found it. After thinking for a few moments on all he had heard, Hawthorn decided that this would be a good time to leave. He had learned quite a lot and had been very fortunate not to have been caught. At first, he wanted to tell Poke what he had heard; but, thinking better of it, he decided to keep it to himself for the time being.

As he entered one of the main passageways that ran up to the different levels of the Keep, he caught the faint aroma of simmering stews. He hadn't realized that it was so late, but now his stomach was fully aware that supper time was near. With a funny growling noise coming from underneath his belt, he trotted up the dimly lit passageway toward his mother's stew pot, being careful not to run into others in the passage who were on their way to a hot meal as well.

After eating two large bowls of stew and several hunks of freshly baked pollen bread, Hawthorn spent the rest of the evening working on a leather sheath for his sting and trying to imagine how an experience could be so frightening that it would cause a battle-hardened soldier to lose his mind. As a result of all these thoughts and a little too much stew, Hawthorne's sleep was troubled that night.

Suddenly Hawthorne woke with a start. Was it his head that was throbbing, or was the whole bed shaking? As his mind cleared, he realized that it was the great drum in the watch chamber that was booming its bass notes throughout the Keep. "Surely it's not morning already," he thought to himself. It was then that he realized the meaning of the drumbeat's rapid cadence, and the truth struck him like cold water: it's a warning! The safety of the Keep is threatened!

Hawthorn quickly pulled on his clothes and then belted on his sting, which was resting in its nearly finished sheath. Although he was hurrying, it took a few moments for him to find everything that he needed. By the time he stepped out into the large main chamber, only a few Larkin were still scurrying about grabbing weapons, while the majority of the warriors were in a group by the door which led to the main passageway. At first Hawthorn wondered why they weren't running up to the watch deck to protect the walls, then he realized that they were all listening to one of the Shaman whom Hawthorn could now see standing in the doorway. Hawthorn walked toward the group, but by the time he arrived everyone had begun to leave. A small number moved out the door, apparently to the watch deck, but most of the Larkin were slowly heading back to their living quarters. It seemed that whatever the reason for the warning, at least for the moment, the Keep was not in immediate danger. Still, Hawthorn was very curious as to what was happening. He noticed that his father and a few others were still talking with the Shaman, so Hawthorn walked over to them. As the young Larkin joined the others, Savin glanced at his son, and laying a hand on his shoulder, Savin returned his attention to the Shaman.

"It's up to you now, Savin," the Shaman was saying. "We know that you will do your best." As he finished this statement, the Shaman looked over at Hawthorn. If it had not been for his father's hand on his shoulder, he would have felt very uncomfortable at that moment.

"I will try, Shaman Rah. It's just that all of this is so strange and so very hard to believe," Savin returned.

"Yes, it is hard to believe—but it happened! This should be a lesson to all of us. Our enemies will try anything to destroy us, even treachery. If it had not been for the wisdom of the Shaman and the Maker's guidance, we might have all been led into some fiendish trap like the Sixth Clan.

"If we discover anything more, we will let you know," the Shaman said as he ended his discourse. With that, he turned and hurried out the door and down the passage, his long robe flowing behind him.

"What has happened, Father?" asked Hawthorn as they walked back toward their quarters.

"Well, Son, from what Shaman Rah has said tonight, it appears that we have had traitors in the Keep."

Hawthorn's eyes widened at the news. "Who?" he whispered.

"The Shaman said that they discovered that Charlock and his nephew, Burdock, were planning to betray the Third Clan into the hands of the Renegades."

"It's . . . It's not true!" breathed Hawthorn, his mouth so dry he could hardly form the words.

Savin continued, "When the Shaman discovered their treachery, they ordered them locked in the cellar below the Keep. On the way, Charlock overpowered the guards, and they both ran back up into the Keep and escaped through a window on the second level. It seems that they took Burdock's mother and sister with them."

"It's not true, Father. I don't believe it!" Large drops began to form in the corners of the young Larkin's eyes as he spoke. "Charlock would never betray anyone! He couldn't! And neither could Burdock!"

"I know how you feel, Son. They were my friends, too."

Hawthorn wanted to tell his father all that he had heard that afternoon, but he wasn't sure how it fit in with what was happening now. After all, he had no idea what happened after he left. Besides that, he wasn't sure his father would understand what he was doing in a place where he shouldn't have been, listening to a conversation to which he had no business listening. So Hawthorn decided to say nothing about what he had heard.

His father was speaking to him again. "The Shaman have asked me to take over your training. Tomorrow I will begin teaching you to hunt and track. If you learn your lessons well, maybe you will get to go on some hunts this season." As he spoke, Savin put his arm across his son's shoulders. Hawthorn looked at his father and gave a weak smile. However, inside, his heart was full of sorrow.

CHAPTER TWO

THE HUNT

The sounds of the woods were fresh and exciting. Some were beautiful and melodious, like the trilling of the wood thrush; others were haunting and mysterious, like the mournful call of the mourning dove or the rustle of a leaf or crunch of a twig coming from the shadows of nearby trees. There were sounds that added to the spacious beauty of the woodlands, such as the harmonious choruses of the mockingbirds, whippoorwills, and peewees; the chirp of the cricket; the *breeee* of the grasshopper; and the airy singing of a crisp breeze through the scented pine boughs many leagues above. Then there were other sounds that brought the full spectrum of fear to any Larkin who heard them: the piercing scream of the hawk, dreaded sky-killer of the day; the roaring hiss of a serpent; the drone of the digger wasp that looked for Larkin-size prey to paralyze and bury with her eggs; and the fierce screech of the owl, sky-killer of the night. All of these sounds, whether melodious, mysterious, or terrifying, were a part of the morning that Hawthorn had spent marching through the woods with nine others on his first hunt.

It was already midday. The ten hunters were marching single file through the woods with Hawthorn in the rear. It had been a difficult march through tall grass and thickets for the last hour, but Hawthorn had hardly noticed. He was still going over in his mind all of the exciting events of the morning.

Even when he was very young, Hawthorn could remember dreaming of going on a Larkin hunt. He had worked hard to prepare for this day. The past

17

few weeks had been full of instruction from his father in the lore of hunting, and Hawthorn had practiced these lessons until his skill and confidence grew. It was then that Savin told his son that he was ready for his first hunt.

Hawthorn had been shaken from his sleep well before daylight that morning. He had dressed and had stepped out of his family's living quarters, which were carved into the cedar wall of the Keep, and walked to the cooking fire in the center of the large living area. A cooking fire was always tended in the living areas for all to use. It was built on a mud and rock foundation to prevent burning the wooden floor. Smoke was removed by way of ventilation ducts carved into the walls and extending to the outside.

Hawthorn had feasted on the honey cakes and hot bowls of lentils that his mother had prepared for him and his father. Even as he thought of the delicious cakes, his stomach began to growl. Since he was starting to get hungry, Hawthorn decided to think of something else. He relived the excitement he and his friend Poke had when they found out that they were both going on their first hunt together. Poke's father, Sycamore, had given him the news the same day Hawthorn's father had told him, and the two friends had been beside themselves with excitement. They had spent the last two days planning and packing and checking. Hawthorn saw himself again meticulously examining each of his weapons and packing his backpack. After their breakfast this morning, he and his father had said their private goodbyes to his mother, then they had marched down to the gate to meet the others in the hunting party. Because this was a big occasion for Hawthorn and Poke, many of their neighbors and close kin had also come down to the gate to see them off and to congratulate the two youths as they were to become Larkin hunters. When the hunting party was prepared to leave, everyone became very quiet, and all of the hunters knelt down on both knees with their heads down. As they did this, two of the Shaman began to say the secret words that they used when they prayed. No one but the Shaman could understand or speak this special language by which the Shaman communicated directly with the Maker. The Shaman said that the reason the Maker had only taught the Shaman His language was to keep those who were unworthy from approaching Him.

After the Shaman had finished speaking the prayer words, they said that they had asked the Maker to bless the hunt and to protect the hunters. Then, as all of the hunters were still kneeling, the Shaman walked by and placed their hands on each of them and bid each one to go and seek food for the good of the Keep. After that, each of the hunters stood up and marched out the gates, waving goodbye to their families and friends. Although this ceremony had been brief, Hawthorn had been very impressed. It always fascinated him whenever the Shaman spoke to the Maker. He thought that it would be such a fabulous and unbelievable honor to be able to speak with the *Maker of All That Is* whenever you wanted. Hawthorn had wished many times that he had that ability. There was so much that he would like to say to the Maker.

Hawthorn's daydreams were suddenly cut short. The Larkin in front of him was screaming something at him, but the words seemed to be drowned out by a deep, droning sound from behind. In an instant, Hawthorn sensed the danger and his right hand shot for his sting. His fingers had just touched the pommel when a tremendous weight slammed into his back, knocking him forward through the air a short distance. He landed on his face and chest, the force of which knocked the breath from him. He felt the powerful insect legs that were gripped around his body, pinning his arms to his sides, and all the while the droning sound was deafening. Hawthorn was helpless to do much more than kick his legs. He could tell from the powerful thrusts being made against his back that the huge insect was trying to pierce his body with its stinger, but it was apparently having difficulty getting around Hawthorn's shield, which was slung behind him and over his backpack. Even so, he knew his death was only a moment or two away.

The Larkin who had been in front of Hawthorn was an experienced hunter named Flint. He had heard the sound and turned in time to see the giant black and yellow wasp descend on Hawthorn. He had tried to shout a warning, but the words were hardly out before the large cicada killer had knocked Hawthorn to the ground and was on him. Flint knew that stabbing the insect alone would not necessarily save Hawthorn from that terrible stinger, which would seek to do its deadly work even as the insect died. Flint quickly ripped off his own shield and heavy backpack as he ran to Hawthorn. Swinging his pack with all his might, he slung it into the body of the monster, knocking it clear of its victim. The wasp rolled onto the grass, buzzing furiously. Righting itself quickly, it flew straight for Flint. He had just cleared his sting from its sheath when the wasp charged him. Flint only had time to make one thrust with his weapon as the huge creature slammed into him.

In its fearless charge, the cicada killer impaled itself on Flint's accurately aimed sting, which pierced the left side of the insect's head and extended through its thorax. Flint gave a painful cry as he was knocked to the ground, the injured wasp writhing on top of him.

By this time, the others, hearing the noise and seeing the fight, hurried to Flint's aid. Almost immediately after Flint hit the ground, Savin was by his side and quickly kicked the dying insect clear of him. Buck, another Larkin, ran over and drove his own sting through the thrashing wasp's abdomen, pinning it to the ground. He then drew his flint knife and carefully severed the stinger from the dying creature and kicked it into some brush nearby.

"Did he get you, Flint?" asked an older hunter named Hawk, kneeling over his fallen companion. Flint was rolling back and forth on the ground, tightly gripping his left thigh and grimacing painfully.

"My leg!" Flint groaned through clenched teeth. "It feels . . . like it's on fire!"

Another of the hunters leaned over the fallen Larkin and began flushing the wound with water from his water pack, a rounded leather pouch used to carry drinking water.

"How does it look, Rush?" asked Hawk after a moment.

"Well-l-l," drawled the burly Rush, finishing his examination of the leg wound, "he's got a nice little rip in the inside of his thigh where the stinger laid the skin open. I've tried to wash the venom out of it, but it's gonna hurt pretty bad for the next hour or so."

Flint being well attended, Savin hurried over to see about his son. Hawthorn was on his knees, trying to dig all of the dirt out of his mouth.

"Are you hurt, Thorn?"

Hawthorn tried to say something, but it came out garbled. Shaking his head in answer to his father's question, he went back to digging at his mouth. Savin pulled his own water pack out and gave it to his son to help him wash out his mouth and clean up his face.

"How's Flint, Father?" Hawthorn asked presently. A large knot was beginning to swell over his right eye.

"It stung him in the leg. It will hurt him for a while, but he'll be all right."

"How's the lad, Savin?" a gruff voice called loudly from the group ministering to Flint.

"He seems to be all right, Hawk," returned Savin as he helped his son to his feet. "He's got a few knots and bruises, but nothing serious."

"Good! Since it looks as though this leg isn't going to be of much use to Flint for a few hours, we might as well camp here and then press on in the morning."

Hawk was a highly respected Larkin of no little ability. Being the eldest, forty-seven seasons, and most experienced, Hawk was the first master of the hunt. He began giving orders to the others in the small band. Despite what feelings might exist between the hunters and the hunt master, his orders were always immediately obeyed. To the Larkin, it wasn't as much a matter of principle as it was a matter of survival.

"Buck, you take Jay and Sycamore and scout the area. Look for any signs of predators. While you're at it, you might look for something to use as a poultice for Flint's leg."

"Lichen works well for that," Sage, the second master of the hunt, informed them.

"Right," agreed Hawk. "Be back here before dark."

Buck acknowledged the order with a single nod of his head. Speaking to Jay and Sycamore, he said, "We'll leave our packs here. Sycamore, bring your bow." With that, the three left their backpacks and quickly disappeared into the brush to the north.

"Savin," Hawk was speaking again, "as soon as you finish tending to the lad, take him and Poke and find us a sturdy bush to sleep in. With Flint's leg like it is, we don't want to be caught on the ground tonight." The order was again acknowledged with a nod.

"Sage, I'm leaving Flint to your care. Rush and I are going back a ways to cover our trail." Shucking their packs, Hawk and Rush trotted off back down the trail in the direction from which they had come.

Night, when it came, was darker than usual. There was no moon, and most of the stars were obscured by clouds. Hawthorn could barely make out the shape of limbs just a short distance from him. He pulled his cloak a little tighter around himself, maybe more out of fear than due to the chill of the air.

Hawthorn and the others were spending the night in a large quince bush. It had been a good choice. The bush was tall enough for all ten of the hunters to get well off the ground. Also, the bush's sharp thorns offered a secondary means of protection against nosy predators. "The trick to sleeping in a bush," Savin had told his son, "is to find a good notch where a couple of limbs meet, pad the seat, and tie yourself in."

What his father hadn't told him was how to convince himself to trust that little rope enough so that he could go to sleep. As tired as he was, the best Hawthorn did was a few short dozes. He had heard the first two watches change. Surely it must be about time for the third watch to begin.

A quick succession of raps was struck against the trunk of the bush, sending the warning vibrating up through the branches. Immediately all were awake with weapons in hand. As Hawthorn untied himself, he heard some movement in the branches below him. In a few moments, an urgent whisper pierced the surrounding darkness, "Here, all!"

Sheathing his sting, Hawthorn quickly climbed down in obedience to Hawk's command. When all had arrived at the limb where Hawk was, he spoke quickly and quietly, informing them of their predicament. "Buck has been listening to some movement in the grass below us for quite some time. Whatever it is has moved right under our bush. All of you bring your bows. We're going to move down into the lower branches to try to fend off an attack if it comes. Savin, you and Sycamore come with me. We'll go down to Buck's level and be the first line of defense. The rest of you stay above us but spread out in the branches. Make no sound, and don't let fly your arrows unless you hear my word."

As quickly as the words were said, each Larkin silently moved down the branches toward the unknown terror below. Hawthorn had descended but five branches when the entire bush began a tremendous shaking, which caused Hawthorn to lose his grip on the trunk. He landed one limb below and managed to hang on, in spite of the great thrashing of the limbs. A roaring hiss thundered from the darkness below, and through the noise screamed a voice, "It comes! It comes!" The same voice let out a short yell which was cut off abruptly. The bush continued to whip about wildly. Hawthorn gripped his limb so tightly that his hands were bleeding.

Almost as suddenly as it had started, the bush stopped its wild shaking. It continued to move, but it was like some great weight was pushing against it, causing the bush to sway slowly. Hawthorn took this chance to climb on top of the limb on which he was hanging. From the darkness not too far below him, Hawthorn heard a voice that he recognized as Hawk's, "Quickly! Move higher! Move higher! The serpent has taken Buck and now is coming for the rest of us!"

Hawthorn worked his way to the trunk and began to climb. He was trying to be sure of his grip and footing, but fear pushed him faster and faster in his climb. He could hear the others climbing just above and below him. As the limbs were getting much smaller, he knew that they must be getting near the top. They couldn't go much farther, and yet the branches continued to sway to the rhythm of the serpent as it slowly climbed the bush, seeking its prey.

"All right, Larkin, we make our stand here!" Hawk was only a branch or two below Hawthorn when he spoke. Those words helped Hawthorn a lot at that moment. Before he had simply been the prey, fleeing the stalker, forced on and on by mindless fear. But Hawk had spoken with such calmness, such firm resolve, that the blinding fear began to melt away. Fear was still there, but it no longer controlled him. He was a Larkin, he told himself, and he would act like it.

"Jay!" Hawk called.

"Here!" came the answer from the darkness below Hawthorn.

"You were on watch with Buck. Do you still have the other lance?"

"I lost my grip on it when the bush shook so wildly. I think it fell all the way to the ground."

"All right! All of you come to my level and spread yourselves around the trunk!" Hawk gave the order, and all moved instantly to obey. "Use your bows and arrows. Shoot for any sound below us. If it gets close enough, shoot for its eyes."

Bow strings twanged, and arrows began to fly down into the darkness. Hawthorn could hear the arrows tearing through leaves and glancing off branches, but still the bush swayed as the serpent came nearer. As Hawthorn notched another arrow and prepared to shoot again, the thought that shouted loudest in his heart was how dearly he wished that he could speak to the Maker and ask for His help.

"Sycamore! Hawthorn! Below you!" rapped a voice on Hawthorn's left. He scanned the gloom directly below his branch and was able to make out the long, blunted head. Fear gripped him tighter, but at least he could see his enemy. Now he had something at which to aim!

The arrows began to rain down on the head of the serpent, but still it kept coming.

"They're bouncing off! The arrows are just bouncing off!" Poke cried out.

"Listen to me, all of you!" Hawk's commanding voice again beat down the fear that was gnawing at each of them. "We aren't going to be able to stop it, so move as far out on your branch as you can. Ride the branches down as close to the ground as they'll reach, then drop. By splitting up, we may be able to . . ." Hawk didn't get to finish his instructions. At that moment, the serpent below them let out a great, hissing roar and began thrashing furiously.

At the sound of the roar, Hawthorn instinctively grabbed for his branch. The powerful contortions of the serpent were causing the entire bush to whip about with tremendous force. Hawthorn knew that at any moment he might lose his grip and be thrown many leagues away.

As suddenly as the terrifying ride started, it ceased. The limbs swayed slowly in recovery to the tremendous thrashing they had just received. There was no longer the roaring hiss of the hungry serpent, just a rustling in the grass below as it slithered away.

"It stopped!"

"Listen! It's going away!"

"What happened, Hawk?"

Hawk was as confused as the rest of them. "I . . . don't know," he answered. "Our arrows certainly didn't do that."

Just then, a voice from far below them broke through the darkness, "A brave lot of hunters all of you are, leaving a poor old Larkin to fight a whole serpent by himself."

It was Buck! Their hearts leaped within them. Not only had he escaped the serpent's jaws, but somehow he had managed to save them all!

"All right, Buck, enough of your foolishness. Now tell us what really happened," Sage said. He was anxious to hear the truth and was getting irritated at the ridiculous stories that Buck was making up about how he had scared away the serpent.

"Yes, please tell us what happened," Poke added. They had finished resetting the watch for the rest of the night, and all were still on the lower branches listening to Buck.

"Well, things happened kind of fast-like, and in this darkness I'm not completely sure myself about all of the details. Jay heard it first. It came from that taller grass to the south of us. The serpent must have sensed us, because it came straight for our bush. We then tapped a warning to the rest of you. By the sound of its movements, we were fairly certain that it was a serpent, so I sent Jay up to tell Hawk what was happening. I decided to move down lower to get a look at it. I thought that if I could see it coming, then I'd be able to warn you a little quicker. But it must have sensed me or seen my movement, because I had only dropped down two or three branches when I looked down and saw two huge jaws coming for me. I barely had time to shout a warning before it hit me. Apparently its mouth hit the lance that I was holding, and instead of grabbing me the serpent just knocked me out of the bush. I fell through some branches and landed on one of the serpent's coils. It took a moment or two for me to realize what had happened and where I was. I guess I moved pretty fast getting away from there.

"I couldn't see anything from where I was, but I could tell by the sound of the fight that you all were having a rough go of it. The serpent had moved quite far up into our bush when I crept back to see if there was anything I could do. I was moving around trying to find a sharp stick or thorn to use for a weapon when I tripped over one of the lances. Even though the serpent was almost up to the top of the bush, there was nearly half of its body still on the ground. I got a running start and ran the lance head between two of the scales on its side and on up into its body. I must have hit something important, 'cause it started bellowing and flopping around like it had eaten a whole hill full of red ants. Pretty soon it fell out of the bush and headed back for the tall grass. I let it keep the lance to remember me by."

Buck had to answer a few questions, and three or four different ones had to retell the incident and explain what had happened to them before they were all satisfied and calmed down enough to try to get some more sleep. But too much had happened that day for Hawthorn; he continued to only be able to doze on and off.

Hawthorn didn't have any problem staying awake during his turn on guard duty. He and Rush held the last watch of the night, and just before daylight they heard some movement in the brush into which the serpent had disappeared. They sounded a warning to the rest, but no attack came. Hawthorn was relieved when dawn finally arrived. This had been his first night outside the protection of their Keep except for the times the clan had journeyed to the Steps for the Great Gathering every five years. On those journeys, the clan spent their nights in strongholds that the scouts had prepared for everyone's protection. But there were no strongholds in which to stay on this trip. Although Hawthorn liked excitement and adventure as well as any other young Larkin, he would enjoy it much more if the adventures were a little less life-threatening.

For breakfast they munched on pieces of dried fruit and drank water from their packs. It was just light enough to see when the small band of Larkin hunters climbed down out of the branches of the quince bush and again began their march. They started quite slowly at first, giving Flint time to work the soreness out of his injured leg, but soon the pace was quickened.

Hawthorn knew that Flint must be in a lot of pain, yet he was hardly limping. He was greatly impressed by Flint's courage and determination. Hawthorn had thanked Flint many times over for saving his life. He even offered to carry his pack for him, but the injured Larkin wouldn't let him. "This will help prepare me for some greater task," Flint had said to him after he had refused Hawthorn's offer.

It was thought at first that, with the injury to Flint, it would not be possible for them to reach the meadow that day. As it turned out, Flint's injury did not slow them up at all. The courageous warrior had forced himself to maintain the brisk pace of the march all day, and they arrived at the edge of the meadow about one hour before sunset.

After a brief rest, Hawk began giving orders, "Flint! Take Jay and see if you two can find a good place for us to spend the night. I'll join you in a moment.

"Buck! You, Sycamore, and Savin go scout the meadow. See if you can find us an active mooflon run. Hawthorn, why don't you go with them? Remember, all of you," Hawk charged them firmly, "we're hunting mooflon, but don't forget to watch out for enemies.

"Sage, you take Rush and young Poke. Be sure our trail is covered for a good ways back. Now off with you," Hawk barked. "There's not much daylight left."

With these words, each Larkin jumped to his assigned duty.

Buck spoke quickly to his scouting party, "Leave your packs here. All of you bring your bows and arrows with you." Quickly each Larkin shed his pack and shield and picked up his bow and quiver of arrows. With the words, "Let's go," Buck led them off at a quick but cautious pace toward the meadow.

Hawthorn was excited to be included in the scouting party. His weariness from the day's march quickly faded as he trotted cautiously behind the others, bow in hand. How he wished that the sun would stay right where it was for a while. There was so much he would like to see and learn. As it was, with so little daylight left, they must move quickly, and there would be no time for the thousands of questions buzzing in his head.

The meadow was a vast sea of grasses that extended across a panorama of rolling hills, the tallest of which, though far distant, obscured the horizon to the east. Hawthorn had heard many stories about the great meadow. There was an abundance of food in this place, but it was also filled with dangers. Hawthorn was impressed with the immensity of it all. He had never been able to see so far in his entire life.

Just then Buck stopped and called them together. He spoke quickly, in almost a whisper. "We will double our efforts. Savin, take Hawthorn and scout north along the edge of the meadow. Sycamore and I will scout south. Remember, be silent, be quick, and be ready for anything. We will all meet back at this spot when the sun is a hand's breadth above that far hill."

With that, Buck and Sycamore trotted off toward the south. Savin smiled at his son. "Come on. Let's go find some mooflon."

They moved quickly through the brush and grasses along the edge of the meadow, stopping frequently to listen. Even though he was alone with his own father, Hawthorn knew better than to ask any questions. What they were doing was serious and dangerous. He must concentrate hard to be alert for any sound, any smell, any movement. The meadow certainly appeared peaceful, but

Hawthorn had learned enough to know that a Larkin could lose his life a thousand different ways in this great sea of grass.

"Over there," whispered Savin as he pointed to the left while they were stopped to look around, "by that bare spot of ground. That looks like a mooflon run." As they moved out into the grass, Hawthorn's heart couldn't help but beat a little faster.

"This is a mooflon run, Thorn," Savin said as he parted the grasses and stepped down into the worn, trough-like path, "or it was a run. It looks like it hasn't been used in quite a while."

"How can you tell?" Hawthorn asked, his curiosity partially overcoming his fear.

"Well, for one thing, there are no claw marks in the ground that they would make in running back and forth. Also there is no fur hung in the grass along the run where they shed it, and there are no droppings in this run like you would normally see. Lastly, if mooflon were using this run, you'd be able to smell them."

"What does . . ." Hawthorn began his question, but he never got to finish. Savin shoved him into a thick clump of grass along the edge of the run and dove in behind him.

"Be still," Savin whispered urgently.

Hawthorn, lying on his back in the thick grass, did not move a muscle. He didn't know why he was lying there concentrating so hard to be still, but he did know this was not the time to ask.

"Hawk!" he heard his father breathe in his ear.

Hawthorn couldn't quite control the little shiver that ran through him when he heard what his father said. He scanned the sky with his eyes, searching for the great killer bird. Hawthorn was beginning to think that either his father was mistaken or that the hawk had left, until he heard that piercing scream that hawks make when they're out hunting. Looking back over his head, he saw it, circling high above the trees. He couldn't tell much about the bird at this distance, but he knew that the hawk, with his sharp eye, could easily count the arrows in his quiver.

The minutes dragged by and still the great bird circled above the two Larkin. Once when the hawk was circling away from them, Hawthorn whispered, "What are we going to do?!"

"Be still," Savin whispered back, "and be ready to move when I say!"

It was a few more minutes before they got their chance to escape. Suddenly, with a terrifying scream, the hawk dropped from the sky like a rock, talons extended. The killer bird hit the grass a short distance away from them, and a tremendous fight ensued. They couldn't tell what the hawk was fighting, but whatever it was, it obviously did not intend to be the bird's supper.

"Now!" said Savin as he jumped up and pulled his son after him. They both raced for the thick brush at the edge of the meadow. Scrambling under some low limbs, they looked back for the hawk. The large bird was still in the grass, but by the sound of things, the fight was almost over.

"What do you think it caught?" Hawthorn asked, eyes wide and breathing hard.

"Enemy, I hope," Savin puffed back. "Let's get back."

Ever alert, they retraced their steps, taking care to stay well back in the brush along the meadow's edge.

Hearing again the scream of the hawk behind them, they both instinctively threw themselves into the nearest thicket. Looking back, Hawthorn saw the form of the large bird climbing into the sky, silhouetted against the setting sun. The long, slender form of a serpent was hanging limply from its talons.

"How fresh was the run, Buck?" Hawk questioned when his scouts returned.

"A lot of recent claw marks and some of this evening's droppings," Buck returned.

"It looks like the main run for a large den of 'em to me," added Sycamore.

"I'd agree with that," Buck nodded.

"What about you two?" Hawk said, looking at Savin and Hawthorn.

"Nothing to the north," Savin said, shaking his head.

"All right then," Hawk clipped with a tone of decisiveness. "Buck, you and Sycamore plan the strategy for a hunt on the run you found. Come tell me the details as soon as you get them all worked out."

Hawk looked off to the west. "The sun has just about set," he said. "We'd better get off the ground before the darkness covers us."

"What was it like, Thorn?" Poke asked anxiously as they gathered their gear.

"Beautiful," he answered, "and scary."

They spent the night in a small cedar sapling. In spite of his weariness, Hawthorn only got a little more sleep than he did the night before. There were several warnings sounded through the night, but nothing came of them. A good hour before daylight all of the hunting party was awakened, and the plan for the day's hunt was explained. After each Larkin's assignment and position was clearly understood, the small band of hunters moved carefully down the trunk of the sapling and into the darkness of the forest floor.

When they reached the edge of the meadow, Hawthorn could tell that dawn was near. The darkness was slowly becoming a gloomy grey. Buck led them south along the edge of the forest. They were moving quickly in order to reach the run and get into position before dawn.

Dawn and dusk were the safest times of the day. Most night hunters had caught their prey and, with bellies full, were settling down to sleep. The day hunters were just now waking and not yet ready to start the hunt. Even so, Hawthorn could not help but be wary. They stopped briefly while Buck and Sycamore got their bearings. Having located their position, Buck led them slowly out into the vast sea of grass. Hawthorn felt very unprotected as he moved out from underneath brush and into the expanse of the meadow. They didn't have to travel much more than a good stone's throw before they found it.

The run was like a narrow roadway, extending north and south and curving out of sight into the meadow on both ends. The smell was the first thing Hawthorn noticed. There was a strong, musty odor. Now he knew what his father meant about the smell of a fresh mooflon run.

The sky was much brighter now, and they had to move quickly. Each Larkin took his place in the deep grasses along the edge of the run. Buck spread them out so that they could cover a good length of the run, with Hawthorn placed in the last position. If any wounded mooflon made it that far down the run, he was to try to put an arrow into it and keep it from getting away. Hawthorn was about as excited as he could be, and he spent the next few minutes trying to calm himself down. If he did get a shot at a mooflon, he didn't want to miss.

From the grasses about two stone throws north came the trill of a meadowlark. At that sound, Hawthorn froze. It was a signal from Buck to warn the rest of the hunters that mooflon were in the run and moving.

Thorn listened intently. He could hear faint movements in the grass-lined run, but they still seemed far away. Before Hawthorn realized what had happened, a large, grey form had rounded the turn in the run and rushed right past Hawthorn. The large creature was already out of range before he could draw his bow.

Hawthorn was furious with himself. Here he was supposed to be a Larkin hunter, and he had let his prey run right under his nose without even being able to get a shot off at him. All he could do was watch the field mouse lumber quickly down the run and disappear around a turn, with two Larkin arrows sticking harmlessly into the skin of his back.

When he heard a roar coming from the north end of the run, Hawthorn stopped berating himself and got ready. He drew his bow string back with the arrow ready. "This time I will have time to shoot," he told himself.

There was a lot of thrashing around the bend to the north of him. With another loud roar, a rather large mooflon crashed into the ground, his head and shoulders just visible to Hawthorn from where he stood. Hawthorn could see the shafts of at least three arrows sticking out of the creature's shoulder and neck.

Even as Hawthorn was counting the arrows, another big mooflon charged past his fallen companion, rounded the turn, and raced toward Hawthorn. As Hawthorn was aiming, an arrow flew from the grass just north of Hawthorn, striking the mouse in the thigh, which caused the animal to stop momentarily. At that exact moment, Hawthorn released his arrow, and instead of hitting the beast's heart, the arrow imbedded deep into its shoulder. With an angry roar, the mooflon limped away. Drawing another arrow, Hawthorn jumped from his place of concealment and ran down the run toward the wounded field mouse. He was only five paces away from the injured beast when he took aim and shot. This time, the arrow struck right behind the shoulder and into the chest in the area where Hawthorn was sure the creature's heart must be.

As realization of the mortal wound rushed through the mooflon, it turned and charged fiercely at its attacker. For Hawthorn there was no escape. Too late, he realized that his foolishness had brought him fatally close to the wounded rodent. As the enraged monster lunged for Hawthorn's chest and throat, there was not even time for the young Larkin to reach for his sting. Instinctively, Hawthorn rammed the end of his bow into the roof of the attacking animal's mouth. This drove the sharp teeth over Hawthorn's head, but an instant later he was slammed into the ground by the force of the charging mooflon. Momentarily stunned by the force of the blow, Hawthorn lay on the ground under the raging beast, groping frantically for his sting.

"Thorn, move!"

He heard the voice behind him through the din of the mooflon's roars. Looking up, he saw that his own bow in the rodent's mouth had been replaced by a long, pointed spear, the shaft of which was held tightly in his father's hands.

Hawthorn knew that the creature would kill both of them if they didn't kill it first. He might get away, but his father certainly would not.

THE MOOFLON HUNT

Ripping his sting from its sheath, Hawthorn grasped the pommel in both hands and, from his knees, thrust the point deeply into the raging mooflon's throat. Instantly, the dying beast rose up on its back legs and released a terrific, gurgling roar. A moment later, the huge mouse crashed to the ground. Releasing the spear, Savin rushed quickly to his son and pulled him clear of the wounded monster's death throws.

"Thank you, Father," Hawthorn gasped as he tried to catch his breath. "I'm such a fool! I almost got you killed!"

"Not to mention yourself!" Savin barked, not a little frustrated at his son. "Nature's not very forgiving, Son, so we've got to use our wits. If you have to rely on experience to learn lessons like this, you won't live very long." Hawthorn's head was dropping lower and lower from shame, and Savin could see that the lesson had been learned.

Putting his hand on his son's shoulder, Savin added with a smile, "You are a foolish young Larkin, but also a very brave one."

Just then, Hawk and Rush came jogging up. "You two all right?" Hawk asked.

"Nothing hurt but one mooflon and a little pride," Savin returned.

Rush reached down and helped Hawthorn up to his feet, saying as he did so, "Thorn, I see you're one of them hunters who likes to give 'em a sportin' chance."

Still very embarrassed by his actions, Hawthorn could only smile weakly and nod his head.

"Have you talked to the lad?" Hawk whispered so only Savin could hear. Savin nodded. "Good. He may not have shown a lot of sense in what he did, but you certainly can't deny the lad's courage—or yours, for that matter."

"We are very fortunate that the Maker saw fit to save us."

"Aye," Hawk agreed. "It was, indeed, the Maker's work."

Now that the actual hunt was over, the real work began, and it had to be done quickly. Time was of the essence. The two dead mice were slit open, and all of their organs were removed. The inside of the body cavity was then rubbed with salt. Next, the large rodents' bodies were stuffed with wild ginger leaves, and the bellies were sewn shut. The ginger helped preserve and flavor the meat, but more importantly, it helped cover the scent. Quickly, litters were made from poles, and the two huge carcasses were strapped on them.

As the sun's first rays crowned the tops of the tallest pine trees along the edge of the woods, the small band of Larkin hunters pushed through the meadow grasses, shouldering their kill and beginning the long journey back to the Keep. The danger now was that the scent of the meat and blood would draw enemies. Because of this, they would only stop for short rests each hour until they reached the Keep.

Each mooflon was stretched on two poles, and it took four Larkin to carry each beast, one at the end of each pole. One Larkin would lead and scout the trail ahead, and one would watch the rear and try to cover trail and scent. Each hour, they would stop for a brief rest and to change the leader and the rearguard.

Hawthorn couldn't believe how heavy the mooflon were. He had wrapped his cloak around the pole to pad it, but even so the muscles in his neck and shoulder had cramped twice, forcing him to quickly shift the heavy load to his other shoulder. The youth in him wanted to gripe and complain and even quit, but when he felt those feelings welling up inside, he would simply look at Flint, his leg still swollen and bandaged, trudging along shouldering his burden, never once slacking his pace or even mentioning the obvious pain in his leg. Hawthorn would remember his words, "This will prepare me for some greater task." With these thoughts in mind, Hawthorn's boyish self-pity would disappear, and a Larkin determination would replace it.

It was late in the afternoon when Hawthorn took his turn at rear guard. He welcomed the rest, but even though he wasn't carrying the heavy litters, he was still very busy. He watched their traveled path for signs of trailing enemies, and occasionally he dropped back a ways to be sure they weren't being trailed at a distance. At the same time, he did his best to cover their tracks. On one of these occasions, he was so intent on scattering brush to cover their trail that he did not notice the dark figure slipping out of the thick grass behind him. When Hawthorn turned to head back up the trail toward the rest of the hunting party, he froze. There, not three paces in front of him, stood a Renegade warrior, war club in hand and dark eyes flashing from behind his frightful-looking wooden mask.

Instantly Hawthorn's sting was in his hand. "Leave me alone!" Hawthorn said, trying to sound threatening. "I don't want to hurt you!" Slowly he began to back away from the Renegade.

A heavy club came down sharply across Hawthorn's arm, the numbing pain causing him to drop his sting. A large, booted foot stepped on his dropped weapon, preventing him from picking it up again. Behind him came an evil, menacing voice, "Don't worry, Larkin," it laughed, "you won't hurt us."

Hawthorn, cringing in pain from his arm, heard other voices laughing around him. Looking up, he saw that two more Renegades had appeared from the tall grass on either side of the trail. From behind, a hand roughly grabbed the neck of his tunic. Angrily, Hawthorn threw himself into the Renegade who held him. He stamped at his captor's foot, driving his heel down hard. There was a howl of pain from Hawthorn's captor. The other Renegades began laughing at the trouble their friend seemed to be having.

Hawthorn whirled quickly, tearing loose from his captor's grasp. He shoved hard at the injured Renegade, pushing him over backwards and then started to run past him down the trail. The falling Renegade managed to reach out and trip Hawthorn as he ran by. The young Larkin fell, sprawling on the path. He tried to jump up quickly, but a sudden painful flash of colors filled his eyes. The colors disappeared into darkness as he dropped heavily back onto the ground and lay motionless.

ChAPTER ThREE

AMBUSH

At the same moment that Hawthorn was confronting the Renegades on the trail behind them, the Larkin hunters carrying the two mooflon were moving quickly along the main path that led from the meadow to the Keep, unaware that disaster was stalking them. Scouts from a large Renegade war party had spotted them as they were preparing the freshly killed mooflon. Carrying word back to the main body of savage fighters, their leader immediately began moving to ambush the Larkin hunting party and relieve them of their fresh meat.

Moving quickly, the Renegades intercepted the path through the woods that the Larkin were taking to return home. The ambush was a Renegade specialty, and it was particularly satisfying when they could inflict some pain on their old enemies. This ambush was craftily set in an area where the brush and grass were thickly pressing in on the sides of the trail. The Renegade leader also sent several of his warriors further back toward the meadow. Their orders were to let the main hunting party pass and to deal with the one or two Larkin who would be lagging behind guarding the rear.

Sage was leading as the Larkin entered the ambush. Tired as he was, his senses were intensely alert. As he moved ahead along the path, the realization came rushing upon him that they were in grave danger. It would have been difficult for him to explain how he knew, perhaps a slight flutter in the leaves off to the left, a faint movement somewhere, or a hint of a new smell in the air. But he knew the enemies were there. He also knew that if he stopped on the trail the Renegades would know he suspected their presence, and that would mean he was a dead Larkin. It was clear to him as well that he had to warn the others. They might all die anyway, but if he could warn them and get them moving to protect themselves before the enemy attacked, some of them might be saved. All these thoughts flashed through his mind in an instant.

Sage acted quickly. As soon as his right foot hit the ground, he pushed backwards with all his might. He spun swiftly and threw himself on the ground. He was conscious of three arrows that flew over his head through the space where he would have been had he not dropped. He sprang up quickly, shouting, "Ambush! Ambush!"

The next two arrows did not miss. But he had seen that the others were responding rapidly to his warning. As his life faded from him, he felt the satisfaction of knowing that he had done what he could to save his friends.

At Sage's warning cry, Hawk yelled, "Down!"

Eight Larkin immediately dropped to the ground as the first volley of arrows flew high of their mark. Poke was a little slow to realize what was happening, and a Renegade arrow hit the top of his acorn cap, tearing it from his head and painfully snapping in two the leather thong under his chin that held it in place.

"Shields!" he heard Hawk yell. Poke grabbed desperately for his shield where he and the others had stored them up on the litters next to the dead mice. The second wave of arrows was zipping into the body of the dead mooflon next to him as he jerked his shield around to cover himself. He felt two solid thumps against his shield when the deadly projectiles hit.

Arrows were flying in from both sides. They were pinned down.

"Hawk!" Poke heard Jay's voice call. "There are no arrows coming from behind!"

"Sage warned us before we were fully in their ambush. That direction is our only hope. In a moment the arrows will stop, and they will rush us. That's when we must fight our way back down the trail. Be ready!"

It didn't take long for the Renegades to realize that, with the mooflon carcasses protecting their backs and the shields protecting them in front, the arrows shot at the Larkin were a waste of time. The trapped Larkin heard a horn blast from the thick brush up ahead and to their right. This was followed by some shouting.

"Get ready, Larkin!" Hawk said so all could hear. "On my word, we move back. Keep your shields up and stay close."

A fierce scream was heard off to the right, which was quickly taken up by Renegades in the grass and brush all around them. From behind his shield, Poke could hear the enemies crashing through the brush on both sides.

"Now!" shouted Hawk. Poke pushed himself up, and with his shield held in front of him and his sting in his hand, he began backing from his place by the first mooflon to join the others. He hadn't taken four steps when the first wave of the Renegades came charging out of the woods to his right, screaming and looking terrifying in their frightful masks. Buck, Rush, and Savin quickly joined him to receive the charge. Most of the Renegades carried heavy war clubs.

As the enemy charged into the waiting Larkin, a short, stocky Renegade with a particularly grotesque red and blue mask chose Poke as his victim. When Poke saw the charging Renegade heading straight for him with his war club raised, the young Larkin was so nervous that he threw himself forward into the attacking enemy. This tactic, in turn, surprised the Renegade, so that when he swung his heavy club at Poke's head, it went behind the young Larkin. As they crashed together, the top of Poke's shield rammed up under the hideous mask and, with a sharp rap, smacked hard into the Renegade's unprotected jaw. Instantly, the stunned enemy warrior crumpled to the ground like a leaf.

Poke, seeing his fallen opponent, quickly moved back to join his companions. He promised himself that he would remember to use that trick again.

The others were busy defending themselves against the initial attack of the closest Renegades. Although several of the enemy had fallen, their numbers were increasing moment by moment as more of the savage warriors poured out of the brush. "Move back! Move back!" Hawk ordered as he saw that the odds were decidedly against them and getting worse by the second.

Trying to stay shoulder to shoulder with his companions, Poke stabbed, dodged, and stabbed again. He wasn't so much fighting an individual opponent as much as he was stabbing at whatever part of an enemy happened to move within striking distance of his sting.

The little band was pushed back by the sheer weight of increasing numbers pressing against them. Then it happened. Rush stumbled and was knocked to the ground by a strong opponent. As the large Renegade raised his club to finish him, Poke stepped over between his fallen friend and his attacker. Poke took the full force of the blow on his shield. The warrior's club crashed into his shield, slamming it into his chest and driving Poke to his knees. The powerful savage raised his club again to finish the stunned young Larkin. Before the blow descended, Buck's sting thrust into the Renegade, and with a grunt of pain, he went limp. Buck had saved Poke, but by doing so he had left himself unprotected. The Renegade who had been fighting with him saw his chance and swung his war club savagely at Buck's head. The Larkin was dead before he hit the ground.

Poke could only yell, "Buck!" as he jumped to his feet and watched in stunned disbelief while his companion fell.

Suddenly Poke felt his shield being jerked away from his arm. He spun quickly and came face to face with a familiar red and blue mask. "See how you like it!" spat an angry voice from behind the mask. Then the Renegade rammed the top of the shield hard up into Poke's lower jaws. The young Larkin collapsed senseless.

Jay had just dispatched an enemy with his sting and had turned to see where he might be needed. As he looked across, he saw Buck and Poke go down. He gave a cry to warn the others and threw himself shield first into the Renegades as they advanced over his fallen comrades. His charge staggered the first few enemies that moved through the gap created by the fallen Larkin. But there were too many of them for him to push back. Try as he might, he was unable to get to Buck or Poke. However, Jay's charge had given Rush enough time to get back to his feet. Rush, too, threw his weight against the Renegade horde, but the two Larkin were only able to slow the advance of the enemy.

"Savin, help them!" Hawk called from the other side of the ring of Larkin defenders.

"Right!" Savin acknowledged as he pushed away from the Renegade that he had been fighting. Hawk and Flint moved in to close the gap where Savin had been.

Savin shouldered in between Rush and Jay to strengthen their side of the circle, but it was still not enough. "There's too many of 'em!" Savin called back to Hawk.

Hawk knew Savin's call was not a cry of fear but a battle report. It told him that they could not hold their position much longer. They must break free from their circle of attackers, and they must do so now!

Hawk dropped the Renegade in front of him, but another filled the spot. As the fresh attacker rained heavy blows down on Hawk's shield, he looked down and noticed the unprotected foot of the Renegade. Like lightening, he drove the point of his sting through his enemy's boot. The Renegade let out a tremendous howl, dropping his war club as he reached for his injured appendage. Hawk threw his whole body, shield first, into the wounded Renegade. Already off balance, the enemy warrior was driven backward with such force that he flew into two other unsuspecting Renegades, knocking them down. As Hawk finished with these three, he realized that he had broken through the circle of enemies. Immediately turning to his left, he charged shield first into the side of the two Renegades who were attacking Sycamore. These two also went down.

"Cover us with your bow from that log!" Hawk yelled to Sycamore over the noise of the fierce battle.

Sycamore instantly sprinted the short distance to the log Hawk had indicated, unslinging his bow as he ran. Leaping up onto the old, moss-covered log, he spun around and, without waiting to catch his breath, began launching his arrows into the ranks of Renegades. He knew all of their lives depended on his accuracy, so his concentration was intense. He shot quickly but made every arrow count.

"Larkin!" Hawk called, "To me!"

Shield to shield, the Larkin warriors fought a retreating battle, backing toward the log.   Sycamore was doing his job. The Renegade numbers were dropping as arrow after arrow found its mark. They had covered about one-third of the distance to the log when Hawk felt that he could spare another fighter.

"Jay, help Sycamore!" he ordered. The Larkin ranks closed as Jay pulled away from the fighting line and sprinted to the log to join Sycamore. The two Larkin archers sent a withering flight of arrows onto the crowd of enemy attackers.

With their numbers dropping rapidly, the ambushers suddenly realized that they were now the ones in grave danger. The demoralized Renegades began to break and run back into the cover of the grass.

"Keep your shields up and move for the log!" Hawk commanded.

With their shields still facing the enemy, they backed as quickly as they dared to their waiting friends. Just as they got to the log, the first wave of Renegade arrows flew into them. Arrows slammed into their shields and dug into the earth around them. They threw themselves over the log as more enemy arrows rained down on them. With grunts and cries of pain, they all hit the ground in a pile behind the protection of the log.

"Who's hurt?" called out Hawk from somewhere under the pile of Larkin. Quickly, they extricated themselves, looking for the injured.

"It's Flint!" announced Savin. Flint was lying on his back, holding his leg and grimacing in obvious pain. There was a Renegade arrow sticking clean through the thick portion of his upper leg.

"Can you . . . believe it?" Flint choked out through clenched teeth. "It's the same leg."

"To the log, Larkin!" Hawk ordered. "I'll tend to Flint."

Rush, Savin, Sycamore, and Jay grabbed their bows and quickly took up defensive positions behind the log.

Looking up to view the line of defense, Hawk called to the Larkin on each end. "Rush! Jay! Watch our flanks!"

Turning his attention back to his injured companion, Hawk examined the wounded leg. After a few moments of moving the leg and feeling the area around the protruding arrow, Hawk announced, "Well, my friend, it could have been much worse. It looks like the arrow missed the bone.

"What's it look like up there, Rush?" the Larkin leader asked.

"There's movement behind some brush to the left, 'bout halfway between us and the trail. Nothing's showing to the right, but I 'spect they're there."

"Is this a defensible position?" Hawk asked as he stuck his head above the log to see for himself.

"It ain't the best," answered Rush, "but I see nothin' better around us."

"It'll have to do," Hawk agreed.

"Savin, help me with Flint," he said as he returned his attention to their injured companion. "Try to hold him still while I get this arrow out of his leg."

Savin sat Flint up and then sat behind him with his arms around him.

"I'll be as gentle as I can, Flint," Hawk said compassionately.

"Just do it, Hawk," Flint said, steeling himself for the pain to come.

Using his sharp cutting edge, Hawk began to saw through the wooden arrow shaft just behind the stone head. With every wiggle of the arrow, waves of pain shot through Flint's leg. It seemed like an eternity to Flint before Hawk was able to snap off the arrow's head. Then Hawk announced, "Okay, Flint, here we go." Savin tightened his grip. Flint, who by now had beads of sweat covering his face, clenched his teeth hard, and Hawk withdrew the shaft from his leg.

Hawk washed both wounds, packed them with some pieces of fungus that he had in his backpack, and bandaged the leg with strips of cloth that Hawk cut from his own cloak. He then gave Flint a long drink from his water pack. "Rest easy for now. We may need you later," he said.

Hawk and Savin moved up behind the log with the others. "What's our situation?" Hawk wanted to know as he peered over the log.

"Wel-l-l," Rush began in his slow, easy voice, "it appears to me that we got ourselves a po-sitional problem."

"Looks to me like they all got scared and left," the youthful Jay excitedly interjected. "I don't see a single one of 'em."

Rush cut his eyes over at his younger companion and hesitated a moment before he responded, "I'll admit that the landscape does seem rather . . . umm . . . . unpopulated at the moment, but I don't think I'd walk out there and test that idear o' yorn. 'Cause if'n you do, you're gonna have several new, feathered pro-trusions stickin' outta yer' thick Larkin hide."

"What do you see?" Hawk asked Rush impatiently.

"That brush off to the left," Rush indicated a thick patch of brush, halfway between them and the trail. "I seen some unnatural movement in there." After a pause he continued, "I figure there's a few more in that thick, grassy patch over there to the right, but if'n we could get Jay to stick his head up a little higher, we'd know for sure." They all smiled at that last remark and looked over at Jay, whose ears were starting to turn red at the good-natured rebuke he'd just received.

"Sure enough," Rush went on, "most of them painted heatherns turned tail and hit the bush. They took our meat with 'em, too." Rush was looking down the log toward Sycamore, whose eyes were anxiously searching the scene of their recent battle. "Syc, if'n it eases yer' mind, I figure yer' boy's still alive."

Sycamore's gaze quickly fixed on Rush. "How do you figure that?" he asked anxiously.

"Wel-l-l," Rush began, "just look out there. There's Sage away up yonder at the head of the trail where he fell, and there's Buck laying where they kilt him. But yer' boy Poke's gone. Think about it. They got no use for a dead Larkin, but a young, live one'll make a purdy decent slave."

Savin quickly looked up at Rush. Rush saw his eyes and knew his thoughts. "Same deal, Savin," Rush answered his unasked question. "If'n we get out o' this here hole we got ourselves into, and we was to walk back down that trail without finding the lad's carcass, then you can put two things in your bag o' truth. The first one is that he's alive, and the second one is that he's with Poke."

"You said we had a 'positional problem'," Jay said. "From our position here behind this log, we can hold off anything they throw at us."

Hawk answered this time, "That's true if they attack from the front, but our flanks and our rear are basically unprotected."

For the first time, Jay looked around and realized how vulnerable they were. "Well," Jay said nervously, "they haven't had time to get behind us yet. Let's move farther back. We . . . we could outrun 'em!"

"Flint can't," Rush said matter-of-factly.

"Don't worry about me," Flint spoke up. "I think Jay's right. Prop me up over there by the log, and I'll hold 'em while the rest of you slip out the back way."

"No! I'm not right!" Jay burst out. "I'm foolish, and I talk when I should be listening. There's no way I'm leaving without you!"

"Nobody's gonna be left behind," Hawk said decisively. "But if we're gonna have a chance to save our skins, we need to have a plan."

"And to have a plan," Rush joined in, "we need to know what we're up against."

"What've you got in mind?" Hawk asked.

"I think we ought'a spread our eyes out a bit," Rush replied. "I'll wager that if Sycamore could work his way down the backside of this here log, movin' easy' like and using that low ground over there, he could make it unseen to that thick stand of brush off yonder to the left. From that point, he could spot any movement against our left flank, and maybe he could get a shot off at 'em from that angle."

Sycamore scanned the ground to the left of their position, studying the terrain. "I can do that," Sycamore stated after a moment.

"While Syc's slitherin' out to our left, I'll be a doin' the same thing off to our right," Rush continued. "I should be able to reach that tree over yonder without them murderin' savages spottin' me. I might even be able to climb up in it from the backside. If I can get up to that second or third limb, I should be able to see about everything they're doin'."

"Anybody got any better ideas?" Hawk asked. No one spoke. "All right then, move out, you two," he ordered. "The rest of us will try to keep the enemies' attention on us."

As Sycamore and Rush began quietly slipping away from the others, Hawk began giving loud orders. They threw dirt and leaves over the top of the log. Occasionally one of them would stick his head up for a couple of seconds and then, just as quickly, duck back down.

It took several minutes for both Sycamore and Rush to get into position. Sycamore found himself about a good stone's throw from his companions. The patch of brush behind which he hid was not as thick as it had looked from the log. He had to remain very still to keep from being spotted by the enemy.

Rush, on the other hand, was behind the trunk of a large sweet gum tree. As long as he kept the trunk of the tree between himself and the Renegades, they had no hope of seeing him. He unlashed a set of climbers that he had brought with him from his belt and quickly strapped on the boot pieces.

Larkin climbers consisted of two boot pieces and two hand pieces. The boot pieces were made to fit the booted foot. When lashed in place, they had a flat, sharp thorn protruding from the front of both feet. By forcefully kicking the toe of a boot into the bark of the tree, this would stick the point of the fire-hardened thorn deep enough to support a Larkin's weight. The hand pieces were short, parallel wooden rods with a cross piece toward the bottom wrapped with leather for a handgrip. The top of the rods had a long, narrow thorn attached to them at a sharp angle so that they resembled hooks. By swinging the hand piece hard against the tree in a downward direction, the thorn would be impaled in the tree bark deeply enough to support the weight of the climber, but not so deeply that it couldn't be pulled back out. By utilizing the climbers, a Larkin who was skilled in their use could literally walk up a tree.

Rush began his assent slowly, testing the feel of the bark. As his confidence grew, he began to climb more quickly. Still, he was careful to be as quiet as possible. Hawk and the others kept up as much noise and activity as they could to keep their enemies' attention on the log.

The first limb on the sweet gum tree left him exposed to the view of the enemy, so Rush climbed on past it to a second limb further up that came off the side of the tree in a wide "V" angle. Rush was sweating profusely and blowing hard when he pulled himself into the notch of the limb. His companions all breathed a sigh of relief when they saw that he had reached a spot of safety.

Rush wasted no time in taking a look around. What he saw gave him concern. There were two Renegades behind the patch of grass which was about two stone throws in front of and slightly to the left of his tree. He could also see three more Renegades behind the brush off to the left. But of greatest concern to Rush was seeing two Renegade warriors crawling stealthily through the grass. One was swinging wide to the left, apparently to attack them from the flank. The other was coming from the right and was heading for the base of Rush's sweet gum tree. Rush scanned the area looking for other enemies.

Behind the log, all were tense. Jay and Savin peered over the top, watching for the enemy attack they expected at any moment. Hawk was behind them, kneeling next to Flint, but his eyes were fixed on the notch of the tree where Rush perched.

Savin felt the breeze as a Renegade arrow shot past his right ear. He heard a "thunk" sound and a groan from behind him as the arrow found its mark. Whirling quickly around, Savin saw Hawk crumple to the ground with a feathered shaft protruding from his left shoulder.

The wounded Flint was reaching for his injured companion. "Savin, help!" he exclaimed. "Hawk's been hit!"

"That arrow came from above us!" Jay said incredulously.

From his perch Rush had seen what had happened. He scanned the trees around him looking for the enemy. Suddenly a movement caught his eye. There, directly in front of him and almost on his same level, was the Renegade archer. The enemy warrior was in a tree very close to Rush's. The Renegade was in the process of pulling another arrow from his quiver as Rush spotted him. He was standing on a large limb and had been leaning against the trunk of the tree to steady his aim. The Renegade was partially hidden from the Larkin behind the log by some leaves, but Rush had an unobstructed view of him.

Unslinging his bow, Rush quickly fitted an arrow to the string, drew it back its full length, and shot. As his arrow struck its mark, the enemy archer dropped his bow and collapsed upon the limb.

Rush leaned over the back side of his tree to signal his friends, but the others were so busy with Hawk that Rush could not get their attention. Waving his arms frantically, he finally managed to get Sycamore to look at him. Using Larkin sign language, Rush warned him of the approaching enemy. Sycamore signed back that he understood, then he silently moved deeper into the brush to hide himself.

By this time the second crawling Renegade had reached Rush's tree. Stringing another arrow to his bow and leaning over the back side of the tree, Rush waited until he was sure that his enemy was completely hidden from the view of the other Renegades.   A single arrow shot from Rush's bow ended this Renegade's murderous career. "Hmmm, the odds are getting better," he thought.

Rush knew that the Renegades would be making their move soon. The sun was setting now, and as it got dark, the enemy would move against them. "But," Rush thought, "they ain't as strong as they think they are. Still," Rush continued to reflect, "even with five of 'em comin' against us in the dark, they could do a lot of damage."

He had to think of a way to reduce the enemies' numbers further. Gazing back at the Renegade lying on the limb of the tree across from him, Rush got an idea. He grinned to himself at the simplicity of it. Looking up, he could see that some of the branches of his tree came in contact with branches of the tree holding the Renegade. He knew he had to move fast to make this work.

Jerking on the climbers again, he moved cautiously out onto the trunk on the back side of the tree and began moving up. He quickened his pace as much as he dared and in a short time reached a limb that extended horizontally into the other tree. Removing his climbers, he ran along this wide limb for most of its length, but as it narrowed, he had to slow his pace. When he reached the point of nearest contact with a limb from the other tree, his heart leaped up into his throat. It was clear that in order for him to reach the other tree, he would have to jump from his limb to the other. He kept telling himself that it would not be a very big jump since the limbs were very close. But he was so high up that the thought of what would happen to him if he missed the limb made his head swim.

He decided that if he thought about it anymore he might not be able to do it, so he locked his eyes on the limb to which he was jumping and threw himself at it. As it was, he almost jumped too hard. He had to grab some small branches coming out of the limb to keep his momentum from carrying him over the opposite edge. As soon as he stopped swaying, he took a deep breath, climbed on top of the branch, and began working his way to the trunk of the tree.

Strapping on climbers once more, Rush carefully let himself down the tree. In a short while he arrived on the limb beside the fallen Renegade. Rush took the remaining arrows from the Renegade's quiver and stuck them in his own. He looked at the tunic the Renegade warrior was wearing. It had many personal symbols painted on it, obviously commemorating various important events and special honors. Rush quickly pulled this tunic off of his enemy and put it on himself. He also grabbed the Renegade's mask.

He then climbed the rest of the way down the tree to the ground. Leaning against the base of the tree was the Renegade's war club. Rush hid his own weapons and the climbers underneath the Renegade's tunic, put on the mask, and took up the war club.

Daylight was fading now as Rush moved cautiously through the shadows until he was behind the patch of grass shielding the two Renegades. He knew that if he shot one of them with his bow, the other one would warn the others and possibly escape. But he had thought all of this through while he was still in the tree. He knew exactly what he had to do.

Rush adjusted the mask, stood up, and strolled nonchalantly up to the two Renegades. They both jerked around suddenly, weapons ready, as they heard Rush approach. When they recognized their companion's mask and war shirt, they lowered their weapons.

"Gort! You idiot!" snarled the taller of the two Renegades. "You about scared the liver outta me! Why didn't you whistle?" Rush just shrugged his shoulders.

"Did you see anything from the tree?" asked the taller Renegade, who was obviously in charge. Rush responded by shaking his head. "Well, I'm glad you came back then," the Renegade leader said. "We'll be getting the signal to attack those scum as soon as Rip and Narick get in position."

A fierce sneeze exploded from the shorter Renegade, who had his mask off. He wiped his nose on the tail of his tunic. From the look of his red, swollen nose and his nasty tunic, this had been going on for some time.

"Would you stop that!" hissed the leader.

"I can't 'elp it!" snorted the shorter Renegade.

"Well, you'd better help it," the leader threatened. "You're gonna get us killed with all the noise you're makin'."

"Wud'm I s'pose to do?" demanded the short one.

"Y'er suppose to do whatever you have to do to keep from attractin' the enemies' attention!" the leader snapped back.

Suddenly three short whistles sounded from somewhere off to their right. "There's the signal," the Renegade leader announced. "It's dark enough now that they won't be able to see us very well. The plan is for us all to slip up as close to that log as we can and then rush 'em. That means," he was glaring at the shorter Renegade now, "in case you can't figure it out, that if we make any more noise, some or all of us will get killed!"

The leader was really getting worked up now. He jammed his finger in front of the face of the short one. "I'm warning you, slime face! If you let out another one of those sneezes while we're moving up, you're gonna wish you hadn't!" he threatened in a whispered rage. With that, the leader spun around and led them out from their place of concealment into the dimly lit undergrowth. The short one swallowed hard and followed after the leader. Rush brought up the rear.

They hadn't taken five steps when the short one suddenly made a frantic grab for the skirt of his tunic and buried his face in it. A muffled sneeze was heard a half second later. As if on cue, Rush swung the war club he was holding and clobbered the short Renegade in front of him.

At the sound of the sneeze, the Renegade leader whipped around and was in time to see his companion collapse under Rush's club. The leader jerked his mask off and just stood there, mouth open, looking incredulously at Rush.

"Wha . . . Why . . . I can't . . ." the leader stammered. He looked down in disbelief at his crumpled companion and then back up at Rush. He tried to speak again. "I didn't mean . . . It was only a threat! Why'd you do that?!" he managed to get out.

Rush just shrugged. The Renegade leader groaned in exasperation and bent over to check on his fallen comrade. As he did so, Rush clubbed him too.

Rush pulled the uncomfortable wooden mask off and headed back through the woods the way he had come. Now that the remaining three Renegades were creeping up through the brush, chances were he wouldn't be able to find them before they started their attack. Since he knew where they were heading, he decided to just be there waiting on them.

Fearing no enemy on this side, Rush ran quickly to the base of the tree where he had started. There he took off the Renegade war shirt and rolled the mask and war club up in it. Then he quickly crawled back into their camp.

"How's Hawk?" was the first thing he said as he returned to his friends.

"He's hurt pretty bad, Rush," Flint said, who was nursing him. "He took an arrow in the upper chest towards his left shoulder. It appears that it missed his lung. We were able to cut the arrow out, but he's lost a lot of blood."

Rush looked at his pale friend and saw that Hawk had fainted both from the pain of having the arrow removed and the loss of blood. "Just as well," thought Rush.

"What about that other Renegade?" Rush asked. "Did Syc get 'em?" Rush looked off to the left toward Sycamore's position. As if in answer to his questioning gaze, Sycamore waved back a Renegade war club he had taken from his victim. "Very good," Rush nodded at Sycamore.

"Okay," Rush spoke to the rest, "here's how she sits, fellers. There's only three of 'em left, but they don't' know they've lost their buddies."

"How are we going to find them, Rush?" asked Savin.

"We don't have to," he answered. "They're comin' to us. Right this moment, them three weasels are slippin' up through the brush to surprise us. In just a minute or two, they should be poppin' up just to the left of the front of our log. So let's all grab our bows, put an arrow to the string, and be ready to give 'em a nice, big, Larkin welcome when they show up."

They didn't have to wait long after they all got into position. There was a sudden fierce cry, and three forms shot forward toward the log. Five bow strings twanged, and the attack was over.

A few minutes later, as Rush and Flint were readjusting Hawk's bandage, Savin spoke up, "Well, Rush, with Hawk out of action, that makes you hunt master. So what's the plan?"

After a few moments of thought, Rush answered. "Wel-l-l, fellers," he said as he turned to face the others, "here's the way I see it. Hawk and Flint ain't doin' no walkin'. Now there's four of us healthy enough to carry 'em, but we'd be goin' so slow, we'd stand a good chance of getting caught out in the open by some Larkin-eatin' varmints. Plus, I'm not sure our good buddy Hawk can last without some help fairly soon."

"So what do we do?" Jay spoke up impatiently.

"I propose," Rush continued, "that we send someone back to the Keep for help while the rest of us find a tree or bush to hoist these two wounded warriors up into for safe keeping."

"Why a tree, Rush?" Flint asked. "We're safe enough right here."

Hawk was stirring now. He was trying to say something, but he was very weak. Flint leaned closer to hear him so he didn't have to exert himself.

Flint sat back up. "Ants!" Flint spoke. "He said 'Ants!'"

"Hawk knows," Rush continued. "There's been enough blood spilt around here that this place is gonna be crawlin' with ants come daylight."

"So which one of us makes the run to the Keep?" asked Sycamore.

"Anyone of us could do it," added Savin. "We all know the way."

"Yep, that's true," Rush replied. "But with Hawk needin' special attention in a hurry, I figure that the most important thing is speed."

After a moment's reflection on Rush's words, they all turned and looked at Jay.

"Then it's me," said Jay resolutely. He was easily the fastest runner in their hunting party. He was one of the three fastest runners in the Keep. He also had the endurance to make a three hour run, which was about how long it would take him if he made good time.

"The moon's coming up," said Sycamore, "so you should be able to see."

"That means the night creatures can see him, too," added Flint.

"They'll see him anyway," groaned Hawk, who was trying to lift his head.

Jay stepped over to Hawk and put his hand on his good shoulder. "Rest easy," Jay said. "They may see me, but they'll never catch me."

"I'm . . . counting on it," Hawk breathed out weakly.

"Jay," Rush called for his young friend's attention. "Do you have any questions on how to get back to the Keep?"

"No," Jay replied. "We're over halfway there, and the trail is pretty clear. With the moonlight, I shouldn't have any trouble seeing the way."

"I hate to put this on you," Rush said to Jay privately, "but if something gets after you, and you get stuck up in a tree or in a hole, Hawk will probably be a dead Larkin."

"I won't let anything stop me, Rush," Jay said resolutely.

"Leave everything here but your sling and a few stones."

Jay laid aside his pack, shield, and sting. He tied his sling around his waist and then sat down and began pulling off his boots. Reaching into his pack, he pulled out a pair of lace-up moccasins with extra thick soles.

"My running boots," Jay announced to the questioning glances. "I always keep them with me in case I need 'em." Jay stood up to test their feel.

Savin handed Jay his water pack, and Jay took a long pull on it. "Well, I guess I'm ready," he announced. "You fellows take care of Hawk and Flint, and I'll be back by daylight with help."

"You take care of yourself," Flint said.

"The Maker be with you, Jay," Rush said seriously as he and Jay gripped each others' forearms in the typical Larkin manner.

"And with you," Jay answered. Turning his back on his friends, Jay leaped over the log, sprinted over to the trail, and disappeared into the moonlit woods.

CHAPTER FOUR

THE LONG NIGHT

It was after sunset when Hawthorn's mind began to win the fight to regain his senses. The first thing he became aware of was pain—a deep, aching pain. Although he was for the moment unable to focus his eyes, he noticed that the pain began to localize in his head. He started to reach up to feel the back of his throbbing head and discovered that he couldn't move. Not being able to remember exactly what had happened, he at first thought that he had been bitten by some large spider and paralyzed. Then he felt the tight cords around his wrists. He found that his legs were also bound.

Suddenly a hand grabbed a fist full of his hair and painfully jerked his head off the ground. Hawthorn blinked, trying to see his tormentor through the tears that were welling up in his eyes. The Renegade began laughing in Hawthorn's face. "Hey! Look over here, Brack!" he laughed. "Da' little scum's wakin' up. I tol' you he'd live. You owe me ten arrows."

The Renegade released his grip on Hawthorn's hair, allowing his head to fall back down. His head hurt so badly when it hit the ground that, for a moment, Hawthorn thought he was going to be sick at his stomach. But in a short while, the intense pain in his head began to settle down to just a dull throb.

Hawthorn began looking around at the Renegade camp. He remembered being caught by the Renegades and trying to get away. He still wasn't sure what had happened after that, but he figured that one of them must have hit him with something—probably a war club. If that were the case, then he was very fortunate to be alive . . . or was he?

"Was it so fortunate to be a Renegade slave?" he asked himself. Then the thought of escape entered his mind. He looked around the camp to get an idea of what he was up against. He could see three Renegades in the camp. None of the three seemed to be doing much of anything. It was as if they were waiting for something or someone.

Hawthorn had not been working on his escape plan very long when a fourth Renegade came trotting noiselessly out of the brush and into the small clearing where they were. "Get ready!" he announced. "They're here!" That apparently was the signal to break camp, because that's exactly what the four of them quickly set about doing.

Soon Hawthorn could hear the sound of rustling leaves and grass as the expected party approached. He could just see their heads as they moved along the trail through the brush. There were fifteen Renegades in the group coming in. When he saw how many were marching into the clearing, his heart sank. As the war party came into full view, Hawthorn was stunned when he saw what they had with them. Eight of the masked warriors were carrying the litters on which were the two mooflon that the Larkin hunters had killed that morning.

"We rest here," ordered a tall Renegade, who was obviously in charge. "Get your packs and be ready to leave when I say." The tall Renegade looked over at Hawthorn. There was so much evil in those cold eyes that it made Hawthorn shudder. "Wolf!" he shouted.

Hawthorn saw an older, grizzled Renegade hurry up the trail toward the leader who called him. The old Renegade warrior was dragging someone with him. It was Poke!

"Keep an eye on our two slaves," the leader said, looking down at Poke and then over at Hawthorn.

"My pleasure," Wolf sneered through a lot of missing and broken teeth. Quickly Wolf jerked a long flint knife from his belt and jammed the point under Poke's chin. "Hey, Greatfighter," he called over his shoulder, "how 'bout I cut their tongues out so they don't do no yappin'?"

Poke was on his tiptoes to try to keep the point of the knife from sinking deeper into his flesh. Hawthorn knew that this was no joke. It was obvious that this mean old snake would have enjoyed cutting both of their throats.

"No, not yet," returned the Renegade leader, whom Wolf had called Greatfighter. "They'd be too weak from loss of blood to help carry the meat."

Disappointed, Wolf put his knife back in his belt and pushed Poke over to where Hawthorn lay on the ground, shoving him down next to his friend. Blood was freely flowing down Poke's neck from the deep cut under his chin. He was trembling and was very pale.

It wasn't long before Wolf was involved in a conversation with another Renegade. Hawthorn slowly leaned closer to Poke and whispered, "What happened?"

"Ambush," whispered Poke in reply.

"The others?" Hawthorn asked with his eyes glued on Wolf.

"Buck dead. Sage dead . . .The rest . . . maybe dead. Don't know."

Hawthorn felt as if his heart had just been pierced by one hundred arrows. He forced himself to ask one more question. "My father?" Hawthorn was searching Poke's face for some sign of hope, but Poke could give him none.

"Don't know," came the answer. "Maybe dead."

"Hey!" snapped Wolf's raspy voice. He was glaring at the two Larkin captives. "You two little vermin wasn't talkin', was you?"

Hawthorn and Poke didn't answer.

"Well, I think I'll shove a couple a dirt clods down yer' throats. That'll stop yer' yappin'."

Wolf bent over and picked up two large clods of dirt and started over to the two Larkin. He stood between them, bouncing the clods in his hands. "Now, my little ones, who's gonna be the first to eat dirt?" he sneered.

"Eat it yourself, you fat old toad!" Poke spat back, without thinking of the consequences.

"Eat this, you scum!" Wolf roared in fury as he lifted his heavily booted foot and drove the heel toward Poke's face. The blow might have crushed Poke's skull had Hawthorn not been alert. When Wolf started his kick at Poke, Hawthorn drove both of his feet at the leg Wolf was standing on. There was a distinct snap as Wolf's knee buckled sideways, collapsing under him. The force being taken out of his kick, Wolf's boot did little more than stun Poke, while Wolf writhed on the ground, holding his knee and groaning in pain. Hawthorn looked all around for a way to escape, but with his hands and feet bound there was none. Looking back, he saw that Wolf, absolutely wild with pain and rage, had his knife out and was crawling for him.

"Stop him!" shouted a voice from across the camp.

Just as Wolf started to throw himself at Hawthorn, three Renegades grabbed him and pulled him back. Wolf roared with anger and fought madly to get to Hawthorn. He even tried to throw his knife at the young Larkin, but one of his captors blocked his arm, and the knife flew wide of its mark. The three warriors finally managed to pin Wolf to the ground and hold him. Soon he began to calm down. From the other side of the camp came the one who had shouted. It was Greatfighter, their leader. He stood above Wolf, glaring at him. "I told you to leave them alone."

"He ruint my knee!" Wolf spat back through clenched teeth.

"You brought that on yourself, you old fool. I told you I wanted them to help carry that meat. When I'm finished with them, you can cut them to pieces for all I care, but until then, I want them unharmed. And I will be obeyed."

Wolf just glared at the Renegade leader.

"Don't make me make an example of you, Wolf," Greatfighter threatened.

After a long wait, Wolf answered. "All right," he panted angrily, still obviously in a great deal of pain, "but when we get back to the Lair, they're mine!"

Wolf looked directly at Hawthorn now. "You're gonna hurt!" he snarled at Hawthorn. "You're gonna hurt so bad!"

Hawthorn knew that it was a promise, and it made him shudder.

"You two get him up and help wrap his leg so he can walk," Greatfighter said to two of the Renegades holding Wolf. "You," he said to the third Renegade, "get some help and tie each of our two slaves to a carrying pole on the litters holding the meat. Be sure to split them up. Tie them to different litters."

Hawthorn and Poke were jerked up roughly. Hawthorn's head was still throbbing, and he had trouble keeping his feet at first. Two Renegades marched Poke off to the second litter, and the end of the leather strap which bound his hands was tied to the pole at the back of the litter on the right side. Hawthorn was pushed up to the front litter and tied to the back pole on the left side.

Hawthorn's mind was racing, trying to come up with an escape plan, but no ideas came to him. He knew that if they reached the Renegade stronghold, he and Poke were dead Larkin. Wolf would see to that personally. If only he could talk to the Maker and ask Him for help! But only the Shaman knew the Maker's spirit language, and no one else was permitted to learn it. If he could talk to the Maker, Hawthorn knew what he would say. He'd tell the Maker how evil these Renegades were, and then he'd ask the Maker to just open up the ground and swallow them up, every last one of them!

"All right! Let's go!" announced the Renegade leader.

Somehow Hawthorn found the strength to lift his corner of the litter. His first few steps were unsteady, but fortunately the going was slow at first, allowing him time to regain strength and balance in his legs.

It was night now, but the Renegades seemed to know their way through the dark woods. The column moved south, laboring through the thick brush.

They stopped several times that night, both to rest and, apparently, to let Greatfighter get his bearings; but the rests were short. In this way, the Renegade column kept moving all night.

It seemed to Hawthorn that an eternity had passed before the sun came up. Shortly after dawn, they stopped again for a short break. Poke and Hawthorn were left tied to their litter polls while a guard sat nearby to watch them.

They were out of the thick brush and had stopped in a small clearing. Sitting there on the coarse, red soil, Hawthorn began looking around. The forest seemed to be changing its personality as they moved south. Hawthorn noticed that there were not as many hardwood trees as there had been. The large, shady oaks, hickories, and elms were being replaced by tall, fragrant pines. Very little underbrush grew under a thick pine forest, so Hawthorn knew that probably they would be forced to carry the litters at a quicker pace.

Hawthorn had no idea how close they were to the Renegade fortress, but he knew that whenever they arrived, Poke and he were as good as dead unless they could somehow free themselves and escape.

Rush chose a young dogwood tree for their place of refuge. It was close to the trail and had some lower limbs that could be easily reached with a short climb. He would have preferred a place much higher off the ground, but getting Hawk and Flint up very high would be too difficult. The fact that it was close by was the main reason he chose this particular tree. Ants were already moving across their recent battleground, drawn there by the smell of blood.

Using their climbers, Rush and Sycamore ascended to the first large branch. They each carried a length of rope made from cocoon silk. Tying their ropes together, they made a loop in one end which they lowered to the ground. Sitting in this loop, Flint used a pair of hand climbers to help pull himself up the tree as Rush and Sycamore heaved on the rope from the branch above. The real chore was getting Hawk up. He was too weak to hold himself in the loop, so Savin climbed up with him. With his arms around Hawk and holding on to the rope that was looped around Hawk's hips, Savin used the foot pieces of the climbers to ascend the tree with him. Rush and Sycamore pulled Hawk up with the rope, while Savin, climbing along with him, kept him from falling out.

It was well past dark when they got Flint and Hawk settled on the wide dogwood limb. Rush, Savin, and Sycamore were exhausted.

"I know you fellers are whipped, but we got us one more chore to do," Rush said to Savin and Sycamore as the three of them sat there on the limb catching their breath.

"What else do we need to do?" asked Savin, a little puzzled.

"We got to make ourselves a couple of bongers," Rush announced.

"Bongers?" Sycamore questioned. "Do you know what he's talking about, Savin?"

"Nope, I've never heard of them."

"That's because I just thought of 'em," Rush said nonchalantly. "Listen, fellers." Rush paused, and they were all silent as they listened to the noises in the surrounding woods.

"Do ya hear that?" Rush asked at last. "There's ants and all kind of scavenger critters movin' over the ground down there where we had our fight. It's a purdy safe bet that some of 'em, maybe a lot of 'em, are gonna find our tree; and I don't care how good you are with your bows, arrows won't stop ants. We might could push 'em off the tree trunk if we had a lance, but we lost those with the mooflon. So I started thinkin', 'How could we protect ourselves if somethin' started up this tree to get us?' That's when I got the idear for a bonger."

Rush then spent the next few moments explaining to them what he had in mind.

"It's so simple," Savin said in amazement.

"If we put one on each side of the tree, that should be all we need," Sycamore added thoughtfully.

"How'd you think of that?" Flint asked from where he was lying nearby.

"Wel-l-l," Rush drawled, "I looked at what we had to work with, and it just... sorta... made sense."

Savin was still wearing the foot pieces of the climbers, so he was selected to climb back down the tree. Once on the ground, he found two large rocks that he was able to roll over to the base of the tree. Savin wrapped one end of the rope several times around one of the rocks and tied it securely so that the rock would not slip out. With great effort, Rush and Sycamore pulled the rock up into the tree. After they had the rock resting on the limb where they stood, they lowered the other end of the rope, and Savin tied the other rock to this end as well. Then Savin climbed back up to give them a hand. When Savin arrived at their limb, he saw that the rope had been untied from the first rock and looped over a limb right above their heads. The three Larkin then pulled the second rock up until it was about halfway up the tree, between the ground and the limb on which they stood.

"You two fellers hold that rock while I fix the other end of the rope."

Savin and Sycamore braced themselves and held tightly to the rope attached to the suspended rock. Rush quickly took in all the slack and looped the rope two more times around the limb above them. Next he tied the end of the rope around the first rock that was resting beside them on the limb. Then with a call of warning to the others, he pushed the first rock off the limb. They now had a large rock suspended on opposite sides of the tree, each one hanging about half way up.

"Okay, Rush," Sycamore said, "how do you use them?"

"Wel-l-l, let's suppose," Rush began, "that there's an ant climbin' up this side of the tree. You just reach up here, grab the rope, and start swinging the rock. Now the trick is to time it so that when the ant reaches the rock's height, you pull the rope in a half circle and cause the rock to crash into the trunk of the tree, making an ant pancake." He demonstrated the swinging technique as he said this, and the large rock crashed into the tree with a resounding thud. "Once the moon gets up a little higher, we should be able to see well enough to hit anything that tries to climb our tree," Rush added.

They took turns swinging the rocks and making them crash into the tree until they felt confident that they each could swing the rocks accurately.

"As tired as we are," Rush began, "I suggest we change the guard every hour. I'll stand the first watch."

"No," Flint spoke up, "I'll stand the first watch. I can't use my leg very well, but my eyes and ears are working just fine. If I see something, I'll wake you up."

"Okay," Rush replied, "that'll be the plan. Whoever takes guard duty, be sure and check on Hawk. Flint, wake me up in an hour, and I'll take second watch. Savin, you take third watch. Syc will take fourth."

"Then it will be my turn again," Flint added.

"Uh … right," said Rush. "We'll just repeat the rotation till sunup. All right? Now let's do some snoozin'."

As Savin and Sycamore each tried to find a place to sleep, Rush went over to check on Hawk. As he leaned over his injured friend, Hawk opened his eyes.

"How ya' holdin' up, Ol' Timer?" Rush said with a sly smile.

"Old Timer!" Hawk growled. "Why, I'll outlive you, Buzzard Bait."

"You sure sound a lot better'n you look," Rush chuckled.

"Well, you ain't no mornin' glory yourself," Hawk shot back. They were both smiling at each other now.

"How about a drink?" said Rush as he lifted Hawk's head and held his opened water pack to his friend's lips. The injured Larkin took a long pull at the offered water. Finally, he laid his head back with a deep, satisfied sigh.

RUSH

"Tastes good," Hawk voiced.

"I got a piece of honey cake and some strips of dried meat I want cha' to chew on," Rush directed. "You need to keep yer strength up."

Hawk ate the offered food, chewing the meat slowly. Finally Hawk looked up at his concerned friend. "Get some sleep, Rush. I think I'll be around for awhile longer."

"You'd better be!" Rush said as he checked his friend's bandage. "I'd hate to think I wasted my last honey cake on ya' if'n you was gonna croak anyway."

Hawk managed a weak smile and shook his head at his crude companion. Rush smiled back as he wrapped Hawk's cloak around him. Satisfied that his friend was as comfortable and warm as he could be under the circumstances, Rush wrapped his own cloak around himself and, using his back pack for a pillow, was asleep in two minutes.

An hour came and went. The moon was up high enough now that Flint could make out shapes of rocks and limbs on the forest floor below. He could not see them, but he could hear the night creatures moving about. He knew that most of them were ants scurrying around, searching for the source of the blood scent they detected. The only creature that he had actually seen was an owl that had flown between their tree and the rising moon, but it had been a long way off and seemed to take no notice of them.

Whenever he would start to doze off, he would pat his injured leg, and with a wince of mild discomfort, he would be wide awake again. Doing this, he managed to keep constant vigil for three hours. He wanted to give the others as much rest as possible.

"Was that something?" Flint thought. He positioned himself to get a better view down the right side of the tree. He sat motionless, staring intently into the gloom below. "There!" he almost shouted his thoughts. "Right there!" His eyes locked on a moon shadow close to the base of their tree. Out of the shadow a tiny creature crawled, moving in an irregular pattern. The ant searched the ground before it, moving closer and closer to the base of the tree. When the ant put its front two legs on the tree trunk, it suddenly stopped. It seemed frozen in that position for a long time. The only thing that it moved was its feelers. After what seemed like hours to Flint, the ant turned away from the tree, only to stop again, sensing the air with its feelers.

Flint was just starting to relax again when—to his horror—the ant suddenly turned and started rapidly up the tree towards them. Forgetting the pain in his injured leg, he leaned against the trunk of the tree and, using the bark as a handgrip, pulled himself up so he could grab the rope of the bonger on that side.

Rush and the others were suddenly shaken from their sleep by a crashing thud and a shudder that shot through the tree. Instantly Rush's hands shot down to his sides, feeling for the steadiness of the limb on which he lay. He had slept in trees too many times to make a sudden move. He pushed himself up and was quickly at Flint's side. They were immediately joined by Savin and Sycamore.

"They work!" was all Flint said.

The three startled Larkin looked down the rope to the large rock suspended at its end. There, stuck to one side of it, was the smashed body of a red ant.

"There's more of them!" Sycamore warned, pointing down at the moonlight and shadows on the forest floor.

"I see 'em!" joined Savin. "There's two over there by that clump of leaves."

"Three," said Rush as a third ant moved out of a shadow near the other two.

"You two watch the other side of the tree," he added after a short pause. "Flint and I will handle this side."

"How's yer leg?" Rush asked Flint.

Flint was staring at the venomous insects as the nearest one started moving toward their tree. "I don't feel a thing," he said at last, never taking his eyes off the ant.

"Here he comes!" warned Rush as the ant began to climb the trunk.

Pulling and pushing, Rush started the great rock swinging again. Right at the moment that he pulled the rope in a curve to swing it toward the approaching ant, he heard Flint shout, "Now!"

There was a resounding *thunk!* The ant fell to the ground with a crushed head.

"Did you see that?" Flint asked anxiously. "As soon as the rock hit, the other two ants turned and headed for the tree."

"We got one on this side now," reported Sycamore.

"The sound of the rocks hitting the tree seems to draw the ants to us," said Flint. "I don't know if this invention of yours is gonna' save us or kill us."

"Do you wanna' stop using 'em?" Rush said as he started the rock swinging again.

"No!" voiced all three Larkin at the same time.

Savin had the other rock swinging as he and Sycamore watched an ant climbing higher on their side of the tree.

"Both ants are coming up!" Flint called out to Rush. "One behind the other!"

Savin had his own problems. The ant was crawling up quickly to meet them. He pulled hard on the rope, causing the rock to crash against the tree. "Too soon!" cried out Sycamore excitedly.

The rock had indeed hit the tree just ahead of the ant, causing it to lose its grip. The insect fell a short way down the trunk, but one of its hooked claws caught on a projection of bark on the side of the tree, and it began its upward climb again.

Rush was more accurate. His rock crashed stunningly on the first of the two ants. The ant's body exploded from the rock's direct hit. As the rock bounced away from the tree, the second ant climbed right past it.

"He got by it!" Flint shouted. "What are we gonna' do?!"

"Grab the rope!" Rush ordered. "Pull the rock higher. Maybe we can knock the ant off." The rock was heaved upwards by the straining muscles of the two Larkin. "Syc, help us!" Rush called. "We can't pull it up fast enough!"

Moving quickly to join them, Sycamore grabbed the rope and began pulling with all his might.

"We're gaining on him," Rush said as he began swinging the rock from side to side.

The rock hit the ant's abdomen with a glancing blow, causing pieces of bark to break loose. It was enough to stop the ant for a second as it readjusted its grip. When the rock swung back, it caught the insect squarely in the middle and sent the creature flying a good stone's throw into the darkness.

Savin's ant was trying a new tactic. Instead of climbing straight up the tree, it began to angle its way up. This confused Savin's aim, and when he brought the rock crashing against the tree this time, he was behind the ant.

"It's climbing around to your side!" warned Savin. Then he added, "From the south!"

Rush was steadying the bouncing rock where they had let it drop back down. He saw the ant's head and front legs as it appeared around the south side of the tree trunk. He pulled the rope hard in the direction of the ant. The big rock swung over slowly and scuffed some bark off the tree just below the ant. This caused the ant to turn and come straight up the south side of the tree.

"Quickly!" Rush called to Sycamore and Flint. "Help me pull the rock up again!" Rush kept swinging the rock, but because of the angle, he was not able to hit the ant.

Savin decided to try something different. Since the ant was already higher up on the tree than his rock could reach, he decided to try to smash the ant with the rope. He got the rock swinging, and then he pulled the rope as hard as he could toward the south side of the tree. In this way, the rock swung around the tree, wrapping the rope around the trunk. The third time he tried it, the second loop caught the ant right behind the head, trapping it against the tree. As the rock swung round and round the trunk, the rope tightened. They each breathed a sigh of relief when they saw the ant's head pop off and tumble to the ground.

"Good work, Savin," Rush offered.

They each intently scanned the moonlit forest floor below them for any signs of enemies. They did see two more ants, but neither of them attempted to climb their tree.

After about a half an hour of relative quiet, Rush spoke up, "I'll tell you what, fellers, with all the activity in the woods around us, I think we better do things a little different. We'll post two guards at a time so we can watch both sides of the tree. Savin, you and I will take this next watch. We'll try to go for two-hour watches to let Flint and Syc get as much rest as they can. But listen, Savin, if'n you start noddin' off, then say somethin', and we'll change the guard sooner."

"I don't think I'll have any problem staying awake," Savin returned as he gazed down at the bodies of dead ants below them.

"All right then," Rush continued. "Syc, you and Flint try to get some rest. We'll holler if'n we need ya."

With a nod of agreement, Flint and Sycamore settled themselves down for some sleep. Rush went over to check on Hawk, and Savin stood leaning against the trunk of the tree, his eyes ranging back and forth gazing intently into the gloom for signs of enemies.

Unseen by Savin were a pair of reptilian eyes gazing back at him from out of the darkness. Those eyes had been watching and waiting for almost an hour. Drawn by the sound of the rocks thumping against the tree, the large, curious lizard had crawled to find the source of the sound. She had watched the end of the battle with the ants and had seen the bodies of the insects fall to the ground. But she had become most interested in the tasty-looking creatures that were defending the branch of the tree. One or perhaps two of these two-legged creatures would just about fill her belly, which had been all but empty for the past three days.

Slowly, cautiously, she began to move toward the tree.

After all the excitement from the fight with the ants, Savin was wide awake. His eyes roved back and forth over the ground below. With the shadows, the dead leaves, and the limbs, Savin almost didn't see the big lizard. She looked like just another dead limb lying there. She was slowly creeping toward the tree, pausing frequently to keep from being seen. She always kept her eyes fixed on Savin. Whenever he looked away, she would move. When Savin glanced back one time, he noticed a slight movement. As he focused his attention on the area where he saw the movement, suddenly the shape of the lizard stood out. The sight of such a terrible enemy — so large, so close — startled Savin, and he gasped.

The great lizard knew she had been spotted, so she burst forward and raced for the tree with incredible speed.

With wide eyes and dry mouth, all Savin could do to warn the others was shout, "Dragon!!" Then he drew back his bow for a shot.

The large reptile literally ran up the side of their tree, never taking her yellow eyes off Savin.

Savin knew that his life depended on his conquering the fear that threatened to paralyze him. With his bow fully drawn, he sighted down the arrow shaft at the rapidly approaching enemy. Bark was flying from its claws as the lizard charged up the tree to claim its prey. Savin was aware that he could not kill so large a beast with just one arrow, but maybe he could stop its charge if he hit the dragon in a painful spot. He wanted to shoot at its eye, but the dragon's eyes were located back on the sides of its head, and he couldn't risk a miss, so he aimed at the fleshy front of the dragon's snout instead. He waited till the terrible creature was so close that he felt that he couldn't miss, then he shot.

The Larkin's arrow struck its mark, sinking half a shaft-length into the lizard's tender nose. With a terrifying roar of pain, the huge beast pulled up and began digging at its face with one front claw while it held onto the tree with its three other feet.

Rush was standing next to Savin now. The maddened dragon broke off the arrow shaft sticking from its nose, leaving the front half of the arrow buried deeply in its head. With blood streaming into its mouth, the great beast shook its head and began to roar at the two Larkin standing just above. Rush grabbed his backpack and, with both hands, hurled it into the back of the throat of the bellowing dragon.

Choking, the big lizard began clawing at her mouth with both front feet. Still clawing and retching, she toppled over backwards, falling a short distance and landing on top of the rock that the Larkin had suspended from that side of the tree. She managed to hang onto the rope to keep from falling the rest of the way to the ground. She bent her neck and coughed out the backpack.

"Shoot for its head, Larkin!" cried Rush.

With bows drawn, Savin, Sycamore, and Rush began to pepper the injured lizard with arrows. Most of their arrows simply bounced off the thick, bumpy hide on top of the creature's head, but a few found their mark in the soft skin of the mouth and neck. This infuriated the beast, and with a hissing roar, she leaped from the rock and charged up the tree again. Crazed by the pain and the rage, she completely disregarded the arrows that struck her now in the nose and the eyes.

When Rush saw that they were not going to stop the creature's fearless charge, he cried out, "Back! Get back!"

Releasing their arrows, the three archers leaped back and grabbed for their stings as the dragon's head, blinded by arrows, topped the limb. In a rage, she was wagging her head from side to side, snapping viciously in all directions.

Flint already had his sting in his hand. As the monster's head appeared over the top of the limb, he hobbled forward, and dodging the snapping jaws, he thrust his sting with all his strength into the dragon's throat and up into its head.

At this new source of pain, the dying lizard let out a gurgling hiss and thrashed its head and neck violently from side to side, knocking Flint off the limb and out into the blackness of the night. As the strength quickly drained from the creature, she threw back her head, and giving one more rattling hiss, she slipped from the limb and crashed into the ground below.

"Flint! Flint! Can you hear me?!" shouted Rush. They each strained to hear a response, listening for even the faintest sound, but they heard nothing from their friend. Rush repeated his call several more times with the same results.

"The dragon hit him pretty hard," voiced Sycamore. "It's hard to tell how far out there he may have gone."

"I'll go look for him," volunteered Savin.

"No," responded Rush, "it's too dark, and this place is crawling with enemies." Looking his two friends in the eye, Rush continued, "You fellers know me pretty well. I ain't one to be givin' up hope when hope's to be had, but I just don't think a Larkin could survive a fall from this high up."

Looking down at the dead lizard on the ground below them, Savin and Sycamore knew he was right. They all three spent the rest of the night watching for enemies, checking on Hawk, and grieving for Flint.

When the moon set, it became so dark that they were unable to see very far down the trunk of the tree. Consequently they were all very tense for the last hour before dawn, but they began to relax a little as the first hint of daylight began to creep across the eastern sky.

When it was light enough to see the ground, Rush announced, "I'm gonna' go see if I can find Flint. If you hear me call, Savin, you come help me. Syc, you'll stay here with Hawk."

Rush used the climbers to descend to the ground. He took a moment to examine the dead lizard. He was grateful that the ants hadn't found it yet. They would definitely have to move to a different place before the ants came, and that wouldn't be long.

He pulled Flint's sting from where it was still embedded in the dragon's throat and cleaned it with some leaves. Then he retrieved his backpack from where the dragon had spit it out. The outside of it was nasty, but the contents were unharmed. He tried to clean it up with some leaves, but he finally just wrinkled up his nose and slung it on his back. He started off cautiously in the direction he felt Flint had been thrown.

He began ranging back and forth, working his way out from the tree, but he saw no sign of Flint. Soon the brush began to get thicker, and Rush had to pick his way through some briars and under some bushes to continue. As he stopped to get his bearings, he heard a movement in the limbs of the bush above him. He quickly whipped out his sting and stood ready for an attack from above.

"I can't tell who you are, but I need some help," he heard a weak voice say from somewhere in the thick branches above him.

"Flint! You're alive!" Rush joyfully exclaimed.

"Rush, help me out of this mess. I'm stuck in these branches."

Rush sheathed his sting and began looking for a way up into the thick, clustered branches. "Are you hurt?" he asked.

"I'm pretty sure my leg's broke," Flint answered.

"Which one?" Rush wanted to know.

"Guess."

It took Rush several minutes to climb up to Flint's level. It was a quince bush, and there were a lot of thorn-like projections coming out of the limbs, so Rush had to move cautiously.

"What happened to yer clothes?!" Rush asked in astonishment when he saw the few tatters that remained on Flint's body.

"I guess what's left of 'em is hanging on all those thorns up through there," Flint answered weakly, pointing up into the bush.

Rush followed Flint's pointing arm with his eyes and saw a clear trail of torn pieces of clothing all the way to the upper extent of the other side of the bush. Rush turned his gaze back to his injured friend. Flint's entire body was covered with scratches. The right side of his face was swollen and severely bruised. His leggings and tunic were mostly missing. The lower part of Flint's right leg was swollen, bruised, and badly lacerated from where it was caught in a V-notch in the limb on which he was lying.

"When I came to," Flint said, "I was hanging head down with my leg caught in this limb. My leg was bent at a really bad angle where it's not supposed to bend. I barely had enough strength left to pull myself up onto this limb."

"Yer leg looks straight enough now," Rush said as he examined Flint's injured member.

"Since my leg was hung up like it was, and not knowing when help would come, I decided to just pull against my broke leg till it straightened out. When I felt the bones slide back in place, I eased up on the pressure."

"You set yer own broke leg?!" Rush asked incredulously.

"Well, I figured it couldn't hurt any worse than it already did," returned Flint. "I was wrong.

"I guess I passed out after that," Flint continued. "It must have been the Maker who kept me from falling off this limb and messing up my leg again."

"You sure do keep Him busy," Rush said as he pulled out his flint knife and began very gently to cut at the limb that had Flint's leg trapped.

After a few moments, Flint asked, "Rush, what in the world happened to me?!"

Rush quickly looked up at his friend, "You don't remember?"

Flint was thoughtful for a moment. "I think I remember us fighting some ants."

"Is that all?" Rush said with some surprise. "You don't remember the dragon?"

"A dragon?" Flint was thoughtful again. "Well . . . yeah, maybe I do . . . but it all seems like a dream."

"Well, this ain't no dream," said Rush, tapping Flint's injured leg with his knife, which caused Flint to wince. "Oh, uh . . . sorry," said Rush sheepishly, and then he bent back over and began cutting on the limb again. Rush related the whole incident from the fight with the ants to Flint's single-handed attack on the lizard.

"I did that?!" asked Flint. This time it was his turn to sound incredulous. "I must have lost my mind!"

"Well, maybe so, but you saved the rest of us," said Rush, "even though you got yerself kilt."

"Nearly kilt," corrected Flint.

"Oh, yeah, nearly kilt," agreed Rush with a half smile. "But if the truth be told, you look more kilt than not."

"If the truth be told," said Flint, "I feel more kilt than not."

Rush continued his narrative, "The lizard, in her death throws, knocked you quite a distance. Fallin' into this here quince bush did most of the damage to you, but it also saved yer life—Ah! I got it!" he said as he cut through the limb trapping Flint's leg.

"Now listen here," Rush said, "hold as still as you can while I splint yer leg with what's left of the branch I cut off." Rush bandaged Flint's leg, supporting it on either side by cut pieces of the limb. With the broken leg securely splinted, Rush began to move his friend out of the bush. In a short while, they were both on the ground, and after a brief rest, they headed for their companions. Flint carried the backpack, and Rush carried Flint.

All the events of the previous day and night were starting to tell on Rush. He had to stop frequently to rest as they trudged slowly through briars and brush. As they approached the tree where their friends were waiting, Rush heard voices. He set Flint down and cautiously slipped forward to scout the situation. He saw several Larkin up in the tree using ropes to lower Hawk, who was being guided down the tree by two others. "Praise the Maker!" Rush whooped. Jay had made it back!

Rush wasted no time in attracting the attention of some of the rescue party. They had all heard of the battle with the ants and the dragon, and everyone was extremely excited to learn that Flint was still alive.

Hawk and Flint were carried a good distance away from the tree with the dead dragon under it since several ants had come very near the area. Once a safe camp was quickly established, the two injured Larkin received medical attention and warm food. Litters were constructed in order to get them back to the safety of the Keep as quickly as possible.

Rush, Savin, Sycamore, and Jay scouted back down the trail toward the meadow. They moved cautiously, painstakingly searching for any sign of Hawthorn.

"Here!" announced Rush. "Right here is where they took him!"

The other three hung back so as not to spoil any of the sign. Rush was the best tracker, so they left him alone as he moved back and forth across the trail, piecing together the events of the previous day from the evidence before him. He spent close to half an hour intensely studying the ground and the brush on each side of the trail. Finally he voiced his conclusions. "He's hurt, Savin, but I think he's alive. At least, the Renegades thought he was when they drug him off. There seems to have been a struggle right here where they took him," Rush pointed out some churned up dirt and scuff marks in the ground.

"How do you know he's hurt?" Savin asked with concern.

"Renegades don't waste no energy on prisoners," Rush answered matter-of-factly. "If'n he was able to walk, they'da made him. But they didn't. Instead, they drug him off through the woods right over here. I reckon they didn't figure any of us would live, 'cause they didn't even bother to cover their tracks."

"That was mighty nice of them," said Savin. "It'll make the job that much easier."

"Wha'chu got on yer' mind?" Rush asked suspiciously.

"I'm goin' after my son, Rush," Savin answered resolutely.

"They've got my boy, too," joined Sycamore. "I'm going with you."

"Now wait a minute!" Rush growled. "It's crazy for two Larkin to go after a whole army of Renegades."

"Three Larkin," Jay said. "I'm going with them."

"Now hold on!" Rush barked with a scowl. "I'm the hunt master of this here expedition, an' I'm the one who's givin' the orders!"

"So what are your orders?" asked Savin.

"My orders are," growled Rush, "that the four of us turn around right now and march back up the trail to camp. We fill our packs with supplies, and then we track us down an army of Larkin-stealin' cutthroats."

"Now you're talkin'!" shouted Jay.

"I thought you said that was crazy," said Savin.

"O' course it's crazy!" Rush returned. "But the best chance we got of savin' those two young 'uns is to catch up with 'em as quick as we can—while they're still out in the open. It'll be a whole lot tougher to get 'em out once they're inside the Renegade stronghold."

"Well, let's go!" said Sycamore impatiently. Then they all ran quickly back to the Larkin camp to get supplies.

CHAPTER FIVE

RENEGADE CAPTIVES

Hawthorn knew that if he and Poke were going to get away, it would have to be during the march. He decided to tackle one problem at a time. The first thing to do was to free himself. The leather strap which bound him to the litter pole had been wrapped several times tightly around both of his wrists. He could not get his fingers to bend far enough to reach the knot binding his wrists, and the other end was tied so far up on the pole that if he tried to get close to that knot, it would become obvious to his captors what he was doing. He decided that his only option was to cut the wrist cord. But with what?

Hawthorn slowly looked around and noticed all the loose bits of rock lying on the dry, red ground where he rested. "During the wet season, this must be a small pool that catches all the run off," Hawthorn thought, "so all the little pieces of rock and debris must just wash right into this spot."

Hawthorn had been sitting on the ground with his arms resting on his knees. Slowly, he let his arms drop between his legs till his hands were touching the ground. There were plenty of small pieces of rock beneath him. Maybe he could find a sharp piece of quartz. He carefully fingered twenty or more small rocks, but none of them had any edge on them at all.

"On yer feet, slave! Rest's over!" snapped Hawthorn's guard.

Again Hawthorn's heart sank. Nothing was going right. In the growing light of the day, the young Larkin stood up and shouldered the litter pole. A deep sigh came from his breast. In two hours he might get another rest, but then, even if he found a sharp rock, he might not have time to cut through the

67

cords. Furthermore, if he did get free, how could he hope to free Poke and escape? Yes, he would have to free Poke. Even if he had a chance to escape, he knew that he would never leave without Poke.

As Hawthorn expected, they were moving at a much faster pace, but always the column kept moving south. Occasionally they would halt for some unexplained reason. "Apparently," Hawthorn thought, "the lead scouts have spotted some sign of danger: ants, perhaps, or maybe a serpent." In any case, he was not allowed to sit down so he still could not search for a cutting edge.

They had not gone far through the pine thicket when they came upon a small, dry creek bed. The gully was not very deep, but the sides were rather steep. Hawthorn and the three Renegades carrying the first litter managed to slide down the steep bank into the dry rocky bed without incident, but as they were scaling the opposite bank, the Renegade in the back next to Hawthorn slipped on a mossy rock and fell, dropping his corner of the litter. This caused the other three to lose their grips on the heavy load. Since Hawthorn was tied to his pole, he fell the short distance with the litter, landing hard on the rocks at the base of the creek bank.

As he tried to right himself, he wondered what else could go wrong. There were bruises and scrapes on his arms, legs, and head, but his right hand seemed to hurt the worst. Lifting his hand, he saw a deep cut in the palm. Looking to see what had cut him so, he saw a sharp, jagged-looking piece of flint sticking out of the bank.

"Hey, you!" a harsh voice barked behind him. "Get on yer feet, and get that litter up the bank."

Hawthorn barely had time to grab the flint before he was roughly jerked to his feet. Gripping the sharp rock tightly, he shouldered the litter pole and climbed up the bank of the creek bed. Hawthorn was bruised, tired, and bleeding, but in his heart hope had revived.

As they marched, Hawthorn sawed at his bindings with his flint cutting edge, and as he worked on the tough leather, his mind was busy trying to think of an escape plan for himself and Poke. Hawthorn didn't want his bindings to fall off, so he didn't cut them all the way through, just far enough so that he could easily break them when he thought the time was right. Now he faced the gigantic problem of finding the right time. He thought he might be able to break loose, grab a knife from the Renegade next to him, and run to Poke before they could catch him. But he knew that he could never free Poke fast enough for them to run away before being caught or killed. The more he thought on it, the clearer it became that, if he and Poke were to have any chance at all, they were going to have to have some type of diversion.

No sooner had this thought entered Hawthorn's mind than the diversion came.

The lynx had been watching the Renegade caravan for several minutes. He was just a yearling, and his hunting skills were not yet honed to sharpness. He had been hunting all day and had caught nothing. He was, therefore, frustrated and hungry. The young cat wasn't sure what he was stalking, but he could smell the mooflon meat, and that was all the information that he needed. His attack was swift and unexpected.

One of the Renegades carrying the first mooflon saw the movement as the cat leaped for them and was able to yell a warning. As the lynx landed in their midst, the litters were dropped, and Renegades began running fearfully in all directions seeking cover. This perplexed the young cat. He had expected to find a large, long, tasty animal, but instead he found two bites of mouse meat and a lot of little creatures scurrying across the ground. So fascinated was the lynx in watching the Renegades run for safety that, for the moment, he forgot about his attack.

This was Hawthorn's chance. He did not even remember freeing himself; it had been an instinctive thing when he saw the cat leaping at them. When the Renegade next to him started to run for a nearby grass clump, Hawthorn tackled him around the legs. The Renegade shouted a curse at him and kicked free, but not before Hawthorn had grabbed the long flint knife the Renegade kept tucked in his boot.

Keeping a careful watch on the lynx, Hawthorn crawled quickly to the back of the second litter. He found Poke crouched behind the mooflon and chewing at the leather straps around his wrists. Poke's face brightened when he saw his friend and the sharp knife in his hand. Hawthorn freed him quickly.

"How do we get away from here?" Poke asked as he rubbed his chaffed wrists. "The Renegades are in the grass and brush all around us!"

"Most of them ran off to the left, away from the cat," Hawthorn quickly responded. "Let's go right."

"Sounds good!" said Poke, jumping up and running quickly towards the brush on the right side of the trail.

Hawthorn rose quickly to follow, but at that moment, the lynx came trotting down the path towards him. It was looking for more Renegades with which to play. Hawthorn wedged himself under the large mooflon carcass and prayed that the cat would not choose now to have supper. But the lynx was having too much fun to eat just yet. It trotted past the hiding Larkin and started sniffing through a thick clump of grass a short distance back down the trail.

Seeing that the cat was occupied, Hawthorn sprinted toward the spot in the brush into which he had seen Poke disappear. The brush was thick, and he had trouble moving quickly without making noise. Hawthorn knew that speed was more important than quiet, so he raced as quickly as he dared through the grasses and undergrowth. Even as inexperienced as he was, it wasn't hard for Hawthorn to tell which way Poke had gone. He came up on a wall of thick grass and saw that some of the blades were slowly bending back up into place. As Hawthorn charged forward to plow through the grass where Poke had gone, an evil, coarse voice stopped him dead in his tracks. "Yer' goin' nowhere, you little scum!"

The voice was coming from the other side of the grass, and Hawthorn recognized it instantly as belonging to Wolf. Silently, Hawthorn eased his head through the blades of grass to see what was happening. There, not two paces in front of him, was his old enemy, and he had Poke.

When the lynx attacked, Wolf had been watching the two Larkin slaves to be sure they weren't eaten by the cat. He wanted them dead, but in his savage hatred, he wanted to kill them, and he wanted them to know that he was the one doing it. Wolf had been far enough back in the line of march that when he saw Poke escape through the brush, he was able to cut him off. There had been a short fight, but Poke was no match for Wolf's strength, fueled as it was by his insane lust for revenge because of the injury to his knee.

Wolf had his back to Hawthorn and was bent over the kneeling Poke. The Renegade had his fingers around Poke's throat, and Hawthorn knew that his friend couldn't last much longer. He also knew that he was the only chance Poke had. He withdrew his head from the grass, took several quick steps back, then charged forward as hard as he could run, throwing himself through the grass wall with all of his strength.

Wolf thought he had heard a noise on the other side of the grass behind him. Momentarily distracted from his murderous business, he turned to glance at the grass wall the same instant Hawthorn burst through like a cannonball, hurtling full force into the startled Renegade. Hawthorn caught him completely off balance. The force of the blow knocked him away from Poke and sent Wolf and Hawthorn tumbling down a short, gravely slope. They landed in a pile with Wolf more or less on top.

"Run, Poke! Run!" Hawthorn yelled at his friend, but Poke had collapsed, unconscious from Wolf's choking grip.

Hawthorn tried to pull himself free from the murderous Renegade, but Wolf, though dazed, was not to be gotten rid of so easily. Grabbing Hawthorn by the hair, Wolf wrapped his arm around the young Larkin's throat. "Yer' mine now!" the evil Renegade hissed through clinched teeth.

At that moment, both Wolf and Hawthorn were startled by voices approaching the wall of grass behind them. "The shout came from over this way, Greatfighter," a Renegade voice called back into the woods.

"He ain't spoilin' my fun this time—at least not with you," Wolf said in a low snarl. Wolf pulled Hawthorn up on his feet and began dragging him deeper into the woods, away from the approaching voices.

Realizing what Wolf was planning to do, Hawthorn tried to cry out, but before a sound could escape his lips, Wolf's powerful arm clamped tighter around Hawthorn's throat, cutting off his air. The captive youth struggled frantically for a few moments, then he fell into darkness.

Hawthorn's vision began to clear very slowly. He was sure he was really awake now and not in a dream as he had previously thought. He hurt too badly for this to be a dream. He discovered that his hands and feet were bound with strips of leather, and he was gagged. He was also being dragged roughly through the woods by the collar of his leather tunic. His body jerked painfully as he was dragged over roots and rocks.

Suddenly Hawthorn was pulled up and dropped hard on the ground. "Oh, yes!" he heard Wolf exclaim in a low voice. "This is perfect!"

The painful drag began again, only faster this time. Hawthorn was towed out of the woods into a small clearing. His heart began to race as Wolf picked him up and began to carry him further out into the clearing. Wolf, still favoring his injured knee, hobbled very cautiously up onto a low, sandy mound. As slowly and as carefully as Wolf was moving, it took several minutes for them to travel even a short distance on the sand pile.

Finally Wolf stopped and laid Hawthorn down on the sand as gently as a mother putting her baby to bed. So surprised was Hawthorn at the Renegade's sudden change in behavior that he began to hope that he might be spared. But at that moment, his hair was grabbed, and his head was jerked back violently. There, not a hand's width away from his own face, was the most evil-looking pair of eyes he had ever seen. The hatred boiling out of those eyes was more than the scared Larkin could stand. Hawthorn tried to look away, but he was roughly jerked back to face his antagonist.

Wolf was feeding on the fear he was causing in the young captive. "Know where you are, kid?" he hissed through a wicked grin. "Red ant mound. You so much as sneeze, and they'll be all over you." Releasing his grip on Hawthorn's hair, Wolf very gingerly walked off the ant mound and disappeared into the woods.

Hawthorn waited until Wolf was out of sight, then he began to scoot his body toward the nearest edge of the mound. He was working on his third scoot when he heard a clicking noise off to his right. Taking a quick look, he saw two large, menacing soldier ants facing him. Hawthorn froze! He knew that the slightest movement would draw the two powerful insects down onto him. As he lay there anticipating their attack, he decided that he didn't know which would be worse: to writhe in agony from the fiery venom in their stings or to be torn to pieces by their powerful jaws.

He held perfectly still, hardly daring to breathe, for what seemed like forever. His muscles began to cramp, but still Hawthorn held motionless.

The sun glistened off their red armor as the two ants stood like statues with only occasional movement from their antennae. Then finally, as if waking from a trance, the ant closest to Hawthorn turned and moved across the mound away from him. A moment later, the second ant followed the first. With an exhausted sigh, Hawthorn collapsed on the sand.

He had just decided to make another attempt at scooting toward the edge of the mound when he saw Wolf returning. In his hands were two long, straight sticks he had found in the woods. The terror that had so recently left Hawthorn now returned in full force.

Wolf cautiously worked his way out to his captive. "Heh, heh, ants ain't got you yet? Well, don't worry," he said sarcastically, "you won't be lonely much longer."

He carefully pulled Hawthorn up into a sitting position. Then he ran one of the tall sticks down between his arms and legs. Very carefully, Wolf worked the sharpened end of the stick deeper and deeper into the sandy soil which formed the ant mound. He had to stop briefly when several ants approached the mound. The insects climbed up onto the nest a short distance from where Wolf was positioning Hawthorn. Both Renegade and Larkin held motionless as the new ants moved quickly across the mound and disappeared into the nest. Hawthorn breathed another sigh of relief, and Wolf continued his murderous task. After a little more work, he had the pole set firmly in place.

Hawthorn realized that the pole was so tall that he would not be able to get his bound hands and feet over the top of it. "Maybe," he thought, "I can pull the pole up after Wolf's gone and can scoot for the woods."

Wolf was very carefully walking away, still carrying the second pole. He got within two or three steps from the edge of the mound and turned around. When Hawthorn saw the evil look on Wolf's face, a shiver coursed through his body.

Wolf spoke, no longer trying to keep his voice quiet. "This is it, kid! You're dead!" he snarled in a loud, fierce voice. Hawthorn thought he felt a tremor in the mound beneath him. "You shouldn't have messed with me," he continued. "When you hurt my leg, that was the worst mistake you ever made. Now you're gonna pay! In ten seconds, you're gonna have more red ant venom in you than you got blood!" With a fiendish laugh, Wolf wrapped both hands around the second pole and jammed it deeply into the ant mound. Wolf began jerking and twisting the pole violently from side to side.

Instantly there was a rumbling and a shaking coming up from deep under Hawthorn's body. Wolf felt it too and laughed louder. "I'd love to stay and watch 'em rip you apart," he laughed, "but we wouldn't want 'em to get me, would we?" Wolf hopped quickly off the mound and hobbled as fast as he could for the woods.

Fear detonated in Hawthorn's stomach. He wrapped his arms around the pole and began pulling with all his strength, but without being able to grip the pole with his hands, the best he could do was to wiggle it back and forth a little.

With a furious explosion, angry red ants burst out of the mound in a dozen places at once. Hundreds of the fierce insects poured across the surface of the mound, looking for the enemy who had attacked their home. Hawthorn, knowing that a horrible death was moments away, let out an involuntary cry of anguish.

At that precise moment, he felt a hard thump as something splattered against his back and shoulders. Then a massive force struck as the ants overran him.

Wolf had hobbled as quickly as he could across the small clearing. He was hurried along by the deep rumbling sound coming from the mound behind him and the clicking of mandibles as the furious red ants rushed out to defend their home. When he got to the edge of the clearing, he heard Hawthorn's cry. He jerked around, hoping to see his victim being torn apart, but the top of the mound was now a seething pile of red ants.

"Too quick!" Wolf thought, shaking his head. "He died too quick!

"I won't make that mistake with the other one," he promised himself. He started into the woods, back the way he had come. Only three steps into the brush he pulled up short. Facing him was Greatfighter, the Renegade chief, and five warriors. Wolf could tell by the fire in his chief's eyes that they had seen what had happened to the Larkin prisoner.

"I told you to leave them alone." There was a deadly coldness in the Renegade leader's voice.

"Now, listen here, Greatfighter . . . ," Wolf began to protest.

"SILENCE!!!" the Renegade leader exploded. "If you can't obey my orders, then I've got no use for you."

"What are you aimin' to do?" Wolf asked nervously, looking from one warrior to another. He noticed that they all had their weapons ready, and they each eyed him menacingly.

Greatfighter pointed a finger in Wolf's face. Angrily he said, "You went against me and killed the kid anyway. Well then, you can take his place." He gave a sharp command to the other Renegades, "Bind him!"

"Now, wait a sec----! " Wolf roared angrily, but his words were cut short.

In that instant, Greatfighter shot forward his lance and had the point touching Wolf's throat. "If this slave gives you any trouble, kill him," the Renegade chief said with an icy calmness that chilled Wolf to the bone.

As the warriors took Wolf's weapons and tied his hands with strips of leather, Greatfighter turned quickly and strode back up through the woods.

"Get him up here with the other slave," he called back over his shoulder. "I'll get the war party together and see how much meat we have left."

With two guards on either side of him and two more behind with war clubs ready, Wolf let himself be led back up through the woods.

CHAPTER SIX

THE HISTORY LESSON

Hawthorn felt as if he were swimming in a sea of blackness as he struggled to regain his senses. The first thing of which he became consciously aware was the pain, a throbbing pain that seemed to come from every part of him. As his mind slowly cleared, the pain increased.

His head seemed to hurt the worst, but there was also a sharp pain that shot through both sides of his chest every time he took a breath. He also suddenly realized that his back hurt, too. Something was poking him in the back. Instinctively, he tried to move. As he did so, the pain in his head exploded with intensity, and a moan escaped his lips.

"Lie still!" a hushed voice not too far away commanded him.

Hawthorn froze and tried to open his eyes. As his eyes focused, he suddenly gasped. He was looking into the face of a nightmare. Above him hovered a large, red worker ant, its menacing pincers opening and closing.

"Do not move!" the voice said again.

Hawthorn closed his eyes and willed himself to be perfectly still. He felt the ant's strange antennae touching his chest, arms, and legs. After a few moments, Hawthorn opened his eyes again and saw that the ant had turned away from him and was examining something else nearby. Painfully, Hawthorn lifted his head a little to keep an eye on the fierce insect. It was then that he realized that he was lying on a pile of dead ant bodies. That explained what was poking in his back.

Hawthorn watched with relief as the worker ant moved further away from him. He heard some movement to his right and tensed in anticipation of facing another ant. Instead he saw a bushy shock of red, curly hair and a pair of green eyes looking at him with concern. Hawthorn focused his gaze on the stranger's face and saw a kind-looking youth only a few seasons older than himself. As Hawthorn studied the youth's face, he saw the furrowed brow clear and the narrowed, tense lips suddenly spread into a wide grin. "Chummy!" the stranger said with delight, "I can't believe it! She worked!"

Hawthorn was thoroughly confused. 'She worked?' He repeated the words as a question.

The young stranger moved around in front of Hawthorn to see him better. He was carefully examining the hurt Larkin's arms and legs for injuries. At Hawthorn's question, the stranger looked up and gave him another broad grin. "Aye, Chum. She really worked!" he returned.

Hawthorn was still confused. "What worked?" he asked again, weakly.

The stranger looked at him with surprise, "Why, my plan, of course. I had to do something to keep the reddies from chompin' on ya."

Hawthorn was beginning to understand. "You . . . you saved me from the ants?" he asked.

The stranger looked up again from his examination. "Now that's a fine thing," he said with a hurt look on his face. "I snatch you from the jaws of death, but you don't know what happened. How am I supposed to be a hero when you don't know you've been saved?"

"I didn't mean to offend you," Hawthorn said, trying to apologize.

"No offense taken, Chummy," the young stranger responded, the grin returning and spreading across his face. "I was just funnin' with ya. You know, trying to keep things light and all that."

Hawthorn's mind was beginning to clear. "I remember being trapped on the ant hill, and all the ants attacking me. Why didn't they kill me?"

"By the look of that huge knot on the back of your head, they very nearly did," came his rescuer's answer.

Hawthorn just happened to look past his new friend and saw the large, red worker ant suddenly turn and start towards them.

"Watch out!" he cried, fear rising in him again. "It's coming back!"

His friend turned quickly and saw the approaching enemy. The stranger looked back at Hawthorn, the smile still in place. "Who? Him?" he replied nonchalantly, flicking his head toward the approaching ant. "No worries, Chummy. They're no problem if you know how to reason with 'em." The stranger pulled two carved sticks about the length of the distance between his elbow and the tips of his fingers out of a sack that hung at his side. The sticks appeared to be wet with a yellowish liquid. The stranger waited till the ant had approached close enough for him to touch. Then he reached out and began rubbing the ant's antennae with the two sticks, one of which he held in each hand. He rubbed and tapped the sticks at different spots along the creature's feelers, using a short, repeated pattern.

Suddenly the ant turned and crawled away.

"How did you do that!?" Hawthorn asked in amazement.

"They're really pretty simple-minded," his friend answered matter-of-factly. "I just told him that I was another worker ant, and so he figured that, since I was over here, he needed to go work somewhere else.

"Say, Chum," he continued, as he looked intently into Hawthorn's face, "you aren't looking so good."

True enough, Hawthorn had turned very pale, and his head was swimming. He tried to say something, but he fainted before he could get the words out.

It was a while before Hawthorn woke up, but when he did, it was more pleasant. He still hurt, but not as badly. He noticed that the pain in his back was gone. In fact, he felt almost comfortable.

Hawthorn discovered that he was no longer lying on a pile of dead ants. He was on a soft bed of leaf mold and was covered by a cloak. When he lifted his head to see where he was, his head started swimming. He tried lying perfectly still, and in a moment the nausea disappeared.

As Hawthorn lay there looking up through the leafy canopy far above him, he thought through all that had happened to him in the last two days. There had been several times when he could have died. He knew he actually should have died while he was trapped on the ant hill. How did he survive that? Who was this funny stranger? Where was he now? Had it all been a dream? If it was a dream, then how did he get here?

No, it couldn't be a dream. The pain was definitely real. His thoughts were cut short by a strange sound coming from high up in the trees off to his left. It sounded like the deep, droning croak of a bull frog, but it was not like any frog that he had ever heard. It was making a different cry now, but Hawthorn knew by the sound that it was the same creature. It was a terrifying howl, and Hawthorn wanted to run, but his injuries made that impossible. His only choice was to lie still and hope that the monster would not come in his direction.

The dreadful screams went on for several more minutes, then they suddenly stopped. The silence actually scared Hawthorn more than the noise.

"As long as the thing was screaming, I could at least tell where it was," he thought to himself. "But now the monster could be anywhere." Hawthorn lay there for quite some time in quiet stillness. He heard nothing but some birds twittering in the distance and the buzz of a few insects as they occasionally flew by. He had just started to relax a little when he heard a noise nearby. Hawthorn tensed and began to feel around for some kind of a weapon.

"No worries, Chummy!" said a cheerful, familiar voice. "It's just me!" From Hawthorn's left appeared his new companion, strolling out of the brush.

"I heard a monster nearby!" Hawthorn excitedly informed the newcomer.

The smile quickly faded from his new friend's face. "Was it coming from the tree tops back yonder?" he asked, pointing up and behind.

"Yes!" Hawthorn answered. "Did you hear it?"

"I think so," returned his companion. "Did it sound like this?" Quickly he dropped a large reed cup with a cord coming out of the back. He held the reed down with his foot, pulled the cord tight, and drew his hand along the taunt cord. An incredible roar emitted from the open end of the reed cup.

Hawthorn jumped at the startling sound. When he looked back up at the stranger, Hawthorn saw that he was grinning broadly again. "It was me!" he laughed.

"Who ARE you?!" Hawthorn snapped. He was no longer just confused; he was also frustrated and getting angry.

"Now don't get yourself all frothed up, Chummy. You'll pass out on me again."

"Would you please quit calling me 'Chummy'!" Hawthorn said, still angry." I am Hawthorn, son of Savin, of the Third Clan of Larkin!"

The smile was gone from his new friend's face, but there was compassion in his eyes. "Listen," he said gently, "I know you've had it pretty rough . . ."

"You have no idea how I've had it!" Hawthorn cut in. "In the past two days, I've been attacked by a wasp, a serpent, and a crazed mooflon! I've been hit on the head with a Renegade war club and made a slave! I've marched all night carrying a dead mooflon. Two of my friends are dead! The rest of them may be dead, including my father! I've been attacked by a lynx, a murderous Renegade, and a hundred red ants! My best friend is still a slave of the Renegades—if they haven't killed him yet! I don't know who you are, where I am, or how I'm getting home! That's how I've had it! And I've just about used up all the patience I've got! I need some answers!" Hawthorn, in his excitement, had raised himself up off the bed. The pain in his head began to increase, and it seemed to him that everything he looked at started spinning around. He collapsed back on his bed as the waves of nausea began to hit him.

"Now there you went and done it," said his companion. "Here, take a sip of water." He offered Hawthorn a drink from a triangular-shaped, skin water bag with a carved, wooden stopper. "Are you all right?" he asked.

"I think so," Hawthorn answered weakly.

"Well, listen here," he said. "You've got to lie really still for a spell. Things must have gotten knocked loose when the ants hit you in the head. If you keep poppin' up and down like that, then all your loose head stuff won't be able to settle back in place. So you just lie still till my brother gets here."

"Your brother?" Hawthorn asked.

"That was all the noise you heard, Chums. I sent him a message on my caller." The young stranger held up the noise-making contraption so Hawthorn could see it. It was a large reed that was as big around as both of Hawthorn's fists together. Only about a hand's width in length, it was open on one end and hollow. There was a wooden bottom, so that it looked like a large wooden cup. A small hole was drilled in the bottom, and a cord had been pushed through the hole and was held in place by a knot tied on the inside of the cup.

"I did it backwards a moment ago just to scare you. You're actually supposed to stand on the end of the cord and pull the cup part up till the string is tight. Then when you draw some rosin up and down the string, it makes a loud noise come out of the open end of the cup. You just point the cup whichever way you want the sound to go," he explained. "My bother and I've got codes worked out so we can talk to each other at a distance. I sent word to my brother that I need his help, and he should be here soon. So why don't you lie still, and I'll try to answer as many of your questions as I can."

The young stranger sat down next to Hawthorn's bed so that he could be comfortable and Hawthorn could look at him without moving his head around. "For starters," his friend began, "let me tell you who I am. I'm Eldan, son of Ripgood the Vigilant, former gatekeeper of Stillwaters, and I am the younger brother of Tobin the Flyer."

"Is Tobin the one you called for help?" Hawthorn asked.

"Yep, that's right."

"Which clan are you from?" Hawthorn wanted to know.

"Clan?" Eldan looked puzzled.

"You know," Hawthorn replied, "which Larkin clan?"

"I'm not from a Larkin clan, Thornbush."

Hawthorn was stunned. "Are you a Renegade?" he asked, not hiding his surprise.

79

"No!" laughed Eldan. "I'm not a Renegade either, although my father was for a while. But he joined the Maker's Children several years before I was born, so technically, that makes me Makerian by birth." Eldan saw the bewildered look on his new friend's face and laughed again. "You don't know what I'm talking about, do you?"

Hawthorn started to shake his head, but the pain stopped him, so he just said, "No."

"That's no surprise," said Eldan. "Your leaders don't think too highly of us."

"The Shaman know about you?" Hawthorn asked.

"Oh, sure," Eldan replied confidently. "At least, the top leaders in your First Clan do. See, the Maker's Children originally came from the First Clan of Larkin. They were all exiled by the High Council of Shaman . . ."

"So you are Renegades!" Hawthorn interrupted.

Now it was Eldan's turn to get frustrated. He quickly stood up. "Okay, you win! I'll leave!" Eldan spun around and began walking away. "Take care of yourself," he threw back over his shoulder.

Hawthorn panicked, "Wait! Please, don't go!"

Eldan stopped. He turned to look back at Hawthorn, a sly smile creeping across his face. "No worries, Chummy . . . I mean, Thornton. I just thought I'd get you back.

"I'll tell you what, Your Honor," Eldan said cheerfully, squaring around to face his patient. "You reserve your verdict till you've heard the whole story, then you can give your judgment on whether I should be declared a Renegade or not."

Eldan threw himself back down on the ground next to Hawthorn and began his story with a question, "Staghorn, have you ever been to the Steps?"

"My name is Hawthorn, and are you talking about where the First Clan of Larkin lives?" Hawthorn was a little surprised by the question.

"Right," returned Eldan. "It's supposed to be the ancestral home of all Larkin."

"It is," Hawthorn returned. "Yes, I've been to the Steps once. I traveled there three summers ago with my parents and most of our clan. I was old enough to make the journey to the Great Gathering that's called every five seasons."

"Well," Eldan queried, "what do you remember about the Steps?"

Hawthorn let his mind drift back to that wonderful time. It was the first time he had ever spent a night outside the safety of the Keep. It was exciting and scary for a young Larkin, and everything he saw and experienced fascinated

ELDAN SON OF RIPGOOD

him. It had taken four and a half days of hard walking along the old trail to reach the Steps.

He remembered when he first saw them. They had been traveling along the bank of a swiftly flowing creek all morning. About midday, they came to a series of three waterfalls resembling stair steps. They climbed the bank until they were at the foot of the uppermost fall. Hawthorn remembered walking out along the ledge leading behind the fall. They must have traveled nearly a bow shot along that ledge, with the moss covered rock as one wall and the cascading water as the other. He remembered that the mist from the splashing water made everything slippery. Passing several guards, they continued their trek until they came to a narrow, slit-like opening in the rock. Passing more guards, they made their way into the great cavern behind the falls that they called the Steps.

Hawthorn had never seen so many Larkin together in one place at one time. Even with all the clans coming together, the great cavern was big enough to house them all. He remembered the long side passages with spacious rooms that the different clans made their homes for the next ten days. He remembered the large, rounded dome room that had a round pool in its center which was fed by a trickling waterfall that fell from the center of the domed ceiling high above the room. He recalled the long, arched hallway lined with lanterns that led to the Larkin cathedral, where they were led in worship of the Maker by the seven High Shaman and their assistants. There were also the friends he had made, the games they had played, the stories, and the food. Yes, he remembered it all. The Steps was a wonderful place.

But Hawthorn wasn't about to give away clan secrets, so he gave Eldan a vague answer. "I remember a lot about the Steps. What are you getting at?"

"Did you get to go in the Treasure Cave below the Great Cathedral? Did you hear about the place down there where old Larkin and some of his sons are buried?"

Hawthorn was beginning to get nervous with Eldan's questions.

"Okay, okay! I won't put you on the spot anymore." Eldan settled himself into a comfortable position, which made Hawthorn think that the story might last a while.

"We originally called ourselves the *Maker's Children*. But I guess it must have been too cumbersome to say all that, so with time, our name got shortened to just *Makerians*."

Hawthorn was beginning to understand a little of all this. "That's what you meant when you called yourself a 'Makerian'."

"Now you got it, Chummy . . . uh, I mean, Sawbrier."

"Hawthorn! My name is Hawthorn!"

"Of course it is, Chummy, and a fine name it is, too. Now stop interrupting me!"

Hawthorn's head was hurting too badly to argue with him anymore. With a groan, he laid his head back down on his bed. He decided to just listen to this crazy Makerian's story and see what he could learn.

Eldan began, "Over twenty seasons ago, there was a Larkin Shaman living at the Steps whose name was Micah. Shaman Micah was an assistant to the High Seven, the rulers of your whole tribe."

"I know who the High Seven Shaman are," Hawthorn cut in.

Eldan ignored his comment and continued his story:

As an assistant to the High Seven, Micah was entrusted occasionally with very special assignments. One particular time he was asked to go into the Treasure Cave and inventory what was there. It seems that the huge door to the cave, which had been sealed longer than anyone could remember, was beginning to rot. Since repairing the door meant that the Treasure Cave must be opened, the High Shaman decided that this would be an excellent opportunity to make sure that they knew what was down there and to be sure that it was all protected.

Guards were placed at the opening of the cave, and no one was allowed in except Shaman Micah and his two chosen assistants. They entered the Treasure Cave with oil lanterns in hand and made their way down the long, twisting, ancient passage. Eventually the cave opened up into a large room. Twelve raised stone slabs were arranged in this chamber, five on each side of a central walkway, with two more stone tables set apart by themselves at the far end of the room. Four short pillars made of stones, one under each corner of the slabs, held up the twelve large, rectangular, flat rocks. On these slabs were laid the bones of the Great Ones.

Mosstar, the last great chief of all the Larkin clans, was laid there, and beside him was his wife, Princess Belladonna. The bones of five of the seven sons of Larkin were entombed there, and in the far end of the room in the center in a place of honor were the remains of Larkin the Great and his wife, Lily.

Micah actually touched their bones! So moved were the three Shaman by this experience that they spent the entire first day identifying those buried there, then reverently recounting each one's life and great exploits. Several times they were overwhelmed with deep emotion.

The three emerged from the Treasure Cave many hours later, speechless from what they had seen. The second day they didn't even enter the cave. They spent the day planning and organizing how they would conduct the inventory. They gathered blank journals and small writing tables and chairs. They discussed how they would handle the various treasures, and in what order they would study the bones and artifacts of each of the Great Ones entombed there. On the third day they assembled all of their supplies and equipment, then passing the guards, they reentered the cave.

They were more prepared this time, but it was still an awesome experience. The first thing they did was to draw a map of the chamber, making specific notes of the placement of each body and each major artifact. It took three full days just to complete this task.

The Treasure Cave itself was a crude rectangle, with the bones of Larkin the Great laid against the center of the far wall, and the bones of his wife lying next to him. The entrance to the cave was directly across the room from Larkin's resting place. An aisle was formed by the ten stone slabs against the side walls, with five on each side. As they entered the chamber, they noticed that the first two slabs on the left were smaller than the others and contained no bones. These were memorials to honor two of Larkin's sons, whose bodies were never recovered.

The first memorial was to honor Oakenboar, Larkin's seventh son. His name was written on the slab, and next to it were laid some weapons and a leather tunic that apparently belonged to him. The tunic at one time had been dyed a deep red. Some of the color could still be seen in places on the old, rotting leather. At the foot of this memorial toward the aisle was a fired clay chest. Carefully lifting the lid, they found personal items that belonged to Oakenboar. There was his chieftain's necklace, carved with Oakenboar's personal symbols. Also in the box was a chieftain's robe, finely woven of colored cocoon silk. Under this were parchments and rolls of leather.

The leather rolls were so brittle that Micah was afraid to try to unroll them. The parchments were covered in a writing unknown to Micah. He assumed that it was a language that the ancient Larkin used in their formal writings which had since been lost over the many years.

After studying these writings for sometime, Micah and his assistants concluded that these might be testimonies

TREASURE CAVE

of those who knew Oakenboar, recounting honorable deeds and events of his life. Micah and the others became intensely interested in deciphering the ancient language. They also decided that it was absolutely essential that they find a way to unroll the leather scrolls so that they could read them.

Directly across the aisle from Oakenboar's memorial was an empty slab. At first they thought that it was just an extra burial place that the builders thought might be needed later, but after closer examination, they discovered that the slab had apparently once been used as the burial place of Mordelay, the first and only High Shaman over the clans of Larkin.

"What do you think happened here?" Shaman Jasper, one of the assistants, asked.

"It looks to me as if the High Shaman may have had some enemies," Micah answered thoughtfully. "He was obviously laid to rest here with the Great Ones, but then some time later, someone came in and removed him from his place of honor."

"They cleaned out his chest, too!" added Shaman Linden, who had been examining the large clay box at the foot of the slab. "Whoever did it was in a hurry. They jerked the lid off and threw it against the cave wall. There are the broken pieces of it by the entrance. The only things left inside the chest are some scraps of parchment and an old, rotted boot."

Jasper was studying the slab. "Whoever it was must have really hated High Shaman Mordelay. They even tried to scratch his name off the slab, but you can still read it."

Back across the aisle, next to the stone memorial honoring Oakenboar, was a second memorial identical to the first. This one, they discovered, was erected to honor Larkin's fourth son, Brahawk.

"I remember a story about him," said Jasper. "Wasn't he the one who was eaten by a lynx while he was protecting his clan?"

"It was a fox," corrected Micah, "and he was on a hunting expedition."

The clay chest at the foot of the memorial contained personal items and more parchments covered with the same strange writing.

Micah was curious. "Linden, make some copies of these parchments. We'll each take some of the copies and use what spare time we have trying to learn this language."

"Why don't we just take the parchments with us?"

"No!" Micah was emphatic. "None of the artifacts must leave this cave!"

So as Linden copied parchments, Micah and Jasper continued their exploration. Directly across the aisle from Brahawk's memorial was a raised stone slab bearing the bones of Princess Belladonna. Even faded with age and covered with dust, her burial gown was startling in its beauty. It was delicately woven of the finest, white cocoon silk. There were thousands of tiny plates of shiny mica that had been cut and sewn in place, covering the gown in a shimmery radiance as the mica reflected the light of the lamps. The chest at the foot of her bier had a few personal items, but most of the space was taken up by several books. The pages were of parchment sewn together; then all of the pages were bound in ageing, leather covers.

Very gently, Jasper lifted the cover of one of the books. "The hand-writing is beautiful, but it's in that same strange language."

Micah studied the writing. "This must be Belladonna's own hand-writing. Most likely these volumes are her personal diary or some sort of journal."

"I'd love to be able to read these!" Jasper wished.

"Whatever else we accomplish," Micah announced, "we absolutely must translate this language!"

Linden looked up from his work of making copies of parchments. "It would sure be interesting to know why this language was lost to us. You would think that if the ancients wrote so much in this language that it would have been preserved—you know, passed down the line and all that."

A look of contemplation fell across Micah's face as he listened to Linden's comment, but he made no response.

On the left side of the room next to the memorial for Brahawk was a burial slab containing the remains of Baden,

Larkin's fifth son and chief of the Fifth Clan. His rotting battle shield was laid across his chest. "Do you think he actually used this huge club to fight with?" Jasper was examining a very large piece of iron wood laid at Baden's left side. It had many thumb-size quartz stones embedded in the large end, and it tapered down on the other end to a carved handle wrapped with leather. "Thunder and skyfire! Try to lift this thing!"

"I don't see any other weapons," Micah said, "and this club looks like it's seen some use."

"This must have been a powerful Larkin," announced Jasper with great admiration.

Across the aisle from Baden were the bones of Mosstar, husband of Princess Belladonna and the last Great Chief of all the clans of Larkin. The three investigators spent much time studying the remains of this famous Larkin.

"Look at all this stuff they laid with him!" Jasper remarked as he fingered small baskets full of jewels and an assortment of ceremonial flint knives with ornately carved handles. The most amazing item that they found by the bones of Mosstar was a silken tunic covered with tiny, carved plates of mother-of–pearl and mica. The tiny plates were sewn onto the tunic in a pattern resembling a fox head on the front and an eagle soaring over trees on the back. "It must have taken years to make this!" he said in amazement as he gently fingered the fabulous garment.

"These must be gifts given by all of the different clans," Micah concluded. "There are pendants and this ornately carved staff. Here's even a portrait of Mosstar carved on a block of cherry wood."

"The people must have loved him very much," Jasper spoke reverently.

"Undoubtedly," Micah agreed. "You know, now that I think about it, I believe that there are actually more legends involving Mosstar than about old Larkin himself."

"Well, one of those legends is true! Look at this!" an excited voice exclaimed near the wall behind them. It was Linden. The excitement of viewing Mosstar's remains had been too much for him, so he left his desk and joined them.

Linden was staring at the wall behind Mosstar's head. "It's really true!" he was saying. "The story is true! It actually happened!"

Micah and Jasper quickly moved to his side. When they saw what had been hanging unnoticed on two pegs driven into the wall, both gave an involuntary gasp almost at the same time.

"The Broken Lance of Mosstar!" Jasper whispered.

"It even has a quartz lance head, just as the stories say," Linden added.

"But that doesn't prove that he used it to kill a huge serpent in order to save Belladonna," Jasper contended.

"What's that on the floor by your feet?" Micah was studying the base of the wall below the lance. Just in front of their feet was a large bundle covered by tattered rags. Jasper explored the ancient bundle at Micah's direction. Very gently he pulled away the rags to reveal the contents of the package. It actually took a few moments for recognition to set in, but when it did, Jasper gasped and jerked upright like he had been bitten.

"What is it?!" Linden yelled as he also jumped back.

"It's Mosstar's proof," laughed Micah.

"Rattles!" stammered Jasper.

Micah was now bent over the bundle. "Thirteen," he announced as he stood up. "Twelve rattles and a button. The snake from which those rattles came was a big one."

"What do you think now?" Linden asked excitedly with a large grin on his face.

Jasper, wide-eyed with amazement, responded, "I . . . I think Mosstar broke his quartz-headed lance while killing the huge serpent that those rattles belonged to and saved Belladonna. But," he added, "I can't prove it." They all laughed heartily at Jasper's newfound faith.

Back across the aisle next to Baden was Larkin's second son, Ramus. He was arranged in a shimmering chieftain's robe woven of thistle down.

"Hey, I just noticed something," Linden was puzzled. "Ramus is the only one of Larkin's sons who doesn't have a shield with him."

"Yes, that's right!" joined Jasper. "There's his sting lying next to him, but no shield! What does that mean?"

"Maybe it means he couldn't use one," Micah said. Jasper and Linden looked questioningly at the older Shaman. Micah returned their gaze. "Look at him. Do you see anything different about Ramus?"

"Well, I never noticed," Linden finally said. "His left arm—it's missing. The left tunic sleeve is empty."

"I didn't know Ramus only had one arm," Jasper said.

Micah agreed, "I don't recall ever hearing that in any of the legends either—only that he was a great warrior."

"I wonder why something that . . . uh, noticeable . . . was never talked about in the legends?" Linden wondered.

"He must have lost it late in life," explained Jasper.

"I don't think so," Micah said, leaning over and closely examining through the tattered tunic sleeve the short piece of bone that had been what was left of Ramus's left upper arm. "The end of this bone is completely healed. This happened a long time before he died. By the looks of it, Ramus may have even been born with this deformed arm."

"But how can that be?" asked an amazed Jasper. "All of the legends about Ramus are of his skill in battle. How could someone be a mighty warrior with only one arm?!"

"You forget, Jasper," Micah said seriously. "These are the Great Ones." An even deeper sense of awe and admiration for these ancient leaders filled each of them.

Across the aisle from Ramus was a slab containing the bones of Lars, the sixth son of Larkin and the first chief of the Sixth Clan. His chest held items similar to the others.

On the same side of the aisle lying next to Lars they found the bones of Larkin's third son, Kaelen the Archer. "You don't have to read the inscription to know who this is!" declared Jasper. "Look at all the bows!"

Arranged in prominent display around the body of the legendary chief of the Third Clan of Larkin were twelve bows. All of them were different. There were long, mid-length, and short bows. Some were straight, some were slightly curved, and two of the bows swept back into a dramatic recurve. The most beautiful of the bows had been placed in Kaelen's hands. It was a large bow of walnut wood that had been intricately carved to look like a fierce serpent with a head on each end. Each scale had been perfectly carved, and the eyes inset with garnets.

Linden was carefully searching through the clay chest at Kaelen's feet. "These are the writings that I'm anxious to be able to read. If only one-tenth of the legends about Kaelen the Archer are true, then he must have been fantastic with a bow and arrow."

Across the aisle from Kaelen was Larkin's firstborn, Jessakin. This great Larkin had been chief of all the Larkin for a time after his father had died. He had been the one to see the need for dividing into clans. Many of the old leather rolls inscribed with the ancient writing surrounded his resting place.

Jasper was examining this famous Larkin leader who was his own forefather. "I always thought he had such an odd name," he said.

"You know, you're right," said Linden. "*Jessakin* does sound really strange—sort of like *Jasper*."

"Now wait a minute!" Jasper growled at his smiling friend. "At least I'm named after a beautiful stone—but what's a *jessakin*?"

Micah and Linden both had to admit that they didn't know where the name had originated. "Maybe some of these rolls or some of the notes in his chest will explain it," Linden suggested.

"Have either of you made any headway on the translating?" Micah wondered after they had been at work for several weeks. Both of his assistants shook their heads.

"Some of the short words that are used frequently are probably words like *a*, *and*, or *the*, but unless we can figure out some of the description and action words, the rest won't help us much," Linden said.

"We must not get discouraged," Micah charged them. "Somewhere among all these parchments, rolls, and journals is the clue that will unlock this language. Let's each be diligent and search for it."

Finding a way to unroll the leather scrolls proved to be a major problem for them. The leather was so brittle and old that the least bit of handling caused them to shatter. After repeated failures in attempting to unroll the leather bundles, they decided to just cut the rolls into strips and then lay the strips end to end. But before they could implement this plan, Micah's wife, Iris, made a suggestion that solved the problem.

"Why don't you just cook them?" she had said over her shoulder as she cleared up after supper. Micah and his two associates, who had shared a meal together to discuss the perplexing problem, were stunned.

"COOK THEM!" Micah almost choked. "My dear, do you know what you're saying?! These leather scrolls are priceless . . . irreplaceable!"

"Well," she returned, still busy with her work, "all I know is that I can take the toughest dried meat and make it as tender as can be if I just cook it long enough."

The three Shaman just looked at each other, dumbfounded. The more they thought about it, the more sense it made. So with a great deal of counsel from Iris, they set about *cooking* the leather rolls. They heated a pot of hickory nut oil, carried it down to the cave, and gently lowered the rolls into the pot. They brought in coals on which to set the pot to keep the oil from cooling. They were scared to do this in the cave for fear of accidentally damaging some treasure, so they made a place well up the passageway. They found that soaking the scrolls in heated oil for ten to twelve hours softened the old leather enough to unroll it without breaking. Not only were they able to record what was written on the scrolls, but they had restored the ancient leather rolls in the process.

They spent five weeks processing the scrolls, making copies of them, then rolling and storing them in newly constructed cedar boxes which were placed at the head of each burial slab or memorial.

Yet after all the work of treating and copying each leather scroll, they were still no closer to understanding the strange language than when they had started.

CHAPTER SEVEN

NEW TRUTH

"So how did they ever figure out how to read that old writing?" Hawthorn wanted to know.

"Don't push me, Chums," Eldan returned, "I was just getting to that part of the story."

As it turned out, it was Princess Belladonna who provided them with the clues to unlock the secret of understanding the ancient words. Linden had spent every spare moment for weeks and weeks pouring over copies of the parchments and rolls but could find no key to solve the mystery. Then he remembered Belladonna's journal.

Princess Belladonna was quite a gifted artist, and many of her journal pages were covered with drawings and sketches that she had made. Many of those drawings had names and descriptions written next to the things that had been sketched. By studying these drawings, Linden soon was able to compile quite a vocabulary list.

Pronunciation was a different problem. No one knew what sounds the strange symbols represented. It was so frustrating trying to translate a language but not knowing how to make the sounds. Even with searching through all the rolls, parchments, and journals, they could find no clue as to how to pronounce the written symbols.

On one of the regular High Days during worship in the Great Cathedral, Micah's mind was still focused on the problem of translating the ancient writings. In the middle of one of the prayers to the Maker, Micah realized that his mind was not on the worship, and he mentally rebuked himself for his lack of respect. He forced his thoughts to concentrate on the words of the Shaman, who was speaking the Maker's prayer language.

Suddenly the idea struck him that maybe the Maker's prayer language and the ancient language they were translating were the same thing. He almost dismissed the thought as soon as he had it, because the prayer language was so holy that it was never to be written down. He had learned the Maker's prayer words the same way every other Shaman had—by being taught by the instructors how to pronounce the words. To keep from treating the holy words with disrespect by writing them, each student Shaman had to learn the Maker's prayer language by oral memorization only.

Micah realized that, since no one actually knew what the prayer words looked like in written form, the ancient language in the Treasure Cave might be it. The legend was that old Larkin himself had taught his sons the special language that the Maker speaks, and they, supposedly, passed it down to clan leaders. It certainly made sense to Micah's mind that the two languages could be the same.

As soon as the assembly was over, he found his two assistants, and they began to compare the symbols of the words that they had translated from Belladonna's journal with the sounds of these same words from the prayer language. They assigned each symbol from a word of the ancient language of which they knew the meaning with the individual sounds making up the word in the prayer language that had that same meaning. After several hours of work, they had a pronounceable alphabet of the ancient language. Once they knew the sounds that each symbol made, they were able to sound out each word on the manuscripts, and as they did so, the words of the ancient language took on meaning.

This was indeed the same language that they had learned for the Maker's prayer words! What an astounding discovery! The three of them were beside themselves with excitement!

At first Micah had been making daily reports to the High Seven about their discoveries, but as the weeks passed and more pressing concerns occupied their attention, the High Seven Shaman had instructed Micah to only make brief weekly summaries of what they had done. At the time that Micah and his assistants discovered how to read the ancient language, there were two major developments requiring the full attention of the clan rulers. The first was a serious disease that was threatening to devastate the Seventh Clan. The second was repeated attacks by large war parties of Renegades. These attacks had been especially severe against the three southern most clans.

So preoccupied were the High Shaman with these situations that they showed only moderate interest in Micah's enthusiastic report. They told him that they were too busy to bother with the specific details of his discoveries. Micah was instructed to complete the task of cataloging what was in the Treasure Cave as well as restoring and preserving what he could. They also told him that unless he found something of utmost importance, he was not to take up their time with verbal reports but rather to submit a written report when he finished.

Micah was very disappointed at the leader's lack of interest in his progress. He understood their pressing concerns with the threats to the clans, but this was a phenomenal discovery that really deserved their close attention.

He finally swallowed his disappointment and decided that one day the importance of his findings would be fully appreciated. With that in mind, he decided to be as thorough in his study of the documents as he could be. He and his assistants would make copies of all the written material found in the cave and keep detailed records of what they discovered and what they did.

By this time, the three investigators had studied every inch of the Treasure Cave except the far end where Larkin and his wife lay. They had walked through this area on their first day and viewed with awe the remains of this revered couple, but now the time had come to investigate this most honored spot.

The patriarch and matriarch of this race of tiny people lay entombed on two slabs of white quartz raised on pillars of limestone. They were lying side by side with their heads toward the end wall of the cave and their feet toward the aisle created by the other burial slabs.

Lily, the wife of Larkin, lay to the right of her husband. Not much was known about Lily except that she had endured many hardships with her husband to come to this place. As he thought about it, Micah was suddenly struck with how little was actually known about both of these great ancestors. There was much mystery surrounding these two.

"Who were they before they came here?" Micah wondered. "From where did they come? Did anyone come with them? Why did they leave where they were?" Given the opportunity, Micah could think of a lot of questions about Larkin and Lily that he would like to have answered.

There wasn't much left of Lily's burial gown. You couldn't even tell what color it had been originally.

"What's all this dust and litter all over Lily's bones?" Jasper asked.

After several minutes of study Micah voiced his opinion. "I can't tell for sure, but my guess is that it's probably flowers."

"They must have covered her in them when they laid her here," Jasper said.

"Yes," Micah agreed, "that's the way it appears to me also."

At the foot of Lily's slab was the same type of fire-hardened clay chest. In her chest were several articles of clothing that had long since rotted, but in the bottom of the chest they found an unusual artifact.

The object was flat, having an overall square shape with rounded corners on one end. The other end had ten long, needle-like teeth projecting from it. The end opposite from the teeth had delicately shaped flowers that were raised up on its surface. The two most prominent flowers each had a small red jewel embedded in its center.

"I've never seen anything like this!" Jasper remarked in amazement.

"Neither have I," voiced Linden, who was looking over Jasper's shoulder. "What do you make of it, Shaman Micah?"

Micah gently picked up the strange discovery. He looked at it carefully from every angle, fingering it delicately. "It must be some article of decoration. By the way the teeth are formed on one end, I would guess that she wore it in her hair."

"That must be it," said Jasper. "With the long teeth sticking into her hair, the pretty part would stick up for everyone to see."

"But what's it made of?" Linden wanted to know. "It looks like slick, shiny stone, but I've never seen a stone that looked like that."

Micah was still studying the strange object. "It's cold, shiny, and very smooth." Micah thumped the side of the object with his finger, and it made a high-pitched ringing sound. "I don't know what it is," he said finally, "but it's not stone."

"Where do you think it came from?" asked Linden.

"The same place as this!" announced Jasper, behind them.

While Micah and Linden had been deep in thought over Lily's beautiful comb, Jasper had turned his attention to the bones of Larkin. Micah and Linden looked up to see Jasper lifting Larkin's sting from where it lay by his side.

"What an awesome weapon!" was all Linden could say.

"It appears to be made of a similar material as Lily's hair ornament," said Jasper as he carefully fingered the ancient weapon. "It's heavy, much heavier than a regular sting, and the shaft is not round like a sting, but flat."

Micah moved close to Jasper to study it. "Are you sure it's the same material? Lily's ornament is a blackish gray color, and Larkin's weapon is a dark brown." Micah thumped his finger against the ancient blade, and some flakes of rust fell away. "Listen to that ringing sound," Micah said. "I think you must be right. It's either the same material or something really close."

"It's got to be something like it," Jasper said, "because it's shiny underneath where this brown stuff fell off."

"The brown flakes must be due to ageing," Micah said thoughtfully.

"Shaman Micah, look at these edges!" Jasper said excitedly. "They've been sharpened! Larkin could cut or slash with it, as well as stab!" Forgetting himself in his excitement, Jasper jumped back, and grasping the sword by its handle, he began swinging it back and forth in wide, sweeping arcs at imaginary enemies.

"Jasper!" Micah barked at him.

Shocked back to reality, Jasper, with a rather foolish look on his face, very gently placed the weapon back beside the bones of its owner.

There was nothing special about Larkin's burial clothes. He was laid to rest in a plain leather tunic, a good portion of which was in tatters. A pair of rotting worn boots was on his feet.

"Except for his place of honor and this magnificent weapon, you would never know that this was Larkin the Great," Linden observed.

"He apparently didn't see himself as great," Micah said. "No beautiful chieftain's robe, no medallions, no jewels on his clothes or his belt, just a plain hunting tunic and some worn boots. He didn't see himself as a king or a mighty ruler. He was the head of his family. He led them, he hunted for them, and he fought to protect them. He never sought greatness, and even in his death he refused to claim it."

"But he was great," Jasper said softly.

"Yes, he was great, though he probably never knew it. His humility makes him greater still," Micah's admiration for his mighty ancestor was growing immensely.

All three of them stood there in reverent silence for a long time. It was Linden who finally broke the quietness, "Hey! Something's missing!"

"What are you talking about?" asked Jasper.

"Larkin has no chest," Linden responded as he searched the base of Larkin's bier.

"No chest?" Jasper didn't understand.

"All the others have clay chests with all their personal stuff and writings at the foot of their burial slab. Even Lily has one, but not Larkin."

"Maybe they did something different for Larkin," Micah suggested.

They began to search that entire end of the cave. They found two clay pots against the wall which were full of jewels of various kinds, sizes, and colors. On a carved shelf mounted high on the wall above Larkin and Lily, they found the huge King Stone of Lanara, the beautiful round emerald as green as grass and as clear as water. This was the very stone over which the terrible Clan War was fought ages ago. But they did not find a container for Larkin's personal belongings.

"I guess he must not have had one," Jasper said after the fruitless search.

"Oh, yes, he did!" announced Linden. "Look down here!"

Linden was kneeling on the cave floor at the foot of Larkin's bier. As the others hurried to his side, they saw him tracing something on the cave floor. "Look! See here? There are scratch marks on the floor."

"Like where a heavy clay chest may have been drug away?" Jasper wondered hopefully.

"It looks like that's exactly what happened," Linden stated as he studied the faint marks. He slowly crawled across the floor toward the right wall of the burial chamber, tracing the scratches. "They go right up to this wall, and then they stop."

"That's odd," said Micah thoughtfully.

"Well, they couldn't have drug it through a solid wall," Jasper said incredulously.

"Unless it's not a solid wall," Micah returned.

Both Linden and Jasper looked at one another as Micah's words sunk in, then both of them quickly began searching the surface of the wall. After a few minutes, Linden found a crevice down close to the floor. As he explored the crack, part of the surface of the wall broke off in his hand. "Hey! Look how easily this piece of rock broke off!" he said with surprise.

"Let me see that," said Micah. He studied the edges of the piece from the wall. He easily crumbled some of the edges off with his fingers. "This isn't stone—it's clay."

"Clay?!" Linden voiced. He quickly reached back into the crevice and pulled hard. Another large piece of the wall pulled off in his hands, revealing a dark opening behind. "You're right, Shaman Micah! It's a false wall!"

With Jasper's help, he quickly created an opening large enough for them to pass through. Grabbing a torch, Linden slipped through the opening, followed by Jasper and Micah. They found themselves in a narrow passageway that led off in front of them a short distance, then curved away to the left.

Linden led the way, carefully following the winding passageway. He stopped frequently to search the floor of the cave for scrapes. At length they turned a corner, and the cave abruptly ended.

"Hey! What happened?" Jasper said with a mixture of surprise and frustration. "There's nothing back here."

"Why would someone go to all the trouble of building a false wall to hide nothing?" Linden was thinking out loud.

"Precisely!" announced Micah. "There must be another false wall somewhere."

Immediately the three of them spread out and began searching the walls, pounding on them with their hands, and listening for a hollow sound.

Linden was the one who eventually found it, but only because he held the torch. He was on his knees scanning the floor for scrape marks that might give him a clue to the location of the hidden passage. When he got to a certain point, the flame on his torch began flickering rapidly. When he moved the torch away, the flickering stopped. His curiosity piqued, he moved the flame back until it began flickering again. Then he moved the flame close to the wall at that spot, and it began to dance even more wildly. The flame actually bent sideways as it was sucked into a faint crack in the wall.

"I think I found it!" he said excitedly. The other two quickly moved to his side. "See! There's a lot of air moving through this crack. Watch how it sucks the flame into it." Linden repeated his experiment with the torch for his friends to see.

"Let's see if we can make an opening," Micah directed.

Jasper found a large rock, and with it he began pounding at the cave wall around the crack. On the third blow, a portion of the wall caved inward. It was short work to make an opening. Linden handed Jasper the torch, and he crawled through the hole.

"This passage is much smaller," Jasper called back to his anxiously waiting friends. "It's very low, and there's only room enough for one."

"Be careful," Micah called after him.

There was silence except for shuffling sounds as Jasper crawled down the small passage. "There's something blocking the tunnel up ahead," he called back from a distance. There were several more minutes of silence. "This is it!" he shouted at last.

"You found the chest?" Linden asked anxiously.

"Yes! Yes! It's here!" Jasper's words shot back. "We're going to need a rope. We'll have to drag it out."

It took a lot longer than they wanted for them to make their way back up to the Treasure Cave; find a long, stout rope; then travel back down to the place where the chest was hidden. They carried extra torches with them this time. Jasper again crawled down the low passageway, dragging a length of rope with him. After a few minutes, they heard him call back, "Okay! Start pulling! I'll help guide it through the crawlway."

It was quite a job pulling on that rope. They had to stop several times to rest. Their clothes were wet with sweat by the time Jasper appeared at the opening, tugging the chest behind him.

It was indeed a clay chest, identical to the ones up in the burial chamber. Carefully they lifted the lid, and inside they found a long, leather roll and two leather-bound books. Micah's heart was in his throat as he gently opened the cover of the top volume and began to slowly read the ancient words. After a few moments, he carefully closed the book and looked at his two companions. Slowly a smile crept over his face. "It's his," he said quietly.

"His?" Linden asked. "You mean Larkin's?"

Micah nodded his head. "It's Larkin's journal . . . in his own hand."

Linden was staggered by the thought. All they had ever known about their great ancestor was from legends passed down from one generation to the next, but now, though he had been dead for centuries, they had before them his actual words and thoughts. The concept was overwhelming, and Linden had to sit down.

"But what's it doing hidden in this hole?" Jasper wanted to know. "Every Larkin would want to know what's in these books."

"I'm getting the impression," Micah gave expression to his thoughts, "that there may be something in these books that someone didn't want every Larkin to know."

After a few more moments of deep thought, Micah issued some orders. "Jasper, I hate to do this to you, but you've had more experience in that small passageway than either of us. I want you to go back and see if there is anything else hidden in there. Be sure to go further back than where you found the chest if you can. But be careful.

"Linden, you and I will try to figure out a way to transport these books and the leather scroll up to the Treasure Cave where we can work on them without damaging them."

They eventually decided to transfer the books and the leather roll from the heavy, clay chest into a smaller, much lighter, wooden box that they could carry more easily.

Arriving at their work table in the Treasure Cave, Micah began to gently lift out the precious volumes. "Linden, you had better go back and be sure Jasper is all right."

"Oh, yes! I had forgotten about Jasper." Snatching up a torch, Linden quickly ducked back into the tunnel opening.

For several quiet minutes Micah simply stared at the ancient journals. Very gently, he rubbed his hand across the leather cover of one of the books. It was so old that the leather had turned black with age. There had once been something etched in the leather, but it had long since faded.

He began scanning through the pages of the two thick books, taking extreme pains to protect each page as he turned it. Both books had been written by Larkin. The first book appeared to Micah to be a journal of some of Larkin's travels. The second book seemed to be spiritual instructions for his sons and their descendents. It was this second book that seemed to demand his attention. Soon he was in deep concentration and had lost all track of time.

Two hours passed before Jasper and Linden stumbled through the opening in the wall. They were both filthy, and Jasper had a large knot with a bruise over his left eye. They both had guilty looks on their faces when they saw Micah.

"I'm sorry we were gone so long, Shaman Micah," Jasper said , "but we made an interesting discovery."

"We found out where that tunnel goes," added Linden.

Immediately they could tell that something was wrong. Micah had not even looked up when they came in. He was just sitting at the table with his head in his hands. His hands were pale, almost white, and he was trembling.

Quickly Linden moved over to check on Micah. "Are you all right?" he asked.

"Get out," Micah said without looking up.

"What?"

"I said, 'GET OUT!'" Micah's head jerked up. A wild fierceness was in his eyes. "I want you both out of here! You are no longer my assistants."

The two younger Shaman were stunned.

"Shaman Micah, what happened?" Jasper blurted out.

"You are no longer needed here!" Micah shot back. "If you don't leave now, I will call the guards!"

"But we don't understand!"

"GUARDS! GUARDS!!'

Immediately there was the sound of running feet approaching from the door. The two Larkin guards burst through the doorway, stings at the ready.

"Remove these two from the Treasure Cave!" Micah ordered. "Their work is finished, and they will not be coming back."

"Shaman Micah, please tell us why you're doing this!" Linden tried again.

"Get them out of here now!" Micah barked at the guards.

The guards quickly ushered out the two disappointed and bewildered young Shaman.

"And make sure that I am not disturbed!" Micah yelled up the passageway after the guards.

Sitting back down at the table, Micah gave a deep sigh, buried his head in his hands, and cried in deep, sobbing anguish. Micah's world was falling apart. He had read things in Larkin's writings that had shaken the very core of his being. He could not handle the presence of his two young associates during his emotional turmoil. Also, he didn't want them reading what he had read. He didn't want anyone to read it. He knew now why Larkin's books had been hidden.

Oh, how he wished he had never seen them! He even thought of destroying them, but he couldn't do it. He thought that he could just hide them again, and no one would know what was in them. But HE knew, and that was the problem. He couldn't ignore it or forget it. He had to deal with it.

It took some time to work through all of his emotions, but when he finally could think things out clearly, he knew he had to know the truth. Once he knew the truth, whatever it was and whatever it cost, that's where he would stand.

So he sat down before the ancient book once more to read the words of Larkin the Great. He would not be devastated this time. He would read the words critically, looking for truth. Then he would let the truth take him wherever it would.

For three days he never left the Treasure Cave. He pored over Larkin's words, taking many notes. He learned about a different God than he knew existed. The Maker that Micah served was aloof, distant, and almost unapproachable. He was a God who seemed to have little interest in the daily difficulties of their lives.

The God that Larkin was writing about was close, very approachable, and concerned even about the number of hairs on one's head. This God knew all things. He spoke and understood all languages, and therefore anyone could pray to Him. The Shaman with their special, exclusive prayer language were unnecessary. The Shaman were actually a hindrance to God's purposes, because Larkin said that the Maker wanted everyone to speak to Him and to know Him personally, like a father.

"A father!" Micah said out loud. "To know the Maker like a father!" Micah had never dreamed of anything like that, and the idea excited him.

The Maker had written a book, and somehow in one of his journeys, Larkin had seen this book of God's, and he had learned to read it. Before Larkin left wherever God's book was, he had copied down many parts of it just as God had written it. Most of the book Micah was studying was taken up with long quotes of the actual words of God that Larkin had written.

Micah was astonished to learn that the Maker had given laws for his created ones to follow, but that even those who had God's laws could not keep them. No matter how hard they tried, no one could be as good as what God wanted. That meant no one was worthy to be in God's presence.

Larkin wrote that the Maker loved his created ones so much that He wanted them to be able to be in His presence. God therefore devised a plan so that no matter how bad anyone was, those who wanted to be His child could be. But it was a very costly plan. The Maker sent His own, perfect Son to come from heaven to the earth, where the created ones were. Larkin called the Maker's Son Jehesus. The Maker sent Jehesus to live with the people of the earth, teaching them what the Maker was like, showing them the Maker's power, and expressing to them the Maker's love. But then, though he had never done anything wrong, Jehesus let himself be tortured and killed in order to take upon himself the punishment that belonged to all the people for disobeying the Maker. But astonishingly, after several days, Jehesus came back alive and showed himself to his followers. Larkin quoted Jehesus as saying that everyone who believed on Him and was bapatized would be saved. Larkin explained that being saved meant that you are made worthy to live with the Maker forever. He also explained that being bapatized was something you did to show that you really believed what Jehesus said. Larkin described it as imitating Jehesus dying, being buried, and coming to life again, but believers were to be buried in water instead of the ground. Larkin wrote that when you came out of the water, you were to trust in what Jehesus had done to save you, and by His power you could pray to the Father through Jehesus, act like Jehesus, and even begin to think like Jehesus. That way others could see what the Father in heaven was like and love Him also.

Larkin had written many stories about Jehesus describing what He said and did while He walked on the Earth. The more Micah read, the more he began to love the Maker's perfect Son. Micah decided that he could get excited about a God who had a son like Jehesus.

Micah made up his mind. The High Seven must know of all this. The truth had been hidden far too long.

chapter eight

THE RESCUERS

Rush spent some time discussing the plan to attempt to rescue Poke and Hawthorn with the leaders of the relief party that had come to their aid. He also told them everything that had happened so they could report it to the Shaman at the Keep. Rush then checked on their two wounded companions. Both were doing well, Hawk surprisingly so. He had drunk two containers of warm meat broth, and his wound was freshly dressed. Rush noticed there was more color in his face and he actually seemed stronger.

Flint's leg had been resplinted, and some fresh clothes were put on him. He was trying to eat and answer questions from the others about his fight with the dragon. The fact that he couldn't remember the fight did not seem to keep him from giving a detailed account of his heroic exploits.

Receiving what supplies their friends could spare, Rush, Savin, Sycamore, and Jay loaded their packs. They also took two of the six lances the relief party brought with them. Bidding farewell to their comrades, the four rescuers plunged into the forest with Rush in the lead. Even though the trail was cold, it was still easy for them to follow. Their attackers hadn't expected any of them to survive, so they had put little effort in covering their trail.

They had only been following the trail a short while when they came to an abandoned camp site. The others waited as Rush carefully examined the area. He ranged quickly back and forth across the small clearing, and then he circled the perimeter, stopping occasionally to examine the ground. Finally, he trotted over to his friends.

"They must have brought both of the young ones here," Rush began, "'cuz the group that took Hawthorn and the main body of warriors who attacked us returned here. Hawthorn's captors came in along this trail we followed, and the rest of the cowards came in from over there." He pointed off to the northeast side of the clearing. "They licked their wounds here, then the whole mess of 'em took off yonder to the south."

"How far behind them are we?" asked Savin.

Rush just shook his head. "Fellers, they got a head start on us you ain't gonna believe."

"How much of a head start?" Jay scowled.

"They didn't make a fire last night," Rush offered.

"What does that mean?" Jay asked again.

"It means," moaned Savin, "that they came back here to regroup and bind their wounds, then they left."

"You mean . . ." Jay began, his eyes getting wide as realization struck him.

"Yes," Savin answered the question before it was asked, "they've been traveling all night."

"So what are we gonna do?!"

"We're gonna hurry," Rush said matter-of-factly. He then took off at a quick trot, leading the way down the trail taken by the retreating Renegades. He had to slow the pace at more frequent intervals than he wanted because Jay was having a hard time keeping up. He had been running all night, and it was beginning to tell on him.

It was at one of these slower times that they passed by a large, moss-covered, rotting log lying on their left, parallel to the trail they were following. There were several large clumps of moss in front of them and on their right. Rush was leading, weaving his way between and around the moss patches, when suddenly something wet and sticky slapped him hard across the face and chest. Instantly he was jerked off his feet and yanked violently to his right. Before he even had time to react, he found himself head first and waist deep in the mouth of a large leopard frog.

The others were completely caught off guard by the suddenness of the attack. Sycamore had been right behind Rush. He had noticed a sudden movement behind the moss clump on the right, but before he could say anything, Rush disappeared. Running forward a few steps, he leaped around the clump, lance at the ready.

All he could see of Rush was his hips and legs kicking wildly out of the huge amphibian's mouth. Rush's backpack and shield were making it difficult for the toad to swallow him. He could see Rush groping for the knife he kept in his right boot.

Sycamore hefted his lance and charged. He buried the lance head deep into the creature's soft, white throat. The toad's response was immediate. Throwing itself backwards, the wounded creature blasted out a painful roar which sent Rush flying out of its mouth. Rush landed with a soggy thud on some moss a short distance away. Savin and Jay quickly ran to his aid.

Sycamore was jerked forward off his feet, but he managed to retain his grip on the lance, which pulled free when the injured frog jumped back. Quickly scrambling to his feet and readying his lance for the frog's next attack, Sycamore began backing toward his friends.

Rush was filthy and his ribs hurt, but otherwise he seemed all right.

"You okay?" Sycamore asked Rush, never taking his eyes off the frog, which was clawing at its injured throat.

"Oh, I'm just dandy!" Rush said sarcastically as he tried to draw his sting from its sheath. "I've got so much toad slobber on me I can't hold on to anything."

"We need to get out of here!" Sycamore said nervously, still watching the frog which was now eyeing them menacingly.

"Quick! This way!" said Jay, heading back the way they had come.

"No! Stop!" commanded Rush. "If we run that way, that hungry fly sucker'll be on us in two hops."

"So what do we do? Fight him?"

"No, not unless we have to," Rush responded, jerking his head around looking for a defensive position.

"Here he comes!" shouted Sycamore as the frog began moving towards them, positioning itself to strike.

"Everyone move back to the log," Rush ordered. "Keep both lances forward."

Savin, who was carrying the other lance, moved up next to Sycamore.

Rush continued, "Jay, cover us with your bow. Okay, everyone, let's move back toward the log."

Moving together, the four Larkin began backing toward the huge, rotting log behind them. The leopard frog moved also, stalking them.

Rush was searching the bottom of the log for some way of escape when he suddenly found it. "Left! Move more to the left." Without looking back, the others followed Rush's directions.

Soon the massive log was looming over them. Rush quickly unslung his own bow and put an arrow to the string. "Alright, Jay, you first!" Rush ordered.

Jay looked back at the base of the log and saw that the ground dipped a little in one spot, allowing a small opening under the log to the other side. Quickly he lowered his bow and wiggled under the log.

"Savin, you're next!" Rush barked, moving up to take Savin's place next to Sycamore.

Savin moved back to the opening and quickly slid his lance, butt first, under the log, then dove after it.

"Now you, Syc!" said Rush.

"Don't you think I should cover you with the lance?" Sycamore countered.

"No! You'd never make it under the log with that lance if you came last. We'd either lose you or the lance. I'll cover you with my bow. Besides, I got a special place in my heart for this ol' mud mucker, and I want to have a word of prayer with him before I leave. Now go!"

Immediately Sycamore turned for the hole, pausing to shove the lance through first. Behind him, he heard a quick, thumping sound, then a terrible croaking roar. He had his orders, so he didn't waste time looking back. He launched himself through the hole to clear the way for Rush.

As soon as Sycamore had turned from Rush to move to the opening under the log, the leopard frog made its move. In two quick leaps, the spotted predator charged the lone Larkin. Rush stood his ground and released his arrow, launching his missile into the back of the huge, gaping mouth. There was a tremendous roar as the arrow sank deep into the soft, tender flesh in the back of the frog's throat. As the frog again clawed furiously at his mouth and throat, Rush made his escape. As his head popped out of the hole on the back side of the log, friendly hands grabbed his shoulders and pulled him through.

"Well, did you have your word of prayer with him?" Sycamore asked.

"Yes, I did," Rush replied with a smile, "and he said he was sorry.

"Come on, let's get movin'." Rush led them to their left. He didn't want to run the risk of meeting their amphibian friend again. Moving about a stone's throw away from the log, they began traveling parallel to it. Once they were well past the end of the rotted, moss-covered trunk and had spotted no enemies, they began to angle back to their right in an attempt to pick up the Renegade trail again.

They had not yet crossed the enemies' path when they noticed that the ground began to get damp. Grass was growing up through the forest litter in thick patches. Weaving around the islands of grass, they finally came to a grassy wall.

Rush called his three friends together. "Okay, fellers, here's the sitchiation. We either back track and go around this grass, which'll put us even further behind, or we push straight through and risk facing whatever might be in there."

Rush saw the grim looks on each of their faces. Neither of their two choices was very appealing. "Jay, see if you can climb up that sparkleberry bush high enough to see how far we'd have to travel through this grass."

Without a word, Jay threw down his pack and shield and pulled himself up into the nearby bush. Ascending the central limb, it was only a short climb to the leaves. At that point the job became easy. Jay simply used the leaf stems like rungs on a ladder, scaling quickly up the tall, straight limb until his weight began to make it sway. At that height he could see over the grass and well beyond it.

"How's it look?" called Rush.

"Well, it could be worse," Jay called back. "We'll have to travel through this grass for about the length of a bow shot, but the grass seems to be a good bit thinner the last half of the way." Jay quickly climbed back down to his friends. As they pondered their next move, the four friends ate a quick meal of the dried fruit they carried in their backpacks.

"I ain't makin' this decision fer ya," Rush began, speaking to his three companions. "I'm thinkin' our best choice is through this grass, but let me tell you fellers somethin', that's a great place to get yerself kilt. So what's it gonna be?"

"I'm with you," said Sycamore resolutely.

"Me, too," voiced Savin.

"How 'bout you, Jay?" Rush asked.

Jay shrugged. "The sooner we start, the sooner we're through it."

"All right then," Rush announced, "let's have at it. I think we'd better carry our shields in our hands. If we hold 'em by the edge, we should be able to drag 'em through the thick grass. Otherwise they'll just get hung up."

Rush cautiously led them into the mass of thick, green blades. It was tough getting the lances through. Savin and Sycamore had to hold them up close to the lance head and drag the long shafts behind them. The jagged, saw-toothed edges of the grass blades clawed at their clothing and skin. In a short time they were all bleeding from numerous cuts on their arms and faces.

Once when Jay was leaning against a piece of grass trying to get his breath a large, black, fuzzy head appeared around the edge of the blade. Jay quickly moved away, trying to put plenty of room between himself and the stinging hairs on the head of the caterpillar. He didn't think the venom in those hairs would kill him, but it would make him wish he were dead. Giving his hairy acquaintance a wide berth, he quickly moved to catch up with his companions.

Whenever there was rustling in the grass around them, they would instantly freeze, remaining perfectly still until the source of the noise moved on. Something big moved close by them once. They had to remain motionless for several minutes until they were sure it had passed.

They had been pushing their way through the thick jungle for what seemed like hours. Rush was sure they had to be getting close to the other side, as the way seemed to be getting a little easier. Pushing on, he led his companions through the pressing forest of tall, green blades.

Rush suddenly froze. "What was that?!" he thought. The others behind him became motionless as well. There was a faint rustling in the grass on their right. No, now the sound seemed louder on their left. The rustling sound was all around them and getting louder by the second. The grass blades on every side of them were vibrating and beginning to move.

"Yiii!" rang Jay's voice in a fearful shout. "They're all over me! Help me, Savin!"

"I'm here, Jay!" Rush heard Savin's reassuring voice. "Be still! I'll try to knock them off!"

"Watch out, Savin! They're getting on you!"

Rush could hear their excited voices, but he couldn't see what was happening to them through the grass. Sycamore was pushing back towards them. As Rush tried to follow, something grabbed his leg. Simultaneously he felt clawing at both of his shoulders.

Instinctively Rush began flailing wildly back and forth trying to beat away his attackers. At that same moment he heard Sycamore yelling. They were all under attack. He felt one of his arms slap something soft. Looking quickly, he caught a glimpse of a black, round body, a little smaller than his own head, tumbling off to his left. Immediately Rush felt sharp claws digging into the right side of his neck. Whipping around, he saw a pair of sharp mandibles snapping in his face. He swung wildly with both arms, sending the creature bouncing off the grass blades to his right. As he continued to flail his arms, he felt the thudding impact as another of the black, round bodies went flying up into the air.

"We've got to get out of here!" Rush roared as he saw more of the creatures popping out of the grass all around him. "We've stumbled into a nest of seed ticks! To me, Larkin! To me! This way!"

Fighting wildly at the scores of bloodthirsty parasites, the other Larkin began moving towards Rush's voice. Rush was bowling his way savagely through the thick blades of grass, totally disregarding the sharp, saw-toothed edges. He paused just long enough to knock one of the bloodsuckers off his leg. No sooner had he done so when another one landed on his back. He yelled and began trying to reach behind him to grab the creature, but he was unable to get his hands on it. He could hear the tick's mouth parts snapping the air at the base of his neck. Suddenly there was a thump, and Rush felt the tick tear loose from his back and sail upward over Rush's head. Sycamore had come up behind Rush and, seeing his predicament, had driven his fist with all his might into the soft underbelly of the baby tick.

Rush didn't stop to look back. He knew their lives depended on how quickly they could get out of this grass, so on he plunged through the towering, thick blades. He shoved ferociously at the grass blocking his way, heedless of the sharp, jagged edges. Despite many cuts and gashes he never slowed his pace. With blood flowing freely down his face and both arms, he threw himself between the grass blades to make a path for his friends, while at the same time yelling continuous encouragement to them. Rush knew that they were too busy to pay attention to what he was saying, but he also knew they were getting separated, and he wanted them to be able to follow him.

Suddenly Rush found himself tumbling out into a small clearing. Pushing himself up off the ground, he spun around and began yelling back into the grass, "I made it out! This way! To me, Larkin, to me! I'm in the clear!"

Sycamore came charging out into the clearing. Rush kept up his calls. Five seconds behind Sycamore, Savin also broke through. He fell to the ground and began rolling furiously, trying to dislodge a fat, black tick clinging to his back and biting at his pack. Sycamore ran over and, with a vicious kick, sent the creature flying back into the grass.

Rush was calling for Jay now. He could hear him in the distance coming through the thick grass. "Keep coming, Jay! Keep coming! You're almost out! Follow my voice!"

There was a muffled cry, then the sounds of Jay's movements stopped.

"No, Jay!!" Rush bellowed. "Don't stop!! Your only hope is to get to us!"

The thrashing sounds began again, and suddenly Jay crashed through the grass blades. His body was almost engulfed by ticks. He had one on each leg, two on his back, and one wrapped around his chest and head.

His three friends were instantly at his aid, knocking and pulling the blood-thirsty parasites off him. Rush yanked the last one from Jay's back, but it had already bitten into his shoulder. When Rush pulled the creature loose, it left a deep wound.

113

Maddened at losing its meal, the creature spun around where Rush had thrown it and charged back at them. Rush whipped out his sting and impaled the tick, pinning it to the ground.

Leaving his weapon embedded in his attacker for the moment, he turned to check on the others. While the bite wound on Jay's back was a deep one, it had not done any serious damage. Savin bathed the wound with water from his pack, and Sycamore made a bandage for him. As it turned out, Rush had more cuts and gashes on his face and arms than all three of the others had put together.

By the time they had all their wounds cleaned and bandaged, the tick had died and Rush was able to retrieve his sting.

"We need to get movin'," Rush said at last. "Jay, are you up for it?"

"Ah, that ol' blood sucker was just tasting the meat. He didn't do much damage," Jay stood up to show that he was ready to go, but Rush noticed that the young warrior wasn't as steady on his feet as he normally was. He took note of that and led them off at a little slower pace to let Jay conserve his strength.

Rush knew that there was no way that Jay could march through the night as tired as he was and with that wound. Actually, they all desperately needed some rest, and they needed a good meal. More dried fruit and some dried meat were all they had in their packs. Rush wished that they had some fresh meat, something to build up their strength.

He led the small band of rescuers at an angle through the brush in order to intersect the Renegade trail that they had been following. It was late in the day when they finally crossed their enemy's path and began the pursuit again. Rush knew that they must eventually camp for the night to give them all, but especially Jay, a chance to rest. It was going to be dark in another hour, and he figured that they needed to start looking for a defensible place to spend the night.

A loud whirring of wings overhead caused them all to instantly dive for cover. Peering from underneath a large blackjack oak leaf, Rush saw a huge grasshopper fold his wings and land a short distance to the right of the trail.

On seeing that it was not an enemy, the other three Larkin crept cautiously out of their places of concealment and moved up to join Rush.

"Do you see the size of that hopper?!" Jay whispered to Savin.

"He's a big one, all right," Savin returned as he watched the gigantic insect feeding a short distance from them.

Rush began crawling toward the big insect with his bow in hand. "What are you doing, Rush?" Sycamore whispered. "That thing is as big as three Larkin."

Rush stopped and looked back at them. "After what we been through the past couple of days, I figure we got to do something to try to build our strength up, and the best way I can think to do that is to eat some fresh meat and lots of it.

"Just look over there, fellers," he said, jerking his head toward the big green bug. "The Maker's done dropped a feast right in our laps. All we got's to do is go get it."

"But, Rush," Savin asked, "how are you going to kill a hopper that big with just an arrow?"

"I ain't gonna' kill him," Rush grinned. "I'm just gonna' stop him so you fellers can run up there an' clobber him. But I got's to get a little closer to do it."

Rush turned and began slowly crawling toward the unsuspecting insect. The creature was so busy feeding that it was oblivious to the approaching Larkin hunter. Rush was able to get very close before he positioned himself to shoot. He drew his bow the full length of the arrow and took aim. The others were still wondering how he was going to stop such a huge grasshopper with only one arrow. There was a sharp "twang" as he released the missile. It struck the large insect in the left rear leg, piercing the shell right above its knee, pinning the leg to its body. The hopper felt the blow and tried to jump, but with only one leg working, the creature only succeeded in flipping itself over on its back.

"HA, HAA!" Rush roared at his dumbfound companions. "He's ours!" Jumping up and whipping out his sting, he charged toward the stricken insect. Stirring themselves from their shocked amazement, the others hurried after him.

As the injured grasshopper thrashed to free its pinned leg, there was a hissing roar, and a large, brown mass flashed up out of the ground, pouncing on the insect.

The Larkin were stunned by the surprise attack of the large wolf spider. Jay felt his knees get weak as he saw the two shiny, black fangs, dripping with venom, stab viciously into the head and upper body of the grasshopper.

"Where'd he come from?!" Sycamore wondered.

"He must have been hiding in a hole in the ground," answered Savin.

At that moment Rush ran back to his friends with fire in his eyes. "Come on, fellers! We got to work fast if we're gonna' save our supper!"

Jay was incredulous. "Rush! What are you thinking?! We can't fight a wolf spider!"

"Why, there ain't nothin' to him 'cept them fangs and them long legs. All we got's to do is flip him on his back and finish him off."

"Oh, that's a great plan, Rush," Jay said sarcastically. "I'll tell you what, you flip him over, and I'll finish him off."

"You got yerself a deal," Rush said resolutely. "Syc, hand Jay yer lance. He's gonna' need it."

As the lance was offered, Jay's eyes got very wide. "Now wait a minute . . ." he started to protest, but Rush cut him off.

"You ain't trying to weasel out, are you? A deal's a deal. I'll flip him, and you finish him off. But we've got to hurry, or that venom will mess up our hopper haunches."

Jay's mouth fell open as Rush turned to the others.

"Grab that long limb over there on the ground," Rush ordered. Savin was standing close to the limb, so he quickly took hold of it and began dragging it toward Rush.

"We want it right here," Rush barked out. He was pointing to a log that was lying on the ground that came up almost to his waist. Sycamore and Savin pulled the limb over to Rush, who positioned it across the top of the log. He put the end of the limb closest to the wolf spider on the ground, with the other end up in the air.

"Okay, that ought to do it," Rush announced.

"What is it?" asked Savin.

"Why, it's a *flip-a-thang*!" Rush said proudly.

"Old Renegade trick?" Sycamore asked.

" Well, if'n it ain't, it ought to be," Rush answered with a smile.

"So what's it supposed to do?"

"Okay," Rush began, rubbing his hands together, "here's how she works. Syc, you and Savin climb up this sapling right here and sit on that limb right above the raised end of the flip-a-thang. When the spider gets over the end of the limb that's lying on the ground, you two jump off together and land on the raised end of the limb. That makes your end of the limb go down, see? And it makes the spider's end go up—real fast. Before he realizes what's happened, he's flipped! That's when you charge in with the lance, Jay, and skewer him."

"And where are you going to be during all this?" Sycamore wanted to know as he and Savin climbed into position.

"Wel-l-l," Rush drawled, "since this is my idear, I figure that I ought'a be the bait. I'm gonna' run up there an' get ol' Fuzzy Leg's attention. When he comes after me, I'll get him to chase me right up this end of the flip-a-thang, and that's when you two jump. Now is everybody ready?"

Sycamore and Savin both nodded their heads as they perched on the limb above the raised end of Rush's invention. Rush looked at Jay, who nervously nodded his head, then knelt behind some brush, tightly gripping the shaft of the lance.

Rush turned toward the wolf spider. He ran toward the large, furry predator, stopping about halfway between the spider and his friends. Unslinging his bow, Rush launched an arrow into the spider's thorax. There was only a muffled rumble from the wolf spider as the arrow bounced off one of its protective plates where the legs attach to the body. Rush jumped, yelled, and waved his arms, but if the spider saw him, it was too busy feeding to bother with him.

"You're going to have to do better than that, Rush!" Sycamore yelled at him.

"Why, I'm down-right offended!" Rush yelled back. "That fuzzy-legged hopper snatcher don't think I'm worth eatin'! I reckon I'll have to learn that rascal what a tasty morsel it is that's over here trying to get 'et!"

Rush cautiously trotted closer.

"Watch yourself, Rush!" Jay called nervously.

"Yeah," added Sycamore, "remember, you're just the bait, not the victim."

When Rush stopped, he was dangerously close to his huge enemy. He yelled again, but the spider still ignored him. Taking careful aim with his bow, Rush let fly. There was a tremendous roar, and the spider leaped backward from its meal as the arrow sank deep in-between two of its protective plates on the thorax.

"Pay attention to me when I'm yelling at you, you eight-legged fur ball!" Rush shouted.

The injured spider whipped around to face the source of his pain. Spotting the Larkin hunter, the maddened wolf spider charged. Rush viewed the oncoming enemy with wide eyes. A high-pitched whine escaped his lips as he turned and ran for his life.

Savin and Sycamore yelled encouragement from their perch, "Good job, Rush!"

"Yeah, good job! He's chasing you for sure now!!"

Rush took a fearful glance back over his shoulder at his gaining pursuer and let out an involuntary "Yiiiiiii!!"

"Hey, Rush!" Savin yelled. "You'd better run faster! He's gaining on you!"

"I am . . . running faster!" Rush yelled back breathlessly.

"No, I mean faster than that," Savin returned.

"I am running . . . faster . . . than that!" Rush screamed.

The huge spider was almost on him when he reached the end of the flip-a-thang. Rush hollered "NOW!!" as he ran past the end of the limb lying on the ground. The spider was right behind him as Savin and Sycamore jumped from their perch. Landing together on the raised end of the limb, their combined weight plus the weight of their heavy back packs brought their end down quickly. But they had misjudged the speed of the spider. Instead of the end of the limb flying up under the front part of the spider and flipping it over backwards, the limb caught the spider under its midsection, sending the startled creature straight up into the air.

Rush looked up and saw the giant spider suspended momentarily above them. "To me, you two! Quick!"

Sycamore and Savin ran quickly to join their friend. Whipping out their stings, they turned just as the fierce killer crashed back to the ground right in front of them. Its charge interrupted by its sudden flight, the great spider was momentarily confused. Suddenly his weak eyes focused on the three Larkin hunters in front of him. He raised his fangs and approached warily.

From his place of concealment, Jay had watched with horror as Rush's plan began to disintegrate. As the spider began to stalk them, Jay knew that his friends were in desperate trouble. Something had to be done quickly, and he knew that he was the one who had to do it. He thought about charging the spider, but he didn't think he could get the spear to penetrate into the creature's midsection. Then suddenly a desperate plan popped into his mind. He knew that it was completely insane, but he couldn't think of anything else. Swallowing hard, Jay positioned the spear on the ground pointing toward the spider. He marked its position with his back pack so he could spot it quickly, then he turned and ran toward the eight-legged killer.

Approaching the creature from its right rear, he began to scream and throw sticks at it to get its attention. At first the wolf spider seemed not to notice, so focused was he on the three prey in front of him.

"Jay!" Rush yelled. "Have you lost yer mind?!"

"Keep still!" Jay yelled. "I've got a plan!" Jay pulled up his bow and sank an arrow into the spider's bulbous abdomen. With a roar, the furious arachnid turned on his new attacker. As soon as he did so, Jay ran for his spear.

"No, Jay!"

"Don't run! You can't get away!"

Oblivious to his friends' pleas, Jay raced on. The spider, seeing its prey in flight, charge furiously after him.

Jay ran with all his speed toward his waiting lance, with the spider gaining on him with every step. When Jay reached his lance, he threw himself down at the butt end. Bracing the end of the lance in the ground with his knee on top of it, he leaned forward and grabbed the shaft of the lance with both hands. With his knee still bracing the end in the ground, he lifted the lance till the point was on a level with the charging spider's mouth.

There was a horrible crash, followed by a violent thrashing that sent clouds of dust and forest litter flying into the air in all directions. Then, as suddenly as it had started, the noise stopped.

Rush, Sycamore, and Savin were stunned at what they saw. Jay was digging himself out of a pile of dirt and leaf litter in front of a dead wolf spider. The charging creature had hit Jay's lance with such force that it had actually impaled itself on two-thirds of the length of the lance.

"I ain't never seen anybody do that before!" Rush was dumbfounded. "Where'd you learn that?"

"What? That?" Jay said nonchalantly as he continued to dust himself off. "That's just an old Renegade trick."

Sycamore laughed, "So Rush isn't the only one who knows old Renegades."

"Seriously," Savin asked, "how did you think of doing that with the lance?"

"Wel-l-l . . ." Jay said out of the side of his mouth, imitating Rush's drawl, "that there's my new invention. I call it my *poke-a-thang*."

They were all laughing now.

"Well, it sure worked better than the flip-a-thang," laughed Savin.

"Now wait just a minute!" Rush jumped in with mock hurt in his voice. "The flip-a-thang would have worked just fine if you two birds had jumped when I said to."

"If we had jumped when you said to, we would have flipped you instead of the spider," Sycamore returned, still laughing.

"I guess I was a bit preoccupied at the time," Rush chuckled.

"Come on, fellas!" Jay shouted at them as he trotted toward the dead grasshopper. "Let's see if we can save what's left of that hopper before the spider venom ruins it!"

"The boy kills one little wolf spider by hisself, and he's ready to take over," Rush commented to his two friends.

Savin just shook his head. "They'll be no living with him now."

The three set off at a trot following Jay.

CHAPTER NINE

TOBIN THE FLYER

"Are you listening to me, Chummy?" Eldan asked with concern.

"Yes," Hawthorn replied weakly. "I heard every thing you said. It's just that my head . . . It's starting to hurt a lot, and when my eyes are open, everything starts whirling around."

Eldan turned away from his friend and began searching through a bag that he had slung over his shoulder. He pulled a small leather pouch out of the bag. The small pouch had a drawstring around the top and some symbols written on the outside. Eldan opened the small sack and pulled out a piece of dried leaf.

"Here," he said to Hawthorn as he put the piece of leaf in his mouth, "chew on this piece of feverfew. It will help with the pain. While you're chewing on that piece, I'll brew up some tea with the rest that will work even better."

Eldan quickly set to work preparing a place to build a fire. After he had cleared a place, he reached into his large bag and pulled out some tinder, consisting of some thistle down and some finely-shredded cedar bark. His curiosity piqued, Hawthorn watched as Eldan pulled out a reddish-brown rock and began to strike it with a piece of flint. As he did so, a shower of sparks exploded from the two rocks, falling onto his tinder. After three or four strikes, the tinder was smoking. Quickly, Eldan blew it into a flame and began to add twigs to it to build it up.

Hawthorn was amazed. "How did you do that?!"

"It's a fire stone," Eldan said, holding up the reddish-brown rock. "Our wise men discovered their use several seasons ago."

Hawthorn marveled at the heavy stone that Eldan handed him. "How did your wise men get such great knowledge?"

Eldan thought for a moment. "Well, when we have needs, much prayer is offered to our Father God, and in time, He answers our prayers."

Suddenly there was a loud cawing in the sky above them. The shape of the large bird circling overhead startled Hawthorn. When he realized that it was a crow instead of a hawk, he relaxed a little. A crow could eat a Larkin if it wanted to, but they weren't hunters. They were more interested in food that was already dead.

Eldan stood up when he saw the circling bird and gave a loud, shrill whistle. As if in response to Eldan, the crow turned and began to spiral down toward them.

"That's my brother, Tobin," Eldan said, still looking up.

"Your brother's a bird?" Hawthorn said incredulously.

Eldan cut his eyes down at Hawthorn with a look of annoyance but didn't respond.

With a flurry of wings, the large, black bird landed in the small clearing just in front of Hawthorn. Hawthorn got another surprise as he saw a Larkin-sized figure slide off the crow's back. He was a burly, deep-chested fellow, a little shorter than Eldan but twice as broad. He had the same green eyes and the same red, curly hair as his brother, but Tobin's face was partially hidden by a thick, curly red beard. He had about as much beard as he had hair, and the result was that his head looked like a small red bush.

As soon as he dismounted, the crow bent down and rubbed its head against the rider. Tobin stroked the crow's shiny black beak and said some words to it. He then picked up a large pack that he had been carrying and walked towards them.

As the bush-headed bird rider approached them, Eldan stepped forward to meet him. "Hey, Bubs," Eldan said to his brother. "I appreciate you coming and all, but you know, you took your own sweet time getting here. What were you doing, sparking the girls again?"

At the last statement, Eldan's brother's eyes narrowed into a fierce glare, his cheeks turned redder than his hair, and a deep rumbling growl came from behind his beard.

"Oh, come on, Bubsie," Eldan said, giving his brother a good-natured swat in the chest with the back of his hand. "Where's your sense of humor? I was just funnin' ya'. Quit growling, will ya? You'll make me think ya' don't love me anymore."

"Eldan!" Tobin growled through clenched teeth.

TOBIN THE FLYER

"I know what you're gonna' say, Tobs," Eldan started again. "You're gonna' say that I talk too much, and I'll admit you've got a point; you sure do. But you know, it's not totally my fault. I wouldn't talk so much if I didn't have so much to say.

"Why are we going on like this, anyway, Bubs? There's a hurt Larkin lying here, and you're wasting time giving me lectures. Come over here, and I'll introduce you to him."

Eldan bent over Hawthorn and said with a smile, "This is my brother, Chummy. I told you he'd come. He's called Tobin the Flyer."

He turned to his brother and said, "Tobs, I want you to meet Prickly Pear from the First Clan of Larkin."

Tobin bent over Hawthorn to look at him. "Prickly Pear?" he asked.

"My name is Hawthorn, and I'm from the Third Clan."

Tobin looked back at his brother. Eldan only shrugged. Turning his attention back to the young Larkin, Tobin began to examine him carefully. "Where do you hurt?" he asked.

"My head hurts the worst, and I get really dizzy if I keep my eyes open too long," was the reply.

"He took quite a pop on the ol' melon," Eldan added, tapping the back of his own head.

"How'd you hurt your head?"

"Which time?" Hawthorn shot back. He then reviewed for them the events of the previous day. He told of the hunting trip, the ambush, and his head injury from that. He told them what information he had acquired from Poke and of their escape and recapture by Wolf. Then he told them how he was staked to a fire ant nest so that he would be killed. "When the ants swarmed over me, one of them must have run into the back of my head pretty hard, because that's all I remember until I woke up on a pile of dead ants, feeling awful."

Tobin looked over at his brother. "Were you there?"

Eldan nodded his head. "Being the good Ranger that I am, I was patrolling Area Eight above the pine forest, looking for a good deed to do. I came on the trail of a Renegade war party and figured that they were up to no good. By the time I caught up with them, the fight with the Larkin hunting party was pretty much over. I saw their two captives and decided that I would try to slip in and free them when they made camp, but they never stopped, except for only very brief rests. I didn't have time to do anything. I was moving parallel with the Renegade column, looking for an opportunity, when they were attacked by a young lynx. There was mad confusion among the Renegades. Moving in closer to see what was happening, I got there just in time to see the two Larkin escaping into the woods away from me. It took me a while to slip past the lynx and the Renegades. By the time I caught up with them, they were into it with another Renegade, who apparently wanted to kill them. He had left Thorny's friend for dead and was dragging Thorny deeper into the woods so his Renegade buddies wouldn't be able to stop him. I could tell that the other Larkin was breathing, but I couldn't get to him before the approaching Renegades got there, so I decided to follow the Renegade with his prisoner and see if I could keep ol' Thornton here from getting his throat cut. Let me tell you something, Tobs, this was one bad Renegade. He staked our friend here out on a red ant nest and then stirred up the nest."

"How did you keep him from being torn to pieces?" Tobin asked curiously.

"Yes!" Hawthorn joined in. "I've been wondering about that myself."

Eldan's mouth spread into a large grin. "Surely you know there's more to me than just a pretty face?"

Tobin rolled his eyes.

"When I saw the murderous rascal heading for the ant nest," Eldan continued, "I figured out his intentions. This Renegade was a powerful-looking enemy, and I wasn't sure that I could stop him without killing him. I also knew that I couldn't stop the ants once they were stirred up into a frenzy, so I decided to turn our little Larkin friend into a red ant."

"What?!" shouted Hawthorn, rising up from his bed. He immediately grabbed his head with both hands as he felt the stab of pain resulting from the quick movement, and then slowly eased back down on his bed.

"Did you use a scent sack?" asked Tobin.

"You're way ahead of me, Bubs. That's exactly what I did."

"Wait a minute," Hawthorn said weakly. "What are you talking about?"

Tobin answered his question. "Each ant has two sacks in his abdomen that contain scented juices. One sack they squeeze out when they're excited. When the other ants smell it, they go absolutely crazy and run around as fast as they can, ripping apart anything that's not another ant from their nest. The second sack contains a scent that tells the other ants that they are a friendly ant from their own nest. They also use that scent to leave trails to food."

Eldan continued his story. "I circled the nest until I found their grave yard for dead ants. I cut into one that looked like it had just recently died and found the two scent sacks. I had to hurry, 'cause things were starting to happen back on the nest. I grabbed the sack, tied it off, and ran back to the nest. I was almost too late. When I got there, the ants were already starting to charge out of the entrances, furious to kill whoever had disturbed them. I couldn't get very close, so all I could do was say a quick prayer and throw the sack at Thornbush."

"Hawthorn!" Tobin and Hawthorn said in unison.

"Uh . . . right. To the Maker's praise, the sack hit him in the back just as the ants got to him. They knocked him around a little bit, but because he smelled like one of them, they passed him by and continued looking for their enemy. Later, when they had calmed down, they thought he was one of their chums who had gone to the great picnic in the sky, so they picked him up and carried him to their grave yard."

"So that's why my ribs are so sore," Hawthorn winced as he felt the sides of his chest.

"You did well, Eldan." There was a look of approval in Tobin's eyes.

"You really did save my life!" Hawthorn said. "I'm sorry that I didn't thank you before, but I didn't believe you. I thought you were crazy."

"Now there he goes again, Bubs. Poppin' my bubble before it even gets blowed up good."

"Thank you, Eldan," Hawthorn said sincerely. "Thank you for saving my life and rescuing me from the Renegades."

"There you go. That's more like it." The grin was back on Eldan's face.

"But how did you know which one of those two scent sacks was the friendly one?" Hawthorn wanted to know.

Eldan looked rather sheepish. "Well, uh, actually. . . I didn't know."

"You didn't know?!"

"You see, Chums, when I cut open the dead ant and got down to the sacks, they both looked the same, and to tell the truth, I couldn't remember which one was which. I really didn't have time to stew about it, you know. After all, your situation couldn't get any worse, so . . . I grabbed one and threw it."

"What?! Oh!" Hawthorn shouted, grabbing his head again.

"Well, you had a fifty-fifty chance, Chummy. That was better than you had without it."

"Eldan could have done no more," Tobin was talking to Hawthorn in a deep, gentle voice. "The choice was actually the Maker's, and He chose to let you live. He's the one you really should thank."

"Yes, but I don't, I don't . . ." Hawthorn's voice was getting noticeably weaker.

Tobin put his finger on Hawthorn's lips. "No more talking, friend. You've got to rest."

They finished brewing the feverfew tea that Eldan had started and had Hawthorn take several swallows of it. Tobin then spent a few minutes looking carefully into Hawthorn's eyes and gently feeling the lump on the back of his head. Finally, he sat back and looked at his brother. "I think he's getting some swelling on the inside of his head."

"He hasn't looked very good for the last two hours," Eldan added, showing his concern. "What do we do?"

"We need to get him to Stillwaters, but he's in no shape to travel. I guess we'll have to do the best we can right here—at least for now."

"Say, Tobs. I remember learning about an herb that helps with swelling."

"Yes, but do you remember which herb it is?" Tobin quizzed his brother.

"Uh ... Grape seed?"

"Dandelion root," Tobin corrected.

"Dandelion root?! . . .Well, yeah, maybe it was dandelion root, but you got to admit I was close."

Tobin let out a deep sigh and rolled his eyes again.

"So, Bubsie, where are we going to get the dandelion root?"

"I've got dandelion root in my pack, along with licorice root and blackberry leaf, which he also needs."

"Well, that's great! So how do we fix 'em?"

"That might be a bit of a problem," Tobin said thoughtfully. "For his body to be able to use those herbs, they need to be in a meat broth, and I didn't bring any meat."

"I don't have any meat either. All I've got is dried fruit and some bread . . . . A meat broth?! Can't we just make a tea out of it?" Eldan asked in frustration.

"Tea won't work with the dandelion root," Tobin answered. "There's something in the meat juices that makes the herb work. I guess we'll have to go hunting, but that may take some time."

"It won't take long if you know where the meat is," Eldan said with the gleam of an idea shining in his eyes.

Tobin had seen that look in his brother's eyes before. "What are you thinking?"

"Follow me, Brother," Eldan said loftily. "I know just where to get the meat." Eldan led the way around the edge of the clearing. They were only a stone's throw from where Hawthorn lay when Eldan stopped and pointed between the roots of a large elm tree.

"There!" Eldan said, grinning triumphantly. Tobin's gaze followed Eldan's pointing finger. In between two of the elm tree's roots was a hole. As Tobin was looking at the hole, two very large, dark brown ants with huge pincers came out of the hole and moved off quickly into the woods. Immediately another large ant carrying a seed in its mandibles came in from the woods and disappeared into the hole.

"You want to feed him ants?!" Tobin said in disbelief.

"Well, no, not the big ones. I was thinking that we could get one of the larvae."

Tobin thought on that for a few moments. "Yeah, I guess a larvae would work okay. But, Eldan, how are you going to get one?"

"I'm gonna' go into their nursery and pull one out," Eldan responded proudly.

Tobin was incredulous. "You've really lost it this time, Brother! Aside from the fact that you'd have to be completely insane to go in there, you would be crawling around for days trying to find the nursery, then you'd never find your way out!"

"Bubsie! Bubsie! Bubsie! Calm yourself. Did you see what kind of ants those were?" Eldan continued. "They were harvester ants, and harvester ants keep their nurseries next to their food storage chambers."

"So what?"

"So, if I give one of the worker ants some of my bread, he'll take it straight to one of the food chambers. If we can slip a rope around him, I can sit behind him on a piece of a leaf, holding on to the rope. He'll sled me right next door to the nursery. If I tie a long piece of rope around my waist, then once I get the larvae, all I have to do is follow the rope back out. See? It's simple!"

Tobin dropped his head in both of his hands and was shaking it back and forth. "Eldan, you've lost your mind! You're not seriously thinking about doing that, are you?"

They both heard a low moan escape Hawthorn's lips as he lay a short distance behind them. "Tobin, our friend over there may die if we don't get your herbs in him, and they won't work without meat. This is the fastest way I know to get the meat." Eldan was searching through his pack as he spoke. He pulled out a long coil of silken rope. Cutting off a short length of it, he threw the rest over to his brother. "Tie that to your rope, and I'll tie one end of it to my waist. While you are doing that, I'll make a harness for the ant with this piece."

Eldan made a large loop in one end of the rope tied with a slip knot. Then he tied a small loop in the other end with a secure knot. He would hang on to the smaller loop as the ant pulled him through the tunnels.

There was a small elm leaf lying nearby, and Eldan chose this for his sled. When everything was ready, they moved it all over next to the hole. They didn't have to wait long. Almost immediately a large, brown harvester ant popped out of the hole. Eldan placed the bread from his pack in front of the sinister-looking insect. Instantly the ant caught the scent of the bread and began feeling for it. This gave Eldan and Tobin just time enough to slip the large loop over the ant's head. Seeing that the rope was in place, Eldan grabbed the other end and quickly sat down on the elm leaf.

Eldan was grinning from ear to ear. "See, Bubs, no prob . . ." But before he could finish the sentence, the ant snatched up the bread and dove back down the hole. Eldan was jerked off the leaf and into the air. He landed face first on the ground next to the hole with a resounding "thud," then was instantly yanked down the hole. Tobin threw himself against the edge of the ant hole. He saw

Eldan bouncing from side to side as he was dragged, face first, down the dark passage.

"Turn loose, Eldan! Turn loose!" Tobin shouted.

He heard Eldan's voice trailing down the dark hole. "No-o . . . oof . . . w-o-o-or-ries . . . aiieeee!!"

Tobin couldn't believe what he had just seen. He thought that he must be crazy, too, to let Eldan do this. Then he noticed the rope being drug after Eldan flying over the edge of the hole. He suddenly realized that as fast as it was disappearing down the hole, the rope would soon run out. He reached for the rope, but he was not quick enough. The end of the rope shot through his hand and down the hole before he could grab it.

"Eldan!!!" he shouted after the disappearing rope.

There was a rumbling noise coming from the darkness of the hole. Tobin had to leap quickly aside as two large soldier ants came charging out of the passage to investigate the disturbance. Tobin moved cautiously away from the entrance of the ant nest. There was nothing to do now but wait and pray for Eldan's safety.

He went back over to Hawthorn. He didn't seem to be in as much discomfort as before. The feverfew tea seemed to be helping him. "You doin' okay, young one?" Tobin asked gently.

"It's not as bad if I keep my eyes closed," Hawthorn said weakly. "Where's Eldan?"

Tobin glanced over at the ant hole. "Oh, he'll be back. We just needed some stuff to help you feel better, and he went to get it."

That seemed to satisfy Hawthorn. He closed his eyes and settled himself into a comfortable position. He didn't notice the look of concern on Tobin's face as he looked back at the hole leading into the ant nest.

"Tobin?" Hawthorn asked a few moments later. "What happened when Micah told the High Seven about Larkin's journal?"

"What are you talking about?"

"Eldan was telling me where the Makerians come from. He got to the part where Micah read old Larkin's journal and found out about the Maker sending his son to show how all people could be his children. What was the Maker's son's name?"

"Jehesus," Tobin answered.

"Yes, that's right, Jehesus," Hawthorn repeated thoughtfully. "Eldan said that Micah decided to tell the High Shaman about what he had discovered, but he didn't get to tell me what happened."

"They kicked him out," Tobin said abruptly. "He told them everything in Larkin's journal. He even read them quotes from it. But it was more than they could handle."

"Why wouldn't the Shaman believe him?" Hawthorn asked curiously. "I mean, Micah was reading Larkin's own words."

"They didn't want to believe him, young one. It would have cost them too much. If they had believed what Larkin said about Jehesus, the High Seven would have had to give up their power and quit being Shaman, and they weren't willing to do that. They were afraid that the truth might get out to others, so they immediately banished Micah and his wife. They brought in Micah's two helpers and ordered them to turn over all the notes and translations that they had made. These notes were sealed in a chest and placed in the Treasure Cave. The door to the cave was then securely sealed so that no one could go in. Then to make doubly sure that none of this information got out, The High Shaman also condemned and banished Jasper, Linden, and their families. An order was issued to all the other tribes that these three families were traitors and that no clan was to receive them or help them in any way."

"That's terrible!" Hawthorn said angrily. "Jasper and Linden didn't even know what it was all about, and their families weren't involved at all!"

Tobin nodded his head. "I guess the High Shaman must have been pretty scared about the truth getting out, so they . . . sort of . . . cleaned house, if you know what I mean."

"What did Micah and his friends do then?" Hawthorn asked.

"Well," Tobin began, "as you can imagine, Jasper and Linden had a lot of questions for Micah. . .

He had not told them the contents of Larkin's journal before because he wasn't sure what the High Shaman would do. Micah thought he was protecting his friends by not telling them what was in Larkin's journal. But since they had all been banished, he started at the beginning and told them everything he remembered from Larkin's words.

They found a small cave in the rocks along the creek a short distance downstream from the Steps. It was big enough to provide protection for their families. Fortunately it was midsummer, and there was plenty of food to be found by foraging in the woods.

They decided to stay close to the Steps and attempt to contact some of their friends and relatives so that they might teach the truth to any who would listen. In doing this, they were able to talk to several of the other clan members. Eventually word got back to the Shaman that Micah's group was close by and trying to tell other Larkin what they knew. This infuriated the High Shaman. They investigated everyone who had had any contact with members of Micah's party and eventually banished more families and individuals. The Shaman then announced a death order against everyone who had been banished. Twice Micah's people were attacked as they tried to speak with friends from the Steps. Finally the Shaman sent bands of guards out to drive the outcasts away.

At that point, Micah knew that it was too dangerous to stay where they were, so he decided that they must leave and find a place where they could raise their families in peace. The thing he regretted the most was leaving the copies of all the manuscripts that Linden, Jasper, and he had made, and he said as much to his friends.

They both just looked at each other and smiled. Then they told Micah something that he didn't know. After they found Larkin's chest hidden in the small passageway, Micah had sent Jasper and Linden to explore the passage while he examined the documents found in the chest. While Micah was reading Larkin's journal, Jasper and Linden had followed the tight crawlway and found that it eventually led to a small opening that came out behind the lowest of the three waterfalls that form the Steps. It would be difficult, but they could get back into the Treasure Cave anytime they wanted.

The first thing they needed to do was to move their families to a safer place. All total, there had been eighteen families banished by the High Shaman. There were one hundred and eight people in all. After sending out scouts, they decided to move their band about a half-day's journey further downstream. There they found a wide overhang of rock, and they made a temporary camp under its protection. While the rest made preparations for a long journey to find a new home, Micah and his two friends took supplies and traveled back to the Steps, being careful not to be seen by guards or foraging parties.

The main entrance of the Steps, as you know, is behind the uppermost of the three waterfalls and is approached from the west bank of the creek. To avoid detection, Micah and the others approached the waterfalls from the east side. They made their way carefully through the brush and grass on the east bank until they were on a level with the lowest of the falls. Somewhere behind this wall of cascading water was the secret entrance to the Treasure Cave. This lowest waterfall was also the smallest of the three. With all the rocks and the low overhang, there was just enough room for them to crawl behind the waterfall on their stomachs, pushing their packs ahead of them as they went. They only had to crawl a short distance before they found the opening, but then Jasper, who was leading, had to spend some time moving rocks and dirt to widen it enough for them to get through. It took some work to get all three of them with their supplies in the small opening. After a brief rest, Jasper kindled a torch and led the way through the long, winding passageway. Two hours later, the three exhausted exiles pulled the last pack through the opening into the Treasure Cave.

Everything was there: all of their copies of the manuscripts, even their tables, blank sheets of parchment, pens, and ink. All of it was just as they had left it.

Micah gave Linden the task of copying Larkin's journals while he and Jasper began packing up all their copies and notes. Micah decided to leave behind an explanation of how to read the language of the manuscripts, in case some honest soul entered the tomb in the future.

It took a day to organize, catalog, and carefully pack all of the copies that they had made. When Micah and Jasper had completed their work, they began helping Linden copy the two precious journals. They worked constantly, one sleeping while the other two copied. Even so, it took most of two more days to finish the work. When they finally finished and had everything stored in waterproof packs, they were exhausted. They ate a meal; then they slept for a long time.

They awoke feeling refreshed and excited. Micah was happier than he had been in weeks. He had no home, but he had a purpose. He would study these manuscripts and learn all that he could about the Lord Jehesus, then he would teach all of his people to know Him, to love Him, to serve Him, and to be like Him.

In solemn reverence, the three friends took one last walk through the treasure room. They took their time, looking at everything in the room. They knew that they would never be here again, but they also knew that for the rest of their lives they would be called upon to tell again and again what they had seen in this place. Very few words were spoken as they viewed the room full of precious relics that composed their history. When they got to the bones of Larkin, Micah put his hand on the bier, bowed his head, and said, "Thank you."

It took close to three hours for them to crawl back through the small passageway with the precious cargo they now carried in their packs. When they arrived at the secret entrance behind the waterfall, they discovered that it was in the middle of the afternoon. Since they were already tired from the long crawl, they rested there until dark, then made their way out from behind the falls. Once they were back on the bank, they lost no time following the creek back to their band with the valuable manuscripts.

Micah spent several days praying to the Maker, seeking guidance on where they should go. After his time of prayer, he felt that they should travel to the Meadow. They needed a source of meat and warm mooflon robes for the coming winter. After discussing his suggestion, the others agreed with his wisdom, and so scouts were sent to find places of protection for the main traveling party to camp each evening. When the scouts returned, the camp was struck, and the great journey began.

They had to travel slowly because of the children who were with them. Though it took much longer than expected, the weather was pleasant, and the journey to the Meadow was peaceful. Once they arrived there, things began to get very difficult. Several heavy storms struck them. Because of the bad weather, their hunts, for the most part, were unsuccessful. Their shelter was inadequate in the rains, and so a number of them got sick. Several of them died.

Unable to find a suitable place to settle, they kept moving south, following the edge of the Meadow. The traveling was long and very hard. They never had enough of anything. Sickness and exhaustion were constantly with them. Four times they were attacked by Renegades. Several more of them died. During one particularly severe battle with the Renegades, one of the enemy fighters, a fierce warrior named Ripfang, burst through the defenders and began attacking the wives and children. He injured several and killed Micah's wife, Iris, before he was struck down. Finally the Renegades were driven off, and the travelers began dealing with the dead and wounded. It was then that they discovered that the Renegade, Ripfang, was not dead but was severely wounded. There was much discussion over what to do with him. Most wanted to kill him, but Micah wouldn't allow it. He told them that Larkin wrote that when Jehesus was being killed by his enemies, he asked the Maker to forgive them, and later, after he came alive again, Jehesus saved many of those who had wanted him dead. Micah said that the Maker was now giving them a chance to be like Jehesus to this Renegade who had caused them so much pain. By his words and his heart, Micah convinced his people that, instead of hating this enemy, they should show him how much Jehesus loved him. So instead of killing him, they fed him, cared for his wounds, and nursed him back to health.

"That is so dumb!!" Hawthorn almost shouted, then winced as pain shot through his head. "He killed Micah's wife; he tried to kill their wives and children, and he was no more than an animal. He deserved to die, and they should have killed him right then!"

"You had better be glad that they didn't," Tobin responded.

"Why?" Hawthorn asked curiously.

"Because if they had killed him, you would have died on the ant hill."

"What?!" Hawthorn was really confused. "All this stuff you're telling me happened over twenty seasons ago. What does any of that have to do with me now?"

Tobin smiled. "It has to do with you, because Ripfang the Renegade was healed by the Makerians and learned to love and trust in the Lord Jehesus. He became a Makerian and changed his name to Ripgood. He won great honors as a protector and defender of those who love Jehesus. Because of his courage, his faithfulness, and his love for the Makerian people, he was made a noble and was allowed to sit on the Council of the Elders. He was granted rank among his people and was given the title of Ripgood the Vigilant. He was made

Gatekeeper of Stillwaters, the Makerian stronghold. He married Laurel, by whom he had two sons. The younger of the two saved your life on the ant hill."

"You and Eldan are the sons of a Renegade?" Hawthorn asked bluntly.

Tobin ignored his rudeness. "Before my father knew Jehesus, he was, in your own words, 'an animal, deserving death', but when Jehesus entered his life, the evil Renegade that he was died, and a new person was born in him. He became more like Jehesus every day, and when he died, he was a Makerian of great honor, full of goodness and faith."

Hawthorn felt ashamed at his earlier response. "I'm sorry," he said. "I didn't know."

Tobin continued his story. "The outcasts continued their journey along the edge of the Meadow for many weeks. They eventually found themselves on the opposite side of it from where they had started, and it was there that they discovered Stillwaters."

"Is that where you live?" asked Hawthorn.

"Yes, Stillwaters is our stronghold. It's a wonderful place. It is very safe, and those who enter it find peace."

"I would like to see Stillwaters," Hawthorn said thoughtfully.

"You shall, young one. As soon as we get you in shape to travel, we will take you there so that you can get well. Our healers have great skill in tending sicknesses and injuries."

They were both quiet for a time. The shadows of the great trees around them were lengthening, and as he looked overhead, Hawthorn detected a faint pinkness to the sky above him. This long day was finally coming to a close.

Thinking clearly was difficult for Hawthorn, but another question came to his groggy mind, "Tobin, how did you learn so much?"

"What do you mean?" Tobin asked absently as his eyes focused on the harvester ant nest.

"You know," Hawthorn returned, "all the stuff you Makerians have, and the stuff you know, and the stuff you do."

Tobin turned back to his injured companion. "What stuff are you talking about?"

"Well, like the fire stones, this tea you made for me that makes my head quit hurting, that loud caller thing that Eldan used to talk to you, and that bird! How did you ever get that huge bird to carry you around?" Hawthorn noticed that the corners of Tobin's eyes wrinkled and his cheeks moved up. He couldn't see Tobin's mouth through all the red hair on his face, but he knew that he must be smiling at him.

Tobin looked up into the trees toward the clearing and gave a sharp whistle. There was some fluttering in the limbs above, and suddenly a large, black form dropped out of the trees and landed startlingly close in front of them. The crow was jet black with a shiny black beak. To Hawthorn, the huge bird seemed to tower over them, and he didn't feel a bit safe in its presence.

Tobin stood up and walked over to the great bird. He made some clucking sounds in his throat as he approached it. In response, the large crow bent its head down and laid its beak on Tobin's shoulder. The red-headed Makerian began stroking the long, black beak affectionately. In a moment, he turned to face Hawthorn.

"This is Nightwing. He's . . . sort of . . . attached to me."

"What does that mean?" questioned Hawthorn, still quite nervous in the presence of the black killer bird.

"Lightening struck the tree in which his mother had made her nest. It killed the mother bird. I found the nest with three eggs in it. I was curious, so I kept the eggs warm. Nightwing was the only one to hatch out. I took care of him and just taught him a few things."

"Just taught him a few things?!" Hawthorn said in astonishment. "That thing's big enough to eat both of us, and it carries you around any place you want to go! That's the most amazing thing I've ever seen!"

"Yep," Tobin replied thoughtfully, still stroking the beak, "he does all right."

"How did you learn all this stuff?" Hawthorn asked again.

"We're no different than you are," Tobin began, sending the large bird away and returning to his place. "The Makerian people are no smarter than the Larkin or the Renegades. But Jehesus taught his followers to pray to the Father in heaven about their needs, so that's what we've done. We are a praying people. We believe in the power of prayer, when it's spoken from a pure heart and directed to our All-Powerful Father above in the name of His son, Jehesus. Jehesus said to expect the Father to answer such prayers. Because we trust the words of the Lord Jehesus, once the prayers are said, we begin looking intently for the answers. These things you've mentioned are just a few of the things the Maker has given us in answer to our prayers."

It was beginning to get dark.

"Let me show you another of the Maker's answers to our prayers," Tobin said as he was searching through his pack. He pulled out a padded, leather pouch that was lined with thick fur. Opening the pouch, Tobin pulled out a long vial made of carved resin with an ornately-fashioned wooden plug in the open end. The vial had a greenish-yellow tint to it. As Hawthorn watched, Tobin shook the vial violently. Suddenly the vial began to glow brightly. Hawthorn was startled by the bright, greenish light radiating from the resin tube.

"What is it?!"

"It's a light stick." Tobin handed the vial to Hawthorn so he could look at it more closely. "We carve the vials out of hardened pine resin, and then they are filled with a mixture we call *moon water* because it shines like moon light. It's really just some juices from glow worms and certain mushrooms. Shake it, and it makes light."

Hawthorn was not only amazed by the brightness of the light, but also by how cool the vial felt in his hands. After examining the light stick for several minutes, Hawthorn handed it back to Tobin.

"Try to get some rest now," Tobin said. "I need to go do a couple of things, but I'll be close by if you need me."

Tobin walked over to the ant nest and hung the brightly glowing vial in the opening, being careful to avoid the soldier ants guarding the passageway. He yelled down into the dark opening once for his brother, but the vibration caused by his shout upset the ant guards, and he had to move away.

Instead of coming directly back to where Hawthorn lay, he disappeared up into the woods. After about half an hour, Hawthorn began to get concerned for his missing friend. Then Tobin quietly appeared out of the darkening shadows. He was dragging an empty bagworm cocoon that he had cut from a cedar tree. The outside of the cocoon was prickly from all the pieces of dried cedar needles stuck to it, but the inside was made of thick, soft silk. With a little effort, Tobin was able to slide Hawthorn into the soft, warm cocoon to keep him from getting chilled in the cooler night air.

Tobin also built up the fire and put small stones in the coals to begin heating up. The pain in Hawthorn's head was greatly reduced by the feverfew tea he had drunk, and now, tucked down in the cocoon, he almost felt comfortable. In a few moments, he was sleeping soundly.

Hours must have passed before he awoke, because the moon was directly overhead. He looked over by the fire where Tobin had been, but he was not in sight. A noise directly in front of him caught his attention, and in a moment, he saw the burly form of Tobin carrying his younger brother. Eldan looked completely exhausted, his clothes were in tatters, and he was caked with dirt from head to toe.

Tobin laid Eldan down next to Hawthorn. Eldan looked over at his friend with weary eyes. Seeing the look of concern on Hawthorn's face, Eldan tried to smile reassuringly. As the corners of his mouth curled into his familiar, broad grin, the dirt plastering his face cracked and fell off in large flakes.

Now Tobin began working next to the fire where there was a large slab of rock with some hollow depressions in it. One of the depressions was just a little larger than a Larkin's head. Tobin had cleaned this one out and emptied his and

Eldan's water pouches into it. Using two sticks as tongs, Tobin began putting hot rocks from the fire into the water. As the rocks cooled in the water, Tobin would replace them with hot rocks from the fire. In this way, he had the water boiling in just a short time. Into the boiling water, Tobin added dandelion root, licorice root, dried blackberry leaf, and cut up pieces of the ant larvae which Eldan had brought back with him. Keeping the water boiling with hot rocks, Tobin cooked his herbal stew. When he felt that it had cooked long enough for all the medicinal properties of the herbs to completely saturate the broth, he drew some out with a cup made from a folded leaf and gave it to Hawthorn and Eldan. He made them both drink two cups of the broth. Tobin then disappeared into the woods again and came back shortly with another bagworm cocoon.

By the time Tobin had Eldan in the soft, warm cocoon, his two patients were feeling the relaxing effects of the herbal broth and were quickly asleep. Trusting in Nightwing to warn him of approaching enemies, Tobin dosed by the small fire.

CHAPTER TEN

MR. WEASEL

Jay knew they were coming. He could hear them as they slithered through the grass and leaves in the darkness around him. He couldn't see them yet, but he knew they could see him. They must be getting close to him now. The sounds of that rhythmic sliding of their long bodies were all around him. His heart was pounding; sweat was running down his face and neck; fear wrapped its icy fingers around his inward parts. Startled by a hissing roar, Jay looked up in time to see fangs and large, gaping jaws falling upon him. He only had time to raise his arms and scream.

"Jay! Jay! Are you all right?!" The only answer Savin got was moans and thrashing.

"Is he okay?" Rush's voice sounded out of the darkness.

There was silence for a moment except for some rustling sounds as Savin felt for Jay in the darkness. Finally Savin spoke, "He's feverish and covered with sweat. I'm having trouble waking him up. He's either having a bad dream, or he's delirious."

"It's got to be his wound," voiced Rush. "Syc, check the sky. How much longer till daylight?"

There was more rustling that trailed off above them. A faint glow of starlight stole in upon them as Sycamore pushed open the trapdoor of the wolf spider's nest. "It won't be long 'til daylight," Sycamore said after studying the sky. "Dawn is just starting to show in the east."

"As soon as it's light enough to see, we need to make a fire and heat some water to bathe Jay's wound," Rush called up to Sycamore.

"Right," returned Sycamore. He stood at the mouth of the opened spider's nest, scanning the dark woods around them, watching the details slowly materializing in the growing light. "Uh-oh."

"What's up, Syc?"

"We've got a visitor."

Savin and Rush climbed up the sloping floor of the nest and joined Sycamore at the opening.

"Over there," Sycamore pointed toward the base of a shadowy bush.

The three Larkin peered intently into the dark shadows under the indicated bush. Out from the shadows into the early morning gloom crept a long, dark, furry form. The creature slipped back and forth across the ground in front of them, stopping frequently to explore clumps of brush, rocks, and holes.

"What is it?" Savin whispered.

"I can't make it out," Sycamore answered.

"Weasel," said Rush out of the corner of his mouth.

"A weasel? Are you sure?"

"Yep, and it appears that he's hungry. I figure he's huntin' fer his breakfast."

"Oh, no!" Savin exclaimed softly. "He's headed right for us!"

Sycamore grabbed the underside of the trap door and quickly pulled it shut as the other two ducked back into the web-lined hole. Sycamore then used the lance to fix the door shut. Outside the trap door, there was a snuffling sound as the hungry weasel tried to find again the scent of Larkin that he had briefly smelled.

"We're in big trouble!" Sycamore announced as he slid down the slopping wall of the spider's nest to join his friends. "Weasels are bad news. Those things never quit when they start after a prey. If he finds our scent, he'll dig us out of here in no time."

There were several loud, roaring snorts coming from the other side of the trap door.

"Too late to worry about it now," drawled Rush. "He's done found us. I reckon I'd better go up and have a talk with him."

"Talk with him?!" Savin almost shouted.

"You're going to talk with a weasel?!" Sycamore asked in disbelief.

"Shor'!" Rush said, surprised at his two companion's ignorance. "Didn't you fellers know? Them critters can be quite reasonable if you just make a good argument."

There was some rustling in the darkness as Rush made his way back up to the door of the spider's nest. "Hellooooo, Mr. Weasel!" Rush shouted loudly through the closed door. The sniffing behind the door seemed to get louder. Rush continued his speech, shouting loudly to be sure the weasel heard him. "Mr. Weasel? Now, I allows that you found us fair and square, and by rights you should get to eat us."

The sniffing and snorting grew even louder.

"But, Mr. Weasel, we got a sick friend down here, and he don't feel up to gettin' et today. As for the rest of us, we got's to take care of our friend here. So, as you can see, it would be mighty inconvenient for us to get et up today. So if'n you'd be so kind as to move along, we'd be about our business."

The loud snorting continued.

"Mr. Weasel," Rush shouted, "you're not listenin' to me!"

The sniffing was really fierce now.

Suddenly, Rush pushed open the trap door and drove his sting deeply into the big, black nose in front of him. There was a terrific howl of pain, and the wounded weasel dashed for the woods.

Rush looked back down at his friends, "I told you them critters was reasonable. You just gotta' make good arguments."

"You made a pretty good one," said Savin, chuckling.

"Yeah," added Sycamore, "I'd say he got your point."

Rush and Savin gently helped Jay out of the dark spider's nest into the growing light of the morning. He was very weak and feverish. They made a bed for him out of dry grass mulch, over which they laid a cloak.

Using a small bow and a stick, Sycamore worked the bow back and forth to kindle a fire. It took several minutes to get a spark to catch in his tender. Then, with a few puffs on the smoldering spark, a small flame appeared. Feeding it very carefully, Sycamore coaxed the flame into a fire. He reached into his pack and pulled out a small, rectangular container made of fired clay. He untied and removed the lid, pulling out several pouches that were inside. He then filled it with water from his water pack and placed the water-filled container on some rocks so that it sat directly over the fire.

As Sycamore was heating the water, Rush and Savin were unwrapping Jay's wounds.

"You're right, Rush. His wounds are becoming diseased."

"I was afeared this might happen," Rush responded. "Tick bites are usually pretty nasty." Rush put his hand on Jay's forehead. "He's one sick Larkin. Looks like we're gonna be here for a few days."

"How long do you figure?" asked Savin, casting an anxious look at Sycamore. Savin could see that he was concerned also.

Rush looked up and saw the worried look on both of their faces.

"Now listen, you two! I know you're worried about the young ones, but nothing's changed. We're gonna find 'em, and we're gonna get 'em back! You got my word on that. But we ain't leavin' Jay, and we ain't splittin' up! Hawthorn and Poke's only chance is if we stick together. Now I want both of you to give me your word that you won't take off after 'em on your own," Rush was standing now. He locked his eyes on Savin, who, after a few moments, finally nodded his head in agreement. Rush's eyes quickly shot over to Sycamore.

"You're right, Rush. We stick together."

Rush's hard look softened, and concern for the two anxious fathers filled his eyes. "I know this ain't the way we planned it, but it'll still work out okay. We'll just have to use the long plan rather than the short plan."

"Hold it. What was the short plan?" Sycamore wanted to know.

"Catch up to 'em on the trail, create a diversion, free our two, and run for the Keep."

"So what's the long plan?"

"Get Jay well, find the Renegade stronghold, slip in unnoticed, find our two, free 'em, slip out, and run for the Keep."

"You got any idea how we're going to do that?" Savin asked.

"Nope, but don't worry about it. We'll figure it out when the time comes. Actually I think our chances of success are pretty good. We've got surprise working for us. They'd never believe we'd be crazy enough to break into their stronghold to get 'em out."

Savin was thoughtful. "You know, Rush," he said, "you might be right. It's certainly hard for me to believe."

"All right, listen up," Rush began. "Here's yer orders. While I'm workin' on Jay's wounds, you two follow the Renegade trail aways so we know which way to go when Jay's better. Try to be back here by midday."

It didn't take Savin and Sycamore long to get their packs and weapons together. There was now plenty of light by which to see. The two fathers, though anxious to be after their sons' captors, showed caution as they followed the trail left by the Renegade war party. They traveled more slowly than they wanted, but they had to be watchful for enemies. Also, the trail was getting cold, and there were places where signs of the war party's passing could easily be missed. Occasionally the two Larkin would leave subtle marks along the trail so that they could find it again when Jay was better.

As they gained confidence in identifying the signs left by their enemies, they were able to move faster. They were both eager to cover as much distance as they could before they had to go back to meet Rush.

It was midmorning now, and soon they would have to turn back in order to make it to their camp by midday. The trail they were following led them down into a dry stream bed. As soon as they descended to the rocky bottom of the shallow stream bed, they were both aware of a faint, creaking sound coming from all around them. Looking up, they saw close to twenty Renegade warriors lining both sides of the stream bank, all with bows fully drawn and their arrows pointing at the two Larkins' chests.

"What's it gonna' be, Larkin?" a voice snarled from behind a frightful mask on a Renegade in front of them. "Slavery or death?"

Savin stole a quick look at Sycamore. They both wanted to fight these Renegades, but they knew that meant certain death. The only chance of rescue their sons had was if they remained alive, so without saying a word, they both lifted their hands into the air, surrendering to their enemies.

Several Renegades quickly ran up to the captured Larkin, took their weapons, and stripped off their packs and shields. Then they bound their hands and put neck ropes on them. "There ain't no doubt about it, Copperhead," said one Renegade in a red and black mask. "Them two was trailin' us."

The one addressed as Copperhead was a muscular Renegade wearing a brown-colored mask that was carved to look like the head of a snake. "There's got to be more of 'em," Copperhead's deep voice growled. "They wouldn't have sent just two. Dagger, take nine fighters with you and scout their back trail. Find the rest of their party. Take 'em alive if you can, 'cause we need the slaves, but if you can't, then kill 'em. If there's too many for you, send back for help."

"Gotcha," returned the Renegade in the red and black mask. Turning quickly from his leader, he went down the ranks of the masked fighters, calling the names of the ones he wanted.

The Renegade sergeant addressed his fighters. "Awright! Now listen, you slugs!" he barked. "Copperhead wants us to scout the back trail of these two captives. We catch those we can; we thump those we can't." He turned to a taller Renegade with a black mask. "Pike, me and you'll take the point. Grunt!" he snapped at a young Renegade with no mask. "You cover the rear."

He quickly turned, and with Pike at his right shoulder, Dagger led his scouting party back down the trail that Savin and Sycamore had been following.

Rush was getting worried. It was well past noon, and his two friends had not returned. He knew they would not have gone after the two boys alone.

They had given him their word, and a Larkin never goes back on his word. He also knew that they would not have been careless in keeping track of the time. Something must have delayed them. The urge to follow the trail and to go look for them was very strong, but he could not leave Jay. He looked over toward the spider's nest that they were using as a refuge. He could see the open door through the brush and grasses just a short distance away from where he stood. He knew that Jay was sleeping just inside the nest.

Rush had been busy all morning. He had done all that he could for Jay, dissolving a piece of salt in the warm water Sycamore had heated up and repeatedly bathing and soaking Jay's infected shoulder wound. After a thorough cleansing and soaking of the wound, he had bandaged it back up again. It must have helped, because Jay's fever seemed to go down, and he had been able to fall asleep. Rush then put out the fire and obliterated any evidence of it. With Jay resting, he decided to look for food close around the mouth of the nest, since ants had dragged off what was left of the grasshopper and the spider during the night. He had ranged a short distance from the spider's nest, looking for edible seeds, collecting a small pile of them in the bottom of the nest.

He had collected another armload of seeds and was about to walk out of the brush with them when he saw the approaching Renegades. He froze, knowing that they could not see him from where he was. They came down the same path his two friends had taken. Rush's heart sank. He knew that Savin and Sycamore would not have let the Renegades walk in on him and Jay without warning them in some way. This told Rush that his two friends were either captured or dead. Rush refused to accept the thought of their being dead, so he decided that until he had facts to prove otherwise, he would believe that Savin and Sycamore were captives.

Reaching for his bow, he thought that he would try to thin out their numbers, but before he drew an arrow he stopped himself. He knew that he must get their attention and draw them away from this area before they spotted Jay. If he wounded one of them here, they might possibly leave one or two Renegades behind with the injured one, and they might find Jay. "No," he thought, "they must all chase me. Once I get them far enough away from Jay, then they'll find out how a Larkin fights."

Slipping his bow back onto his shoulder, Rush took a deep breath and strode boldly out of the brush into full view of the enemy. He waited until he was sure that they had seen him before he looked in their direction. On seeing the Renegades, Rush gave a shout and ran back into the woods away from where Jay was lying.

A few arrows were shot his way, but they were hastily launched and only flew through the leaves around him. There was a lot of yelling and shouting behind him. Rush stole a quick look back and saw that they were all after him at a full run. He also saw something else. He was outdistancing them. "Bunch of slow Renegades," Rush thought.

He forced himself to a slower pace because he didn't want to lose any of them—yet. Rush made a mental note of the sun's position. He wanted to keep track of the time, and he had to know the direction in which he was running so he could find his way back to Jay. As near as he could tell, he was running northwest. Dodging brush and leaves, Rush did his best to maintain that direction until he had gotten the enemy band far enough away to feel that Jay was safe.

After he had been running for several minutes, Rush took another look back. "Those guys are doing better," he thought, "especially that one in front."

In a few more minutes, Rush looked back again and gave a little start. The lead Renegade had left the others behind and was gaining rapidly on Rush. When Rush turned back around to look where he was going, he had a smile on his face. He maintained his speed, allowing the lead Renegade to get closer. When Rush could hear the footfalls of his rapidly approaching enemy, he increased his speed slightly.

The Renegade runner was right behind him now, almost within striking distance. Rush sped up again, and so did his pursuer. They were speeding past brush and grass, rapidly outdistancing the other Renegades.

Just as the fleet-footed warrior got close enough to use his war club, Rush, who was still smiling, suddenly stopped and doubled over. The Renegade, who was just raising his war club to attack, was caught completely off guard. Unable to stop, he ran full speed right into the doubled over Rush, making a complete flip in the air and landing full on his face.

Glancing back at the approaching warriors, Rush stood up and made a quick survey of the surrounding woods. He decided to keep going in the same direction in which he had been running. Running past the motionless, prostrate form of the injured Renegade, Rush continued on, checking frequently to be sure the war party was following him. He came to a patch of thick brush with a rabbit trail running through it. Not seeing any better options, he sprinted down the trail at full speed. The rabbit trail had some twists and turns in it, and in places, the brush closed in very tightly on either side. As Rush quickly rounded a tight turn in the trail, he ran into a limb extending out over the path at head height. He hit the limb hard, and it staggered him. The pain clouded his mind for a moment. Holding the limb for support, he reached up and felt the large knot rising under his right eye. He looked back down the trail but saw no approaching enemies.

"They'll be here soon," he thought. He could hear them coming in the distance. Just as he started to duck under the limb and keep running, an idea popped into his mind. The smile was back on his bruised face as he grabbed the limb into which he had run and began bending it back around the trunk of the bush from which it grew. With muscles straining, Rush bent the limb back until it touched the trunk of another bush a little further away. He grabbed the trunk and held it tightly, clamping the bent limb between it and his body. With his free hand, he reached into his pack and pulled out a coil of silken rope, one end of which he quickly tied around the bent limb and the trunk. He secured the rope with a slip knot. Then holding onto the rest of the rope, he backed deeper into the brush. He positioned himself so that he could see the Renegades as they approached his trap.

He was right; he didn't have long to wait. He let the first seven Renegades pass, but as the last two got even with the bent limb, he pulled hard on the rope.

There had been a lot of tension on that limb. It shot around like an arrow. There was a very loud *whack*, and both Renegades were flying through the air, going back the way they had come.

As realization of what had happened struck, there was a lot of shouting and screaming among the other Renegades. This gave Rush time enough to pull in his rope and take off through the thinning brush. Again Rush checked his direction. "Almost due north," he thought. He wasn't ready to lose them yet, so he made lots of noise as he ran.

The Renegades were absolutely furious now. Rush could hear their screams and threats as they ran in pursuit. "They'd better save their breath," Rush chuckled to himself. Rush maintained his course, making sure he left a good trail to follow. After running for almost a quarter of an hour, he was forced to a sudden stop. A dry creek bed barred his way to the north.

"Should I go left or right?" he wondered, peering up and down the bank. Suddenly a new idea popped into his head, and the smile began to spread across his face again. The problem was that, to make his plan work, he had to cross this creek bed before the Renegades got there. He looked over the edge of the bank. It was climbable, but it would take too long. By the time he got down to the creek bed, the Renegades would be there, and he'd be an easy target for their arrows. "I guess it won't work," Rush thought, and resolved to go left along the bank.

He hadn't run five strides when he saw exactly what he needed. A young sassafras sapling was growing out of the bank, not fifteen paces in front of him. One of its lower limbs extended out over the creek bed. The smile was back on Rush's face.

Quickly he ran over to the edge of the bank and moved enough of the dirt and rocks to make it look like he went over the edge of the bank at that spot. Then carefully, so as not to leave any tracks, he hurried over to the sapling. It was small enough that Rush could reach around it, so he grabbed it and began to climb up. He reached the limb and began scooting out along it. When Rush was about three quarters of the way across, his weight caused the limb to bend. He turned around, and as the branch bent toward the other bank, he slid down the limb. "Perfect!" he thought as his feet touched the ground on the opposite bank. Releasing the branch, he quickly threw himself on the ground just as the Renegades raced out of the brush across the creek bed from where he lie.

There was a small log laying along the bank just in front of him, so Rush crawled behind this. Cautiously he peered over the log, watching his enemies. They apparently had not seen him drop from the limb. Some were studying the edge of the bank where he had left intentional signs. Others were scanning the bottom of the creek bed, trying to spot him. Scouts were sent both up and down the creek bank a short distance looking for signs.

Soon it appeared to Rush that a decision had been made, because ropes were thrown over the edge, and the leader and four of his followers slid down into the creek bed. As the last one was sliding down the rope, Rush stood up, bow in hand, and launched one arrow across the narrow ravine. The arrow struck the unsuspecting Renegade, causing him to release his grip on the rope and crash into the rocks below.

Rush quickly dropped behind the log again. There was much screaming and yelling down in the creek bed. The two scouts up on the creek bank came running back when they heard the shouting.

Rush jumped up again and shot an arrow at the leader. The Renegade scouts up on the bank spotted Rush as he shot and shouted a warning. Dagger, the Renegade leader, heard the warning and turned toward Rush right as the arrow arrived. It struck his thick, wooden mask between the eyes. The force of the blow knocked him backwards to the ground. Dagger screamed with pain and anger. He ripped his mask off, the arrow embedded in the front. He had a small wound in his forehead where the point of Rush's arrow had pierced through the back side of the Renegade's mask.

Immediately several arrows from the creek bed and from the bank above were sent flying toward Rush, who quickly ducked behind the log again.

The two scouts on the bank were ordered to keep Rush pinned down with their bows while the other Renegades crossed the creek bed and climbed up the other side.

Every time Rush popped up to shoot, one or two arrows would fly past his head. By crawling back and forth along the log and jumping up in different spots, Rush was able to get enough shots off to keep the Renegades in the creek bed pinned down also.

"This ain't gonna work!" Rush thought to himself as he realized that he would run out of arrows before they did. He was trying to figure out his next move when he noticed that the branch on which he had climbed across the creek began to move. Staying behind the log, he moved back until he could see the full length of the branch. A smile began to spread across his face.

The two Renegade scouts on the other bank had discovered the limb that Rush had used as a shortcut across the creek. Both of them were working their way up the sapling and out onto the limb. They were trying to hide themselves with the large, mitten-shaped sassafras leaves, but Rush spotted them almost immediately.

"Whoo-wee!" he whispered to himself as he watched the two Renegades moving stealthily along the branch towards him. "Those two birds are just eat up with *the dumbs*." He let them crawl on until they were about half way across the creek. At this point, Rush notched an arrow to his bow string. "It's hard to feel sorry for someone with no more sense than these two," he thought as he launched an arrow that struck the last of the two climbers. The pierced enemy fell like a stone.

The Renegade who was left on the limb saw his companion drop. He jerked his head back around and, looking through the leaves, saw Rush drawing out another arrow. Rush was far enough back behind the log that the Renegades in the creek bed could not shoot at him. Too late, the Renegade realized the foolishness of his position. He couldn't go forward, he didn't have time to go back, and his friends couldn't help him. As he saw Rush draw his bow, he took the only choice he had left. He jumped.

"He ain't too smart," Rush thought, "but he's got guts!" Rush peeked over the log and into the creek bed to see what had happened to him. "You lucky toad!" Rush laughed out loud. The Renegade had landed on his chest in a pile of soft sand that was between two jagged-edged boulders.

At his laugh, several Renegade arrows were launched in his direction, but seeing them coming, Rush ducked behind the log.

Dagger decided to make his move. Leaving two of his warriors to keep Rush pinned down, he led the others in a charge forward. Rush heard them coming, but they were too close to the bank now for him to shoot at them without exposing himself to Renegade arrows. They would be up the bank soon. He might get one or two of them, but they would certainly get him.

Keeping low, Rush moved quickly into the woods, following what appeared to be some sort of old trail. When Dagger and his warriors reached the top of the bank, they could hear Rush moving through the woods ahead of them. Dagger quickly waved for the other two Renegades in the creek bed to join them.

Rush was moving quickly now. He was trying to put distance between himself and his pursuers, so he didn't hold back. As he broke through some grass in his way, he ran right into a large, furry form. Realizing his danger, Rush quickly leaped backward. The startled animal yelped and jumped forward, whipping around to face the threat.

"Mr. Weasel!" Rush shouted, the familiar smile back on his face. Facing Rush was a large, dark brown weasel with fierce eyes, snarling lips, and a swollen red nose. "Mr. Weasel," Rush spoke to the snarling creature, "how about follerin' me back down this trail aways? There's some fellers back there just dyin' to meet you."

As Rush spoke, he picked up a rock lying at his feet. Taking careful aim, he threw it hard at the predator's sore nose. As Rush turned to run back down the trail, he heard a roar of pain behind him. Rush ran as hard as he could, knowing that the enraged weasel would be on him in a moment. Rush could hear the brush crashing from behind as the weasel charged after him. He willed his legs to move faster.

Dagger and his four remaining warriors had all reached the top of the creek bank, and he was just turning to lead them into the woods in pursuit of their enemy when suddenly Rush burst out of the brush running furiously. He ran right through their midst before the startled Renegades had a chance to react, knocking over Dagger and another Renegade as he went by. Rush never slowed down as he ran south along the edge of the bank.

The Renegades were just picking themselves up when the maddened weasel exploded through the brush. Rush could hear the screams and the growling as the weasel vented his fury on the Renegades. Continuing to run for a few more seconds, Rush stopped at the edge of the bank and looked back. He grimaced as he saw what was happening. There was nothing more to fear from this war party, so his mind turned to Jay. Descending the steep bank, he quickly crossed the dry creek bed. Rush waited till he felt the weasel was too busy to notice him, then he scaled the bank, staying partially hidden behind a pine tree root that had been exposed by erosion from the creek.

Even though Rush pushed himself to try to get back to Jay as soon as possible, it was late in the afternoon by the time he found his way to the spider's nest. Rush's heart sank as he entered the nest. Jay was not there. The bedding that he had been lying on was undisturbed, and the cloak that had been covering him had been thrown aside, but he could find no other sign of Jay. Rush crawled out and began to search the ground for signs of a fight, but there were none.

"He was too weak to fight," Rush groaned to himself. "Whoever or whatever it was must have crept up and just took him."

Rush was sick at heart and just about physically exhausted. He sat down on the ground holding his head in his hands. What was he to do? He was so tired and upset that he couldn't think straight.

He was sitting in that same position when, with a solid *thump*, something alive smacked into him, rolling him over. Whatever it was had a very soft body and was clawing against his back and side, trying to get away. At first Rush thought it was a small tick, but when he grabbed it to pull it off of himself, he realized that it was a harmless aphid.

"A fine protector you are —" he heard a voice near him call out. Rush turned quickly, and there, standing nearby, was Jay, another squirming aphid tucked under his arm. "— leaving a poor, defenseless, sick Larkin to fend for himself!" Jay pulled the squirming creature out from under his arm and lifted it over his head with both hands.

"Jay!" Rush laughed as the second aphid landed solidly against his chest, knocking him over again.

CHAPTER ELEVEN

STILLWATERS

The sharp cry startled Hawthorn from his sleep. He jerked his head up quickly to see what was happening, and the familiar throb began to pound in the back of his head, only not as intense as before.

"Better lay still, young one," the familiar voice of Tobin called to him. "You're far from well."

At hearing Tobin's reassuring voice, Hawthorn eased his head back down onto his bedding.

There was another cry. "Yeeow!! Bubs, you're killing me!!"

"Hold still, Eldan! If I don't clean up these scrapes, they'll fester."

"Well, you could be a little more gentle about it—Yeeow!!"

Eldan was sitting on a stone over by the fire. He had his tunic off, and Tobin was using some warm water to clean off the dirt that was caked on his chest and back. With much yelling, growling, and fussing from both of them, Tobin managed to clean away the grime from his brother's body.

Hawthorn, who had been watching the cleaning process with amused interest, was shocked at the extent of the scrapes, cuts, bruises, and lacerations covering Eldan. "Oh, Eldan! Look at what's happened to you! I can't believe you did that for me. You could have been killed!"

"Oh, go on, Chummy. It was just a walk in the creek. I had the whole thing under control—Yeeow!! Would you take it easy, Tobs?!"

"I'd hate to see what you would look like if you had lost control," Tobin mumbled as he continued to work on Eldan's back.

"You're frettin' like an ol' mother possum, Bubsie," Eldan laughed. "It's just a couple of scratches."

"Yeah," Tobin said sarcastically, "just a couple of scratches. One covers the entire front of your body, and the other one covers your back! Eldan, this hair-brained scheme of yours almost caught up with you this time!"

"Calm yourself, Bubs. It all worked out. I made it back okay, and I'm a hero," Eldan said loftily.

"You only made it back by the Maker's grace, and you're a NUT!" Tobin shot back.

"Jealousy does not become you, Tobs," Eldan flipped back at his brother, who only growled in response.

After cleaning the terrible scrapes, Tobin pulled a leather pouch out of his pack. Removing the wooden stopper, he squeezed out a handful of a greenish salve, which he began applying liberally to Eldan's injured body.

Hawthorn's eyebrows shot up. "What's that stuff?"

"Wound balm," Tobin muttered through his bushy red beard.

"It's great stuff, Chummy," smiled Eldan, who was obviously feeling better as the ointment began to take effect. "Our healers make it out of aloe and golden seal juices. It keeps festers away from a wound and greatly relieves the pain."

"Then you can rub some on my head when you're through with Eldan," Hawthorn said, half jokingly.

"Sorry, Chums," Eldan returned. "It only works on outside pain, not inside pain."

"Your head still hurting?" Tobin asked with concern in his eyes.

"Not like it did," Hawthorn answered. "Whatever you put in that soup I drank helped a lot. I feel like I should be back on my feet tomorrow."

"I wish that were true, young one. But the fact is, when the herbs you drank wear off in a few hours, you're going to feel just as badly as before, and if the swelling in your head starts coming back, then you could die."

"Would more of the herbs help me?" Hawthorn wanted to know.

"Yes, they would," Tobin acknowledged. "You need to drink a broth of those herbs and some others every few hours for three or four days. It takes that long for a head injury like yours to heal. The problem is, we've used up all of those herbs that I had with me."

"Can you get some more?"

"I can," Tobin answered, "but I really think the best plan would be to take you to the herbs."

"Do you think that's going to work?" asked Hawthorn. "I still get dizzy when I sit up, so I don't think I would be able to walk very well."

"You won't have to walk," Tobin said. "Nightwing will take us."

"Oh, no! Not the crow!"

"No worries, Chummy. That bird's as gentle as can be . . . wouldn't hurt a fly. No sir, Chummy, nothing to fear from that one. You'll be as safe as in your mother's arms." Turning to his brother, Eldan added, "By the way, Tobs, you're not gonna make me ride the ol' feather duster, are you? Not that I mind, of course. It's just that all that air would be bad for my wounds."

"Scratches," Tobin growled.

"Uh . . . right, scratches," Eldan began again. "So you and the bird take Thornton here and flutter on over to Stillwaters. I'll be along directly."

"I thought you said the crow was safe," barked Hawthorn nervously.

"And that he is, Chums, that he is. But it's my health . . . you know . . . air poisoning? I just can't afford to get diseased from all that air around my wounds."

"Scratches," growled Tobin.

"Uh . . . yes, that's right, scratches. You see, it would be too great a risk."

"But what about MY wounds?! Won't the air poison them?!" Hawthorn countered.

"Chummy, your wound is on the back of your head, and the air will be hitting you in the face. So, you see, you'll be just fine. No sir, no worries for you. So just climb right up on the ol' bird with Tobs and sail off into the clouds. I can see it now! A beautiful sight! Just beautiful! Wish I was going with you! Yes, sir! But I can't let myself get diseased. I got to do the responsible thing, you know, and take care of these wound . . . uh . . . scratches."

"It's just as well," Tobin said. "Nightwing might have some difficulty carrying all three of us."

"Well, there you have it," Eldan said, beaming. "I'll just see you two fellows off, then I'll stroll on home."

"Don't push yourself, Eldan. You didn't lose much blood, but severe scrapes like that can really take a lot out of you. Keep this wound balm with you and use it frequently." Tobin pulled the pouch containing the medicinal salve out of his pack, along with some bread and dried fruit, and handed these to Eldan.

"Listen to him, Chummy. Frettin' over me like an ol' granny. Ah, but he's a good ol' Bubbsy. Love's me to death, he does."

"Just help me get him loaded on Nightwing," Tobin interrupted.

Tobin gave a short whistle, and the huge, black crow seemed to fall out of the tree and land gently on the ground in front of him. Reluctantly, Hawthorn allowed himself to be lifted up and helped over to the huge bird. Tobin made some clucking sounds, then lifting his right hand high over his head, he brought it down low. In response, Nightwing dropped to a sitting position and lowered his chest and neck until they touched the ground.

"But what if I fall off?!" Hawthorn blurted out as he was lifted and carried over to the great bird.

"Don't worry," came Tobin's reassuring voice. "You'll be tied to me."

"But . . . what if YOU fall off?!" Hawthorn returned as he was pushed up onto the bird's shoulders.

"Then you and Tobs can have a nice little talk on your way down."

"WHAT?!!"

"Eldan!" Tobin growled as he hopped up behind Hawthorn and tied a piece of rope around them both.

"Don't yell at me, Tobs. I'm just trying to lighten the mood."

"You're not helping," Tobin shot back.

"Well, YOUR mood could certainly use a little lightening."

"Nightwing, up!" commanded Tobin, and the crow jumped to its feet.

"Whoa!!!" shouted Hawthorn, grabbing for feathers.

"Ah, Chummy, what a striking figure you cut, sitting there so gallantly astride the noble bird."

"I don't want to do this!!" Hawthorn screamed, looking for a way to get off.

"Nightwing, fly!"

"No! Wait! Yiieee-e-e . . ." Hawthorn's shriek trailed off as the crow shot into the air.

"It's a beautiful sight, Chummy! Just beautiful!" Eldan shouted after them.

Slinging his backpack gingerly over his shoulders, Eldan started back through the woods in the direction of the red ant nest where he had first found Hawthorn.

With a loud thumping of wings, Tobin's crow flew higher and higher. Out of sheer terror, Hawthorn threw himself on the bird's neck, grabbed feathers with both hands, and buried his head in them.

After a while, the furious thumping of the enormous wings stopped, and there was quiet, except for the wind rushing by Hawthorn's ears.

"You ought to take a look, young one," Tobin said calmly. "You may never get a chance to see these sights again."

At first Hawthorn clung even tighter to the bird's neck, but the quiet and Tobin's calm voice gave him courage. Slowly he lifted his head and opened his eyes. What he saw absolutely astounded him. So mesmerized was he by the view that he forgot his fear. Off to his left for as far as he could see was a sea of deep green. After a few moments he made a sweeping motion toward all the green below him and said to Tobin, "What is it?"

Tobin, who had flown with Nightwing many times and who was quite familiar with the bird's-eye view of the world, was surprised by the question. "What is it? Why, it's the forest . . . the woods where you live and hunt."

Hawthorn had spent his whole life living under towering trees. His world consisted of earth, brush, grasses, and rotting logs. His mind simply couldn't comprehend looking down on hundreds of thousands of trees.

"That's the woods?!" he finally asked incredulously. "It's so . . . so . . . much!"

"Well said," chuckled Tobin. "It is much, and it goes a lot farther than you can see."

"What is that large, brown area?" Hawthorn asked, pointing down and to the right. "Is that the meadow?"

"Yep," came Tobin's reply.

"This is unbelievable! The meadow is so huge! I had no idea it was that big, and yet I can see the whole thing from up here."

With clucking sounds, whistling, and pressure from his heels, Tobin directed Nightwing's flight. They turned westward and were soaring over the large sea of grass.

"It's all going by so fast!" Hawthorn exclaimed. "We've almost crossed the Meadow!"

"Yep," Tobin said in his ear. "I'm always amazed at how fast Nightwing can travel. It takes two complete days to walk across the meadow, and that's if you don't run into trouble. But it only takes a few moments for him to fly over it."

"You've actually walked across the meadow?!"

"Most of us have, many times," Tobin answered. "It's the main way we get from Stillwaters to your part of the forest."

Hawthorn was stunned. "But the serpents, the thick grass, the predators, the dangers . . . How can you possibly do that?!"

"It's not as difficult as it seems," was all the answer Hawthorn got.

By now they had reached the far side of the meadow and were flying over the rich green of the forest again. After a few more moments in the air, a silvery light beam flashed up through the trees. They were soaring straight for the flash of light. As they came closer to it, the flashing, reflective silver began to spread out in the forest below them.

"What's that?" asked Hawthorn, captivated by the rounded, mirror-like area in the midst of the sea of green below him.

"That?" Tobin paused. "That is Stillwaters."

NIGHTWING

Maybe the herbs were wearing off, maybe all this was just more than Hawthorn's mind could handle, but the old throb began to come back, and dizziness began to set in. It was just at this time, while they sailed noiselessly high above Stillwaters, that Tobin gave Nightwing the command to descend. The great crow pitched over onto his right wing and began a tight spiral toward the ground.

Tobin had tried to warn him right before they started down, but Hawthorn was unprepared for the rapidity of their spiraling descent. He grabbed wildly for the neck feathers in front of him. He was unable to stifle a cry as they spun earthward. Hawthorn was dizzy, nauseous, in pain, terrified, and weak. His mind said, "No more!", and he lost consciousness, sinking into blissful, peaceful darkness.

When Hawthorn awoke, he noticed several things at once. Though his head hurt and he was a little nauseous, he actually felt more comfortable than he had in days. Whatever he was lying on was so soft that he sank down into it. As his eyes began to focus, he discovered two odd facts: the sun was shining directly on him, but at the same time, he seemed to be lying inside some kind of dwelling.

He couldn't keep his eyes open too long, or things would start spinning again. So he lie there with his eyes closed, marveling at the feel of the soft bed. Somewhere in the distance he heard singing, but it was like no song he had ever heard before.

Larkin seldom sang. In fact, the only singing with which Hawthorn was familiar was the two or three tonal chants that the Shaman sang during the Great Gathering assemblies. Hawthorn usually fell asleep as the Shaman chanters droned on and on.

What Hawthorn heard now was completely different. He couldn't make out the words, but this was most definitely singing, and it was beautiful. There was nothing monotonous about this. There was a high, ringing melody of many different tones, and others were singing other tones at the same time that made a most wonderful harmony.

"Where am I?" he wondered again. "And where is Tobin? Maybe this is Tobin's dwelling at Stillwaters." He tried to open his eyes again and was relieved that this time his head didn't swim as badly. As his eyes focused, he was amazed at his surroundings. He was lying in a room that was made of wood. There were no boards or beams that he could see. The room appeared to be carved out of one piece of wood, like the rooms of the Keep, but these walls were not just smooth wood. The walls and the ceiling were covered with carvings that had been painted in dazzling colors. There was a round window cut out of the wall through which the sun's rays poured. A relief carving of a beautiful grape vine surrounded the window. The carved vine had leaves painted a dark green all over it, and there were numerous branches of purple grapes. On the wall below the window was a carved nature scene with a river and a waterfall cascading over some rocks. Patches of spring flowers were all around. There was so much to look at that it made his head hurt.

Looking to his right, he saw that beside his bed there was a small table with delicately carved legs and a round top. On the table sat a blue bowl filled with a brown liquid that was steaming. As he moved his head over to examine the contents of the bowl, he became aware of the strong smell of sage. His eyes followed the fragrant steam as it rose from the bowl, then he noticed something else.

The ceiling of the room was also covered with brightly painted carvings. He was amazed at the detail. It was like looking up through a patch of beautiful flowers at a blue sky, patched with big, white, fluffy clouds. There were colorful insects of various types crawling and hiding on the stems, leaves, and petals of the flowers. There were bluebirds, cardinals, and yellow finches carved and painted in such a way that they appeared to be soaring through the sky. Two of them were chasing after flying insects. Never in his life would he have ever imagined a room like this one.

Suddenly the door opened, and in walked a finely dressed lady carrying a steaming blue pitcher. "Oh!" she said looking at Hawthorn. "You're awake. Are you feeling better?"

Hawthorn wanted to answer her, but the words failed him. His strange surroundings, the dizziness in his head, and now the sudden appearance of this lady asking him questions overwhelmed him.

"Don't try to talk right now," she said smiling. "You must wonder where you are and what has happened to you. Just rest now. When you're better, we will have plenty of time to talk."

Just then three children came running into the room.

"Can we see him now, Cawi?" said a wide-eyed little boy with curly brown hair. He was pushing his way around the lady with the pitcher in an attempt to get a better look at Hawthorn. "You said we could see him when he was better. Is he better now?!"

The little boy, who couldn't be over four seasons old, was being pursued by two girls. Hawthorn guessed the younger girl to be about eight seasons old and the other one maybe two seasons older. Both girls looked remarkably like the lady who stood between them.

"I'm sorry, Cari," the older girl apologized to the lady. "He got away from us. You know how he is."

The lady with the pitcher stooped down and got eye to eye with the little boy. "Robbie," her tone was not sharp, but it was firm. The little boy had obviously heard that tone before because his large brown eyes immediately snapped to the face of the lady. "He's not well yet. We need to let him rest."

"You mean he's still hurt?"

"Yes, he's still hurt, but you can help him."

A look of pure excitement lit up the boy's face when he heard this. "What 'cha want me to do?" he asked.

"Go find Father," she said with great seriousness, "and tell him that our guest is awake now."

"Okay, Cawi," he said earnestly. "I'll go get him!"

"I think he's in his study," said the youngest girl.

"I know where he is!" said the boy indignantly. The little fellow then went running out of the room yelling, "Faaaa-therrrr!!!" The two younger girls ran after him.

The lady with the pitcher looked over at Hawthorn and tried to suppress a laugh. "Please forgive him," she said to Hawthorn, "but he is so excited that you are staying here with us."

Hawthorn studied his nurse more carefully as she walked over to the table next to his bed and poured more of the steaming, brown liquid into the bowl. A stronger scent of sage filled the room. She had large, dark brown eyes that seemed full of energy and life. Her face was rounded, and her cheeks had a slight, pinkish glow. Her thick, light brown hair cascaded in waves down her back almost to her waist. The white dress she wore, while simple, was very pretty. It had a high neck, long sleeves, and its hem touched the floor. Around the neck and cuffs of the sleeves were embroidered tiny purple flowers. She also wore a purple sash around her narrow waist.

"She's not really beautiful," thought Hawthorn as he looked at her face, "but there's something about her that's very attractive." His mind struggled for the right word. "Radiant!" he thought. With her bright, expressive eyes and her engaging smile, radiant was the word that, to Hawthorn, seemed to sum up his impression of her.

She had finished pouring the liquid and was starting to leave.

"Please don't go yet," Hawthorn found his voice.

She stopped and turned around; her eyes were wide and questioning.

"Where am I?"

Her eyes softened, and she smiled at him. "I'll answer a few questions for you, but then you really need to rest. You're in the home chambers of Taumis the Gentle, Healer of Stillwaters."

"I'm at Stillwaters?" Hawthorn asked.

"Yes. Tobin the Flyer brought you in from across the meadow three days ago. You have had a serious head injury and are staying here until you recover."

"Who are you?" Hawthorn felt compelled to ask.

"My name is Carineda, and this is my home."

"The children that came in . . ." Hawthorn began.

"They do get pretty excited when we have guests," Carineda broke in, "especially Robbie. I hope he didn't upset you."

"No, not at all," Hawthorn answered. "I like him. You'll have to bring him back so he and I can talk."

"I don't think I could keep him away from you if I wanted to," Carineda said giggling. "But he'll be doing all the talking—you'll just have to listen."

"Are they yours?" Hawthorn asked.

"Mine?" Carineda replied with a confused look.

"Yes, yours. Are they yours?" he asked again.

"Are what mine?"

"The children."

"The children?!" Carineda gasped. "You think I'm their mother?!"

"Well, I just thought you might be, since they look so much like you," Hawthorn stammered, realizing that he had somehow offended his gracious hostess.

"They're my brother and sisters," she said, glaring at him.

"Please forgive me, my lady. After all the kindness you've shown me, I would never knowingly offend you."

Carineda studied Hawthorn for a moment. When she saw his sincerity, she cocked her head and asked him a question, "How old do you think I am?" Her face was serious, but her eyes had a mischievous glint.

Hawthorn had this nervous feeling in his stomach, like he was about to get in trouble. He could see no way out of this other than to just be honest. "I . . .uh . . . well, I mean, I figured you were about twenty-five seasons."

"Twenty-five seasons!!" she exclaimed. "Where do you get that?!"

As fuzzy as his thinking was, Hawthorn knew a lot depended on how he answered this question. "You know," he began, "you really don't look twenty-five, but you seem so mature. And then, when you were dealing with the children, you were so confident . . . and the children had such respect for you that . . . I just assumed that you must be that old."

She looked at him without speaking for several moments. Finally a smile began to slowly spread across her face. "I'm impressed," she said, the mischievous look still in her eyes. "You handled that very well. You must have had a lot of practice talking your way out of trouble."

Now it was his turn to study her face to see if he was still in trouble. The laughter in her eyes gave her away, and he returned her smile. "Caution is telling me to keep my mouth shut, but you've made me very curious."

"Curious about what?" she returned.

"Well, how old . . ." Hawthorn stopped himself. He didn't want to get himself in trouble again if he could help it. "Excuse me, my lady, but what I meant to ask was, what should I have guessed your age to be?"

Carineda laughed out loud at Hawthorn's diplomacy. "This is my fifteenth season," she answered.

Hawthorn's mouth dropped open, and Carineda laughed again at the silly look on his face. "You're playing a joke on me," Hawthorn finally said.

"No," she said, still laughing, "I've never (hee, hee) been more serious (ha, ha, ha)."

"Come on," Hawthorn said, getting frustrated. "You're not really just fifteen, are you?"

"Yes, I am."

Hawthorn knew many Larkin girls who were fifteen and sixteen seasons old, but none of them could come anywhere close to matching Carineda's grace and maturity.

"You are just fifteen?! How is that possible?!" he blurted out.

"It's possible, because fifteen seasons ago I was born," Carineda responded. She did not understand why her age was so amazing to this young Larkin, and it was starting to annoy her.

"But— but—" Hawthorn stammered, "you're so . . . I mean, you're . . . you're a lady!"

She was taken aback by Hawthorn's open admiration of her, but she could tell that he meant it innocently. Hawthorn was embarrassed by his foolish reaction and his own immaturity. "Please forgive me, my lady. I should have listened to my caution earlier and kept my mouth shut."

Sensing Hawthorn's embarrassment, Carineda tried to come to his rescue. "I appreciate your compliment," she said, smiling at him, "but I am not really a lady—at least not yet. I am working on it, though. But until I'm able to reach that honor, you really shouldn't refer to me as 'my lady'."

Hawthorn started to apologize again, but before he could get the words out, she continued. "Why don't you just call me Cari? That's what my friends call me."

Hawthorn, who had been too embarrassed to look her in the eye, raised his head and saw her gentle smile again. "My friends call me Thorn," he smiled back at her.

ChAPTER TWELVE

REUNION

After their talk Cari had insisted that Hawthorn rest, which he had been more than happy to do. Hawthorn discovered that he was not as well as he had thought that he was. After a few minutes of talking with Carineda he was unable to focus his eyes, and the old headache began to come back.

Cari spent several minutes looking very carefully at Hawthorn's eyes and had him describe for her how he was feeling. She then left for a short time, returning with two different liquids for him to drink. The first was a dark green drink that was very bitter. The second one was a reddish-brown tea that had a pleasant mint taste. Shortly after that, Hawthorn got very tired and slept a long, dreamless sleep.

When he awoke it was night time. There was an oil lamp illuminating his room, and someone was touching his head. His whole body felt very heavy, and it was hard for him to see clearly. When he was able to focus his eyes, Hawthorn saw a nicely dressed, middle-aged Makerian with a dark brown beard leaning very closely to him. The stranger had dark eyes that looked stern because of his furrowed brow.

"Well, hello," the Makerian said in a deep, gentle voice, his eyes no longer stern.

"Who . . . Who . . ." Hawthorn mumbled weakly. It was all he could make his mouth say.

"Don't try to speak. The medicines you've been given are very strong, and you're still feeling their effects. It will be some time before you will be able to speak clearly.

"My name is Taumis. I'm a healer, and you are staying in my home. I believe you have met most of my children already. My daughter, Carineda, has been taking care of you."

Taumis spent a few more moments examining Hawthorn. Finally he sat back, his soft eyes studying his young patient. "You are quite fortunate, my young friend," Taumis began. "Your injuries were severe, but the Great Father Above has seen fit to say 'yes' to the many prayers that have been offered for your recovery.

"It will be several more days before you will be able to walk without getting dizzy, but as nearly as I can tell, you should recover fully. I hope you will forgive a father's pride, but I gave my daughter, Carineda, full responsibility for your care." Taumis noticed a questioning look on Hawthorn's face.

"Oh, she's quite an accomplished healer for her young age, and a gifted herbalist." Taumis leaned forward and intently examined Hawthorn's eyes again. "Yes . . . yes . . . I'm quite proud of how she handled these injuries. Her choice of herbal mixtures and the timing of their administration were quite good." Taumis was talking more to himself now than to Hawthorn. He seemed lost in his thoughts for a few moments.

"You'll have to excuse me, my friend," Taumis finally said. "I forget myself. You must try to rest now while the herbs are still working on you. If you feel up to it, we may let you try to sit up tomorrow."

Taumis left the room for a short while, but soon he returned with the familiar blue pitcher. He poured the steaming contents into the bowl on the table beside Hawthorn's bed. The strong smell of sage seemed to fill the room. "That should help you sleep," said Taumis. "Be at peace, young Larkin," Taumis spoke sincerely. "The Maker has granted you your life back." Taking the pitcher and the oil lamp, Taumis left the room, closing the door behind him.

Lying in the comfortable bed in the darkened room, Hawthorn did feel at peace. Breathing deeply the heady aroma of the sage mixture, he actually felt good . . . good and . . . sleepy.

It seemed to Hawthorn that he had only closed his eyes for a moment, but when he opened them again the bright rays of the sun were streaming through his window. He felt a lot better. He didn't have nearly as much trouble focusing his eyes, and when Carineda and her father came in and sat him up in bed with some cushions behind him, he only felt some momentary dizziness.

The nausea had left him as well, replaced by a ravenous hunger. Cari was concerned that Hawthorn's stomach might not be able to handle too much at first, having been so long without solid food, so she started him with a bowl of hot porridge made of finely ground briar root, vetch seed, and honeysuckle nectar. Hawthorn wasn't too impressed with the appearance of the contents of the bowl that was handed to him, but the smell was encouraging. His hunger overruled any reluctance he had about eating it. Hawthorn dug his spoon deep into the hot, golden soup and filled his mouth. Suddenly his eyes flew wide. "Murffl. . . libbic!" He was trying to say something through a mouth full of porridge. He was able to get out, "Dish stuff ish goof!" before he buried his head in the bowl and began shoveling the tasty, thick soup into his mouth shamelessly.

Cari began to giggle at him. Her father only stood there nodding his head, an enlightened look on his face. "I'd say the boy's better," he said dryly.

Hawthorn finished the first bowl and made short work of a second. He literally begged for a third bowl full. He sounded so pitiful that Cari finally gave in, but she drew the line there. "You've been sick for too long," Cari stated emphatically. "We've got to take it easy on your stomach until you get used to eating solid food again."

After observing Hawthorn for a short while as he sat up and ate, Taumis, seeing no signs of dizziness or nausea, excused himself to go check on some other patients.

Hawthorn decided that if he couldn't eat any more, then he wanted to talk. He figured that, since Cari probably had about as many questions as he did, that he would be polite and tell her about himself. He told her about his family and his friends. He told her about growing up in the Keep, but he was careful not to tell her its exact location, nor did he mention anything of its defenses.

Cari seemed genuinely interested and asked occasional questions about what he was describing to her. She seemed especially interested in how the Larkin worshipped the Maker. He saw her eye brows knit together in an expression of concern when he told her of the Shaman and how that they spoke to the Maker on behalf of the people.

After this there was an awkward silence for a few moments which Cari broke by asking Hawthorn how he had gotten hurt. Grateful for the change in subject, Hawthorn began telling the story of his first hunt and the Renegade ambush in which he had received his first blow on the head. Hawthorn saw tears of compassion forming in the corners of Cari's large, brown eyes when he told of his uncertainty of whether his father survived the ambush or not. He told of being a Renegade prisoner with Poke and of the harsh treatment they had received from their captors. He told her of Poke and his attempted escape and recapture by Wolf. His memory of being staked on the fire ant nest was kind of vague due to his second head injury, but Eldan had told him what had happened, so he related Eldan's version.

"What happened to your friend?" Cari asked.

"You mean Poke? I truly don't know. Eldan said he was sure Poke was still alive when Wolf tried to kill me. If they didn't kill him for trying to escape, then he's probably a Renegade slave."

They both sat in sad stillness for a while. This time it was Hawthorn who broke the silence. "Tell me about your family, Cari."

Cari brightened, remembering that part of her job as a healer was to keep her patient's spirits up. "Well," she began, "you met most of them. I have two brothers and two sisters. My older brother's name is Raken. He's not at Stillwaters right now, because his company is patrolling the south woods. He's a second season Ranger, and we are all very proud of him. I'm next in line. Then there is my sister, Clarea, who is ten seasons old, and my other sister, Nollie, who is eight, and my little brother, Robbie, who is almost four."

"Robbie must be the little fellow I met yesterday." Hawthorn remembered his first encounter with Cari's brother and sisters.

"Yes," Cari smiled, "that was Robbie."

"He seemed quite curious."

"Curious!" she laughed. "It takes all of us and the Maker's grace to keep that little boy's curiosity from getting him hurt."

"I like him," Hawthorn said smiling. "You'll have to be sure to bring him to see me soon."

"Oh, I'm sure that you will get all the time with Robbie that you will want." They both laughed at that thought.

"Tell me about your parents," Hawthorn urged.

"You've met my father," she began. "He is a noble. His title is Taumis the Gentle, Healer of Stillwaters. He really is a gentle Makerian. He has such compassion for the hurts of others. I guess that's why he devoted himself to learning the arts of healing. But he can be stern when he needs to be— especially if you're not taking your medicine like you are supposed to," she smiled.

"I haven't met your mother yet," Hawthorn said. "Tell me about her."

The smile faded only slightly from Cari's face. "My mother died nearly four seasons ago, giving birth to Robbie."

"Oh, Cari! I'm sorry! I didn't know," Hawthorn stammered out.

"It's all right, Thorn," she said still smiling. "I understand. I really don't mind talking about it. She and I were very close, and I do miss her terribly, but in a way, I envy her and the time she has had in the glorious presence of the Maker and his wonderful son, Jehesus. I wouldn't take that away from her for anything."

This all sounded rather strange to Hawthorn. He had heard Eldan and Tobin talk about Jehesus, but he had heard and seen so many new things that he was having trouble dealing with it all. Now Cari's words confused him even more. The thought of death had always scared Hawthorn, and his defense had been to just not think about it. Cari seemed completely at peace with death— even excited about it.

Cari could tell Hawthorn was deep in thought about something she had said. She decided that he would talk about it when he was ready. Realizing that her patient had been sitting long enough, she helped Hawthorn lie back down in his bed. Promising to let him sit up longer in the afternoon, she left him to rest.

Hawthorn lay there trying to think through all that had happened to him and all the things that he had heard, but the more he thought about it, the more bewildered he became. Here he was being cared for by a people that he hadn't even known existed, who possessed knowledge that he had never dreamed possible, and who were telling him things of which he had never heard before. Growing weary by all the mental exercise, he drifted off to sleep.

He was awakened about midday by a knock on the door. In walked Cari, her two sisters, and little Robbie. Each one was carrying containers of some wonderfully smelling food.

"Cawi says we gonna fatten you up," Robbie announced, grinning.

"And I think we can do better than porridge this time," Cari added.

"Bring it over!" said Hawthorn excitedly, his mouth already starting to water.

"We're going to let you have all you want, Thorn," Cari said, looking sternly at him, "but you have got to promise me that you'll eat it slowly. I don't want you getting sick."

"I promise! I promise!"

This meal turned out to be the finest feast Hawthorn had ever eaten in his life. There were honey cakes made of cattail flour and millet seed, steamed green briar shoots basted in sunflower oil, baked fish with herbs, roasted acorn meats with ginger sauce, and blackberry crumb pudding with nectar topping. To drink they brought him a large mug of sparkleberry cider. True to his word, Hawthorn took his time eating it, but he ate it all, savoring every bite. He had eaten good food before, but nothing like this. Finally Hawthorn leaned back and let out a deep, contented sigh. "That was wonderful!" he murmured in ecstasy.

"We're glad you liked it," Cari laughed, her two sisters giggling behind her.

"Look at that!" exclaimed Robbie with wide eyes. "It's all gone! Cawi, he ate more 'dan Waken does when he comes back from patwol!"

"I was really hungry, Robbie," Hawthorn said sincerely, "and the food you made for me was so good that I just had to eat it all."

"Hey!" said the little boy with a suspicious tone. "How'd you know my name was Wobbie?"

"How'd I know?!" Hawthorn responded in mock disbelief. "Why, you're famous. Every Larkin within . . .." Hawthorn thought for a moment ". . . uh, two leagues of here has heard of Robbie, son of Taumis the Gentle, Healer of Stillwaters."

"Weally?" Robbie asked.

"It's the truth; I promise."

Robbie seemed completely satisfied with Hawthorn's answer. "You know sumpin'?" Robbie said with absolute sincerity, coming up and leaning against Hawthorn's bed. "I'm gonna be a wanger like Waken when I'm big and stwong."

"I'll bet you will be a good one too.

"Hey, why don't you climb up here with me, and you can tell me all about your big sisters," Hawthorn added.

"Sure!" Robbie said excitedly, and he started climbing.

"Robbie," Cari said, "remember what I said?"

"Oh, yeah," the little boy said with disappointment.

Turning back to Hawthorn, Robbie said, "Cawi said dat we can't stay wiff you vewy long cause you got guests coming."

"Guests?" Hawthorn questioned, looking at Cari.

"They should be here soon," she responded.

"Who are they?"

"I'll let them introduce themselves," she answered evasively. Cari quickly set the kids to work collecting dishes and making Hawthorn comfortable. Shortly after they left there was a knock at the door. In walked Tobin with two others.

"How are you feeling, young one?" Tobin asked through his red bush of hair and beard.

Although he could not see his mouth, Hawthorn could tell by the wrinkles in the corners of his eyes that Tobin was smiling at him. "Tobin!" Hawthorn cried out in genuine delight to see one of his rescuers again. "I'm so glad to see . . ."

Hawthorn stopped in mid sentence as he looked past Tobin to the faces of the other two visitors. His eyes flew wide, his mouth dropped open, and it was several moments before he could make words come out of his mouth.

"It's really you," a deep voice spoke, strong with emotion. "I, truly, never thought I'd see you again, Hawthorn."

"Charlock! Burdock! How did you get here?!"

Hawthorn's two old friends each came over and, in turn, extended their right hand and arm to Hawthorn, who reached out with his right arm to each of them. They grasped each other's forearm in the typical Larkin greeting.

"We'll tell you our story," Burdock said, "but first, you tell us what happened to you."

Cari brought some chairs into the room for Hawthorn's guests. A moment later she returned with a tray containing mugs of cider for each of them.

Hawthorn told his story again in as much detail as he could remember. His knowledge of the actual ambush was very sketchy, and he could give them no more information than what Poke had told him.

They began asking him for news of friends and family members back at the Keep. Hawthorn did his best to tell them everything he could remember.

"Now it's my turn," Hawthorn said to his old teacher. "What happened, and how did you get here?"

"I suppose the Shaman told everyone that we were traitors," Charlock growled.

Hawthorn nodded. "They made all of you sound pretty bad. I knew it wasn't true, but I couldn't figure out why the Shaman turned against you."

"Well, it's good to know that you had faith in us," added Burdock.

"It had little to do with faith," Hawthorn confessed. "I was in the passage outside the assembly hall when you and your uncle were waiting to see the Shaman, and I overheard Charlock say that he thought the ones who rescued you weren't Renegades but were lost Larkin who had been missing for several seasons."

"Why, you little spy!" Charlock snapped.

"I'm sorry, Charlock. I know I shouldn't have been there. I'll admit that I was curious, but I didn't go there intending to listen in. I went there hoping to see how Burdock was doing."

"I'm glad he heard it, Uncle," said Burdock. "At least someone there knows the truth."

"But I don't really know any more than that. You were called back in by the Shaman after that. The next thing I knew, both of you, as well as

Burdock's mother and sister, were all escaped traitors. At least that's what I was told."

"But you didn't believe that," Charlock prodded.

"No, I didn't," Hawthorn responded. "That explanation made no sense at all.

"I figured that the Shaman didn't accept Charlock's explanation of who the rescuers were and that they thought you were both crazy. Convinced that you had both lost your minds, they decided to lock you up, but you overpowered the guards and escaped."

"It would save you an awful lot of trouble if we just leave it at that," said Charlock thoughtfully.

"No!" Hawthorn said firmly. "I want to know the truth."

"Your explanation was partly correct," Charlock began. "The Shaman pretended, at first, that my idea about lost Larkin being out in the woods helping others was ridiculous. They tried hard to convince us that the rescuers had to have been Renegades. But Burdock and I both knew that couldn't be true, and I said as much. I should have kept my mouth shut, but by that time I was furious at their deceit. Once they were convinced that we knew the truth, they had no choice but to get rid of us."

"Get rid of you?!" Hawthorn exclaimed. "Why?! What truth are you talking about?"

"The truth about these people, Hawthorn," Burdock responded. "The Makerians."

"We didn't learn the whole story until later," Charlock began again, "but we knew enough to know that there was another group of people out here besides the known Larkin tribes and the Renegades. I couldn't understand why the Shaman felt so threatened by the knowledge of these people at first, but we understand now."

"It's Jehesus, isn't it?" asked Hawthorn with a look of understanding.

"Yes," Burdock nodded. "The Shaman don't want anyone to know about Him."

"The Makerians have the knowledge of Jehesus," said Charlock, "and if the Larkin learn about Jehesus, then the Shaman are out of a job. The basis for their power among the tribes is that they are the only ones who know the prayer language. Since no one can talk to the Maker but them, the people are afraid not to do everything the Shaman say. The people don't know that the Maker sent His son, Jehesus, from the great heavenly place. They don't know he came into this world to show us how much the Maker loves us and to teach us that everyone can talk to the Maker."

"You can even be the Maker's child," Burdock said excitedly, "if you just trust in Jehesus enough to do what he says!"

"If the Maker is your father," Charlock was saying, "then you don't need a Shaman or anyone else to talk to Him for you. As His son, you can speak to Him yourself, any time you care to."

"But the Shaman should want everyone to know the truth!" Hawthorn said indignantly.

"You're right, Hawthorn," Burdock responded. "They should want that, but keeping their power is more important to them than the truth."

"Getting back to our story," Charlock broke in, "the Shaman intended to lock us up until they could decide what to do with us."

"Some of them were actually talking about killing us!" Burdock added.

"You must have misunderstood them," Hawthorn said skeptically. "Larkin don't kill their prisoners."

"Not only did they talk about killing us," Charlock said, "but, as upset as they were at us, I believe they actually would have done it. That is why we decided that if we could escape, we would.

"As the guards were taking us down to the cells, I had a chance to whisper to Burdock to be ready. Our chance came when we got to the cell chamber. The cells were all empty, as they usually are, so the only guards were the four taking us down there. As one unlocked the chamber door, I spun around and grabbed two of the guards and slung them into the one opening the door. The three of them went crashing into the cell chamber and sprawled onto the floor. The fourth guard turned on me, but Burdock threw himself into him from the side and drove him into the wall. As he bounced off the wall, I grabbed him and threw him in on top of the others. Before they could get to their feet, Burdock had slammed the door and bolted it shut.

"We ran quickly back up to the second level where our living quarters were. We grabbed bread, pouches of dried meat, and fruit that we had stored, as well as some robes, our weapons, and our hunting packs.

"It made me sick to think of taking Burdock's mother and sister with us, but I knew that the Shaman would just use them to get to us. As it turned out, when they heard what had happened, they both refused to be left behind. There was a ventilation window near our living quarters on the second level, so we let ourselves down the outside of the Keep with a rope and then slipped off into the shadows.

"We traveled by moonlight," Charlock continued. "We moved cautiously through the woods, and although we didn't hurry, we kept moving without a rest for the first two hours. I knew that the Shaman would spend two or three hours searching the Keep before they would figure out that we had left.

"After several hours, I found a small bush in which we could spend the rest of the night. This was all very hard on Burdock's mother and sister, as you can imagine, but they never complained. We tried to make them as comfortable as we could, and then Burdock and I took turns being on guard.

"Just as dawn was breaking we were attacked by an owl, but the bush was thick enough that the killer bird couldn't reach us as it swooped by. The owl then landed next to the bush and began tearing away branches trying to get to us. Finally Burdock and I drove the great bird away with our arrows.

"By this time it was light enough to see, so we breakfasted on dried fruit and bread, then we struck out again. My plan was to try to find Burdock's rescuers. The problem was that Burdock was never really sure where he was from the time they pulled him out of the creek until they brought him back to the Keep. He did remember that the whole time he was with them they were traveling almost due east. Since that was all that I had to go on, I set our course due west from the Keep.

"We traveled slowly, taking our time. We had a big head start on any search party, and I honestly didn't think that they would bother to send one after us. As we traveled west, we ranged back and forth through the woods, looking for signs of Burdock's rescuers. About midday, we came upon a small clearing spotted with thick clumps of tall grass. As soon as Burdock saw them, he shouted something about grass islands. I thought he had gone crazy on me."

"I recognized the place," Burdock explained. "After Laver and his men rescued me, the last place we spent the night before they took me to the Keep was in that clearing. As we left the next morning, I saw all the clumps of grass and thought that they looked like grass islands in a sea of sand."

"So I asked Burdock if he remembered where they had made camp," Charlock took up the story again. "Well, yes and no,' he says to me. 'It was inside one of these clumps of grass.' I told him that I thought that was pretty crazy, because you never knew what was inside one of those things. 'Not this one,' he says. 'It's hollow.'

"So we started searching in the grass clumps, and we eventually found it. It really was amazing! From the outside, it liked like a big, thick clump of grass. But just a short way into the grass, it opened up into a small clearing in the center of the grass clump. The floor of the clearing was soft sand, with a rock wall around the inside edge of the grass. There was a small cave built into the rock wall on one side. It was a great camp site—big enough for twenty warriors and completely invisible to anyone on the other side of the grass.

"When we checked the fire pit, we found the coals were still warm, so we figured that they had come back there to camp after they had taken Burdock home. Since we had nothing else to go on, we decided to just stay there, hoping that they would come back. We waited there for three days, and then late one night after we were bedded down, someone climbed into the camp. Burdock was standing guard, and they both saw each other about the same time. When our visitor saw Burdock, he ran, but we called after him, and he stopped.

"As it turned out, he was one of Laver's men who had been sent on ahead to get a fire going and to heat some water, because they were bringing in a wounded Renegade. They had been attacked by some of them. As the Makerians were defending themselves, one of the enemy warriors was wounded in the head, and they were going to try to help him.

"About two hours later the rest of the party arrived, and the leader of the group was my old friend, Laver. We all stayed there seven days nursing the Renegade. It was funny at first because to begin with the fellow thought they were going to eat him. Then he thought they were just going to torture him. Then he thought they were trying to fix him up to make him a slave. When he finally understood that they were taking care of him simply because that's what Jehesus would want them to do, it almost shocked him to silence. It was two days before he would say anything, and when he did, he only wanted to know one thing: 'Why?' Laver and two of the others spent a lot of time with him explaining about Jehesus. When he was well, they offered to take him home, but he didn't want to go. He wanted to stay with them and be Laver's slave. Laver laughed and told him that they didn't have slaves, but if he wanted to stay with them, they would take him to their elders, and he could ask them. After I explained to Laver what had happened to us, he made us the same offer.

"As we traveled to Stillwaters, Laver explained what had happened to him years ago. While out with a party of Larkin hunters, they had run into a swarming army of red ants. They had tried to outrun them, but they were unable to. He and some of his men became separated from the others and were surrounded by the mass of venomous insects. The marching column of killer ants was slowly closing in on them. Just as it looked like the bugs were about to find them, the Makerians appeared, walking through the column of red ants. They poured some ant scent over Laver and his men and led them right through the mass of insects to safety. The ants seemed to not even know they were there. One of the Larkin hunters had fallen and broken his arm as they had run from the ants, so the Makerians took them all to Stillwaters. Later Laver and his men became followers of Jehesus and decided to stay with the Makerians.

"When we came to Stillwaters, they fed us and took care of us. We had lots of questions, so they explained their history to us. After we learned about Jehesus, we wanted to become his followers. Once the elders were convinced that we knew what we were doing, they let us stay and become Makerians."

"You know, Hawthorn," said Burdock, "I'm sure the elders will let you stay too. We'd be happy to speak to them for you."

"Burdock!" Charlock snapped. "You're putting too much on this lad. All of this has to be almost overwhelming to him. Besides, he has a family back at the Keep whom he loves very much!"

"I still have a lot of questions," Hawthorn agreed, "but it's beginning to make sense to me. I'm totally amazed at what I've seen and learned, and I wouldn't be a bit surprised to wake up and find out that it was all a dream. But I know it's not. I'm fascinated by the stories I've heard about Jehesus, but I don't know what to do with Him. Learning about Jehesus goes against everything I've ever been taught, and part of me wants to reject Him. But if the stories about Him are true, then I know that I will want to believe in Him."

"I'm sorry, Hawthorn. I never meant to pressure you. I guess I'm just excited about what we've found here."

"That's all right, Burdock, I understand. I'm sure I'd be the same way."

"As soon as you're able," Charlock said, changing the subject, "we want to have you come and stay with us. Burdock's mother and sister are anxious to visit with you also."

"Thank you. I'd like that very much.

"Tobin," Hawthorn said, looking over to his quiet friend, "How is Eldan doing? I remember he was scrapped up pretty badly."

"I'm starting to get worried about him," Tobin replied, his eyes showing concern. "He should have made it back to Stillwaters two or three days ago, but he hasn't showed up yet."

"Shouldn't someone go look for him?" Hawthorn asked anxiously.

"A patrol of Rangers was heading out yesterday. They were to cross the meadow using the same trail Eldan should have used to come here, so I asked them to keep an eye out for him."

Tobin could see Hawthorn was really upset by Eldan's disappearance. "Now, listen here, young one. You know how Eldan is. He probably got another one of his loony ideas and is trying to work it out."

"But he's hurt!" protested Hawthorn. "He should have come back here."

"You're right," Tobin agreed. "He should have. But Eldan never was one to put *should's* ahead of *could's*. Don't worry about Eldan, Thorn. He may be crazy, but he's not stupid. I'm planning on going out on Nightwing tonight to see if I can contact him. If I hear anything, I'll let you know."

"Thanks, Tobin," Hawthorn said earnestly. "I would appreciate that."

CHAPTER THIRTEEN

ON THE TRAIL

"I thought you'd done got yerself et up fer shor this time," Rush said with a relieved look on his face. He tossed the aphid off of his chest and sat up.

"Well, I didn't get et up," Jay returned, "but it was no thanks to you! There I was—defenseless, sleeping, trying to recover from my fever—all the while trusting in my good friend, Rush, to look out for me and protect me, and where were you? Out picking daisies."

"Pickin' daisies?!" Rush responded with a hurt look on his face. "Now lookahere, Jay, I didn't mean to leave you. It all happened so fast. See, there was these Renegades . . ."

"Renegades?!" Jay asked in mocking disbelief.

"Well, yeah, and then. . ."

"And there had to be at least ten of them, right?" Jay interrupted with a sarcastic tone.

"Uh . . . right, right, there was about ten of 'em, and then . . ."

"And you fought all ten of them by yourself, right?"

"Burn yer hide, Jay, I ain't makin' this stuff up!" Rush was getting frustrated. "I know it sounds crazy, but—Hey! What are you laughin' at?"

Jay had been trying hard to keep from laughing, but as Rush got more and more desperate to try to tell what had happened, Jay couldn't hold it anymore. At first a giggle escaped his tightly pinched lips, then another, and then the dam broke. Jay was now on his knees, laughing so hard his sides ached.

"Yer laughin' at me, ain't cha?"

"Yeah!" Jay managed to get out, still laughing uncontrollably. "Rush, your face was priceless!"

"Why, you little sneak!" Rush snorted as realization hit him. "You were awake!"

"Yeah!" said Jay, laughing.

"You saw those ten Renegades!"

"Yeah!" Jay said, still laughing.

"And you knew I had to deal with 'em all by myself!"

"Yeah, I did!"

Rush turned his back on his friend.

"Oh, come on, Rush," Jay said, still giggling. "Don't get your feathers ruffled. Can't you take a joke?"

Smack! A fat aphid slammed into Jay's chest, knocking him to the ground. Great sobs of muffled laughter began to emanate from under the aphid's fat body as it lay on top of the prone Larkin.

It took several minutes for Rush and Jay to quit laughing. When they finally did get control of themselves, they took turns telling what had happened to them.

Jay's fever had broken in the late morning. When the Renegades showed up and spotted Rush, all their yelling woke Jay up. He lifted his head up and looked out of the spider's nest in time to see the Renegades chase Rush into the woods. He knew Rush had intentionally led them off to protect him. A feeling of helplessness overwhelmed him as he thought of Rush and the others outnumbered by enemy warriors. The thought made Jay angry. He wanted to help his friends but couldn't. He finally decided he could try to get some strength back and gather some food stuff that might be close at hand in case they had to hide in the spider's nest awhile longer.

He took one of the seeds that Rush had brought in, broke some pieces off of it, then pounded the pieces with a rock until it was a coarse meal. Mixing that with water, he made a nutritious paste, which he ate. When he felt strong enough, he got up and carefully began moving about looking for supplies. He found a number of edible seeds and roots which he brought back and stored in the bottom of the nest. After each trip, he took time to rest and eat more seed paste.

On his fourth trip out, he found a plant that appeared to be some type of mint with which he was unfamiliar but was covered with aphids. From the ground all the way to the top of the plant, every stem had aphids attached to it, sucking juices. Jay walked over and began to feel around on the back of one of the aphids attached almost at ground level. The soft insect seemed oblivious to Jay's touch. Jay was searching for the small bump that he knew was located on the lower portion of the aphid's back. When he found the small papillae, Jay began to stroke it very gently. Within a few moments the aphid's body gave a slight shudder, and a large drop of a thick, golden liquid as big as Jay's hand rose out of the bump. Excitedly Jay scooped up the honeydew in both hands and began taking deep drinks of it. A look of ecstasy crossed his face as he tasted the deliciously sweet juice.

About this time he felt a shake in the mint plant. Looking up, he saw three ladybugs had discovered the herd of succulent aphids and, landing on the upper stems, had begun devouring the insects as quickly as they could shove them in their mouths. Unwilling to sacrifice this newfound source of nutrition to the voracious appetites of the ladybugs, Jay grabbed two of the aphids and carried them back to the nest. That's when he discovered that Rush had returned.

Jay had been unaware of what had happened to Sycamore and Savin, so Rush filled him in, sharing with Jay his concerns at seeing the Renegade scouting party coming in on the same trail on which their two friends had left.

"Do you think the Renegades found them?" Jay asked.

Rush nodded his head. "I'm almost sure of it."

"Do you think they're dead?" Jay's voice was very soft.

After a long pause Rush finally said, "There's no way to know fer shor. But as far as I'm concerned, they're captured 'til proven otherwise."

Jay nodded his head. "Then it's up to us to get 'em all out," Jay said resolutely.

"That's the way I see it," Rush agreed.

They stayed at the nest for two additional days to give Jay more time to regain his strength. On the third day, Jay was feeling like his old self and was quite insistent that they push on. They let the aphids go, but they left their stockpile of seeds and roots in the bottom of the spider nest in case they needed to hide there in the future. They closed the trap door and carefully secured it shut with some sharp stakes.

In the last three days, they had seen five scouting parties of Renegades pass their hiding place: three were going out and two were coming in. With all this traffic, they knew that they must be getting close to the Renegade stronghold. The two Larkin, with this knowledge, moved out cautiously. The trail was easy to follow, being worn by all the movement on it, but their caution kept their pace almost to a crawl. Twice during the day they had to dive for cover as they heard the approach of enemy patrols.

"This isn't working," Jay whispered in Rush's ear as they lay under some leaves, watching the second Renegade war party march by.

After the danger had passed, Rush looked over at his friend, "I gotta agree with you. We're getting' no place follerin' this trail. Tell ya what let's do. Let's move off the trail about a stone's throw to the left and move parallel with it. We'll stay close enough to be able to slip back over and be sure we haven't lost it. That way we can move faster with less risk of being spotted."

"Anything's better than what we're doing now," Jay agreed.

Rush led them in a way that was perpendicular to the path they had been following. He stopped about twenty paces out and turned right, moving parallel to the trail. For the most part, this plan seemed to be working pretty well. The going was a little rougher off the trail, but they made much better time since they didn't have to be as cautious. In this manner, they traveled most of the day, occasionally scouting out the trail to be sure they hadn't lost it.

They were moving through a stand of hardwood trees with some thick underbrush. As they walked clear of the brush, they found themselves in a small clearing surrounded by tall oaks. Relieved at the easier walking, they moved across the leaf-scattered clearing.

Buzzzz . . . whap!

Rush, who had been leading, was suddenly struck in his chest by something that knocked him completely off his feet and into a surprised Jay. Rush quickly rolled over and began frantically grabbing for his shield slung across his back. "Hornets!" was all he had time to yell.

Before the word had gotten out of Rush's mouth, Jay was pulling his own shield around to the front. He was trying to slip his left arm in the shield's straps when a second hornet slammed into it so hard that the shield was driven back into Jay's face, knocking him to the ground also. "They'll be all over us in a second!" Jay screamed, frantically trying to get back up on his feet.

"Don't run, or we're done for!" Rush commanded. The droning sound of many wings grew louder as hornets began to shoot rapid-fire out of the nearby hole in the ground which was the entrance to their nest. "Back to back!" Rush shouted as he stood up, using his shield to knock aside the oncoming insects. "Fight 'em back to back!"

Jay understood Rush's plan and quickly spun around, slamming his back into Rush's just as five hornets hit them at one time. They braced their legs and pushed hard into each other's backs, holding their shields in front of them with both hands as the furious insects clawed at them or rammed their venomous stingers at them. The two companions jabbed and slapped at their attackers with the edges of their shields.

"We can't do this forever!" yelled Jay over the deafening sound of the attacking hornets.

"Let's try moving away from their nest," Rush yelled back. "Stay back to back, and we'll move toward those trees to your right."

Jay took a quick look to his right and saw the large trees that Rush had spotted nearby. "I'm ready! You call it, Rush, and we'll step together."

"Okay! Step!" Rush called, and they both took one step to the side—Jay to his right, Rush to his left.

"Again! Step!" They side-stepped once more.

"Step!"

"Hold it!" shouted Jay. "One's got my foot!"

He shoved right and left with his shield to give himself some room, then drove the bottom edge of his shield down hard into the claw gripping his foot. "Okay, go!" Jay called, and they took another step.

Fifteen or twenty hornets raged all around them now, but only five or six of them could confront them at one time. Rush had hoped that the hornets would eventually tire and leave them alone, but as time went by, they actually seemed to be getting madder. Step by step Rush and Jay slowly worked their way farther away from the hornets' nest and closer to the trees. The fight had already lasted several minutes, and sweat was streaming down their faces and arms. Rush could feel his arms getting tired, and he knew Jay couldn't last much longer. Stealing quick glances over his left shoulder, Rush searched the area around the base of the trees for some way of escape. He knew he had to think of something quickly, or they weren't going to make it.

"Rush! I see a hole!"

"Where?" Rush panted back.

"It's in the base of that tree!" Jay returned.

"Which one?"

"Those three trees closest to us—it's in the one to the right."

"I can't see it." With his shield held so closely in front of him, Rush was unable to see the base of the tree that Jay had described. Rush moved his head over to the edge of his shield to peer around it and almost got a stinger in the face. Cautiously, he tried again and was able to get a quick look at Jay's tree. Rush saw a small crevice at the base of the tree where two large roots came together to join the trunk. The hole looked to be about chest high to a Larkin and about shoulder-width.

"That's our best chance. Let's go for it," Rush decided. "Toward the hole . . . step . . . step . . . step . . ."

With hope stirring in their despairing hearts, they moved with purpose toward their objective. As they got close to the tree, the hornets had less and less room to attack them from the tree side. This forced the furious insects to concentrate their assault on the other three sides. The hornets seem to sense that their foes were trying to get away, and they actually intensified their attack. Whether it was Rush and Jay's weakening arms or the ferocity of the crazed hornets, it became harder and harder to hang on to their shields.

As Rush and Jay stood back to back next to the crevice, they tried to decide how one of them could climb into it without leaving the other one exposed to attack. The hornets actually made the decision for them. As they stood there debating their next move, Jay's shield was suddenly ripped from his hands.

"Go!" cried Rush, and instantly Jay dove for the crevice. At the same time Rush drove himself backwards and to his left after Jay, keeping the shield in front of him. Rush's shield, being too large to fit through the opening, effectively blocked the hornets from following them. Rush hung on to the straps on the back of the shield, pulling as hard as he could to keep the furious bugs from clawing it away to get at the two Larkin.

Jay found himself in the dark recesses of the tree cave, sprawled on something soft and spongy that smelled like rotted humus. "Help me, Jay!" he heard Rush call.

There was just enough light coming in around the top and bottom edge of Rush's shield for Jay to find his way over to him. "I'm right here."

"Help me hold the shield! My arms are givin' out!"

Jay grabbed the strap on the right side, and Rush seized the left one. They braced their legs against the sides of the crevice and held on tightly. The maddening drone of fifteen to twenty pairs of wings continued incessantly.

"Watch out!" cried Rush, quickly spreading his legs wide. A long stinger had suddenly been thrust under the bottom of the shield and began darting back and forth where Rush's feet had been.

Holding on to the shield with his left hand, Jay unsheathed his sting. Bending low, he jabbed his sharp weapon under the shield. He felt a hard jerk and the hornet's stinger rapidly disappeared. Jay was just starting to feel some measure of satisfaction when another stinger came thrusting back under the shield close to his own feet. Now it was his turn to jump. Almost at the same moment, two more stingers came jabbing through the opening at the top of the shield. Jay could feel some of the venom peppering his neck and cheek. "Don't these things ever give up?!" Jay yelled.

"I'm tellin' you," Rush drawled, "these critters need to find something better to do with their time."

"Oh, no!" Jay spoke, with panic in his voice.

"What is it?"

"Something's got me!" Jay was now stamping violently.

"Are you stung?" Rush wanted to know.

"No! Yiii!" Jay was now stamping his feet and whipping the backs of his legs with his sting. "Something's crawling up my legs!"

"Oh! Yeesh! They're on me, too!" Rush was stamping now.

"What are they, Rush? Ticks?!"

"They're too small," Rush spat through clenched teeth. He was holding the shield and alternately stamping his legs and swatting his pants with his free hand. "There's not enough light to see 'em. They're too hard to be ticks, and they're not biting or stinging, just crawling."

"There's got to be hundreds of 'em!" Jay returned. "Oh! Ah! No! They're crawling up inside my pants!"

"Stop it! Stop it!!" Rush screamed and began throwing himself repeatedly into the wall. "Help me, Jay! Help me! They're all up inside my shirt!"

"I've got all I can handle!" was Jay's answer.

"Jay! Augh! They're crawling all over me! Help me! Please, help me! I'm ticklish!!" In spite of the torture they were enduring, they both maintained their grip on the shield. "I gotta get outta here, Jay! Are the hornets gone?"

Jay glanced through the top crack. "Not yet! There's still a few of them out there!"

Rush let out an agonizing cry and continued slapping himself and stamping his feet.

They were under Jay's shirt now. "Oh! Eeh! Aack!"

"Yeow! No! Geesh!"

Both Larkin were jumping, stamping, slapping, and throwing their bodies in all manner of the most violent gyrations. After several more minutes of their wild dancing, Rush cried out once more, "Check again, Jay! Check again!!"

Jay steadied himself and peered out, searching for signs of their recent attackers.

"Well?" Rush barked.

As miserable as he was, Jay knew that it was certain death if he made a mistake here. "It's clear!!" he finally yelled, releasing the shield and diving through the opening.

With a fierce roar Rush charged after him. Both Larkin rolled violently across the ground, frantically pulling off their clothing. There were literally hundreds of small black and orange insects covering their entire bodies. Still yelling, they began desperately pulling, slinging, hitting, and shaking the crawling creatures off themselves.

It took several agonizing minutes to get the last of their tormenters pulled off and thrown away. They both stood there breathing hard, looking at each other. Jay suddenly burst out laughing. Rush, seeing how absolutely ridiculous they looked, joined him. They laughed long and hard, releasing the tension of the recent battle.

Regaining some measure of control, they began putting their clothes back on. This took some time, because they had to thoroughly search each article of clothing for hidden insects. "It's a good thing that was a nest of ladybug nymphs you fell into instead of spider babies," Rush chuckled.

Jay suddenly sobered. "Oh, yeah! You're right!" he said seriously, plucking another of the elusive crawlers from the back of his hand. They spent the next few minutes in silence as they finished dressing and gathering their discarded weapons.

"I think we need a new plan, Rush," Jay announced as he tugged on his boots.

"What'cha mean?" Rush wanted to know.

"Well, following the trail didn't work. We almost got spotted by two different Renegade scouting parties. So then we tried moving parallel to the trail, and the results were worse. I just think we need to try something else."

"Think about what you just said," Rush chuckled. "You don't want to walk on the trail, and you don't want to walk off the trail. What else is there?"

"We could walk above the trail," Jay said with a sly look.

Rush thought on that for a moment. Then he searched the limbs on the trees around them. "I'm game for that," he finally announced, nodding his head.

"We should be able to follow the trail more accurately without having to worry about scouting parties or hornets!" Jay added enthusiastically as he searched through his pack for his climbers.

Rush took a few minutes to find the best tree for their purpose. The first thing he needed was a tree with long, spreading limbs that extended into other tree's limbs, and the limbs needed to be going in the general direction of the way they needed to travel. He found a large hemlock close by that he thought would suit their purposes very well.

Walking over to the base of the tree, they began strapping the claw-like climbers on to their feet and hands. Rush led the way. The bark on the hemlock was rugged and crumbly, which made the climb more difficult. After considerable effort, they both made it up the tree to the appropriate limb. Once on top of the limb, they removed their climbers and got their breath.

FOLLOWING THE SKY TRAIL

183

They began making their way along the limb, moving away from the trunk. Branches from a nearby tree crossed the limb on which they were traveling. When they got to the first of these branches, Rush stopped and spent some time studying the direction of the trail far below them. Then he began closely examining the limbs of the nearby tree to decide which one offered the best route to follow. The branch that intersected their limb the farthest out seemed to Rush to be their best choice.

To reach the desired branch, they had to travel out to the very extremity of the limb. As its diameter got smaller, the branch on which they walked began to move and sway under their weight, making the journey much more perilous. They had to move with great caution to the spot where the new limb crossed their own.

The new limb never actually touched their own but extended over the top of their limb at a height of about four Larkin above where they stood. "So how do we get to it?" Jay asked, holding tightly to the swaying limb as he looked up at the small branch a short distance above their heads.

Rush was looking up too. "We'll just throw a rope over it and shinny on up. It's gonna take both my hands to throw the rope, so you'll have to hang on to me."

"And who's going to hang on to me?" Jay wanted to know.

"Wel-l-l," Rush said out of the side of his mouth, "I reckon you'll just have to hang on to yerself."

Jay scooted over next to Rush, and sitting on the limb, he put his right arm around a small branch that came up out of the limb next to where he sat. The other arm he wrapped tightly around Rush's legs.

"Okay," Jay announced, "I think I've got you."

Rush released his grip on the small branch which he had been holding to keep his balance. Quickly he reached into his pack and pulled out a coil of silken rope. He tied several knots in the end of it for weight, then prepared to throw the rope. "All right, here we go," Rush said to alert his friend to hold tight.

Rush carefully measured the distance with his eye, then using only the movement of his right arm to propel the rope, Rush tossed the line toward the limb above them, causing very little movement in the limb on which they stood. The knotted end of the rope flew up and over the branch above them, falling very closely to where Rush stood.

"There you go," said Rush with great satisfaction. "Easy as falling off a log."

"I wish you wouldn't use that expression," Jay said as he peered the great distance to the ground below them.

Rush grabbed both sides of the rope that looped over the branch above them and began to climb. It took less than a minute for him to climb up the rope to the branch above, but getting his burly frame up on top of the limb was more difficult. With the help of a small, jutting side branch close to the rope, Rush was able to finally pull himself up onto the higher branch.

Then Jay began the climb. With Rush's help, he too was shortly sitting on top of the new branch. Rush recoiled his rope, and placing it back in his pack, led the way along this new path in the sky.

Since they were now moving toward the trunk of the new tree, the limb was getting thicker, which made the walking much easier. When they had covered two-thirds of the distance to the trunk, Rush halted and began examining the limbs as they came off the other side of the tree. Comparing these options with the direction of the Renegade trail below told Rush the limb to which they needed to go next. As they got to the trunk of the tree, they stopped to unpack their climbers once again.

"We'll circle the trunk to the other side," Rush informed Jay as they strapped on their climbers, "then we'll need to go up the tree a ways. That second limb up on the other side should be the one going our way."

"It's a mighty long way to the ground from up there," Jay said, looking up at the limb that Rush had selected.

"When you walk the sky trail, you got to follow it where it goes," Rush shrugged.

As before, Rush led the way. They worked their way around the trunk to the other side, then they began ascending the tree. The tree they were climbing was a white oak, and because its bark was tighter and smoother, the climb was much easier than the first tree. Reaching the selected limb, they again removed their climbers and began following the limb away from the trunk.

Jay had never been this high before, and he was amazed at how small things looked on the ground. He could still make out the thin line of the trail snaking through the forest, but they were much too high to see anyone traveling on it. As they approached the end of this limb, Jay could see that there was a problem. The limb had a sharp bend in it to the left. The branch from the next tree that they needed to reach approached this bend but didn't touch it. Because it was the closest spot to the next branch, they stopped at the bend to decide their next move.

Jay surveyed the distance between where he stood and the branch they needed to reach. There was about half a stone's throw of open space between the two limbs—way too far to jump. Looking down, Jay got dizzy just thinking about the fall.

"Looks like we've reached a dead end." Jay said.

"What'cha talkin' about?" Rush said with a surprised tone. "This ain't no dead end. This is what's known as an *opportunity*. All we need is just a little help," Rush said looking around, "and we've got it made."

Rush looked back down the limb the way they had come and spotted a short side branch containing a cluster of five large acorns. Trotting back to this short branch, Rush pulled the coil of rope from his pack and tied the end to the small twig from which the cluster sprouted. When this was securely knotted, he wrapped another part of the rope just a short distance from the tied end to the limb on which they stood. This rope he also knotted in place securely. Pulling his flint knife from his boot, he began cutting at the small twig holding the acorns. In a short while the weight of the acorns broke the twig at the place where Rush had cut it. The acorn cluster now swayed back and forth below the main limb, suspended by Rush's rope, which was still securely fastened to the acorns and to the limb.

"Help me pull these up," he spoke to Jay.

"What are we doing?" Jay wanted to know.

"This is the help we need to get to the other branch. We're makin' a *nut-knocker*."

Jay knew better than to ask too many questions. He figured that they would all be answered shortly. After pulling their load of acorns back up onto the limb, Rush had another request. "Let me borrow your coil of rope."

Again without comment, Jay reached into his pack and pulled out the rope, handing it to Rush. Taking Jay's rope, Rush securely tied one end of it to the end of his own rope, the other end still being fixed to the cluster of acorns.

"Now," Rush said, as he handed Jay the free end of the length of rope. "Take the rope and tie it real tight back up there by the bend in the limb."

Obediently, Jay took the rope and moved carefully back out to the limb's end. As he stood there near the drop off, he called back to Rush, "Right here?"

"Yeah, that's good. Right there. Tie 'er off good 'n' snug."

He still wasn't sure what Rush had in mind, but he was familiar enough with Rush's ideas that he figured his life might possibly depend on what he was doing, so he took special pains to tie the rope securely. "Okay," Jay announced, as he returned to Rush.

"Good 'n' tight?" Rush wanted to know. Jay simply nodded his head. "All right. Help me carry these acorns back up the limb 'til we take the slack out of the rope." With this accomplished, Rush then surveyed the length of the rope as it extended down the right side of the limb on which they stood. Satisfied that no branch or projection from the limb would catch the rope, Rush turned to Jay and the acorns. "We're all set!" Rush announced smiling.

"So what's going to happen?" Jay wanted to know.

"I got it all figured out. See, what 'cha do is, you shove these heavy oak nuts off the side of the limb. Since they're tied to the rope, and the rope's tied to the end of our limb, then the nuts will swing. The weight of 'em should swing 'em hard enough so that they'll fly over and hook on that side branch of the limb over there that we need to get to."

"Sounds reasonable. Let's shove 'em off."

Just as Rush had planned, the weight of the acorns caused the whole length of the rope to swing in a large, sweeping arc. As it reached the opposite limb, the rope hit the side branch of the other limb, but the acorns did not flip over the branch and catch there. Instead, the rope bounced off, and the acorns came swinging back.

"Hmmm . . . didn't seem to work," was all Jay said.

As soon as the rope stopped its violent swinging, Rush hurried out to the end of the limb and began pulling up the rope. "Help me pull this up, Jay. I know what the problem is. I got it all figured out. We just need to give them acorns a little more speed."

Jay hurried up to his friend and, without any more comment, helped pull the acorns up. It turned out to be a bit of a job hauling that load of acorns up two lengths of rope. After getting their load securely up onto the limb, they rested. Then carrying the cluster between them, they walked it back up the limb until the rope was tight again.

While taking another break to rest, Rush explained his new and improved plan. "Now all we gotta do is to lift the acorns, and this time instead of just dropping them off the limb, we'll throw them up into the air as far as we can. The extra distance falling will increase their speed, and that should do the trick."

Jay nodded his head thoughtfully. "Whenever you're ready," he said to Rush.

"All right," Rush barked. "Here we go. Lift!" Each one taking a side, they hoisted the heavy cluster up to chest height. Taking a moment to get their balance, they steadied themselves to heave the load as high as they could. "One . . . two . . . three . . . GO!"

With every muscle straining to the uttermost, they launched their burden almost three Larkin high before it dropped past the limb. Watching the swinging rope with eager anticipation, they saw it sweep across the open space and again smack against the branch on the other tree. The end result, though, was no better than the first try.

Rush was stunned. He had not even considered that his idea wouldn't work. Shoulders drooping, he was momentarily at a loss to know what to do next. He stood there staring at the swinging acorns.

"Hey, Rush! How about a little help?"

Startled, Rush looked up and saw Jay standing at the end of the limb pulling on the rope. Rush quickly moved down the limb to his friend, and together they pulled up the heavy acorns once more.

"Wel-l-l," Rush said slowly, with a great deal of disappointment in his voice, "I guess we'd better get these ropes off. Then we'll climb down."

"Climb down?!" Jay said, appalled. "You mean you're giving up?"

"I'm not givin' up going after our friends," Rush said, a little hurt. "But I don't see any sense in wasting time playin' with these acorns anymore."

"So just because YOU'VE run out of ideas, you think getting across to the other limb can't be done. Is that right?" Jay asked accusingly.

Rush's eyes narrowed as he studied his friend's face. "If you've got a better idear, let's have it," he finally said skeptically.

"Help me carry this thing back up the limb," Jay laughed.

When they reached the extent of the rope, they set down their load and sat down to rest. "Now, Rush," Jay began with a superior tone in his voice, "your idea would have worked if we could have raised the acorns ten Larkin high before we dropped them, but there's no way to raise it that high. So since we can't increase their speed by dropping them from a higher point, we should be able to accomplish the same thing by increasing their weight."

"I already thought of that, Jay, but there's nothing to tie to the acorns to increase their weight. There ain't any more acorns reachable on this limb, and it's not worth the effort to climb to other limbs and try to carry them back to here."

"Rush," Jay said loftily, "I am absolutely amazed at your lack of imagination." Jay began rummaging through his backpack. When he straightened up, he was holding a rolled-up, long leather strap that he used for tying things. He flashed a broad grin at Rush, then quickly began to tie himself to the cluster of acorns.

Rush was shocked when he realized his friend's intentions. "What do you think you're doing?!" Rush blurted out.

"It's my new invention," Jay said. "I call it my *Jay-knocker*." By now Jay had himself securely strapped to the acorns. "Now, Rush, help me lift this thing."

"Jay! You're not serious about jumping off this limb."

"Dead serious," Jay returned, laughing.

"Don't say that!" Rush was almost in a panic. He couldn't believe what was happening. "Jay, listen to me. Think about what you're about to do. This is insane!"

"No more insane than some of your ideas," Jay retorted. "You got us up here in the first place."

"But you could die doing this!" Rush pleaded.

"Yeah, but if I live, it'll make a great story."

Lifting the acorns with great effort, Jay backed up until the rope was tight. Then with a big grin and wild eyes, he jumped off the limb.

JAY!" Rush yelled.

"Woo-hoo-hoooo!!"

Jay held on for all he was worth as he swung wildly toward the other limb many leagues above the ground. The air rushed by him so quickly that he felt like laundry flapping in the wind. The rope pulled against him as he arched up toward the coveted branch, slapping into the limb a short distance from where he was tied to it. With the sudden stop, Jay's added weight caused the acorns to sail past the limb and to flip over it twice.

"Jay! Are you all right?" He heard Rush's worried voice calling.

"I'm not sure," Jay mumbled, hanging upside down close to the end of the branch of the new tree.

"What?"

"I said, 'Sure'!" Jay yelled back.

Making certain of his grip on the branch, Jay untied himself from the acorn cluster. Pulling himself into a more secure position, he untied the acorns and let them fall away. Then he took his end of the rope and tied it tightly to the limb.

"Okay, Rush, it's your turn," he yelled over to his companion. "Untie the rope from the end of your limb and swing over."

"What?!" came the startled reply. "You expect me to do what you just did? I'll come hand over hand, but I'm not swingin'."

"Rush, where's your spirit of adventure? You may never get another chance to do something like this," Jay said with enthusiasm. "Besides, if you don't swing over, we lose both ropes, which it's sure we'll need to escape with our friends."

Rush had no argument to this last statement. Rush looked over the edge of the limb to the ground far below and began to feel sick to his stomach. Resolved to his fate, Rush began to slowly untie the rope. He looped the rope around the upper thighs of both legs before wrapping it twice around his waist and securing it tightly with multiple knots.

Jay observed all of these preparations with excited delight, frequently yelling over encouraging words to his nervous friend. When Jay could see that Rush was almost ready, he yelled out one more suggestion, "As soon as you're ready, Rush, strap on your climbers. That'll make it easier for you to grab the limb and climb up on it when you reach the top of your swing."

Grateful to postpone the death-defying feat for as long as possible, Rush carefully fitted his climbers onto his hands and feet. When there were no other preparations to make, Rush stood up looking very unsure of himself.

"Now back up 'til the rope is tight . . . okay, good. All right! You're ready. Show me what you're made of!" Jay yelled encouragingly.

Rush knew that thinking about it would only make it harder, so leaning back until he could feel the strong pull of the rope, he simply closed his eyes and jumped.

He dropped like a rock, the rope catching and swinging him across the open expanse so quickly that he almost didn't have time to be afraid . . . almost.

Reaching the bottom of its arc, the taunt rope swung him rapidly upwards toward the new limb. Rush had enough presence of mind to open his eyes, knowing that he must grab the limb to keep from swinging back from where he came. The velocity of the weighted rope swung him up to the level of the bottom of the limb just as it began to lose its momentum. It wasn't exactly what Rush wanted, but it was close enough, and he fiercely jabbed the points on his hand climbers into the bark on the bottom of the limb. The climbers held, and Rush found himself suspended at a dizzying height from the bottom of the limb close to the trunk.

"You made it!" Jay laughed with delight as he ran over to above where Rush hung. "That was absolutely amazing, Rush! You should have seen it."

"I'm glad you enjoyed it," Rush growled, still suspended under the limb. "Now help me get out of this mess."

"Oh, okay. Uh . . . I'll untie the rope and pull you up."

"Well, HURRY, why don't cha?!" Rush barked. "I'm feelin' mighty insecure right now."

Jay quickly loosened the tied end of the rope, then hurried to a spot directly above his distressed friend. He took up the slack and wrapped the rope once around the vertical trunk of a nearby branch that grew up out of the limb on which he was standing. "Okay, Rush. I'm ready. You try to climb while I pull."

"Pull hard!" Rush yelled. He felt his body moving upwards as Jay began taking in the rope. Rush made a quick grab for a higher place with his left hand. As the climber bit into the bark, he pulled hard to keep himself moving up. He did the same thing with his right hand, repeating the process until he was able to dig his foot climbers into the bark to help his climb. Both Larkin were sweating profusely and out of breath before Rush was lying safely on top of the limb. It was several minutes before either of them spoke. Rush finally broke the silence. Sitting up, he looked over at his grinning companion and spoke, "I do some wild stuff, but you're crazy!"

"I'm not crazy," Jay said, with a hurt look on his face. "I'm just . . . uh, dangerously creative."

Chapter Fourteen

THE LAIR

While Jay gathered and recoiled the ropes, Rush visually scouted the Renegade trail. He was still staring intently at the forest floor when Jay joined him with their packs.

"I think we're close to their stronghold," Rush volunteered. "The trail comes out of the woods right here close to us. It seems to go across that open space, then disappears into that rocky bluff on the other side of that clearing. My guess is that they've got themselves a cave over there." Jay's eyes intently followed all that Rush was pointing out to him. "Let's go down from here and scout it from the ground," Rush decided. "We can't see enough detail from up here to tell what we're up against."

Strapping on their climbers, they descended their tree on the opposite side from the trail. They moved cautiously, trying to avoid detection from possible enemy sentries. When they reached the ground, they repacked their climbers, then moving stealthily through the brush, they scouted parallel to the trail until they arrived at the clearing. The two Larkin eased noiselessly through the brush on the fringe of the clearing. Rush found a spot where they had an unobstructed view across the open area, though they themselves remained hidden.

"I was right," Rush whispered as he peered across the clearing. "Look straight across to that bluff. There's a cave in the base of it, and it looks like they got two warriors guarding the entrance."

The clearing in front of them was covered with coarse sand and patches of short, dried grass. A few small thickets of briars could be seen randomly scattered about. The bluff that Rush referred to was more than a long bow shot away. Following Rush's direction, Jay let his gaze fall upon the rough, rocky wall straight across from them. He noticed a crack at the base of the bluff that extended straight up the rock face for almost half of its height. The crack was wider at the bottom than at the top. As Jay scrutinized the opening at the base of the rock wall, he could just make out two tiny figures on either side of the opening.

Both Larkin sat in silence for a few moments. Then Jay spoke, "It'll be dark soon. We can slip across the clearing then and try to find a way in."

"We could do that," said Rush thoughtfully, "but chances are pretty good that that's the only way to get in. If it is, then that means we'd have to fight those two to get by 'em. The end result would be, we'd get the whole muckeree of them varmints all stirred up, and we'd wind up gettin' ourselves caught or kilt."

"So how do we get in?" Jay wanted to know.

"I been doin' some thinkin' 'bout that," Rush said smiling, "and I think I've got a plan. I figure one or two of them scouting parties we've seen go down that trail ought to be coming back home soon. So if I put on my varmint suit and slip in amongst 'em as they march by, I'll just stroll right in with 'em like I own the place," Rush laughed. He was already pulling out the Renegade clothing and mask.

"I'm glad I kept this club," Rush said as he untied the weapon where he had strapped it below his pack.

"So what am I supposed to do?" Jay said with his hands on his hips.

"You'll have to wait here till I scout the place out and figure out a way to get our bunch out," Rush returned, pulling on the Renegade tunic.

"Well, I don't like it!" The anger was rising in Jay's voice. "The plan was for both of us to go in. Your idea could take days, and once you get in there, you may not be able to get back out. If this thing drags on, how am I supposed to know if you're okay, or what I need to do?"

The sun had sunk behind the western woods, and the shadows were lengthening. Rush completed his change of clothes and packed away his stuff. With the wooden mask slid up on top of his head, Rush hid his shield under some dried leaves.

"Now hear me out, Rush," Jay said anxiously. "I think I've figured out a way to get us both in." Jay unsheathed his sting and began sketching a rough map on the ground. "We're right here," Jay said, stabbing the ground, "and over here is the Renegade cave. Now if we wait till dark, we should be able to ease our way across that clearing without being seen. We can follow this line of briars till we get close."

Jay was completely absorbed in drawing out his plan. He was oblivious to the fact that Rush was paying no attention to him. Rush was peering past Jay into the darkening woods behind his friend. After a few moments, Rush reached up and pulled the mask down so that it concealed his face.

By now Jay had covered most of his plan, so he looked up at Rush to see if he was in agreement. It startled Jay to see Rush standing there with the mask on. As Jay stared at his friend, he saw Rush slowly lift his hands over his head as if he were surrendering.

"What are you doing?" Jay said in a confused tone.

"Point your sting at me," he heard Rush whisper through the mask.

Jay now noticed that his friend's eyes were not on him but on something behind Jay's back. The small hairs on the back of Jay's neck began to stand up as he realized that danger was near. He did as Rush had whispered and lifted the point of the sting until it pointed at Rush's chest.

"Looks like we got here just in time," growled a menacing voice behind Jay.

Jay quickly whirled around and saw two Renegades coming at him with war clubs raised. Several others could be seen behind them coming quickly out of the gloomy woods. Jay was preparing to defend himself when suddenly he was grabbed violently from behind and thrown down roughly. A booted foot stomped on his sting, pinning it to the ground. A hand grabbed a fist full of Jay's hair and jerked his head back. A knife point was held up against his throat, and he was looking into the hideous face of a Renegade mask. "You made a big mistake coming here, Larkin," the voice behind the mask snarled. "I'm gonna make you wish you had never been born."

Jay looked up into the cold eyes glaring at him through the mask and saw the right eye wink at him. Suddenly he realized that it was Rush who was threatening him.

Jay knew now what had happened. While he had been so absorbed in explaining his plan, Rush had spotted the Renegades sneaking up on them through the woods. He had pulled his mask down over his face and gotten Jay to point his sting at him. By pretending to be captured, Rush had taken suspicion away from himself and focused all the attention on Jay. When Rush grabbed him and threw him down it was to keep Jay from being hurt by the other Renegades. Even Rush's threats were a way of trying to protect Jay. If Rush could convince the other Renegades that he had some claim on Jay, maybe they would leave him alone.

"Good thing we showed up when we did," the Renegade leader said to Rush.

"I guess it was," Rush said casually. "You headed in?"

The Renegade leader nodded.

"How about we tag along?" Rush asked, jabbing a thumb at Jay.

"So that's it," the Renegade said with a snarl. "We escort the prisoner in, but you take the credit. If it weren't for us, you'd be Larkin fodder right now! So as far as I'm concerned, he's my prisoner, and I'm takin' credit for his capture!"

The Renegade's grip tightened noticeably on his war club, and Rush saw a threatening look in his eyes. Rush met his gaze with hard eyes of his own. "I don't care who takes credit for him," Rush snarled equally as threatening. "But once we get him in there, he's mine." Rush glared at all of the Renegades standing before him. "I mean it! I'm gonna make this Larkin suffer long and hard, and none of you are gonna interfere!" As Rush glared at each one, they all averted their gaze from his vicious eyes.

The Renegade leader laughed nervously. "You'll have your fun. As soon as we get through the gate and report in, he's all yours.

"Grunts!" the leader shouted over his shoulder. The Renegades with no masks or ornaments ran forward and saluted the leader. "You two grunts take charge of the prisoner. Bind him and keep a close eye on him. If he gets away, you'll both find yourselves slaves again, and I promise you that I'll make sure you never get another chance to be warriors."

Rush was taking all this in. Apparently Renegade slaves could eventually earn the right to become warriors, but they were not allowed masks, ornaments, or even names until they had proven themselves.

The two grunts ran quickly over to Jay and began tying his hands. After securely binding him, they put a lead rope around his neck. With the captive in tow, they quickly formed ranks and marched off. Rush placed himself in the middle of the Renegade troop close to Jay. They marched out of the woods and into the clearing, following the trail as it ran straight across to the crack in the bluff. They got to a place in the trail where a white rock that was just within bowshot of the cave stuck up from the center of the path. At this spot the troop halted. At a signal from the guards at the cave, the leader advanced and made some sort of communication with one of the guards who had come forward to meet him. Apparently satisfied, the guard turned back to the cave and gave a signal. At the same time, the leader turned to face his troop and indicated that they were to advance.

When they reached the mouth of the cave, they halted again for a few moments. A third Renegade had appeared from the cave's dark opening and was talking with the leader. Rush concluded that this was a captain, and the Renegade troop leader was reporting in. Standing at the mouth of the Renegade Lair, Rush became aware of a muffled drumming sound coming from somewhere deep within the dark cave before him. The Renegade leader turned and called for the Larkin prisoner, and the grunts in charge of him drug Jay up to the front of the formation. To avoid unnecessary questioning, Rush stayed where he was. He was hoping that the leader would be too prideful to mention that Rush had helped capture Jay. He really hoped that the leader wouldn't mention Rush at all. After a few minutes, the signal was given, and they marched on into the cave. A wave of relief flooded over Rush after he passed the guards at the gate.

Jay had been kept at the gate with the leader, the two grunts, and the captain. They were trying to find out who he was and what he was up to. Rush felt pretty sure that the troop leader wouldn't mistreat Jay too badly, because he had seen the fear in the leader's eyes when he threatened him earlier. But Rush wasn't sure what the captain might do. He knew Jay wouldn't give them any usable information, but he was concerned for his safety.

It was several more minutes before Rush saw the leader coming down the passageway with Jay and the two grunts. The leader had taken off his mask and was walking up to Rush. He was shorter than Rush, with a dark, swarthy appearance. His hair was jet black, greasy, and laid tightly against his head. The Renegade was grinning as he approached, and Rush was startled at the appearance of his teeth. Each one had been filed to a sharp point, giving him the appearance of some fierce animal. "Okay, he's all yours," grinned the leader.

"Good!" Rush snarled. "I'm gonna borrow these two grunts for a bit." Without waiting for a reply, Rush turned and barked an order to the two guards. "Take him to the cells!" The two grunts immediately grabbed Jay and pushed him down the dark passageway.

Rush was actually delighted at their good fortune. Not only were they both inside the Renegade Lair, but he also had two guides to show him around. All he had to do was to be careful how he phrased his orders so that the grunts would not know that he had no idea where he was going.

They were led down the long, main passageway. Torches burned at regular intervals from holes cut into the rock wall. The passage had a downward slope and gradually widened. After a short march, they rounded a curve, and Rush could see more lights in the distance. As they trudged toward the lights, Jay suddenly stumbled and fell. The Renegade in front spun around and, seeing

Jay on the ground, pulled hard on the rope around Jay's neck, choking him. "Get up, you worthless pile of . . ."

"Hey!" Rush snapped, jamming his war club under the Renegade's nose. "You leave one mark on his neck, and I'll clobber you so hard you'll have to eat through your belly button!"

The grunt's eyes flew wide, and the rope immediately went slack.

"Nobody, and I mean nobody," Rush growled, cutting his eyes over to the second Renegade, "lays one finger on this Larkin but me. You two got that?!"

Both Renegades swallowed hard. "Y-y-yes, sir," they stammered.

"How about a little help here?" Jay called up from the sandy floor of the cave. Both grunts seemed eager to assist Jay back to his feet, and in a moment the procession began again.

The beating of the drums was much louder now. Mixed with the relentless rhythm were the shouts and yells of large numbers of people. The wide passageway down which they traveled led into a large, cavernous room. It was like a gigantic meeting hall, all naturally formed out of solid rock. The ceiling was somewhat dome-shaped but was not exceptionally high. One could sling a rock and easily hit the stone roof. What the room lacked in height, it made up for in width and breadth.

The noise in the huge room was almost deafening. Many drums made from hollow logs were placed all around the room and were being fiercely pounded by three and four Renegades each. Literally hundreds of Renegades could be seen milling about the room. Many fires were burning in different parts of the cavern, but around a very large one in what appeared to be the center of the room, there were large numbers of the enemy. All of them were screaming and throwing their bodies around in time with the rapid drum cadence. Rush was mesmerized by the scene. The great crowd of Renegade warriors seemed to have been dancing for quite some time. Sweat was literally streaming from their bodies, and they had worked themselves into a wild frenzy.

Their guides led Rush and Jay around the right side of the great room. They walked by three passageways before the grunts led them down a tunnel which was not very well lit. This passage sloped downward rather steeply. A torch was flickering a short distance further down the tunnel, causing long shadows to dance on the floor, walls, and ceiling. When they reached the torch, the passageway made a very sharp turn to the left. Following their guides, they descended deeper and deeper in the Renegade Lair.

Another torch could be seen in the distance. The savage cries and drumming sounds began to fade as they traveled further into the cave. As they

THE RENEGADE LAIR

approached the second torch, the most noticeable sound was the crunching of their own feet on the gravelly sloping floor. The torch was protruding from a hole cut into the rock wall, and Rush observed that the tunnel they were traveling down seemed to end there. On closer inspection, he saw that a wooden door had been built into this wall. In the door was cut a small window about head height, with several wooden bars running up and down and side to side across it. There was a guard, of sorts, on duty. The Renegade guard, bored with his monotonous task, was sitting with his back propped against the wall, snoring loudly. So deeply was he sleeping that he did not hear their approach.

When they saw their resting comrade, both of the grunts cut their eyes at Rush. Observing their looks, Rush realized that they expected him to respond to this situation. "Wake him," Rush growled in a low voice.

The grunt who was leading immediately bent over, picked up a fist-sized rock, and threw it viciously at the sleeping guard. The hunk of sandstone hit the rock wall just above the head of the guard with a loud "crack" and exploded into hundreds of fragments. "Eeeow!!" the guard screamed, rolling back and forth in the dirt, holding the side of his face.

"Get up, you!" Rush snarled threateningly.

The injured guard looked up with a mixture of anger and fear in his eyes. There were many small cuts on the right side of his face where the tiny rock fragments had peppered him.

"I should crush your skull right now for sleeping on guard duty as a lesson to these two," Rush growled, shaking his club in the guard's face, "but I figure that'd be lettin' you off too easy. I'm makin' it my mission in life to be sure you become the perfect guard. Stand at attention when I'm talking to you!" The scared guard quickly snapped to attention. "You're a mess! You got dirt all over you. Clean yourself up! Where's your weapon?"

The guard looked down at his empty hands and then furtively glanced around for his discarded war club. "I . . . uh . . . well, I think . . . uh . . ."

"WHAT?!" Rush screamed into his face.

"It's over by the wall, sir!"

"Well, get it! And if I ever see you without it being in your hand, I'll make you eat it!"

The guard scrambled to get his club, dusting himself off in the process. The other two grunts were laughing at their comrade's predicament. Jay seemed to be enjoying the proceedings as well.

The guard was back at attention, a little cleaner, with club in hand. Rush surveyed his quarry with a critical eye. "Are you sweating, grunt?"

"Uh, yes, sir," the guard answered.

"Well, stop it!" Rush barked. "Now get over there and get that door open! We've got a prisoner."

With a confused look on his face, the guard turned, threw the bolt on the door, and jerked it open. Rush nodded at the two guides to lead the way. As the party passed through the door, Rush glared at the guard. "I'll be back," he snarled.

The guard made an involuntary nervous jerk at this statement. After they passed through the opening, the door closed behind them. Behind his mask, Rush grinned as he heard a whimpering sigh coming through the barred window in the door.

They were led down another passageway, this one with a few more torches than the previous one. The tunnel they passed through now continued to slope downward but was formed in a long, right-hand turn. After several minutes of this spiraling journey, the turning passageway straightened out and opened into a wide path with a few scattered boulders. They marched on for about the length of a bow shot and found themselves at another rock wall with a wooden door. Again they found another guard. Fortunately for him, this one was awake.

"We have a prisoner," one of the grunts said. The guard walked over to the entrance, jerked back the bolt, and pulled open the door. They walked into a small, well lit room with a very tall ceiling.

There was a guard in this room also. He sat behind a rough table just to their right as they entered the room. There were thick, wooden bars built into the floor and ceiling on each side of the room. There was another door, which had a barred window in it, in the far end of the room. Rush noticed that the far door could be bolted from inside the room.

"What's yer business?" the guard snapped at them as he set aside the acorn flask out of which he had been drinking. Rush could tell by the smell and manners of this guard that his flask contained wine and that he had been taking frequent pulls at it.

"Our master here's got a prisoner for you," the first grunt said.

The guard stood up. He was a little unsteady on his feet. He shuffled over in front of Jay. Taking the rope off Jay's neck, he grabbed him by the tunic and slung him hard into the wall.

"You can go," the guard said. "He's mine now!"

The guard himself was suddenly grabbed by his tunic and slung face first into the rock wall next to Jay.

"I don't think you understand," Rush said from behind his mask. "He's not your prisoner; he's mine."

The guard turned around to face Rush, his nose and lips beginning to swell. "Who do you think you are?!" the enraged guard yelled. "Why, I'll . . ."

The guard, eyes wide with terror, suddenly dove to the floor as Rush's war club smashed powerfully into the cave wall right where the guard's head had been. Rolling over, the guard looked up to see Rush standing over him, war club raised.

"I think I'm the guy who's gonna flatten yer head if you let any harm come to my prisoner. Now you listen up, you drunken sot. This Larkin is mine, and nobody's gonna hurt him but me. Got it?"

The guard spat some dirt out of his mouth and mumbled something. Rush's club descended with tremendous force. The guard screamed and rolled to the side. The club's head drove into the ground, spraying sand and gravel over the guard's head.

"I got it! I got it!" the guard screamed.

"Good," said Rush. "Don't forget it. Now get up and take real good care of my prisoner."

Never taking his eyes off Rush, the guard rose and helped Jay to his feet. He pulled open the heavy, barred door to the cell nearest them and started to shove Jay in. Then he stopped himself. "Uh . . . would you step in here?" the guard murmured to Jay while looking at Rush.

"Maybe," Jay said nonchalantly. "How about untying my hands first?"

The guard cut his eyes over at Rush, who nodded his head. Reluctantly, the guard unbound Jay's wrists. "Okay," the guard said to Jay after his hands were free, "now in."

"How about something to eat?" Jay asked innocently.

"This ain't no inn!" the guard barked.

"I think this will do," said Rush. He was picking up a dish containing a good-sized piece of roasted meat that he had found on the guard's table.

"Hey! That's my supper!"

"You drank your supper," Rush returned as he handed the dish to Jay.

"This will do nicely," Jay said pleasantly, taking the dish and strolling nonchalantly into the open cell. "Wake me in time for breakfast," he said over his shoulder.

The guard slammed the cell door shut and wedged a long pole against the door and the floor. "There!" he said in frustration. "Are we done now?"

"No, we're not," Rush spoke, staring at the guard. "Take me to the other slaves."

"They're down in the mines right now, but the guards will be bringing them back here in about an hour. You can look at 'em then."

202

Rush jammed his club under the guard's nose, "Take me to the other slaves NOW!"

"I can't leave this post," the guard pleaded. "I'm on duty!"

"These two will cover for you 'til you get back," Rush said, indicating the other two grunts. They started to argue, but one look from Rush stopped all resistance. "Lead the way," Rush demanded.

The guard swallowed hard and walked the length of the room to the far door. Drawing back the bolt, he pulled the door open. In a basket next to the door were several torches. The guard picked one up, lit it from a burning torch protruding from the wall, and led the way through the dark opening.

As Rush followed the guard it became immediately apparent that they were walking through no small tunnel. This was actually an immense room, the ceiling of which disappeared into blackness far above. The floor was littered with rocks and huge boulders, but there was a worn, sandy path through all the fallen rocks on which they traveled. In spite of all the debris around them, the trail was clear and level, and they were able to walk at a quick pace. They traveled the trail in this way for nearly a quarter of an hour, coming eventually to a fork in the path. The left fork continued down the length of the room. The right fork descended through an opening under a large bolder. They followed the right fork and began making their way into the deeper regions of Renegade Lair. The narrow passage descended steeply in a series of turns, then flattened out into a straight tunnel, the end of which sloped upward slightly before descending again in another curving passageway.

A distant roaring sound began to reach Rush's ears as they moved down the tunnel. The further they went, the louder the noise became. Suddenly the narrow, descending tunnel opened up into a very large cavern. From where they stood, Rush could see the tiny specks of many torches flickering in various areas of the great room. The path before them led down into the middle of this huge area.

Rush now recognized the roaring sound. It was the sound of a rushing river. The guard led the way down the worn trail toward a small cluster of torches. As they approached the torches, two figures could be seen standing in the light. "There you go," said the guard, pointing to the two figures just ahead. "See them two? The tall one on the left is Shard. He's the slave boss. Can I go now?"

Rush nodded. "Just remember what I said about my prisoner." The guard swallowed hard, then turned quickly and hurried back up the trail. Rush turned away from the retreating guard and walked toward the light. At his approach, both Renegades turned and stared hard at him. When they saw the garb and mask of a Renegade warrior, they relaxed.

"You need sumpin'?" Shard asked, eyeing Rush suspiciously. Shard was a tall Renegade. He was taller than Rush and almost as broad. He wore a coarsely-woven kilt that appeared reddish brown in the torch light. A tan shirt covered his chest and arms, and a wide leather belt was strapped around his waist. The only weapon Rush could see on the slave boss was a long, braided leather whip coiled at his side. There were two more things Rush noticed about Shard as he approached him: one was the no-nonsense air of authority he possessed, and the other thing was that he was very dirty.

"I understand you got some new Larkin slaves down here."

"Yeah, I've had some new 'uns come in. What about it?"

"I want to see if it's some of the ones who jumped me a few days ago."

"I'm tired of you guys comin' down 'ere an' killin' off me workers!" Shard flashed fire in his eyes. "I ain't havin' it no more, see?!"

"Oh, I don't aim to kill none of 'em—yet," Rush returned smoothly. "I just want to, sort of, introduce myself to 'em."

The corners of Shard's mouth turned up just slightly, forming a faint grin, and he chuckled to himself. "Awright, you can see 'em, but if any of 'em can't do dey work tomorrow, I'm comin' after you, and don't think I cain't," Shard said as he grabbed the whip at his side. "I could peel 'da hide clean off ye' 'fore ye could get close enough to swing 'dat fightin' stick o' yorn."

Rush glanced down at the whip, then back up at Shard's fierce eyes. "I believe you could at that," Rush said. "Don't worry; I want these Larkin to live a long time."

Shard turned to the grunt standing nearby. "Show dis warrior where da new slaves is workin'. Dey should be mining flint below da ferry on dis side of da river."

The grunt saluted and turned to Rush. "This way, master." The grunt led the way into the gloom. The path they walked was lined with white rocks. In the dim torch light the outline of the path was quite distinct. The sounds of swift water were very near, and as they topped a small rise, Rush could see that a stone's throw ahead of them was a swift, underground river. On this side of the river directly in front of them a wooden dock was built. A large rope fastened to stout beams ran from this dock across the river to the other side. There were torches flickering on the opposite shore a distance of about a bow shot. In the light of these torches, Rush could see a similar dock to which the other end of the rope was attached. Floating in front of the distant dock was the ferry. It was a rectangular-shaped raft with low side walls. It was large enough for well over twenty Renegades to be carried at one time. A rope ran through small openings on each end of the raft so that those in the raft could pull it back and forth. Two large oars were placed one on either end to propel the raft when only one or two Renegades were in it.

Turning to the right, his guide led Rush down river along a rocky path that ran parallel to the bank. Rounding a large boulder and topping a rise revealed a lighted area just ahead. As they approached this torch-lit area, Rush saw what appeared to be a rock quarry. There were many slaves here and much activity. Most of the work being done was directed at the face of a towering boulder that appeared to be solid flint. Using hammers with quartz heads and pry rods, thin slabs of rock were being flaked off the surface of the huge flint boulders. These large sheets of flint were then broken into smaller pieces by slaves with hammers. Other slaves would then load the pieces into baskets and carry them to another area where they were dumped into piles. Slaves at these piles would work through the razor sharp flint pieces, looking for the ones most suitable for flaking into arrowheads, spear points, knives, and ax heads. Rush noticed that blood was streaming down the arms, legs, and hands of almost all of these slaves where they had been repeatedly sliced by the sharp flint edges.

Rush's anger began to rise as he saw what these poor people were being forced to do. "Where are the new Larkin slaves?" Rush growled at his guide.

"I don't know," the grunt shrugged. "They're around here somewhere."

A low snarl began to rumble from behind Rush's mask. He locked his eyes hotly on the insolent guard standing next to him. Slowly Rush's war club rose until it touched the grunt's nose. "Find 'em!" Rush demanded.

Eyes wide with fear, the grunt stammered a 'yes, sir' and sprang forward toward the slaves working on the flint boulder.

Rush watched the guard for a few moments and then began his own search. The dim light of the torches plus the fact that all the slaves were filthy made the task difficult. Unable to recognize any of his friends at the boulder, Rush moved toward the other slaves working on the piles of broken pieces. Suddenly Rush gave a start. There ahead of him, just pouring out his basket of broken flint, was Sycamore. Looking around, Rush noticed several guards nearby.

Walking over to his friend, Rush stuck his war club in Sycamore's chest. "You!" He could see the anger burning in his friend's eyes. Rush was chuckling behind his mask. "Out of line!" Rush snapped as he pushed Sycamore backwards with his club. "I've got some business with you."

Sycamore glanced around him. Rush knew he was thinking of fighting him. "You try anything, and either I'll kill you or the guards will," Rush said, loudly enough for the guards to hear.

Realizing that resistance was useless, Sycamore turned around and let Rush push him toward a large boulder nearby. Just as they passed behind the huge rock out of sight of the guards, Rush spoke. "That's far enough," he said, glancing around to make sure they could not be seen.

"What do you want with me?" Sycamore demanded, bracing himself for the expected beating.

"Boy, Syc," Rush said, raising his mask. "You sure make a great slave. I'll have to remember to tell your wife that when we get back home."

"Rush!" Sycamore exclaimed in excited relief. "I should have known it was you. How did you get here?"

"I put on this varmint suit and snuck in. Where are the rest of our bunch?"

"They're on the other side of that pile of flint over there, sorting."

"Lead me to 'em," Rush said, pulling his mask back down.

Sycamore led the way, with Rush occasionally shoving him in the back with his war club and growling threats. They made their way around behind the huge pile of hammered stone, where small groups of slaves were sitting around the base of the pile sorting through the broken flint for those pieces best suited for knife blades, arrowheads, spear points, and other tools.

Sycamore finally stopped before a group of four slaves busy at this task. Looking carefully at each of their dirty faces, Rush recognized Savin and Poke. Rush's eyes searched the faces of the other two slaves but saw no one he recognized. Rush looked at Sycamore. "Isn't there another one?" Rush growled.

"No," Sycamore returned sadly, his gaze dropping to the floor.

Rush's heart sank within him at hearing this. "You two!" Rush barked, pointing his club first at Poke, then at Savin. "Get up and come with me."

Rush directed his friends behind a small mountain of discarded flint pieces a short distance away. Once assured that they were not being watched, Rush revealed himself to Savin and Poke. "Where's the lad, Savin?" Rush asked with fear in his voice.

Savin opened his mouth to answer, but words wouldn't come. Instead, tears began to wash clean streaks down his dirty face.

"They killed him, Rush," Sycamore said. Then he, too, was overcome with emotion. For the next few moments the four friends wept in silence.

"When?" Rush finally asked.

Poke then retold his story. "The Renegade war chief was so mad at Wolf for killing Hawthorn," Poke said as he finished, "that he made him a slave to take Hawthorn's place."

"You mean that Wolf character is down here?" Rush asked.

"Yeah. He's swinging a hammer over at the boulder."

"Well, I've got business with him right now!" Rush growled.

"No, Rush!" said Savin. "If you kill him, they'll never let you down here again."

"Just forget him, Rush, and tell us how we're getting out of here," Sycamore wanted to know.

"Wel-l-l," Rush drawled, "I ain't quite worked that out yet. I need to scout this place and see if I can figure the best way out. In the meantime, I'll try to slip you fellers some weapons and extra food to keep yer strength up."

"Where's Jay?" Savin asked.

"We only had one varmint suit, so he had to come in as a prisoner. He's up in the cells, waitin' on you."

"So how'd you get down here in the slave mines?" Sycamore wanted to know.

"Oh, these Renegades are right accommodating. All you got to do is ask in the right way, and they'll do anything for you. They think I've come down here to beat you three up. It might help our cause a little if you fellers would smear some of the blood from yer cut hands onto yer faces. Then when they're leading you back up to the cells, if you'd groan and limp a little more than usual, it would make my masquerade a little more convincin'."

"Now, listen up," Rush spoke. "I don't mean to stay in this rat hole any longer than I have to, and I ain't leavin' it without every last one of us. So buck up and be ready, 'cause when the time comes, we'll probably have to move quickly."

A horn sounded in the distance.

"That's the signal for us to head back to the cells," Sycamore informed Rush.

"Then we better be heading back," Rush said. "I'll try to scout around this place tomorrow and gather some weapons. Then I'll try to slip back down here to check on you fellers the day after, if I can. Just be ready to move at a moment's notice, and don't lose heart."

CHAPTER FIFTEEN

MAKERIAN HOSPITALITY

"How are you doing, Thorn?"

"I'm fine, Cari! I'm fine! You worry too much."

"Well," Carineda returned, "you staggered some when we went around that turn. I don't want you losing your balance and hitting your head again."

"I just took that turn too fast, that's all," Hawthorn responded.

Hawthorn had improved enough that Carineda had been getting him up to walk. Up to this point his walks with Cari had consisted of walking around their living quarters. Today, however, Cari had decided that Hawthorn was ready for a little longer excursion.

After a hardy breakfast they had set out. Exiting their living area, Cari led Hawthorn along a wide, well-lit hallway. Quick movements still made his head swim, so he took slow deliberate steps. Hawthorn had been improving rapidly. He actually felt strong and almost back to his normal self. He was very glad to be out exploring the Makerian stronghold.

They turned left into an adjoining passageway and continued walking. They quickly emerged out into a large, circular central area. There was a wide walkway extending out from the walls on which Hawthorn and Cari now stood. To Hawthorn's left the walkway spiraled upward in a sloping curve as it followed the curve of the wall. To the right the walkway spiraled downward to the lower levels. A wall that was about chest high bordered the outside edge of the walkway.

"This is the central passage of the Refuge," Cari announced.

"The Refuge?" Hawthorn questioned.

"That's what we call this place," Cari answered.

"I thought it was called Stillwaters."

"Stillwaters is what we call the whole area where we live," Cari explained, "including the Refuge, the water, and even the surrounding woods. If we want to refer specifically to this fortress in which we live, we call it the Refuge. This open area we're standing in is the central passage. It's the main way we get from one level to another: all of the halls are connected to this large walkway. From here it's just a short trot to whatever level you need to reach."

Hawthorn noticed that there were indeed a lot of people moving up and down the passageway. He walked across to the retaining wall and looked over the edge. He could not see the bottom. "How far down does it go?" Hawthorn wondered out loud.

"Quite a long ways," Cari said evasively.

There was a large, circular stone tower located in the center of this central area around which the walkway spiraled. The rock tower came up out of the depths of the Refuge and extended up as far as Hawthorn could see.

"Can I ask what that is?" Hawthorn questioned, pointing at the stone tower.

"That is a chimney," answered Cari. "It was built four seasons ago."

"It sure is big."

"There are large work rooms in the lower levels of the Refuge where our wise ones and builders work to develop and build new things to help us. The chimney allows the smoke and heat to get out.

"What kind of new things?"

"Oh, all kinds of new things," she answered vaguely.

"Can we go down there, Cari?"

"I don't have permission to take you down there, but we can go up to the next level to my favorite spot. It's a place where you can get the most beautiful view of the lake. Come on."

Hawthorn allowed Cari to lead the way up the spiraling walkway. A number of people passed them as they moved slowly up the curving ramp. Hawthorn felt awkward since he was an outsider, but he could not detect any uneasiness or suspicion in any of the people he met. In fact, he was very impressed with how friendly everyone was. Almost everyone they met spoke at least a few words of greeting, and those few who didn't speak smiled and nodded at them. Back home he might walk from the top to the bottom of the Keep twenty times and still not have more than five people even make eye contact with him, much less speak to him.

"Let's go this way," said Cari as she led him through an arched doorway to the left. The passageway that they entered led directly away from the central passage. A short walk brought them to the end of this tunnel where they could go either left or right. Cari pulled Hawthorn to the left. "It's just a little farther," she said coaxingly.

Cari stopped in front of a set of carved, double doors. Without hesitation, she turned the handle and swung the right door open. Passing through the opening, they walked into a wide hallway. This hallway ended a short distance ahead in another set of double doors. Off of each side of this short hall were paired sets of heavy doors. There were also what appeared to be many tall cabinets built into both walls.

"What is this place?" Hawthorn whispered.

"You will see in a moment," replied his guide.

When they reached the second set of double doors, Cari again pulled the right one open. Bright light flooded the room. As Hawthorn's eyes adjusted to the intense light, he realized that these doors led to the outside. They walked through this doorway out onto a large balcony that had been carved into the side of the huge cypress stump that served as the Makerian stronghold. Hawthorn took four paces forward and reached the retaining wall of the balcony. It came up a little past his waist. The young Larkin stood silent for several minutes bathing in the sunlight and drinking in the view.

The Makerian refuge was located on the northern end of Stillwaters Lake. From where Hawthorn stood, he could see the entire eastern shoreline. To his extreme left, the northern shore came quite near to the Refuge. Hawthorn guessed the land to be about two bow shots away on that side. To his extreme right, Hawthorn could view most of the southern shore many leagues away. A large number of cypress trees grew along the edge of the immense pond, and the shore line was dotted with numerous cypress knees— the tower-like, knobby projections growing up out the water and the ground from the roots of these trees.

Hearing some noises coming from overhead, Hawthorn looked up and saw a large beam projecting from the top of the Refuge, which was eight levels above the balcony on which he stood. The tip of this large beam extended well out over the water. To the end of the beam were attached two ropes. One rope hung straight down, terminating in a small bundle that was suspended above the water at about one-half the height of the Refuge. The beam's second rope was also attached to the distant end of the beam, but this line, instead of hanging downward toward the water, ran back into the Refuge. Leaning over the balcony wall for a better look, Hawthorn saw that this second line disappeared into an opening in the wall two levels below where he stood. As he watched,

Hawthorn could see that this second rope was being drawn into the opening. The pull on this line resulted in a gradual bending of the tip end of the long beam. As this second rope was continually drawn tighter, the long beam bent more and more. This, in turn, dropped the bundle closer to the surface of the water.

A third rope could be seen running from the top of the suspended bundle, curving back toward the refuge and disappearing into a large opening several levels above Hawthorn. This third rope remained slack during this whole procedure.

"What's all this?" Hawthorn asked, fascinated by what he saw.

"They're going to try to catch a fish," Cari answered.

Hawthorn took that information and studied the activity a little more closely. "How does it work?"

"Do you see that small package just going into the water?"

Hawthorn looked in the direction that Cari was pointing and could see that the bundle at the end of the first rope was now low enough to touch the water.

"Well, that package," Cari continued, "contains things that some of the fish in the lake really like to eat. The fishers attach the package of bait to that rope by hanging it on a sharp hook carved out of bone that's tied to the end of the line. When a fish bites the bait, then the fishers release the bent beam. When it springs up, the fish is caught."

"How do the fishers know when a fish is biting the bait?" Hawthorn wanted to know.

"Watch," was Cari's answer.

As Hawthorn continued to watch the line, it was lowered into the water, and he saw something that he had not noticed before. A piece of wood was attached to the line being lowered into the water. As the line was lowered far enough for the wooden piece to touch the water, Hawthorn could see that it floated. He gave a little laugh as he recognized that the wooden float had been carved into the shape of a fish.

"When the floating fish gets pulled under the water," Cari explained, "then the fishers know something has bitten the bait."

"That's amazing!" Hawthorn said, looking over at Cari. "How did they think . . ." Hawthorn didn't finish his question. Looking past Cari, he saw a strange object moving across the water to the north. "Cari! What's that?!" he exclaimed, pointing excitedly at his new discovery.

Cari turned quickly to see what had distracted her friend. A rectangular, barge-like craft cruised into view around the north end of the Refuge. The barge was steered by a large oar attached to the stern which was controlled by a Makerian standing in the rear. Two paddle wheels, one on each side, powered the boat. A long crank, being turned by a crew of two more Makerians, connected the two wheels. As they turned the crank, the boat glided swiftly across the water in the direction of the north shore.

"That's the paddle barge, which we also call the *Turtle*. We use it to move supplies and sometimes people back and forth between the shore and the Refuge."

"Those people in the middle are making it go, right?" Hawthorn asked.

"That's right. The faster they turn the crank, the faster the paddle wheels turn, and the sooner you get where you want to go."

"How do they change directions?" Hawthorn had no experience at all with water craft and therefore knew nothing about how they worked.

"There are two ways that you can turn it," Cari explained. "The first way is by the pilot who is standing in the rear. That long pole that he is holding is a steering oar. The part down in the water is wide and flat, like my hand, only bigger. Whenever the pilot wants to go left, then he pushes the pole to the right, and that makes the flat part of the oar move to the left. As water hits the blade of the steering oar, that causes the nose of the barge to turn to the left. To turn right the pilot simply pulls the oar pole to the left.

"If they need to turn the barge quickly, then the crew disconnects the crank rod connecting the two paddle wheels, and they can turn the wheels separately. By turning the one on the left forward and the one on the right backward, then the barge will turn to the right amazingly fast. Reverse the direction of the paddles, and you spin the barge to the left. It's really pretty simple once you get the hang of it."

Hawthorn was absolutely dumbfounded by what he saw and heard. "That may seem simple to you, but to me it's like a miracle. I've never even dreamed of anything like that."

They were both silent for a few moments. Finally Hawthorn spoke, "Everything is so . . . so wonderful here. I keep telling myself that it can't be real, but it is real. Everything I've experienced here is so far beyond what my life is like. Your medicines are so much better than ours. Your inventions and discoveries are like miracles to me. Your religion seems wonderful. Everyone appears so happy, so at peace. There's no fear of death here. You talk with the Maker whenever you want to, and it seems as if He talks back to you. Cari, it's too much for me. I can't understand it. It all fascinates me, but it's so amazing that it scares me too." Hawthorn looked into Cari's eyes with a desperate gaze. "Please help me to understand!"

"I'm sorry, Thorn. I thought showing you around Stillwaters would be enjoyable for you. I never meant to cause you more distress."

"It's not you or this place, Cari. I don't want to hide from the truth. I just want to make sense of it.

"Twenty or so seasons ago," Hawthorn continued, "your people were still Larkin. With all the hardships that the Makerians have had to go through, how could your people know and be able to do so much more than the Larkin in such a short time?"

"All that you have seen," Cari answered, "can be explained very easily. Our Lord Jehesus and His Father, the Great Maker of All That Is, has poured out His great blessings on us."

"I've heard that before," Hawthorn responded with irritation in his voice. "But why would the Maker bless the Makerians and not the Larkin?"

"The Maker has blessed the Larkin, hasn't He?" Cari asked. "From what you've told me, the Larkin clans are strong and well. He's given you health, strength, and plenty of food, hasn't He? He's kept you warm in the winter. He's protected the clans from their enemies. He's even spared your life several times in the last few days. I'd say the Larkin have been very blessed by the Maker."

"You know what I mean, Cari. Why would the Maker show you so many wonderful inventions and discoveries and not show them to the Larkin?"

"I can think of several reasons, Thorn, but I really think it all boils down to the fact that we asked the Maker for them." As Hawthorn thought on these words, Cari continued, "As soon as our leaders discovered that through faith in Jehesus anyone could pray to the Maker and that the Maker listens to and answers the prayers of His children, we became a people of prayer. We pray about everything. Whenever a decision needs to be made, or if we have some special need, each of these things is presented to our Heavenly Father."

"So you have someone to pray for each of these things?"

"No, it's not like that. Our leaders discuss with the whole tribe the needs or important choices that come up, and we each begin praying about these things. But we don't just say one prayer. Jehesus taught us to be persistent in prayer, so we keep praying for as long as it takes until the Maker provides the answer."

"You mean all of this wonderful 'stuff' has come from prayer?"

"That's right. Once a need has been presented to us, we all begin praying. It may take a while, but eventually an idea comes to one of the builders or one of the wise ones that's the perfect solution. All of the things you see here and have mentioned are the answers for problems about which we prayed."

Suddenly Hawthorn heard a distant shout from far above, followed by a thump and a roaring *whoosh* sound. Large drops of water began to splash all around them. Cari gave a squeal and ran to the back of the balcony. Looking out for the source of all this disturbance, Hawthorn saw a gigantic sunfish flopping vigorously from the end of the fishing line.

"They caught one! They really caught one!" Hawthorn exclaimed. "Thunder and sky-fire! That thing is huge! Why, it must be eight Larkin long!"

Hawthorn watched in fascination as the large fish was slowly drawn into the Refuge by means of the third line. It took several minutes before the carcass of the sunfish disappeared into a wide opening in the side of the Refuge several levels above.

"What will they do with it now?" Hawthorn asked, his gaze still riveted on the opening above him.

"Well, after killing the fish, the next thing they will have to do is remove the scales. This is really the hardest part, but with some hot water and hard work all the scales will be detached. Next they will skin the fish. That's quite a job as well, because they will try to take the skin from each side off in one solid sheet. After that, one crew will start working on the skins while the rest will begin cutting off the meat. We cook some of the meat fresh to eat now. The meat that remains will be dried or smoked for long-term storage."

"What will they do with the skins and the scales?" Hawthorn wanted to know.

"The scales will be separated according to size, and the skins will be scraped, stretched, and tanned. After being dried, softened, and oiled, the skins will be turned into clothing that's light, comfortable, and entirely waterproof."

"Waterproof?!"

"That's right. You can wear it in a soaking rain and stay dry. How about that?"

"Did you get that from prayer?"

"Yes, we did."

"But what about the scales? What do you do with them?"

"Oh, my!" she said, a little bewildered. "We do hundreds of things with them. The larger ones are cut and used to make body armor and shields for the Rangers and guards, soles for boots, combs, handles for brushes, eating and cooking utensils, and lots of other things. The smaller ones we use for making things like buttons, fasteners for ropes and straps, and decorations for clothing. Strung together they make beautiful curtains and shades. When you cut them into squares and glue them together with resin, they make waterproof containers.

"THEY CAUGHT ONE! THEY REALLY CAUGHT ONE!"

216

"We use almost every part of the fish we catch," Cari continued. "The air bladders are used for storage containers. The small bones are used to make needles, awls, and pins. The rib bones are long, curved, and springy, so we use them as springs in beds, couches, and chairs to make them more comfortable. Most of the organs of the fish we use for food. The intestines we scrape and wash and use to make sacks or pouches for storage. You can also take some of the cleaned intestines; stuff them with meats, vegetables, and seasonings; tie off the ends; and bake them. That probably doesn't sound very appetizing, but they are delicious!"

"So you're telling me," Hawthorn returned, "that all of those things came from praying?"

"I am absolutely convinced," Cari answered seriously, "that all of these things are special gifts that the Father in heaven has given to us because of the requests and prayers that we have made to him through the Lord Jehesus, His Son."

Hawthorn turned away from his friend in silence. He stood leaning against the balcony wall, gazing out across the rippling surface of Stillwaters. He remained there for several minutes, deeply in thought. Finally a noise drew his attention to the north shore. Looking to his left, he saw that the Makerian paddle barge had pulled away from the shore and was churning toward the Refuge loaded with large baskets full of grain and seeds. Watching the two Makerians cranking the paddle wheels, his eyes followed the strange craft until it disappeared around the north end of the Refuge. Turning to his companion, Hawthorn smiled. "Cari, I think I'm ready to learn more about Jehesus."

Cari smiled back, her eyes bright with excitement. "Let's go find my father."

Hawthorn spent most of the afternoon and part of the evening listening to Cari's father tell him stories about Jehesus. At first he was suspicious and a little defensive, but the more he listened, the more fascinated he became. He heard of many amazing things that Jehesus did to show his power. Hawthorn had many questions, and Taumis patiently answered each one.

Hawthorn heard about things called sins. Taumis explained that these are bad things that people do that hurt Jehesus and the Maker very much. Taumis told him of a very bad place called hell, a place of fire and agony where the Maker will put all the bad people and enemy spirits.

Hawthorn thought the hell place was a good idea. He had always figured that there should be a place like that for all the Renegades. He was taken aback when Taumis told him that hell was a place for all people: Renegade, Makerian,

Larkin, and anyone else who did not come to the Maker's Son, Jehesus, to be forgiven of their sins.

Then came the really hard part. Taumis tried to explain to Hawthorn that everyone who was old enough to make decisions for themselves had sinned against the Maker; therefore, everyone deserved to be thrown into the hell place. That thought was more than the young Larkin could handle. Renegades in the hell place made more sense, but not Larkin, and surely not himself. It was very late before Hawthorn's mind was able to push all of these thoughts aside and find relief in sleep.

For the next two days Cari took Hawthorn for longer walks. Each morning and each afternoon the Makerian nurse made sure her patient was challenged physically. Hawthorn's strength and balance returned quickly. There was no dizziness now, and the headaches were long gone.

For four hours in the middle of every day but one, Cari disappeared for what she called her classes. The one day she did not go to classes was on the first day of the week. Hawthorn discovered that this was a special holy day when all of the Makerians stopped all their work and spent the day praising the Maker and Jehesus, reading the sacred words, praying, and spending time with family and friends.

Every day for the Makerians started and ended with prayers. There were also quite a few scattered throughout the course of the day as well. But the prayers Hawthorn heard from Taumis and his family on the morning of Holy Day seemed different. To Hawthorn, the prayers seemed to have a little more excitement in them, like each one knew something was about to happen. But after they all finished praying, nothing did happen—except breakfast.

Now breakfast was something about which Hawthorn could get excited. They ate honey cakes topped with sliced pecans and strawberries, plus there were cups of blueberry nectar to drink. After breakfast Hawthorn was looking forward to a hot cup of mint or sassafras tea like they usually had, but today he was told that there was no time for tea.

They hurried to clean up the dishes before they were called to a special Holy Day meeting of all the Makerians. Taumis told Hawthorn that they began every week by using the first day to praise the Maker, to worship Him and His Son, and to encourage each other in following Jehesus.

"You're welcome to come with us if you would like to," invited Taumis. "Many of us will meet together later this morning for a time of praise and prayer."

"I am very curious," Hawthorn responded, "but are you sure that it's all right for me to be there?"

"Why, certainly. We would all be honored to have you."

"But won't the people be offended since I don't share their belief in Jehesus?" Hawthorn asked.

"No," Taumis said thoughtfully, "they might feel sorry for you, but they would still be honored that you came. Afterward we've invited some friends and relatives to come share a meal with us to honor the Lord Jehesus."

As it turned out, Hawthorn almost felt sorry for himself. The Makerian meeting took place in a huge, vaulted chamber that was called the great hall. There were several rows of tiered benches lining three of the walls. The fourth side of the great hall made up the front of the room. On this open end of the room stood a large, wooden table behind which were arranged several chairs.

"Is this the holy place where you worship the Maker?" Hawthorn asked Cari as they entered the great hall.

"Well," Cari responded, "we do worship the Maker here sometimes, but the great hall isn't a holy place. Normally it's used when our leaders want us all to discuss important things that are happening or problems that we need to work out. The reason that we meet here is that this is the only room in the Refuge large enough to hold all of us.

"It's always enjoyable when we can gather all of us together in one place to worship, but the really important stuff happens later, when we meet in our homes with smaller groups of people."

There were almost three hundred people in the room, but they were not crowded. It would take many more to fill the great hall. This was not a hushed, solemn assembly. There was a tremendous amount of noise as everyone visited with each other. Hawthorn was introduced to more people than he could remember.

Everyone began to quiet down suddenly, and at the same time Hawthorn became aware of singing coming from the other side of the room. Looking around, the young Larkin finally spotted five or six Makerians seated among the people across from him who appeared to be doing the singing. Hawthorn was stunned by the beauty of the music. Then it came to him. This was like the singing that he had heard when he first woke up after his injury. What was amazing to Hawthorn was that the singers were all singing the same song, but they were each singing different notes. They were singing the same words to different music, yet it all fit into one song.

After several moments of harmonizing in this way, they reached a point in the song when everyone in the great hall suddenly joined them in singing—that is, everyone except Hawthorn. He was so startled that he jumped. Cari, who was sitting next to Hawthorn, wasn't singing either; she was giggling. Hawthorn was completely entranced by the beauty of the music. He didn't want them to stop, and for quite some time they didn't. Whenever they finished one song, someone in the crowd would start another. Many times the person calling for the song would make some comments about what that song meant to him or her. They sang song after song. They sang about the greatness of the Maker and the wonderful things He had done. They sang about Jehesus, the beauty of His life, the great sacrifice of His death, and how the Maker raised Him to life again. The love, the joy, and the excitement that flowed from their hearts made Hawthorn almost wish that he believed in Jehesus.

At the end of one of the songs, another Makerian stood up and began to speak to the people, "May the Maker, our God and Heavenly Father, bless the reading of His holy word." Then the speaker unrolled a piece of parchment and began to read,

"'The preaching of the cross is to them that perish foolishness, but to us which are saved it is the power of God. For it is written, I will destroy the wisdom of the wise and will bring to nothing the understanding of the prudent. Where is the wise? Where is the scribe? Where is the disputer of this world? Has not God made foolish the wisdom of this world? For after that in the wisdom of God the world by wisdom knew not God, it pleased God by the foolishness of preaching to save them that believe. For some require a sign and others seek after wisdom, but we preach Christ crucified, to some stumbling blocks and to others foolishness, but to them who are called, Christ the power of God and the wisdom of God. Because the foolishness of God is wiser than people and the weakness of God is stronger than people. For you see your calling, brethren, how that not many wise, not many mighty, not many noble people are called: but God has chosen the foolish things of the world to confound the wise; and God hath chosen the weak things of the world to confound the things which are mighty, and the base things of the world and things which are despised, hath God chosen, yes, and the things which are not to bring to nothing the things that are: that no person should boast before God. But by His doing you are in Christ Jehesus who became to us wisdom from God, and righteousness and salvation and redemption, that just as it is written let him who boasts, boast in the Lord.'"

When this Makerian finished reading the holy words, he sat down. Then another Makerian stood up where he could see all those who had assembled.

"My brothers and sisters, after hearing such wonderful words, I am strongly moved to pray to the Maker, our Father. But before I pray, I wonder if there are others among you who also feel moved to pray, who would like to join me?"

As the speaker was finishing his words, several others stood up. Before they could start their prayer something was said from the crowd to the left of the speaker. Immediately, two of those who had joined the speaker hurried over to the left and began to help an older Makerian to his feet. He was so feeble he had to be helped to a chair that the speaker had pulled out for him.

"That's one of our nobles," Cari said in Hawthorn's ear. "He is called Melchus the Prayer. You have never heard anyone pray like he does."

After Melchus was finally seated, the prayer began. The speaker started the prayer, and after he finished, the others each prayed in turn. They praised the Maker and His Son, Jehesus, in many different ways and with much feeling. Hawthorn was impressed with their deep thoughts and meaningful words. The last one to pray was Melchus the Prayer. When his turn came, he lifted up his hands and began to pour out his heart to the Maker. The power and emotion in this Makerian's words to his God were so moving that Hawthorn felt his heart deeply stirred. Looking around, the young Larkin noticed several of the Makerians around him wiping away tears as Melchus' passionate words brought them all before the very presence of their Heavenly Father.

After the praying was finished and as Melchus was being helped back to his place, another older Makerian with white hair arose. He began teaching the people about some things that he thought were important in the holy words that were read earlier. He encouraged them not to live their lives trusting in their own power, but to trust in the Maker to give them power through faith in Jehesus to do mighty things for God. Several questions were asked by different ones in the crowd, and a lively, open discussion ensued.

"Well, what did you think?" Cari asked as they were eating dinner a short while later. Eighteen neighbors and relatives had joined Taumis's family for a large meal. It was the custom of the Makerian families to have a lot of people share their midday meal with them each Holy Day.

"I've never experienced anything like that in my life," Hawthorn replied in earnest.

"But did you like it?" she persisted.

"Yes, I did, but I didn't understand some of it. I absolutely loved the singing. It was so different. I've never heard all the different types of singing before."

"Different types? Oh, you mean the parts."

"I guess so," he answered.

"Some of our people discovered that music has four parts, just like a year has four seasons. The main tune of the song, the melody, we think is like the season of the year where you do your most work. So we call it the summer part of the song. The high harmony part that the women sing we call the spring part. The harmony part that the men sing we call the fall part, and the really low part we call the winter part. With a little practice, you can find the four parts in almost any song."

At this point they were interrupted by Cari's father, who announced that they were now going to share in eating the bread and drinking the grape wine that represented Jehesus' death on the cross. Taumis explained, primarily for Hawthorn, that this was done to remember the sacrifice that Jehesus had made for them so that those who believed in Him could have their sins forgiven. He said that it was a special meal that Jehesus had commanded all of his followers to share in regularly in order to remember him. Prayers were offered for the bread, then for the cup of wine. These were passed around the table, and each one there took some of the bread and drink.

Hawthorn felt uncomfortable participating in this ritual, so he just passed them both to the next person without taking any. After the regular meal was over, all the visitors stayed. They spent the entire afternoon together, talking mostly about Jehesus. It seemed to Hawthorn that these Makerians actually expected Jehesus to show up among them. Someone told a story about Jehesus saying that just as Jehesus showed love and faithfulness to his followers in the story, He expressed the same love and faithfulness to his followers today. At this point different ones told how they had experienced the love of Jehesus during the past several days. Hawthorn was quite touched by a couple of the stories. In every case, the person ended up expressing how deeply they loved the Lord Jehesus for how He had revealed Himself to them. Several times during the telling of these events people would just spontaneously speak words of praise to Jehesus or to the Maker. At one point, as someone was praising Jehesus, several others joined in. Soon almost everyone in the room was telling Jehesus how much they loved Him and how good they thought He was. There was more singing, and although it wasn't as impressive as what he had heard in the Great Hall earlier, Hawthorn still loved it. Someone began talking about how he had hurt Jehesus this past week by getting angry and saying hurtful things to his family. Then before the whole group, he asked each member of his family to forgive him. There were some tears and some hugging, after which several different ones prayed for this Makerian and his family. At this point, others also told of personal failures, needs, or concerns. It made Hawthorn think about some of the failures in his own life. He was not surprised to see that much praying was done for each of these people. Although it made Hawthorn uncomfortable to hear the people speaking so openly about their problems, he thought that it would be great to have a group of people like that with whom to share your troubles and to encourage you. All things considered, Hawthorn enjoyed the day, and he thought it was a wonderful way to start a week.

The next morning after breakfast, Cari took Hawthorn for their regular morning walk. Since Hawthorn seemed to have fully recovered his balance and was rapidly regaining his strength, they decided to walk to the top of the Refuge. "Do you think you're ready for a little faster pace today?" Cari asked.

"Yes, I've been wanting to stretch my legs."

"Okay, let's go," Cari nodded. With that she turned and set off up the central passage at a rapid walk. The pace was a little faster than Hawthorn had anticipated, and he was being left behind. He pushed himself to go faster and slowly began to catch up with his companion. Hawthorn thought that after they had spiraled up two levels that Cari would have to slow down, but she didn't. Even in her long dress, she maintained the brisk pace level after level until finally they emerged into the bright sunlight on the watch deck. Only then did she stop.

Hawthorn had kept right with her the whole way, but he was hurting. His breathing was heavy, his leg muscles were burning, and he was sweating. It was some consolation to him to look at Cari and see that she, too, was breathing hard, and her face was wet and flushed. "You did pretty well," she said, smiling at him.

"That was a little more stretching than my legs were expecting," he responded.

"You've been inactive for a while, so I thought you needed the exercise. Plus," she added with a sideways smile, "I wanted to see if you were doing as well as you said you were."

"So did I pass the test?"

"You did all right," she smiled back.

As Hawthorn caught his breath, he began to look around. By turning in a circle, he viewed the entire shore line of Stillwaters. To the southwest, he noticed a tall waterfall cascading from a steep, wooded bluff. The bottom of the falls was hidden by trees, but he could see the break in the shoreline where the water from the falls fed into the lake.

The watch deck itself was bustling with activity. On the east side was the support structure for the long fishing beam, the bottom of which was anchored solidly to the floor of the west side of the watch deck. Some maintenance work was being done on the beam and its support. One crew was doing some kind of repair work on the supporting timber on the east side that lifted the large beam up in the air. He heard some distant yelling from above, and looking up, he could see several Makerians who had climbed out to the very end of the fishing beam doing some work on the rope attached to the end.

""That's not a job I'd want," Hawthorn said out loud as he watched the men working on the end of the beam.

"It's not as scary as it looks," Cari responded.

"How do you know? Have you climbed out there?"

"Several times," was Cari's answer. "I personally think that climbing the perch is a lot scarier."

"What's the *perch*?" Hawthorn wanted to know.

"That's the perch," said Cari, pointing up and to the right. Cari was pointing to the top of a tall, branching cypress limb that was growing up from the west side of the watch deck.

"I had no idea that the Refuge was carved into a living tree!" Hawthorn exclaimed as he gazed up at the swaying branches of the limb growing far above his head.

"When our people were looking for a safe place to make their home many years ago, they found this cypress stump out here in the lake where it had been blasted by lightening. That limb was all that was left of the original tree. Over the years it has been able to get enough nourishment to stay alive, but it doesn't get any bigger."

"Why do you call it the *perch*?" Hawthorn wondered.

"We named it that for several reasons. You see the steps carved into the surface of the limb? That allows us to easily climb up into its branches. Our guards perch up in the upper limbs to watch for enemies. Sometimes the fishers will climb up to spot where the fish are. Also, Tobin the Flyer sometimes uses that large side branch as a place for Nightwing to land."

"Could we climb up there a little ways?"

"Well, we don't have time right now, Thorn. I've got to go change and get ready for my classes."

They started back down the spiraling central passage at a much slower pace than when they came up. This was as much to let their eyes adjust to the dimmer light in the interior as to rest their legs.

"What are your classes like, Cari? Are they for teaching you how to be a Makerian lady?"

"No, not these classes. They are more for teaching us different skills."

"You mean like sewing and cooking?"

"No," Cari giggled, "not exactly. I'll tell you what: let's hurry back, and I'll see if I can get permission for you to come to class with me, then you can see for yourself." There was something about this suggestion that made Hawthorn a little uneasy, but he agreed.

After they got back to the family quarters, Cari left to go find one of her instructors. Ten minutes later she came flying into the room. "You can come!" she yelled as she ran through the family room where Hawthorn and Robbie were playing and on into her bedroom.

Not quite ten minutes later, she came walking back out. The transformation momentarily stunned Hawthorn. The beautifully feminine, long dress had been replaced by a rough leather tunic and leggings, and the tunic was belted with a dark green sash. Her long, flowing hair had been pulled back and coiled tightly behind her head, and in her hand was a tall, worn fighting staff. "I'm ready!" she grinned.

Hawthorn stood speechless. He had never seen her dressed like this. Because Hawthorn was usually resting or playing with Robbie during Cari's class time, he had never actually seen her when she left for class or when she came back. The silence was broken by a knock at the door. Cari ran to it and pulled it open. Two girls Cari's age, dressed just like her, stood there. Both carried staffs.

"Are you ready to go, Cari?" the shorter of the two asked when they saw their friend.

"Yes, I'm all set. Come on, Thorn, let's go." Hawthorn walked over, and Cari introduced him to her friends. The shorter girl was Cari's cousin, Mistral. Hawthorn remembered her being at yesterday's big dinner. The taller girl was one of their close friends, Kaya. Hawthorn was spared the embarrassment of trying to think of something to say by Cari's cousin.

"Come on, let's go, let's go!" she said impatiently as she pushed Kaya encouragingly down the hallway.

For the second time that morning, Hawthorn found himself rapidly ascending the sloping, curved walkway that led up to the watch deck. He followed the three girls out to the large, central area of the open deck. There they joined nine other girls all close to the same age, all dressed the same, all with fighting staffs. Standing with them were four Makerian warriors. Cari pulled Hawthorn up to a very muscular, intimidating-looking Makerian and introduced Hawthorn to him, "Sir Koran, I want you to meet my guest and friend, Hawthorn the Larkin. Hawthorn, this is my chief instructor, Sir Koran."

Hawthorn extended his right hand. He intended to grasp the forearm of Sir Koran in the customary Larkin greeting, but instead Sir Koran grabbed

Hawthorn's extended hand with a firm grip and shook it. Cari introduced Hawthorn to the three other warriors. Each of the three gripped his hand warmly and greeted him. Hawthorn noted that they all called him "Sir Hawthorn".

"You are welcome to be here, Sir Hawthorn," Koran said with some authority. "I hope that you will find our class interesting. There will be much activity in this area in just a few moments, so I suggest that you find a comfortable place to sit over there by those storage boxes. You should be able to see everything quite well from there." Hawthorn thanked Sir Koran, bowed respectfully, then retired to the storage boxes.

"All right, let's begin!" Koran spoke to the group. "Ladies, form!" he barked.

Immediately the girls jumped into two rows of six girls each, all standing at attention with their staffs on their right side. Koran then called on one of the other warriors, Sir Lorris, to lead them in a prayer. Hawthorn didn't know if he would ever get used to all the praying here. He understood why they did it, and he knew that if he felt that he had the right and the ability to pray to the Maker that he'd pray to Him all the time as well. Sir Lorris offered a very sincere prayer asking the Maker to protect each one and to stir each girl's character to work hard to develop her skills so that she would be able to serve others, protect the weak, and please the Lord Jehesus.

After the prayer Sir Koran had some announcements. "Ladies, listen carefully. The training schedule for this week is as follows: tomorrow's training class will be on the bow and arrow; the next day we will use the sling and bo-lo; the following day we will ferry to shore to study wood lore and tracking; the day after that we will work on sting and shield. We'll spend the last day of this week reviewing defensive strategy and attack planning."

"Oh, Sir Koran," came a voice from the back row of girls. "If we play war again, can I be a Renegade?"

"You were a Renegade last time, Myna," came another voice from the back row.

"I was not! I got captured by the Renegades right when everything started, and I had to sit in their silly ol' jail the whole time!"

"Ladies!"

"Then you started helping them."

"Ladies!"

"Well, I got bored."

"Ladies!! Form!!" Sir Koran directed. "I know our guest did not come to hear us argue, so form the circle, and we'll warm up with the staff dance."

The girls quickly formed a circle, all facing inwards with the end of their staves resting on the floor in front of them. Koran walked around the outside of the circle and assigned each girl a number, either one or two. "All right, does everyone know who your partner is? Good!" Turning to the other three warriors with him, Koran ordered, "Start the song."

It was then that Hawthorn noticed that the other three warriors had musical instruments with them. One had a flute; one had a small hand drum with shakers attached to its sides; the other one had a long-necked, hollow gourd with strings attached to it. They began to play a slow, happy song; the second warrior keeping time on his hand drum with slow, steady beats.

As the song began the girls started moving in time with the drum beats. They bounced their staves, turned to the right, twirled them, bounced them, turned to the left, and twirled and bounced them again. When they completed this cycle, they turned to their partner and swung three hard blows against their partner's staff—each attacking and parrying in turn. Then facing center, they twirled their staffs, bounced them, and turned to the right. This last move caused the circle to rotate to the right two steps. Then they repeated the whole thing again. They did this again and again. Each time the beat of the music got faster and faster. Soon the girls' movements became so fast and furious that Hawthorn had trouble keeping up with them. He thought that they would not be able to continue this much longer, but the fast music continued, and so did the dance. Finally the dance ended, and Koran seemed pleased.

"Very good, ladies. I only saw one or two missteps. Now that we're all warmed up and loose, let's begin the training session for today." Koran and his team of instructors began showing the girls defensive and attacking moves with their fighting sticks. They practiced them over and over at half-speed. Then with gloves, pads, and helmets, they practiced them full speed.

Hawthorn was especially observant of Cari. After watching her speed and skill with the staff, he decided that he didn't want to fight her. In fact, it was quite clear to him that all of these girls were very skilled with this weapon.

"What do you think, young one?" spoke a deep, gruff voice from behind him. Hawthorn turned quickly and saw Charlock standing near.

"Good morning, Charlock. I didn't hear you come up."

"So I noticed," his older friend returned.

"They're very good," Hawthorn said, turning back to class. "Their training is so hard and intense."

"Every Makerian must be ready to defend themselves and their home if attacked. There are so few of us, and our enemies are many and strong.

"I have some news for you, Hawthorn," Charlock continued. "The Council of Elders has called you to appear before them and the nobles of Stillwaters."

Chapter sixteen

BEFORE THE COUNCIL

"I'm scared, Charlock," Hawthorn said as he paced nervously back and forth in a large room in Charlock's living quarters. "What will they do to me?"

"What will they do to you?!" his old friend shot back. "Why, they'll hang you up by your toes and pull all your teeth out!" Charlock paused and frowned. "What will they do to you? You're a guest here, Hawthorn. They have invested a great deal of time, effort, and food to make you well. If they were planning on harming you, do you think they would have gone to all that trouble?!"

"No," Hawthorn returned a little embarrassed, "I don't guess they would."

"You've got nothing to fear from the council, young one," Tobin joined in. He was seated at a table with Charlock as their nervous friend paced the room. "The council will try to help you if it can."

"What is this council?" Hawthorn wanted to know.

"It's sometimes called the Great Council. It's also called the Council of Elders and Nobles."

"Are they, like, your leaders?"

"The elders are the real leaders," Charlock said.

"That's right," added Tobin. "The elders are the ones we look to for guidance and direction. The nobles are more like counselors and advisors."

"So what do I tell them?"

"The truth," Charlock said sternly. "Always tell them the truth. If you can't tell them the truth, then politely refuse to answer their question."

"They will want to know who you are and why you are here," Tobin informed him. "Tell them your story, but try to be as brief as you can. They really do want to hear what you've been through, so tell them. But don't waste their time with a lot of unnecessary information. Also, Hawthorn, if you don't have to bring up Eldan's little adventure in the ant nest, I would appreciate it if you didn't, and if Eldan had any sense, he would appreciate it too." Tobin exchanged a knowing look with Charlock.

"Sure, Tobin, I won't bring it up unless they ask me." Hawthorn stopped pacing and sat down again at the table with his two older friends. "You said there are five elders and how many nobles?"

"Eighteen."

"That's a lot of people," Hawthorn said thoughtfully. "Will they all be there?"

"Most of them will be."

"How do I address them?"

"With respect," was Charlock's typical, stern response. "You may use words like *esteemed elders*, or h*onored nobles*, and always remember to say *sir*."

"There will be one lady there," Tobin added, "Betony the Benevolent. You should address her as m*y lady*."

After a moment of thoughtful silence, Hawthorn had another question, "What are the elders like?"

"They are great leaders," Charlock answered without hesitation. "If you knew them as I do, Hawthorn, you would feel the deepest respect and appreciation for these five Makerians."

"Aye, Charlock," Tobin said warmly, "you speak my heart's words as well.

"The Maker poured out great blessings on us when He gave us these leaders," Tobin addressed Hawthorn. "The oldest is Micah, about whom I have already told you."

"Micah is still alive? How old is he?"

"I believe he is seventy-five seasons now. His eyes are clear, his mind is sharp, and his heart is true."

"What about the other two Shaman who were Micah's helpers?" Hawthorn asked. "What were their names? Jasper and somebody?"

"Jasper and Linden," Tobin answered. "Jasper was asked to serve with the elders just last year. He is the youngest of the elders. I believe he is fifty-eight or fifty-nine seasons old."

"What about Linden?"

"Linden died many years ago of an illness. The sad thing is that, if we knew then what we know now, he probably could have been saved. That is sad for us, not for Linden. I envy him the time he has had with the Maker and the Lord Jehesus.

"The other three elders are Rizopus, Nettle, and Coriander," Tobin continued. "They all love the Lord, and they love us. Their wisdom and insight are amazing. Don't try to fool them, Hawthorn. They will see right through you."

"Tobin the Flyer is himself a noble," Charlock interjected. "He is very familiar with the elders and every member of the council. He and I have offered to be your attendants at the council meeting. We will offer you advice if you need it or answer any questions you may have."

"I can't tell you both how grateful I am for your help, and these clothes you've brought me are the finest I've ever worn."

"Your clothes looked a bit rough for all they'd been through," Tobin said with a sideways glance. "We wanted you to make a good impression on the council, so we thought we'd dress you up in some of Eldan's old clothes that he has outgrown."

"Tobin and I have a plan to try to help you," said Charlock, "but it will have a much greater chance of success if the council will support it."

"A plan?" Hawthorn asked excitedly. "What is it?"

"We'll tell you our idea on the way to the council meeting," Charlock responded. "Are you ready to go?"

"No," Hawthorn said nervously, "but we might as well get it over with."

When they arrived at the council hall, they were met outside the large double doors by a young Makerian not much older than Hawthorn.

"Hawthorn, this is Anselm," Tobin said by way of introduction. "Anselm is one of the council ministers."

They shook hands in the typical Makerian way of greeting.

"What's a council minister?" Hawthorn questioned. He was curious at such a grand title being applied to such a young Makerian.

"Council ministers are just servants of the council," Anselm answered with half a smile. "A lot of things need to be done in order for the elders and nobles to be able to do their work most efficiently. Whatever needs doing, the council ministers are available to serve.

"It will be my privilege to introduce you to the council in just a few moments," Anselm continued. "How shall I introduce you?"

"I am Hawthorn, son of Savin, of the Third Clan of Larkin."

"Do you have a title I should use?"

"No, I'm just a youth," Hawthorn responded humbly.

"He's a Larkin hunter," Charlock stated to Anselm. Hawthorn started to protest that statement, but Charlock quickly cut him off.

"Did you lie to me about killing the mooflon?" Charlock asked in his typically gruff manner.

"No, but . . ."

"Then you are a Larkin hunter."

"But, Charlock, I have not yet been given that honor by my clan."

"That's because they don't yet know that you killed the mooflon. Since we know, we will give you the honor now.

"You will introduce him as 'Hawthorn, son of Savin, a Larkin Hunter from the Third Clan,'" Charlock instructed Anselm.

"I shall do so, sir," Anselm responded respectfully.

In a few minutes a small panel on one of the large double doors opened up, and Anselm stepped up to the opening. He held a short conversation with someone on the other side of the door, then the panel was closed.

"Sir Hawthorn," Anselm said formally, "the elders and nobles of the council will entertain you presently."

It wasn't long before the large doors cracked open. A brown-haired young lady in a long, yellow dress appeared and nodded at Anselm. "It is time," he announced. "Sir Hawthorn, if you and your honored attendants would follow me please." Turning, Anselm stepped confidently toward the large doors as they both swung wide to allow the party entrance into the council chamber.

Hawthorn was immediately impressed with the large room he entered. It was not nearly as large as the great hall where they had worshipped the Maker, but the room was still spacious. The council chamber had six sides. The ceiling was arched and extended almost three stories. The three walls in front of Hawthorn were almost entirely covered with shelves and cubby holes, and all of this space was filled with books, parchments, and scrolls.

A balcony ran around the entire chamber. Ladders with handrails reached up to the balcony at several places around the large room. From the balcony up, all six walls were covered with shelves, cubby holes, and cabinets of various sizes, all containing books, records, and charts. Hawthorn was stunned by the sheer volume of written material.

He followed Anselm out to the center of the room. Before him was a beautifully carved walnut table. Behind this table sat two Makerians, one very old and one very young. The old one, obviously, was one of the elders. Hawthorn assumed the young one to be a scribe or recorder.

Flanking this table on either side were two other carved tables sitting at angles to the central one. Behind each of these tables sat two elders. To

Hawthorn's right and left were seated the nobles. The chairs were arranged in two rows, with five in front and a second row of four behind them raised a little higher than the front row.

Hawthorn noticed maybe eight to ten other young Makerians stationed in various locations around the room. Two more were positioned close to the nobles' chairs. Another council minister was seated at a table near the back wall. A large stack of books was placed on top of this table, and the young Makerian seemed to be busy with some sort of research. Two more ministers were seated in the balcony awaiting orders to retrieve some needed book or chart.

Anselm began addressing the council. With a few flowery phrases he introduced Hawthorn to the council members using the title of *Larkin Hunter*. If he hadn't known better, Hawthorn would have thought that he was an important person.

"Welcome to Stillwaters," said the old Makerian seated directly in front of him. "My name is Micah. Seated at the table to my right are my fellow elders, Coriander and Nettle. At the table to my left are Elders Jasper and Rizopus."

Hawthorn felt a bit awed by this Makerian about whom he had heard so much. Micah's hair was very white, with bushy, white eyebrows shading his pale blue eyes. His white beard was trimmed short, and he had a large nose. Hawthorn bowed respectfully to each of the three tables.

"Seated to your left and right are many of our distinguished and honored nobles," he continued. "They are here to give the elders counsel and advice, but I'm reasonably sure that your two attendants, Tobin the Flyer and the Good Charlock, have explained to you who we are.

Micah continued gently. "You must be a little intimidated by all of us here. Please do not feel as if you are on trial. We want you to know that we consider you our guest here at Stillwaters, but we do have some questions that we would like to ask you."

"Yes," snapped a voice on Hawthorn's left, "like 'Who are you' and 'What are you doing here?'" The questions came from a bald, very thin elder sitting at the outside end of the left table.

"Listen to you, Nettle," returned the elder sitting next to the first speaker. "Here we are telling this young Larkin that he is our guest, and you start barking questions at him like he has stolen your bowl of plum pudding." The second speaker was almost the exact opposite of the one called Nettle. He had a thick, white beard down to his belly, which was quite large and round. Hawthorn remembered that this was Elder Coriander, and the young Larkin instantly liked him.

233

"Now don't start in on me again, Coriander!" Nettle responded. "I'm just trying to get some information."

"Well, show some compassion to the lad. He has obviously been through a lot, and he is probably feeling a little scared right now."

"Compassion?" Nettle questioned. "Why, I've got all the compassion in the world. Just ask anybody. But compassion won't get the job done."

"Just don't be so hard on the lad," Coriander persisted.

"Certainly, certainly. I understand your concerns, and I will try to be gentler.

"So," Nettle addressed Hawthorn again, "Who are you, and what are you doing here?"Coriander rolled his eyes and shook his head.

"I believe we already know who he is," Micah spoke. "Could you please tell us about the circumstances that led to your being brought to us?"

Hawthorn tried to remember all the proper terms of respect that he had been taught as he began his speech. He told them briefly of the hunting trip. He mentioned his father, his friend Poke, and Poke's father. He told them about the mooflons they had killed. He described his capture and the ambush of their hunting party, though he omitted some of the torment through which Poke and he went. He briefly told of their escape and recapture and of Wolf's attempt to kill them both. He spoke in greater detail when he described how Eldan rescued him and cared for his head injury. As Hawthorn was telling about the part Tobin the Flyer had played in helping him, he noticed that his friend, who was standing beside him, shifted nervously. To ease Tobin's discomfort, Hawthorn moved quickly through that portion of his narrative. As Hawthorn finished his story, he took time to thank Taumis the Gentle, his daughter Carineda, and their family for nursing him back to health. "I owe the Makerian people my life. I hope that someday I will be able to repay you."

"Young friend, you owe us nothing." It was the voice of Micah. "All that has been done for you is what the Maker wanted; we have only done His will. The Maker and His Son, Jehesus, love you very much, and it is His desire that we communicate His love to you. What we have done for you is our way of showing you that love. If you feel that you have a debt to pay, then you owe it to the Maker, not to us."

At this point, Micah called for Taumis the Gentle to report on Hawthorn's physical health. Taumis sat in the second row of seats to Hawthorn's left. He stood and gave a report on Hawthorn's head injuries, his treatment, and his recovery. He described Hawthorn's injuries as severe and called it a difficult case. He then explained that his daughter Carineda had been given responsibility for treating Hawthorn. During the most critical period, Cari had sat by Hawthorn's bed for two days, refusing to take a break even to rest. She had constantly monitored his condition, changing his medication time and time again in response to the changing needs of her patient.

Hawthorn stood there amazed at Taumis' report. He had had no idea of all that Cari had done to save him.

As Taumis finished his report to the council, he stated that Hawthorn was now considered fully recovered and fit to travel, although he did mention that it would be very bad for Hawthorn if he received another head injury anytime soon.

"Thank you, Taumis the Gentle," Micah nodded, "and please express to your good daughter, Carineda, our most profound thanks for the diligent and faithful service that she has rendered to our Larkin guest."

Turning to Hawthorn, Micah spoke again, "Your healer has declared you fit to travel. You should be able to return to your home by accompanying the next Ranger patrol heading in that direction, if that is your wish."

Hawthorn swallowed hard, cleared his throat, and spoke, "Honored Elders and Nobles, I am very grateful for all of the care and kindness that you have shown me. I do wish to return to my home, but not until I find out what happened to my father and friends, and not until I have done everything in my power to help rescue my friend from the Renegades. I have no right to ask you, but I have no one else to whom to turn for help. Will you please help me rescue my friend Poke and search for my father and friends?"

"Do you realize what you are asking of us, Larkin?" snapped Nettle.

"You ask a hard thing," came the voice of Jasper from the right.

"The search for survivors of the ambush would not be so terribly hard," said Coriander.

"No, of course not!" Nettle answered. "The Rangers could do that during their normal patrols. But freeing Renegade slaves is another matter all together. You know where Renegades put their slaves."

"Exactly," Jasper spoke again. "To free this Larkin captive, a rescue party would have to enter the Renegade Lair. We would be risking a number of lives."

"You have said nothing, Rizopus," Micah spoke. "What are your thoughts?"

The Elder Rizopus was a thin, balding Makerian with a gray, scraggly beard and a very prominent chin. As he spoke, Hawthorn was struck by the fact that Rizopus had no teeth. "Fer myself," Rizopus grinned a big, toothless smile, "I would love to deprive the Renegades of another slave. I wouldn't want any of our people gettin' kilt over it, but if'n it could be done, it would certainly be worth thinkin' about."

235

"Most Honored Elders and Nobles, may I speak?" Charlock's deep, gruff voice boomed across the hall.

"Certainly, Good Charlock," Micah responded. "Your counsel is welcome."

"To attempt to rescue someone from the Renegade stronghold would be extremely dangerous, and I can understand your reluctance to undertake such a venture. My reason tells me that it is indeed a foolish thing to attempt, but my heart will not let me walk away from it. This young Larkin here, his friend Poke, and their families—I know them. I know them well. I spent most of this last year personally training this young Larkin and his friend, Poke, in the ways of a hunter and warrior. They are like my own nephews. My conscience will not let me rest until I have done everything in my power to help my friends. Hawthorn and I will go together to the Renegade Lair and do what we can."

When Charlock finished his short declaration, there were a few moments of thoughtful silence.

"Honored elders and nobles, may I speak?" It was Tobin the Flyer. Micah nodded, and Tobin continued, "In the short time that I have known Hawthorn, son of Savin, I have found him to be a Larkin of noble character. He is honest, and he has the courage to seek truth. Also, as you have heard, he is loyal and faithful to his friends. If he and Charlock are going to try to save their friend, then I must help them."

"You could all be risking your lives for nothing," Nettle challenged. "How do you know that Hawthorn's friend is still a captive? He could have escaped, or he could have been killed before he even reached the Lair."

"What you say is certainly possible," answered Tobin. "But we have evidence to indicate that several members of Hawthorn's hunting party are being held captive in the Renegade stronghold.

"Yesterday, Captain Bannock and his squad of Rangers returned. They had been scouting the southeast woods." As he said this, Tobin turned and pointed up on the wall behind him and to his left.

As Hawthorn looked back to see where Tobin was pointing, he was shocked. Though the upper portion of the back three walls above the balcony was shelves of books and charts, below the balcony, the back three walls had been carved and painted into a detailed relief map of the land surrounding Stillwaters. The Stillwaters Lake could clearly be seen in the center of the huge carving. It was painted a brilliant blue, and on its northern end was painted the Refuge. To the east of the lake was a small line of green trees, then the expanse of the meadow. The meadow was painted a golden brown color and had several white lines crisscrossing through it. Hawthorn decided that these white lines must be trails. The young Larkin instinctively let his eyes move past the meadow and on eastward through the green forest to the area where his own home was located. To his further surprise, he saw that the precise location of the Keep, the home for his own clan, was marked with a bright yellow spot. As he let his eyes move over the map, he saw that the home for each Larkin clan was similarly marked. When Hawthorn looked at the southeast area of the map to which Tobin was pointing, he saw a bright red spot placed on top of what, to Hawthorn, looked like a carving of a mountain. "That red spot must be the location of the Renegade Lair," he thought to himself.

"As the Rangers moved through the area to the west of the Renegade stronghold, they were contacted by my brother, Eldan," Tobin continued. "He sent a message to me through Bannock that he wanted me to meet him in the woods west of the Renegade Lair as soon as possible. Last night I flew out on Nightwing and was able to talk with Eldan.

"It seems that when I flew off with Hawthorn to bring him here, Eldan decided to go back to see what had happened to Hawthorn's friend, Poke. He found the place where Poke and Hawthorn had been captured after their escape, but Poke had been carried away."

"That's an encouraging sign," Micah said thoughtfully.

"Yes, it is," agreed Tobin. "It means that Poke is alive, or at least he was at that time."

"It also means that he was in good enough shape that they thought he would make a worthwhile slave," said Coriander.

"Eldan thought that if he hurried, he might have a chance to get to the Renegade Lair in time to see in what kind of shape Poke was," Tobin continued. "He traveled as quickly as he could through the forest, arriving at the Lair without being detected. Eldan saw a Renegade scouting party arrive with two captives dressed like Larkin, neither of which were youths.

"Hawthorn had said that he and Poke had been traveling with a large Renegade War party and that they were the only two captives, so Eldan figured, and I agree with him, that these two were probably part of a Larkin rescue party. The Larkin would never send just two warriors on a rescue mission, so Eldan backtracked, looking for signs of other Larkin.

"Eldan eventually found where the Larkin had camped and where they had run into the Renegade scouting party. He found where two of the Larkin had escaped through the brush. He trailed them for some distance toward the Lair, but he lost their trail when they apparently climbed into the trees to travel. By this time, it was obvious that they were headed to the Lair, so Eldan made his way back there as quickly as he dared. When he arrived in the Lair's vicinity, there was some commotion. Apparently at least one and possibly both of the Larkin he had been trailing had been captured."

"So that means you can expect no help from the Larkin," came a sharp voice from the table at the left.

"Maybe and maybe not, Elder Nettle," Tobin continued. "We all know of the resourcefulness of our Larkin neighbors. It's very possible that their capture might be part of their plan to enter the Lair to get to their friends."

"Excuse me, Noble Tobin," Nettle interrupted, "but what difference does it make whether it was planned or not? They are still captives of the Renegades, and they're still locked up in the slave mines, and no one can escape the slave mines."

"They can if we help them," Tobin returned confidently.

"Now how in the world do you expect to do that?" Nettle shot back.

"Don't attack him, Nettle."

"Coriander, why do you have to criticize me?! I'm only searching for facts."

"Well, it sounds like you're hunting for snakes."

"Snakes! Well, I never! Coriander, I'll have you know that I'm being just as kind and caring as I know how to be."

"Now, I agree with you there."

"Please continue, Noble Tobin," Micah said.

"Snakes!" muttered Nettle under his breath. "What a thing to say."

"Eldan wanted to talk with me," Tobin continued, "because he remembered something that our father had told us. All of you, except maybe Hawthorn here, know my father's history. Being a Renegade of high rank, he was put in charge of guarding the Lair for a time. One of his patrols discovered a crevice in the rock high up on the hill above the Lair. Some time later my father took with him three other Renegades and explored this crevice. What he found was a chimney-like passageway that dropped into the depths of the cavernous home of the Renegades. Using ropes and projecting rocks, they descended this shaft, coming out eventually in the upper part of a large room near the slave mines in an unused portion of the cavern."

"Noble Tobin," Nettle said condescendingly, "if the Renegades found the crevice, then you know it is well guarded."

"There is a very good chance that it is not guarded at all. At that time my father was not well liked by some of the Renegade leaders. Not knowing what might happen in the future, he decided to keep this information to himself."

"Why would he want to keep that information to himself?" asked Jasper.

"He was concerned that if his enemies gained enough power, they might throw him in the slave mines. If that ever happened, then he would be able to escape through the shaft."

"But the other Renegades who were with him—surely they would have told," Nettle reasoned.

"Those three Renegades were very loyal to my father. If he had been made a slave, they would have been too. They were as eager to keep the secret as my father. These three all died before my father became a Makerian. At the time my father passed this information on to my brother and me, he felt certain that he was the only one who knew about the crevice."

"Don't you think it's likely some other Renegade patrol would have found it just as your father did?" Nettle cross-examined.

"It is possible, sir, but I don't think it likely."

"And why not?!" Nettle wanted to know.

"Because my father and his friends hid it. They covered it over with bark, brush, and rocks. Then they marked the spot in a secret way so that they could find it again."

"Then how will you find it?"

"My father drew a map and described on it how they marked the spot."

"Honored Elders and Nobles," Charlock's commanding voice boomed across the room, "we are well aware of the risks of undertaking such a plan, but we've thought it through. The plan is a good one. Loyalty to friends and family demands that Hawthorn and I try to help them. We appreciate the help offered to us by Tobin the Flyer and his brother more than we will ever be able to show them. We are not asking the elders to organize a rescue mission. We are simply letting you know that we have to try to help our friends. If you feel so moved, we would be grateful for any supplies and equipment that you would be willing to let us use."

"If I were twenty seasons younger, I'd join you," Rhizopus said in earnest through a toothless smile.

"If you were twenty seasons younger," Nettle retorted, "you'd still be older than dirt." Coriander shot a hard look straight at Nettle.

"A-And I mean that in the nicest way possible," Nettle quickly added.

The meeting with the elders and nobles had been over almost two hours when Tobin came in to report the elder's decision.

"Have you been meeting with the elders and nobles all this time?" asked Hawthorn.

"They had a few questions," Tobin answered, "and there was more discussion about what we intend to do. But most of the time was spent in prayer."

"Do they support us?" Charlock wanted to know.

"Well, they aren't willing to send a Ranger troop with us, but they have prayed for our success. We have permission to take all the supplies and equipment we think we might need, and word is being sent to all the Rangers and guards in the Refuge to see if any might want to volunteer to go with us."

"That's wonderful!" Charlock had a surprised tone in his voice. "That's a great deal more than I expected."

"I expected them to supply us," Tobin said, "but the offer to solicit volunteers for us was a special blessing."

"Do you think we'll get some volunteers?" Hawthorn wanted to know.

"Hmm," Tobin said thoughtfully, "I think it would be safe to count on at least five."

"Five!" Hawthorn said excitedly, "Do you really think so?"

"I will be very surprised if we don't get at least that many. There are a fair number of former Renegades among the Makerians, and most of them would give a lot to try to make right some of the wrongs in their past."

"So they can go to the Maker's home when they die?"

"No, young one. When you are ready to make Jehesus Lord, part of doing that is trusting completely that when Jehesus suffered and died, his death paid the full price for all of your sins. So when these former Renegades made the choice to trust in the Lord Jehesus, to repent of their sins, and become his followers, every one of their past sins was paid for by the blood of Jehesus. The Maker forgave them, made them His children, and gave them the right to live with Him and the Lord Jehesus in heaven forever. The sacrifice of the Lord Jehesus was so perfect and so precious to the Maker that not only are all of their past sins forgiven, but any sin they commit in the future is forgiven also, as long as they hold fast their trust in Jehesus firm to the end."

"But if that's true," Hawthorn asked, "why are they so anxious to make up for what they've done? If the Maker's forgiven them, then they should forgive themselves."

"It's not a matter of forgiveness, young one. It's a matter of responsibility and duty. Even though the Maker may forgive our sins, there are still consequences that we must face. If you steal something, the Maker can forgive you, but you still have to deal with the consequences of your theft. The people from whom you stole are still without their possessions. True repentance requires that you give back what you stole, or if you can't, then you work to make restitution.

"Hawthorn, some of these former Renegades participated in ambushes and attacks on innocent people. Some of the people they killed; others they captured and made slaves. If you were one of these former Renegades and had given your life to do the Maker's will in every area of your life, and you had the chance to go back and try to free some of those slaves, would you volunteer?"

"Yes, I would have to," Hawthorn answered thoughtfully.

"I think we can count on some volunteers," Tobin said confidently.

As it turned out, they got twelve volunteers. They would have gotten quite a few more, but several of the Ranger patrols were away from Stillwaters at this time.

It took a day and a half to assemble the rescue team and pack the supplies and equipment. Hawthorn was absolutely stunned to find that Cari was a part of the team.

"Charlock, do you see who's here?! Carineda, the daughter of Taumis the Gentle, is standing over there, and she said she was going on the rescue with us."

"It's all right," Charlock said calmly as he was going over the supply packs. "Her father gave permission for her."

"But, Charlock," Hawthorn said anxiously, "we can't let her go. It's too dangerous!"

Charlock stood up and looked directly at his young friend. "We need a healer with us. There's no telling what kind of shape those poor souls will be in when we get them out."

"I know we need a healer, but not Cari!"

"Listen to me." There was a bit of a growl in Charlock's voice. "She is the best healer who's able to go with us right now."

"But what if we have to fight Renegades?"

"Didn't you see how she handled a staff? Well, she handles a sting, shield, a bow, a spear, a bo-lo, and darts equally as well. She handles a sling better. And if you're concerned about how she handles herself on the trail, don't be. She's completed two expeditions already. This will be her third. Now do I need to say anymore?"

"Yes. What's a bo-lo and darts?"

Charlock chuckled under his beard. "I'll show you when we go to the weapons room."

When all the supplies for the rescue mission were packed and checked, the word was given to sling packs. The rescue party marched out of the store room and down the hallway. Hawthorn had no idea where they were going, but he figured that they would eventually wind up at the Renegade Lair, so he just followed along.

They came out onto the central passage and began marching down the spiral walkway deeper into the Refuge. Since he was carrying a heavy pack, Hawthorn was glad that they were going down instead of up. They had traveled down the wide, spiraling walkway for several minutes, then they were led into a wide, arched side passage. This passage had several heavy doors on either side. After this, they passed through a set of tall, double doors which opened into another short hallway. This brought them to the main gate of the Refuge. The main gate consisted of two very thick and very heavy doors which appeared to Hawthorn to be carved of iron wood. The gates were open, but their party stopped just inside them for several moments while Charlock and Tobin talked with some guards at the entrance. This was fine with Hawthorn; he needed the time to let his eyes adjust to the bright sunlight reflecting in through the open doors.

As they marched through the gate, Hawthorn's eyes were busy. They were walking out onto a wide and tall covered porch that had been carved in the side of the Refuge about two-Larkin high above the surface of the water. The outer edge of the large porch had been carved to form a thick wall about chest high. Narrow notches through which archers could shoot had been cut into the wall at frequent intervals along its length. Looking up, Hawthorn saw that suspended above them was a large and heavy door-like slab of iron wood cut to fit the gateway through which he had just walked. It was hinged to the top of the frame of the main gate and was suspended by strong ropes running from the outer end of the suspended door and extending up into holes in the roof. Obviously the plan for this structure was for those ropes to be released from above if enemy troops overran the wall and tried to storm the gates. The huge, suspended door would swing down, sealing the entrance. Those inside would then lock the door in place and close the double doors of the main gate. Any enemy would have to chop through two thicknesses of iron wood to get in. Looking back up at the roof, Hawthorn could see many holes cut through it. By using those holes in the chamber above, the archers would make short work of anyone trying to chop through the gates.

They marched out to an opening in the center of the wall where a drawbridge-like ramp had been lowered to the surface of the water. At the lowered end of the ramp waited the Turtle, the large, rectangular watercraft Hawthorn had seen moving across the lake.

"All right!" Hawthorn said to Cari, who was standing near him. "We get to ride on the Turtle!"

"Sorry, Thorn," Cari responded. "Our packs and equipment get to ride, but we have to walk to shore."

"Walk! You can't be serious."

"There's not enough room on the Turtle to carry all of us and our supplies without having to make three trips there and back, and that would take most of the day. So we let the Turtle haul our packs, and we walk to shore through a tunnel that runs under the lake and comes out over there on the shore."

It only took a few minutes for the volunteers to store their packs and equipment on board the barge, then Charlock led his party back into the Refuge. As they made their way along the main hallway, Charlock stopped next to two sentries. He spoke to them a few moments, then showed them a piece of parchment with a wax seal on the bottom. After viewing the parchment, one of the sentries nodded to Charlock. Walking over to a nearby door, he opened it and invited Charlock in. Charlock turned and motioned for Hawthorn to follow him. Hawthorn couldn't see much in the darkened room at first. He saw the dim form of the sentry standing in the middle of the room. The sentry reached up and grasped a round object suspended from the ceiling. As he shook the sphere, yellowish-green light burst from it, revealing a room full of hand weapons.

"Take your pick," Charlock said. "The Council has given their permission for you to arm yourself from our stores." Hawthorn was bewildered by the mass of weapons. "Well, don't take all day. Get a move on!"

With a start, the young Larkin began searching around him for what he needed. To his right were several boxes full of flint knives. They all seemed well made. The first one he picked up was a little too long to fit in his boot. His second choice was better. It was the right length with a good, sharp edge. The carved, wooden handle with leather wrapping was a little thicker than he liked, but he would get used to it. He also picked out a sling, a short bow with recurved ends, and a quiver of arrows.

"You'll need one of these," Charlock said from the other side of the room. He was holding up a sting and sheath. Charlock helped him find one that was a good length and balanced for his arm. There were rows of plain, rounded shields hanging from the walls. Some were made of wood covered with leather, but some were carved from large fish scales. Hawthorn picked up one of the scale shields. It was so light he doubted that it would be much protection.

Charlock unslung his own shield. Its surface was painted a dark green, and his own personal emblems were painted on it in black. He turned it over so Hawthorn could see the inside of his shield. It was made from a large fish scale.

"You trust it?" Hawthorn asked.

"It's tougher than wood and a whole lot lighter."

Hawthorn grabbed a scale shield and slung it on his back. Charlock started to leave. "Wait a moment," Hawthorn stopped him. "What are the weapons you were going to show me?"

Charlock stopped, looked at his young friend, then walked over to a bin and pulled out what looked to Hawthorn to be a giant arrow. It was a long shaft as thick as three of Hawthorn's fingers, with a heavy spearhead on one end and feathers on the other.

"This is a dart," said Charlock, fingering the large, feathered shaft. "You throw it with one of these." From another wooden chest, Charlock had pulled out a carved, wooden stick as long as the distance between his elbow and the end of his fingers. The stick had a leather-wrapped handle on one end, and it was carved into a hook on the other. A fired, clay ball had been fitted to the stick near the hook end for weight. "You hook the handle into the end of the dart, then using the handle, you throw it like a spear. The weighted handle lets you throw the dart with a lot more power than without it."

Hawthorn studied the weapon for a few moments. "Okay, now what's a bo-lo?"

Further down the wall, Charlock found some long pegs with a lot of leather straps hanging from them. He reached up and pulled one of the straps. Charlock held it out from him at about head height. The strap hung down from his hand. At the level of his waist the strap divided into two. At the lower end of these two straps were tied two round rocks, one to each strap.

"What do you do with that?" Hawthorn wanted to know.

"Well, I don't have room to show you here, but you whirl it over your head and throw it at your enemy. You want the bo-lo to hit them right here, where it splits. Then both weights fly around and around them, tightly binding them."

"Are we going on an expedition, or are you guys going to play in the weapons room all day?" It was a Ranger in their group that everyone called Turk.

Charlock's cheeks were red as he replaced the bo-lo and headed for the door. "Come on," he growled as he passed by Hawthorn.

They returned to the central passage and descended two more levels before they marched into a sloping side passage. The opening to this passage was unlike the others Hawthorn had seen in that this one was protected by two heavy ironwood doors similar to what he had seen at the main gate. Two sentries stood guard beside the two open doors.

Charlock stopped just long enough to say a few words to one of the guards and show him the parchment he carried. Returning Charlock's sheet, the guard nodded and waved the party through.

All the other passageways through which Hawthorn had traveled in the Refuge had been level except for the spiraled central passage. This one they had just entered sloped steeply downward. There were several places where the passage dropped off so severely that the walkway had been cut into stairs. After descending for quite some time, the sloping passage eventually began to level out. Hawthorn realized that this passage was carved through one of the roots of the great cypress stump that formed the Makerian refuge. He felt uncomfortable when he thought of all that water over his head.

He noticed some odd designs carved into the wooden walls. Every so often in this level part of the passageway, Hawthorn saw circles cut deeply into the wall. They were very noticeable because the center of each circle was painted a bright red. It didn't make sense to him at first until he saw two guards stationed in this part, both of them carrying large hammers.

Hawthorn's heart leaped into his throat when he realized the purpose of the hammers. This passageway was obviously the main way to get from the Refuge to the shore. That made it the best way to get enemy forces into the Refuge. In order to protect the Refuge from enemy attack, several circular plugs had been cut into the wall and painted so they would be easily spotted in a hurry. If an enemy force tried to get through this passage, the guards would hit the plugs with their heavy hammers, driving out the plugs and letting in the water.

"That would pretty much stop an attack before it ever even got started," Hawthorn thought to himself.

Soon they were climbing steps. Hawthorn was very glad he wasn't carrying his heavy pack. After a while the way became very steep, then it became steps that circled straight upwards. After a long, spiraling climb, Hawthorn found himself in a small room with two guards standing on either side. He followed his party through a small doorway and enjoyed the smell of fresh air pouring through. A short hallway led to a second doorway through which streamed bright sunlight.

It took a little while for Hawthorn's eyes to adjust to the brightness. He heard some voices to his left, and turning, he saw the paddle barge being unloaded where it had docked in a special place close by on shore. Looking past it, he saw the Refuge for the first time. Even from this distance, it was quite an impressive stronghold.

Turning around, he wanted to see what the land gate to the Refuge looked like. Spread out along the land bordering the shore was a forest of cypress knees. These were the woody projections from the roots of the cypress trees that stuck up from the ground. They were broader at the base than at the top and formed wooden towers of varying heights. The one immediately behind him contained the gate to the Refuge. He noticed that many of the other cypress knees had doors and occasionally windows carved in them. He didn't know if these were other passageways or dwelling places. He saw so many people coming and going around him that Hawthorn finally decided that a lot of the carved cypress knees must be dwellings.

He had to hurry to catch up with the rest of his party as he saw them marching off to the west parallel to the shore. "Hey, Turk!" Hawthorn called as he saw the Ranger moving toward the back of the line.

"Well, there you are. Charlock sent me back to be sure that you didn't get eaten by a snappin' turtle."

"Thanks," Hawthorn said nervously, unsure of whether Turk was kidding about the snapping turtle or not. "I'm not very familiar with this area, but aren't we headed away from where we need to be going?"

"Well, bog me down! You're quite a sharp cookie, you are. You're right as rain, Thorny, old boy. The Renegade's Lair is way off to the southeast, and we're headed west. I guess that would seem a bit peculiar if you didn't know what we were doin'."

"So . . . what ARE we doing?" Hawthorn wanted to know.

"Well, I suppose you might call this a shortcut."

"A shortcut?"

"Um-hmm, in a manner of speakin', o' course."

"Do you think you could tell me a little about this shortcut?"

"Yeah, yeah, I suppose I could; but, uh, well, you know—some things a person's just got to experience for hisself. Why don't we just let it be a surprise? You like surprises, don't cha?"

Hawthorn felt a familiar nervous knot beginning to form in his stomach. He didn't like surprises. He didn't like them at all.

STILLWATERS

ChAPTER SEVENTEEN

THE WOMPUS RAT

Rush was getting edgy. He had had almost no sleep for the last three days. His only hope to remain undiscovered in the Renegade Lair was to try to blend in unnoticed among all his enemies. So far he had been able to do this by staying on the move. Fortunately the Renegades were not very disciplined or organized. Consequently, there was a lot of random moving around with everyone pursuing their own concerns, except for the occasional work detail that came marching through.

When the last patrols had come in and the gates were shut, most evenings were consumed with a lot of eating, drinking, boasting, fighting, telling the latest news, and playing of games. The games mostly involved a lot of wagering and usually ended in more fighting. This went on until quite late, at which time most of the Renegades would wander off to their various sleeping quarters. That's when the chance of discovery became greatest for Rush.

The Renegades were divided into five separate tribal groups, and for good reason, none of them trusted each other. The top leaders of the five tribes formed a kind of council that made laws and decisions for all the Renegades. From all Rush had heard and seen, there was a great deal of jealousy and hatred expressed among them. In the three days he had been in the Lair, Rush had seen two Renegades killed in fights.

Whenever they went to bed, for protection they always slept with their tribal group. Rush didn't dare sleep with any of the groups, since they would have quickly discovered that he didn't belong with them. The first night he spent in the large, central cavern pretending to be so drunk that he passed out with several other Renegades who actually had drunk themselves unconscious. He thought that was a pretty good plan until the drunk closest to him got sick. Between the smells and the snoring, he got no sleep that night. The next night he found a deep crevice behind a boulder in the dark tunnel leading to the slave cells in which to sleep. He was hidden well enough, but the rocky floor of the crevice was so uncomfortable that he wasn't able to sleep much then either.

Though he was tired, Rush had not wasted his time. After much careful thought, he had finally decided on a plan of escape. But he didn't like it, because its chances of success were not very good.

The plan itself was quite simple. He would pick a quiet time when most of the Lair was asleep, then descend to the slave cells, overpower the guards, and free the slaves. He would provide them with what arms and supplies he could sneak from the Renegades. At that point, the really difficult part of the plan would come. He and the fifty or sixty slaves would have to ascend into the main part of the Lair, slip past the sleeping tribal groups, and work their way quietly up the passage leading to the main gate. They would next have to overpower the gate guards without alarming the whole Lair, open the gate, and flee into the forest. At least that was what was supposed to happen. Rush knew that there were many things that could go wrong in a plan like this, but it was the only plan he had, so he accepted it. If something did go wrong once the escape was begun, they would either have to fight their way out or face being killed or recaptured.

Rush knew that it was more than he could hope for all of them to get to the main gate without being discovered. He figured that their best chance of success was for him to try to provide enough weapons for the slaves to effectively defend themselves.

He decided to use the crevice in the slave cell tunnel to store the weapons and supplies he got. So far he had managed to collect seven knives, four bows, fifteen arrows, five war clubs, six cloaks, and two water packs. He knew that he would be able to lift more weapons later in the evening when all the drinking would start up again.

Food, on the other hand, was much harder to come by. He had only been able to garner a small sack of dried meat and about the same amount of dried fruit. He knew that he had to come up with more food, because if they made it out of the Lair, they would have to move fast and far. For the first day or two they would not have time to hunt for food.

With all of his moving around through the Lair, Rush had been able to locate the store rooms, but getting into them would require some planning.

Because all of the Renegades were thieves and not to be trusted, there were at least three guards posted at each store room at all times. Rush decided to try to get into one of the store rooms as soon as the drinking and partying started that evening.

As it turned out, the Renegades actually helped Rush implement his plan. The three scouting parties that had been sent out that morning had all been very successful in finding food. All total, five large mooflon had been brought in, as well as a huge supply of wild grapes, blackberries, and grains. Everyone was very excited about their success, and a wild celebration started early in the evening.

Rush pretended to be partially drunk as he staggered into the passageway where his targeted storeroom was. As he approached the three guards, they eyed him suspiciously. Rush threw up his hand to them in a carefree greeting. He took a long drink from his wineskin, and as he did so, he leaned his back against the smooth rock wall and slid down to the floor. Finally, he lowered the wineskin and gave the three guards a wide, silly grin. "Thunderation!" Rush laughed. "What a feast! I ain't never seen so much food and drink in all my life!" As he said this, he took a very large bite out of the roast in his hand. The grease from the meat ran down his beard, and Rush rolled his eyes back into his head and hummed in ecstasy as he chewed.

"Say, that looks pretty good, mate. How's about sharin' a bite with three poor blokes stuck on guard duty?"

"I ain't givin' away me supper!" Rush growled. "Besides, there's meat and grog aplenty out there. Why don't you go get your own?" With that Rush pretended to take another long drink from the wineskin.

"Say, Gash, why don't we?" said one of the guards, whose eyes were riveted on Rush's wineskin.

"Why don't we what?" mumbled the guard who was called Gash.

"Why don't we go get some food and drink for us?"

"Cuz we're on guard duty, you lunkhead! The cap'n would flay us if he finds us gone."

"But all the best food and drink'll be gone by the time we get off duty! Here's an idea," the scheming guard continued, "I'll slip off to the party and gather enough for the three of us and come right back. The cap'n is too busy getting' drunk to worry about us, and if he does show up, just tell him I got sick and had to run to the loo."

The one called Gash, who apparently was in charge, took all this in as Rush made a great show of thoroughly enjoying his meal. Gash's stomach finally overruled his fear of the captain. "Awright!" he finally growled, "but I'm goin', not you!"

The other guard was obviously disappointed but said nothing.

"Hey!" Gash spoke to Rush, "How 'bout standin up and coverin' for me if someone shows up 'afor I get back?"

"Sure," Rush said, his mouth full of meat. Gash left his war club and walked quickly down the passageway. After Gash had left, Rush began to laugh. He laughed harder and harder.

"What's so funny?" one of the guards asked.

"You two just got slickered!" Rush laughed coarsely.

"What do you mean?" the first guard asked.

"If you two think he's comin' back here with an armload of goodies, you're dumber than you look!" Rush rocked back and laughed loudly.

"Why, that no good slime ball!" the schemer spat.

"You mean Gash is gonna stick us with guard duty while he goes to the party?" the other guard asked.

"He already has!" the first guard shouted at him. "And here we are . . ."

"Like a couple of saps!" Rush finished his sentence for him and laughed unmercifully at them.

The first guard glared at Rush and began walking purposefully down the passageway.

"Hey! Where are you goin'?"

"You can stay here suckin sap if you want to, but I'm getting' me some grog!" the first guard yelled over his shoulder as he disappeared down the passageway.

The lone guard looked down at Rush, who was still laughing. "You ain't leavin' me here with dis while you go stuff yourself!" he shouted and ran after his companion.

As the last guard disappeared, Rush quickly jumped up and slipped the bolt on the door. He pulled a short torch out from under his tunic, lit it from the one on the wall, and slid inside.

"The mother lode!" Rush said to himself as he looked around at the large room full of supplies. There were piles of sacks filled with seeds and grains. There were bins full of roots. There were hundreds of bunches of dried herbs suspended from overhead beams. Rush lifted the lid on a large, fired-clay box. "Yes!" he whispered. The box was filled with strips of dried meat.

Rush grabbed a nearby sack of seeds and dumped them out. He then quickly filled the large sack full of dried meat. Next he scooped up the seeds and put them in the box. Lastly, he put a thin layer of meat on top of the seeds so that it looked like the box was still filled with meat.

He left his sack of jerked meat there and continued searching other boxes. He stopped in front of another container that was filled with dried fruit. He again dumped out a nearby grain sack and filled it with the fruit. He had just refilled the box with the grain when he heard a voice shouting on the other side of the door.

"Please don't beat me, Cap'n!"

"So you want to be party guys, huh? Well, you can party all you want to right here, 'cause for the next week this is your home, and if I come down here, day or night, and one of you birds is missing, I will personally cut your ears off. Got me?!"

"But, Cap'n," a scared voice stammered, "what are we gonna eat?"

"I'll send you food and drink—if I think about it."

"Hey! What's that door doin' open? If there's somethin' missin' outta that storeroom, yer all loosin' an ear right now!"

When Rush first heard the voices, he had grabbed his torch and ran to the back of the storeroom looking for a place to hide. He found a dark tunnel on one side of the back wall leading slightly downward and to the left. Without hesitation he ran down this passage. The tunnel ended suddenly. It was filled with a large refuse pile. Rush put his torch out quickly as he heard the Renegades enter the storeroom.

"These torches on the wall—light 'em up!" barked the gravelly voice of the captain. "Light 'em all up! We're gonna search this place from top to bottom. I want to know what's missing."

The light from the torches began to reach further and further down the short tunnel where Rush was hiding. Instinctively he backed further away from it. As he did so, his heel caught on an object, and he tumbled over backwards into the refuse pile.

"Yo, Boss!" a voice cried out close to the entrance of Rush's hiding place. "Our thief's back here. I just heard him movin' around in the trash pit."

Rush sat up quickly. His mind raced for a plan. He looked for another way out, but there was none. Hiding was out of the question in such a small room. He would either have to fight his way out, or . . . his eyes looked down at the object over which he had tripped. It was an old, dried-up mooflon skull. The rest of the rotted carcass lay nearby. Suddenly a grin began to spread over the Larkin's face. He quickly grabbed the skull and began tying it to the top of his head with some strips of leather he pulled from a pocket. He then drew the hood of his cloak over the top of the skull on his head and tied it under the lower jaw bone. This made Rush look like some kind of a tall monster with a rotted skull for a head. Peering out from under his cloak, Rush reached down and yanked the lower part of the two front legs off the carcass. Holding these by the long bones, he poked the two sinewy claws out from under his cloak to look like the monster's hands. Just then he heard the approach of the Renegades.

"You sure he's in there?" the Renegade captain growled as he walked up to the guard standing near the door to the trash pit.

"He's there all right. Who do you think it is?"

"Probably one of the grunts trying to get some extra food," one of the other guards volunteered as the rest of the Renegades walked up.

"Well, if it is," barked the captain," I'll make him eat his own ears!"

"You sure got this thing about ears, don't cha, Boss?"

"Do you wanna keep yours?" the captain shot back at the speaker.

"Uh . . . Yes, sir, I do."

"Then quit yappin' and go get that thief!"

The guard leaned into the opening leading to the trash pit and yelled into the darkness, "Come on out of there, you! We know you're in there!"

Some scratching and low snarling sounds came out of the dark opening.

"Dat don't sound like no grunt to me," said Gash, who was standing close to the doorway. "It sounds more like some kind a' varmint."

"Yeah, a big varmint."

"Cut that drivel and go get him!" yelled the captain.

"But, Boss, what if it's some terrible cave beast?"

"Yeah, or maybe a demon?!"

"You yellow-bellied, slime-faced, weak-kneed, gutless, worthless cowards! You're all a bunch of worthless cowards! I spit on all of you!" the captain screamed.

He lifted his own war club and started toward the doorway.   "Follow me, if you dare, ladies," he sneered over his shoulder.

He could hear some snarling back in the trash cave, but it was too dark to see.

"Grab some of those torches on the wall!" he yelled back at the nervous followers. "Let's light this room up!"

Quickly, in response to his orders, three of the closest torches were pulled down from holes in the wall and were moved toward the cave entrance.

"I think I see him back in there," voiced the captain as the light from the advancing torches began to cast a glow into the dark room. "Awright, you! This is it! I'm gonna . . . what the . . . oh, no—NO!!"

The captain's stunned voice was drowned out by an absolutely hideous, screaming roar.

What he saw was a tall, demonic form. It stood upright like a Renegade, but its hands were fearsome claws. Its face was that of some long dead creature, with black, sunken eyes and large, terrible-looking, sharp teeth locked in a skullish grin. The terrifying creature let out a horrible roar and charged at him. A bone-chilling scream erupted out of the captain's gaping mouth. Dropping his club, he spun and fled back up the short passage, bowling over five Renegades in his escape. All of the torches were dropped in the frantic effort of the terrified guards to escape the charge of the screaming demon.

One of the Renegade guards was fatter than the others, and he was slower getting up. Rush pounced on him, slashing his shoulders with one set of claws, which left the guard's leather tunic shredded. The guard yelled and leaped to his feet. Rush swung the other set of claws, and they sank deep into the large, protruding rump of the retreating Renegade. A portion of the seat of his pants remained hanging from the demon's claws as the guard ran away.

In four more seconds the storeroom was completely emptied of Renegades. Rush could hear their screams fading as they fled down the outer passageway. "This is so fun!" Rush laughed to himself. "I could make a career of this—if it smelled a little better," he added, sniffing at one of the decaying claws.

Rush decided to keep his new costume in the hopes of getting a chance to use it again. He emptied a sack of seeds out onto the trash pile and put the skull and claws in it. He also found two war clubs and a knife that had been dropped by the hastily retreating guards. These he placed in the sack with the skull. He quickly ran to the front of the storeroom and found his sacks of food. Shouldering these, he peeked out of the opened door. Seeing that the passageway was empty, he made a quick dash down the hall with his load.

There was so much commotion in the large, central chamber that Rush was able to enter unnoticed. A small crowd was gathered a short distance away from where he stood. He thought that he recognized some of the voices, so he moved over a little closer to hear what was being said.

"I'm telling you blokes, it was the most horrible thing I ever saw. It nearly kilt poor ol' Muckly there."

"What was it, Cap'n?!"

"It weren't no livin' creature. It was a demon!"

"A demon? What kind of demon? What did it look like?"

"It was big and was wearing a black robe. Its bony fingers had fierce-looking claws."

"And they felt fierce too, mates!" the fat Muckley whined as his wounds were being treated.

"Its face," the captain continued, "was a rotting skull with a long nose and huge fangs."

256

"I knowed it!" a grizzled, old, toothless Renegade spat out. "I know'd it fer sure as soon as I heard it. Cap'n, you done stirred up a wompus rat!"

"That's bad, right?" asked one of the guards tending to Muckley.

"Bad?! You ain't seen bad till one of them thangs gets after you."

"What are they, Stargazer?"

With his audience spellbound, the old Renegade named Stargazer began to tell all the legends he'd ever heard about wompus rats. "Why, them thangs is the badest, meanest, viciousest demons they is. They lives in holes deep in the ground where death dwells, and when they gets hungry, they slips up on a victim and rips his heart out!"

"Mercy on me!" squealed Muckly, in a rather high-pitched voice. "He was goin' fer my heart!"

Rush slipped away from the excited Renegades and headed for the tunnel to the slave cells to hide his stuff. "I ain't had this much fun since that night I sewed up my brother in his own sleepin' bag," Rush giggled to himself.

"No! Absolutely not! I will not climb onto that *whatever-it's-called* until you tell me what we're doing here!"

"I told you, Thorny. It's a load lifter, and it's part of the shortcut we need to take."

Turk, Hawthorn, and several of the rescue party were standing at the base of a gigantic water oak tree, which was located on the northwest side of Stillwaters Lake. The land surrounding this part of the lake sloped steeply upward away from shore. The roots of this giant tree gripped the rocky, forested hillside a good three bow shots from the shoreline, and yet so tall and massive was it that its huge branches extended far out over the surface of the water.

Turk was trying to coax the young Larkin into climbing onto a wooden, raft-like platform with low rails on all four sides. Ropes attached to each corner came together a short distance above the platform, forming one large rope that ran straight up into the branches of the great tree, reaching to a dizzying height.

"All you got to do is just get on the lifter, and she'll take you right up as pretty as you please—no climbing or nothing."

"But why do I have to go up there, Turk? I thought we were marching to the Renegade Lair."

"Yep, yep, we're goin' to the Lair. We sure are. But first we need to go up there," Turk said, pointing straight up.

257

Hawthorn was starting to get a look of panic on his face. "Look, Turk, I don't handle heights very well, okay? So I'll just let you guys go up there, and I'll wait here for you to come back down."

"The problem with that is that we're not comin' back down."

"What?!"

"Well, at least, we're not comin' down here."

Turk could see the look of confusion and fear on the face of his young charge, and he decided to take a different approach. "Boy! You sure do make it hard to keep a secret, Thorny. Okay, I'll tell you what. I'll give you a little hint. We ain't marchin' to the Lair. We're flyin'."

"Flying!" Hawthorn was stunned. "How are we going to—oh, yeah. I know how we're flying: Tobin's bird. That's why he didn't march out with us."

Turk just smiled at him.

"All right, all right," Hawthorn tried to reassure himself. "I can do that. It's a big bird, and I don't have to look down. Yeah, I remember now. The flying part's not so bad. The going up and the coming down—that's the bad part." Hawthorn took another deep breath. "But I can do it for Poke."

"That's it! That's it!" Turk said, slapping him on the back. "Do it for ol' Poke! Climb aboard. Lively now!" Hawthorn was less than *lively* as he reluctantly climbed onto the lifter with the rest of his comrades. "Okay, mates," Turk said cheerfully as he jumped over the rail and onto the deck of the lifter. "We're ready to go. All secure?" Turk shot an inquiring glance at each member of his party. "Good.

"We're all set," he said to another Makerian standing a short distance away. "Send us up."

The Makerian nodded his head. Before him a large, red sheet was spread out on the ground. Shaking out a large, white sheet of about the same size, he covered the red sheet with it. Then shading his eyes, he stared intently up into the branches until he saw the signal for which he was looking. "Hold on," he cautioned. As soon as his words were spoken, there was a sudden lurch, and the lifter began to rise into the air.

The ascent was slow and steady. As they rose higher and higher, the Makerians standing around the railing began pointing out to one another various objects and places of interest in the distance. They tried to interest Hawthorn in the beautiful view, but he couldn't be coaxed out of his place. He was sitting in the perfect center of the lifter with knees pulled up to his chin.

They had been steadily rising for several minutes when Hawthorn happened to look up, and he saw a large, square object coming down toward them. In another few minutes, he could see that it was the underside of another load lifter that was descending. It passed them by just a short distance away, and Hawthorn could see that it was loaded with acorns.

"The rope from our lifter goes up into the tree and runs over a crank wheel that's been built onto the main branch up there, then comes back down and attaches to the other lifter." A young Makerian Ranger named Kordilon was talking with Hawthorn, trying to take his mind off the trip. "Did you see all the acorns piled on it? Well, the reason they do that is to counterbalance our weight. That way the workers up there turning the wheel don't have to labor so hard to lift us."

"I was wondering how this thing worked," Hawthorn said.

"It's really pretty simple, but it works well. We mostly use it for hauling acorns."

The trip lasted several more minutes. Soon Hawthorn could clearly see the wheel that was pulling them steadily upward toward a great limb. As they got closer, Hawthorn studied the construction of the machine. It was indeed quite simple in the way it worked, but even so, Hawthorn thought that it must have taken a genius to think of it. The framework holding the wheel was built of beams which rose above and to the side of the huge branch on which it rested. There was a platform built on either side of the hub of the wheel. On this stood eight Makerian workers, four on each side. These eight shared the work of turning the crank that turned the wheel. The rope ran through a deep groove around the top rim of the wheel. When they turned the wheel, this pulled the rope which raised the load lifter on one side and lowered the other one.

Hawthorn's thoughts were interrupted as the lifter came to a stop. They stepped off onto a loading dock built onto the side of the limb. The number of Makerian workers that Hawthorn saw was surprising. Looking around, he didn't recognize any of the rest of their group.

Turk led them off the dock onto the large branch. They marched single file down the length of the limb, occasionally passing workers heading back toward the loading area. They walked on for several minutes. Hawthorn felt comfortable enough to look below. When he did so, he saw that they had walked well past the shore of the lake and were now far out over the water.

Even though the great limb extended a long way from the shore, it was still quite large when it came to an abrupt end. Apparently years back the end of the limb had broken off, and then, over time, it had healed itself into a blunted knot. Hawthorn was surprised to see a large wooden building attached to the knotted end of the limb. As they marched up to this impressive structure, he could see Charlock standing in the open doorway waiting on them.

"I'm glad to see you ALL made it," Charlock said to Turk.

"All accounted for, Gen'ral," Turk replied, cheerfully giving Charlock a knowing wink.

"Hurry up and get 'em in here; we need to keep moving," Charlock growled.

"Step lively, troops! The gen'ral's in a hurry."

Once inside, Hawthorn took a moment to look around him. The inside of the large room was remarkable. It was formed with large, carved beams and wide, wooden boards pegged in place to form tight-fitting walls. There was even a smooth floor formed of the same wooden boards. The room itself was alive with activity. All of the members of the rescue party were being fitted with shoulder harnesses made of wide straps of some woven material. There was also another harness device that was stepped into and pulled up until it was firmly fitted around the waist.

Turk and another Makerian ran over to Hawthorn and, without any explanation, began unslinging some of his weapons. Then they started fitting the same set of harnesses on him. "What's all this for?" Hawthorn was curious.

"Safety," was Turk's reply.

"Safety?"

"Sure, safety. We don't want anybody fallin' off, ya know."

Hawthorn thought back on his last flying experience. He wished that he'd had some type of harness then. All he had had that time was just a rope that Tobin had tied around both of them. That didn't make him feel very secure, especially as the huge black bird began to spiral downward.

Hawthorn looked at the wide straps securely fastened around his shoulders, chest, and hips.

"First group on deck!" a voice across the room shouted loudly.

Hawthorn turned toward the voice. It was one of the Makerian workers who was not a member of their party. He was standing in the opening to a wide hallway. Behind him a short distance, Hawthorn could see a large, wooden deck and, beyond that, blue sky.

At the call for the first group, Hawthorn saw several of their party pick up their weapons and walk past the worker down the hallway to the open air. Hawthorn was unable to see anything else because Turk grabbed him and spun him around to face him.

"Hey!" Hawthorn protested. "I was just trying to catch a glimpse of Tobin's bird."

"You can sightsee later," Turk cut him off. "I've got to be sure your harness is tight enough." Turk worked on Hawthorn's harness for quite a long time and still seemed to be dissatisfied with it.

"Group two on deck!" came the shout.

Hawthorn instinctively tried to turn, but Turk wouldn't let him. "Hold still! I'm trying to get this right!" Turk still seemed unhappy with something about Hawthorn's harness, so he drug him over to the far side of the room and began going through all the harnesses hanging on the pegs and comparing them with Hawthorn's. This too went on for quite some time. Hawthorn wasn't sure what was wrong, but he was starting to get a little nervous.

"Third group on deck!" came the call.

"That's us," Turk said cheerfully. "Follow me." He immediately left Hawthorn and started walking back across the room toward the hallway opening.

"Hey! What about my harness?!" Hawthorn cried anxiously.

Turk glanced down at his nervous companion's harness and then quickly looked back up. "It's fine. Come on." With that, he turned and disappeared down the hallway. Confused, Hawthorn quickly hurried after him.

Walking through the short hallway, Hawthorn followed Turk onto the large, open-air deck and stepped into the bright sunlight. Looking around, Hawthorn was surprised to find that neither Tobin nor his bird were there. Turk was walking hurriedly toward the right side of the deck. He looked back briefly and motioned for Hawthorn to quickly follow.

Turk was moving toward six sets of steps. Each set was spaced about ten paces from the others. Each had ten individual steps going up to a small platform about three-Larkin high above the very edge of the deck. A short ladder extended from this platform to another one directly above it. About head height above this second platform, an upright beam supported a wooden arm. Suspended from the extended end of this wooden arm was a very strange-looking contraption adorned with a crown of maple tree seeds.

The seeds from maple trees have a large wing attached to them. When these seeds are released, the weight of the seed on one end and the large, papery wing on the other cause the seed to whirl rapidly. The rapid, spinning motion causes the seed to drop slowly to the ground.

Six very large maple seeds had been used to construct the machine suspended before Hawthorn. The seed ends of the six maple seeds were firmly attached to one another in a circle. The large wings of each seed extended out away from the center of the circle, all of them turned in the same direction and cocked at the same angle. A wooden spool with a large hole running through it was located in the center of the circle with all of the seeds connected to it. Through the center hole of this spool extended a smooth pole. A cap above and an enlargement in the pole below kept the large circle of seed wings in position. The central pole hung down almost touching the deck where Hawthorn stood.

Attached to this central pole were three shorter rods, all fixed crossways to the central pole, and all three connected to each other with ropes attached to each end. The first crossways rod was near the bottom of the central pole, the second was about halfway up, and the third one was near the top. Extending from the central shaft were two long, narrow poles forming a tail-like structure. One of these long poles was attached close to the top at the level of the uppermost crossways rod, and the other was attached at the level of the lowest rod. These two poles pointed straight back. They were about the length of three Larkin and were connected to each other at the very end by a wide piece of colored cloth. Ropes were attached from the ends of the two lowest crossways rods and were secured to the end of the tail.

Workers were busy mounting one of these machines to the arm at the top of each set of steps. Looking back to his right, Hawthorn saw the open door to a large store room. Inside were suspended many more of the maple-seed machines.

"Hey, Turk! What are those things?" Hawthorn asked.

"They're called *whirly bugs*. Sometimes we just call 'em *whirlers*. Now hurry on over here. We got to get a move on."

"Well, wait a minute," Hawthorn protested. "Where's Tobin and the bird?"

"They ain't comin' here," Turk grinned.

"Not coming here?" Hawthorn was getting very confused. "What do you mean, they're not coming here?! You said we were flying on his bird to the Lair."

"Well, now, Thorny, that's not what I said."

"You said we were flying!" Hawthorn shot back.

"That's right," Turk countered, "but I didn't say HOW we were flying."

"Well, how else can we fly if not on . . ."

"All clear!" came a shout from one of the raised platforms at the edge of the deck. Two Makerians were harnessed onto a whirler, one standing on the middle cross-rod and holding the top cross-rod by the ends, and the other Makerian standing on the lowest cross-rod and holding the central shaft. With his eyes wide and his mouth open, Hawthorn watched as the arm suspending the whirler was swung out until the whirly bug was suspended out over open space.

"Ready?" cried the worker who swung the arm out.

"Spin it!" called the Makerian standing on top.

The worker grabbed a wooden ring below the circle of maple seeds and pulled hard. The ring had been attached to a long cord that had been wound around the spool. On yanking the cord, the maple wings began to spin like a top.

"Release!" called the top Makerian.

A second worker standing on the platform above pulled a pin, and the whirler with its two passengers dropped from sight.

"WHAT!!" Hawthorn screamed.

"Keep watching," Turk said reassuringly.

Sure enough, Hawthorn saw the whirler reappear some distance away, its fan blades spinning rapidly. The two Makerians were actually flying the thing across the pond.

Hawthorn looked at Turk with wide eyes. "You expect me to fly on one of those?!"

"Surprise!" Turk grinned. "Now hurry up, we're running short on time. Help us out, will ya, fellas?"

Two rather large workers stepped up behind Hawthorn and escorted him quickly to the nearest, suspended whirler.

"Wait a minute! Wait a minute! Not so fast! Can we talk about this?! Turk! Why didn't you tell me about this?!"

"Because you'd still be standing at the base of the tree if I had," replied Turk.

In just a few moments, the two workers had Hawthorn strapped in place on the bottom position of the whirler. "Put both feet on the bottom cross piece, lean back against the straps, and hold on to the center pole," Hawthorn was instructed. "You should keep your bow and arrows where you can reach them quickly."

"Why?" wondered Hawthorn.

"Sometimes birds think the whirlers are bugs and try to eat them."

"Oh, great!"

By this time Turk was strapped into position directly above him. Turk had both of his feet spread wide as he stood on the crosspiece just above Hawthorn's head. Hawthorn figured that he should stand like that also, so he spread his feet out wider. As he did so, the cross piece on which he stood tilted to his left. Because all of the crosspieces were roped together at the ends, that made all three of them tilt to the left.

"Whoa, Thorny!" cried Turk. "I'm doin' the steerin', not you. Bring your feet back near the center pole."

Hawthorn quickly complied.

"Okay, Hawthorn, here's how it works. To turn slowly to the right, lean your weight on the right side of the crosspiece. To turn left, lean left. To turn quickly to the right or left, push forward on the right or left cross piece with your feet, like this." Turk leaned back on the harness around his waist and pushed the right crosspiece forward with his foot. This caused the tail of the whirler to swing to the right.

"There's a small rod running next to the central pole where your hands are. Do you see it?"

"Yes," Hawthorn answered, fingering the small rod.

"Follow the rod up to just above your head, and you'll see a handle sticking out from it. If you push that rod up, it rubs against the spool attached to the whirling blades. That slows the blades down, and you'll go down faster."

"I don't want to go down fast!"

"Well, sometimes you need to," answered Turk. "All right, Thorny, are you ready to go?"

"No!"

"Great!" smiled Turk. Then he turned to the workers on the platforms next to them. "We're ready, fellas."

"Would you guys like for us to offer a prayer to the Maker for your safety?" asked one of the workers.

"Oh," replied Turk, "he don't believe in prayin'."

"Please pray for us!" Hawthorn cried out.

The workers and Turk all smiled at each other. Then they all pulled off their caps, and one of the workers pronounced a brief prayer to the Maker appealing to Him for protection and success in their mission. As he finished, they each said, "Amen." Hawthorn didn't know what it meant, but he said it too.

"Okay, let's go," announced Turk.

"Swing it!" commanded one of the workers.

The worker standing on the top platform swung the arm out away from the deck.

"Whoa!" cried Hawthorn as he looked down and saw the surface of the pond many, many leagues below. He gripped the central pole tightly and closed his eyes.

"Ready?" called the worker.

"Spin it!" answered Turk.

The worker jerked hard on the cord that was wrapped around the spool, and the blades began to spin rapidly overhead. Turk waited a second or two to be sure the blades were rotating correctly, then he called out, "Release!"

There was a click; then their whirler dropped into open air.

Hawthorn felt his stomach shoot up into his throat. They actually only fell a short ways before the spinning blades caught the air and held them.

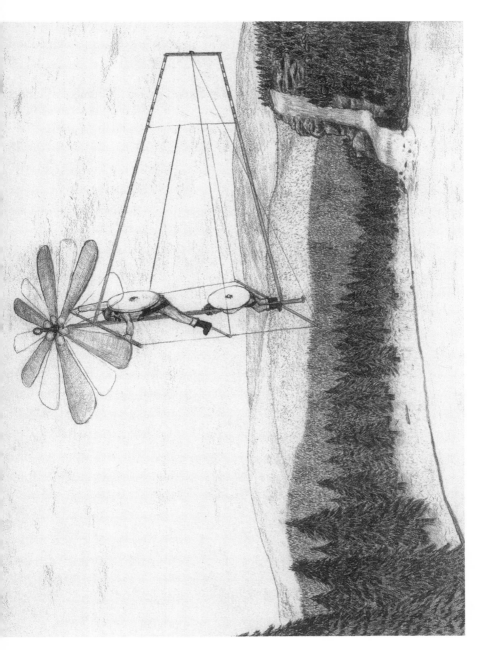

Hawthorn still had his eyes closed. The noise of the spinning blades sounded a lot like the buzzing of a bumble bee.

"Isn't this great, Thorny?" called out Turk from overhead.

"Yeah, great," Hawthorn called out, his eyes closed and hands clutching the central pole as tightly as he could.

CHAPTER EIGHTEEN

SCOUTING THE LAIR

Turk and Hawthorn whirled through the sky, following the line of whirly bugs carrying the rest of their comrades. Hawthorn tried to calm himself and enjoy the adventure, but there was a breeze behind them causing their whirler to bounce around like a wind-blown leaf. When he finally opened his eyes, he was amazed to see the southeastern shore of Stillwaters passing beneath them.

Turk pulled back with his arms and pushed forward with his feet as they caught an updraft at the end of the lake. Their whirler soared up and over the tops of the cypress trees bordering the shore. When they reached the open air above the tree tops, the wind really pushed them along rapidly. In a very short time, they were buzzing across the southern end of the meadow.

Looking down, Hawthorn saw several larks far below them leap up out of the grass and chase some flying insect. This made Hawthorn nervous, and he began trying to figure out how to notch and shoot an arrow while hanging on for dear life to the central pole of the tossing whirler. He finally decided that, if a bird came after them, they were in trouble.

They followed their friends across the meadow and then down into the trees along the southeastern border. That's when the trip really got exciting. Hawthorn watched trees rush closely past them at an alarming rate. They jumped limbs and dodged trunks so fast that all Hawthorn could do was close his eyes and hang on. The bouncing, jerking, and swinging went on for some time as they raced through the thick woods. Finally they slowed down and began to spiral toward the ground. Looking down between his feet, Hawthorn saw the tiny figures of the rest of his party moving around on the ground below them. As he watched, the tiny forms grew larger very quickly. Hawthorn cried out as the ground rushed up to meet them. Just in time, Turk pulled back, and the rapid descent came to a halt. Their whirler hovered just a very short distance above the ground, then slowly dropped, touching down with only a slight jar.

Several Makerian Rangers ran up to hold the whirler upright so that Hawthorn and Turk could unstrap themselves without the flying machine falling over on them. As soon as they were safely standing on the ground, the whirler was tipped over, picked up, and carried to a crevasse in the base of a nearby oak tree. Their whirler was hidden in the crevasse with the rest of the Makerian flying machines, and the spot was marked so that they could be retrieved some time later. Charlock called the party together and immediately led them on a march to the east. After traveling through the woods for about an hour, the forest floor began to slope upward. The further east they traveled, the steeper the climb became. Just when Hawthorn felt he couldn't go much farther, Charlock called a halt. While everyone else rested, Charlock had one of the rangers use his caller to send signals up into woods to the east. From off in the distance and above them was heard the answering call. After a brief rest, they continued their climbing march.

They had only been marching again for a short time when they heard a distant crunching sound approaching as some forest creature bounded toward them through the steeply sloping woods. Everyone quickly dove for cover as a large, muscular gray squirrel burst through the brush into their midst.

A small cheer went up as the Makerians came out of hiding to greet the intruder. Hawthorn climbed out from behind a large oak leaf and was stunned by what he saw. There, sitting on top of the squirrel like the king of the woods, sat Tobin. Hawthorn moved up to join the group gathering around Tobin and his furry friend.

Turk, who was standing next to Hawthorn, shot an elbow into his friend's ribs. "Close yer mouth, Thorny," he laughed. "You look like y're infested with pine bore beetles."

At that point, Tobin, who had been greeting the Makerians as they came up, noticed Hawthorn. "Good day to you, young Larkin," he said through his red, bushy beard. "I don't believe you've met Chatter yet." Tobin leaned over and scratched the neck of his furry steed. Chatter had been sniffing the ground intently since they had arrived. On feeling the affectionate rub of his master's hand, he lifted his head and twisted it back, presenting Tobin with an ear that he could scratch if he were so inclined.

"It's a blessing to see you, good Tobin!" the gruff voice of Charlock interrupted their greeting.

"And you, sir," Tobin returned the formal greeting.

"Have you found a place to make our base camp?"

"Eldan has found a good location about an hour's march straight up the slope from here. It might save us some time if Chatter and I ferry you up."

"Yes, of course," Charlock said thoughtfully. "Time is most precious. How many can you carry at a time?"

"I have places for five to sit behind me."

Charlock was silent for a moment as he considered the most efficient use of his resources.

"Goodclaw! Gilly! Stoke!" Charlock barked. The three Rangers quickly presented themselves before their commander. "Goodclaw, you've got more field experience than any other Ranger here. You're in charge of setting up our camp. Gilly, you're one of the Vigilants, aren't you?"

"Yes, sir. I've been a gate guard for eight seasons."

"Good! I want you in charge of security. Stoke, you supervised the packing of all our supplies and equipment. Tobin and his friend here have been kind enough to haul them from Stillwaters to our base camp. You're in charge of unpacking and organizing them for us. You three will join Carineda and me behind Tobin as he gives us a ride up to the site of our base camp.

"Graceson!" Charlock called. The lieutenant for the first Ranger troop came forward.

"Yes, sir!"

"I'm leaving you in charge here. Keep them moving uphill. Rest when you must.

"Turk!"

"Yes, sir!" Turk responded.

"Turk, I've put Graceson in charge," Charlock announced.

"I understand, sir."

"As lieutenant of the second Ranger troop, you'll be his second in command."

Charlock turned back to Graceson. "Once we get to the base camp," Charlock continued, "I'll send Tobin and his squirrel back down to ferry the rest of you up."

"It'll take him two trips to get the rest of us," Graceson responded. "Is there a specific order in which you want me to send the troops with Tobin?"

"Probably," Charlock grunted as he gave Carineda a boost up onto Chatter's back. "I'll think about that on the way up and tell Tobin whom to bring next."

Two Rangers boosted Charlock up. Grabbing handfuls of gray fur, Charlock climbed up to the last seat in the long, wooden saddle strapped to Chatter's back. He jumped into his seat behind Cari and quickly tied himself in. He jammed his feet into two holes in the base of the seat in front of him and grabbed two handles on the back of Cari's seat. "I'm in!" he shouted. "Let's go!"

Tobin turned and looked at the five faces behind him. "All set?" He saw all five nod. "All right then, let's go! Chatter! Up!"

The huge squirrel leaped to his feet.

"Chick, chick!" Tobin spoke, and Chatter whirled to the left, heading back up the steep hill from which he had come. "Fly!" Tobin called, and they disappeared in a burst of dirt and dry leaves.

Hawthorn was standing near Turk. "That is the most amazing thing I've ever—" Hawthorn stopped himself and thought about all the amazing things he had seen in the past few days. "That's really amazing!" he finally said.

"Let's get moving, Turk," Graceson ordered.

"Right!" Turk responded. "Form up, troops! Let's march!"

It took less than half an hour for Tobin to return. The dust hadn't settled before Tobin began calling out the names of the next group to be transported up to the base camp.

"Marsh, Blesstis, Sammal, Turk, and Hawthorn!"

"Come on, Thorny ol' boy!" Turk said enthusiastically. "This is great! We get to snatch the gravy."

"Snatch the gravy?"

"Well, sure! Never walk when you can ride, I always say."

"But, Turk, did you see how fast that thing runs?"

"Hey, Hawthorn, listen. It's not like falling off a whirler. If you fall off the squirrel, you hit the ground in no time!"

"If you're trying to encourage me, Turk, it's not working," Hawthorn grumbled. "Can't someone else take my seat? I'd really rather walk."

"Sorry, Thorn, orders is orders. Charlock must need you up there. Don't forget, time is critical if we're going to save your friend."

Without another word, Hawthorn walked over and started climbing up onto Chatter's back. He took the next to last seat. As he was trying to figure out how to secure himself, Turk climbed up behind him.

"Tie yourself in with those two ropes on either side of the seat. Yeah, like that, but you'd better pull it tighter than that. Okay, good. Now, your feet fit into those two holes down there. That's right! That's right! Jam 'em in there good and tight. Now, just grab ahold of those handles on the back of the seat in front of you, and you're ready."

With Hawthorn strapped in, Turk quickly secured himself in the last seat. "We're ready, Tobin!" Turk called.

"All set?" Tobin asked. He took time to make eye contact with each passenger. They each returned his questioning gaze with a nod. "All right, let's go!"

The commands were given, and Chatter whirled around and shot back up the hill so quickly that Hawthorn didn't have time to yell. He had quite a ride up that hill. Chatter didn't run so much as he leaped and bounded. It required a lot of leg and arm strength to keep from bouncing in the seat.

"Hey, Thorny!" It was Turk yelling at him from behind.

"What?" Hawthorn yelled back.

"Try shifting your weight back and forth in the seat, in rhythm with the squirrel's leaps."

This was a new idea for Hawthorn. He looked at the others in the seats in front of him and noticed that they were all riding much more smoothly than he was. He tried to imitate the way they were moving back and forth. After a few minutes of experimenting, he found that if he shifted his weight forward and backward at just the right time, the ride became much smoother for him as well.

"Hey, this isn't so bad!" he yelled back over his shoulder as he began to get the hang of it.

"Look at you!" Turk laughed. "You'll be wanting your own squirrel next!"

After fifteen minutes of climbing, they came to a very rocky place. Chatter had no trouble climbing the jagged-edged rocks even with the load on his back. As they topped the ridge, they found themselves standing on a flat, sandy plateau that ran up to the foot of a limestone bluff a little less than a bowshot from where Chatter now stood. Looking left and right, Hawthorn could see that the sandy area was about twice as long as it was wide. It was bordered on three sides by sharp rocks and by the steep bluff behind.

"Hello, the camp!" Tobin called out.

"Over here, Tobin!" came a voice from across the plateau.

Tobin spoke some more words in the squirrel's ear, and Chatter trotted across the open sandy area toward the rocky limestone wall opposite them. Hawthorn could see their packs stacked up against the base of the bluff and three Makerians busily opening the packs and laying out equipment and supplies. The Makerians were Goodclaw, Carineda, and Stoke.

"Where are the rest of them?" Tobin asked.

"Out scouting," the answer came from Goodclaw.

"Let's go, troopers!" Stoke barked at the new arrivals. "I need every one of you breaking down the packs—NOW!"

They all quickly dismounted and trotted over to help with the packs. Even Tobin slid off and went over to help, since Chatter needed to rest before he made another run down the hill. As they completed the task of unstacking all of the packs, Stoke went though and identified each one according to what they contained.

"These are camp supplies; take them over to Goodclaw. These two and that one over there are medical supplies and bandages. Cari is setting up the aid station down there under that overhanging rock. Take those to her. This pack and that one are climbing equipment. Just leave them right there for now."

"Hey, Stoke! Are all these food?"

"Um . . . let me see. That one is; that one is; so is that one and that one, but that long one is a weapons' bag."

"Where's the weapons' bag?" Marsh wanted to know.

"Over there in front of Blesstis," Stoke answered.

"Bring it over here, Blesstis, and put it with these others."

"Sammal!" Goodclaw called out after a few minutes. "You and Marsh help me set up the camp. Turk! You and Blesstis help Stoke unpack the equipment. Hawthorn, you help Carineda unpack her supplies."

"Looks like Chatter's ready," Tobin announced. "We'll be heading down for the rest of them."

"Right," Goodclaw returned. "Hurry back; we've got a lot to do."

Hawthorn watched his friend ride off, then turned and trotted along the rock wall to the overhang where Cari was setting up her aid station.

"Hi, Cari! What do you need me to do?"

"Hey, Thorn. How about moving all these packs back up under this ledge?"

"Okay."

"Set them up side by side in order, starting with number three."

Hawthorn looked down at the pack he had just picked up. Sure enough, there was a number five written on it. He looked over at Cari. She was using a large slab of rock that was almost waist high as a work table. She was setting up packs one and two on it. Apparently those first two packs contained the supplies and materials that she used the most. The rest of the packs contained all the rest of the medicines, herbs, and other things she might need. She knew exactly what was in each pack, and by lining them all up in order, she could walk right to anything she wanted. Hawthorn was impressed with her organization.

"Is that like you want it?" he asked when he had all the packs arranged.

She took a quick look from her work. "That's great! Now how about digging me a fire pit right over there next to that end of my table?"

Hawthorn found a flat rock with a sharp edge and began scooping out sand in the spot where Cari had pointed. He was almost finished when he heard a familiar voice cry out, "Hey, Chummy!"

Hawthorn looked up to see a young Makerian with a mop of thick, curly red hair and a silly grin on his face running towards him. "Eldan! Is that you?"

"It's as me as you can get, Acorn!"

"Hawthorn, Eldan, my name is Hawthorn!"

"It certainly is, Chummy, and don't you forget it. Say, you look a lot better than the last time I saw you."

"You do too," returned Hawthorn, noticing that most of the scrapes on Eldan's arms and face were almost healed.

"Hey, Eldan, Charlock told me you saw some of the Larkin prisoners being taken into the Lair. Can you tell me what they looked like?"

"Well, let's see," Eldan said thoughtfully as he scratched his thick crop of curly hair. "As I recall, they looked a lot like prisoners."

"I'm serious, Eldan! I'm trying to figure out . . ."

"Calm yourself, Chummy. I'll tell you all about it on the way. Let's go."

"Where are we going?"

"You've been selected to go with Turk, Tobs, and Yours Truly on a scouting mission into the Lair," Eldan answered.

"Really?! All right! But why me?"

"'Cause if we happen to spot some of the prisoners while we're in there, you're the only one who can tell us if any of them are your people. Now come on; they're waiting for us."

"Cari, I've got to go," Hawthorn said to his friend.

"Yes, I heard," she answered. "Be careful, both of you. I'll start praying for you right now."

"Well . . . thanks," Hawthorn returned.

"We sure do appreciate that, Miss Cari. We do! We do!" Eldan spoke with enthusiastic sincerity. "You're a treasure! Just a real treasure! You know I've said that before."

"Yes, I know, Eldan."

"There, you see? I didn't just make that up; it's a known fact! You're the most treasurest person . . ."

"Eldan!" Cari interrupted. "Don't you and Hawthorn need to be going?"

"Yep, yep, that we do. Now lookee there! You did it again. Put us back on the right path when we's about to wander off. Why, you're just a treasure,

Miss Cari! An absolute treasure! Come on, Thornton. Shake a leg. You've made us late with all your gum flappin'."

"ME?!" snapped Hawthorn as he ran after his retreating companion.

As they waited for Tobin to return with the last of the troops, Eldan, Turk, and Hawthorn put together four bundles to take with them. They packed climbing equipment, bandage material, and some food. Hawthorn was given two of the light sticks—the hollow resin vials containing chemicals which, when shaken, glowed a bright green. One of these he hung around his neck; the other he placed in his pack. They each took a bow and arrows. Hawthorn wanted to take his sting, but Turk thought he might have a hard time climbing with it, so the young Larkin left the weapon behind. After Tobin returned, Charlock called the four together for a meeting. He had five objectives for them. First, they were to descend into the Lair and find the prisoners. Second, they were to mark the way in and out for the main rescue attempt. Third, he asked that they find out how many guards there were and how the slaves were being guarded. Fourth, they needed to figure out the best way to free the slaves and get them out. Fifth, they were to return with the information.

"You're askin' a lot of us," Turk spoke.

"Just do your best," was Charlock's reply.

"Which one of the five is the most important one?" Eldan wanted to know.

"The fifth one," Charlock stated firmly.

"This could take some time," Tobin said thoughtfully.

"I know," answered Charlock. "We need the information, so take the time to do a good job. But keep in mind that the longer we sit here, the more likely we are to be discovered. Any questions?"

There were none.

"All right then, let's pray about this."

The four Makerians fell to their knees, and they began to cry out passionately to the Maker, asking for His protection and guidance. Hawthorn knelt with them but said nothing. He was getting used to the spiritual fervor of these people. It still made him uncomfortable, but he understood it, and he respected them for it.

To save some time, they decided to ride Chatter up the hill to the hidden entrance into the Lair. Each member of the scouting party shouldered his pack, a water pouch, and a coil of rope. When everyone was securely mounted, Chatter was sent scurrying up the hill. The secret entrance actually wasn't very far from the camp, but the climb would have cost them time and energy.

Tobin knew exactly where to go. He and Eldan had followed their father's map earlier that day and had found the hidden entrance, just as their father and his Renegade companions had left it years before. The opening was a small crevasse that was just big enough for one person to descend at a time. It opened into a rock chimney that dropped straight down.

Tobin had them all rope themselves together with Eldan leading, Turk next, then Hawthorn, and himself in the rear. With no more fanfare, they set off.

Using the sharp rocks protruding from the wall, Eldan descended into the Renegade stronghold. Giving one another plenty of room, they each lowered themselves in turn. As the darkness engulfed them, they used the glow sticks suspended around their necks as a source of light. The climbing was not extremely difficult, but it was slow and tedious. The straight drop eventually became a steep slope of boulders and rock outcroppings. Eldan would try one way down, then have to stop and backtrack when he came to a dead end or drop off.

They had been climbing for over half an hour but hadn't gotten very far. The lack of progress was frustrating, but no one said anything. They each knew Eldan was doing his best and that they themselves could do no better.

"Hey!" Turk called out in a subdued voice. There may not have been a Renegade within a hundred leagues of where they were right now, but just knowing that they were descending into a portion of the Renegade stronghold made them anxious to be as quiet as possible.

"What is it, Turk?" Tobin responded from the darkness above Hawthorn.

"As difficult as it is finding a path down this thing, shouldn't we be marking our trail, since we've got to do this again with the rest of the troops?"

"Yes, you're right. Does anyone have anything with them that will leave a mark on stone?" It was silent for a moment.

"I have a piece of quartz. That should work," Turk finally responded.

"All right," voiced Tobin. "Turk, mark our trail using arrows to indicate the right path."

They continued on in this way for only a short while when Turk called out again.

"Hey! Look at this."

"What is it?" Hawthorn asked.

"Just come here, all of you. You too, Eldan."

In a few minutes, they were all perched within touching distance of Turk.

"What'd you find, Turkey?" Eldan piped up.

"I was getting ready to scratch an arrow on this rock, but there's already a mark on it. Look!"

Turk held his glow stick close to the flat rock where he had started to draw, and sure enough, a strange figure was distinctly visible where it had been scratched into the limestone rock.

"What is that?" Hawthorn asked.

"I don't know," replied Turk, "but some person definitely put it there."

"It looks like a long *V* that's curved. Maybe it's an arrow" said Eldan.

"It doesn't look much like a *V*," Hawthorn thought out loud. "I think it looks more like a claw."

"Or a fang!" announced Tobin.

"Yes! A fang!" Eldan burst out. "Why, Bubsy, that's it! That's it!"

"What's it?" asked Hawthorn.

"That fang has to be the symbol our father made years ago."

"How do you know?" asked Turk.

"Because his Renegade name was Ripfang."

"Well, it makes sense."

"Of course, it makes sense, Turkey! Do you think the only thing Tobs uses that ol' noggin of his for is to sprout red fuzz?"

"That's enough, Eldan," growled Tobin.

"Why, he may look dumb as a rock, but let me tell you, that boy's a thinker!"

"Eldan!"

"So what does it mean?" asked Hawthorn, pointing at Ripfang's symbol.

"I think it means," Tobin answered, "that our father is going to show us the way down. Let's follow the way the fang points and see if it doesn't lead us to another mark."

They began their descent again with renewed vigor. A few minutes later Eldan called up to them, "You're right as rain, Tobs. I found another fang, but this one points to the right."

"Keep lookin' fer those marks, Eldan," Turk called back. "We'll follow 'em all the way to the bottom."

The more of the marks Eldan found, the more confident he became in following them. They were making good time now since they did not have to explore or backtrack. They continued at this pace for well over an hour when suddenly a sound froze them in their tracks.

"Did you hear that?!" Hawthorn whispered loudly to Turk.

"It sounded like a horn," Turk answered.

"Shhh!" Eldan hissed at them. "Tuck in those lips, you two. You're flappin' 'em too much."

"Remember," Tobin spoke softly from just above them, "if we can hear them, they can hear us. Let's move as carefully and as quietly as we can."

They continued descending the rock-strewn slope, following the path marked out by Ripfang years before, but this time they were much more cautious—a misplaced foot or a cascade of stones and they would be as good as caught. Twenty more minutes of climbing passed, and no other sounds were heard. Then suddenly Eldan hissed a warning. Everyone stopped and dropped behind nearby rocks. Hawthorn saw Turk slip his light stick inside his tunic to block its light. He quickly did the same. Leaning over his rock, he looked into the blackness. Hawthorn saw several small, flickering yellow lights moving in a line some distance below them. He could also hear noises coming from the lighted procession: yelling and an odd snapping or popping sound. Tobin joined Hawthorn behind his rock.

"That's why we came, young one."

"What is that, Tobin?"

"Those are your friends," he answered. "The guards are bringing the slaves up from the mines."

"What's that popping sound?" Hawthorn asked.

"Whips," was Tobin's one word reply.

Hawthorn had to wipe tears from his eyes as he watched the slow, agonizing march of the slaves along an unseen path below them. It took several minutes for the last torch to finally pass by and disappear. The four scouts remained hidden until they were sure there was no one below them to hear their descent.

"You know," Hawthorn spoke to Tobin, who was near him, "we watched them walk along that path for a long time. That means that this cave place we're in must be enormous."

"It would be very easy to get lost in here," Tobin agreed. "That's why you should always remember to look behind you as you go through a cave."

"Why?" Hawthorn asked.

"Because the rock formations look totally different when you're leaving a cave than when you're walking in. When you're going into the cave, look behind you, so you'll remember what the formations look like when you're coming back out."

"Hey, guys!" It was Turk. "We're movin' down."

They began the final descent with renewed determination and energy. Even so, it took thirty more minutes to reach the trail at the bottom of the cavern. While they were resting next to the trail, they strengthened themselves with a meal of seasoned, dried fish and honey cakes.

"What's our plan, Bubs?" Eldan asked as they finished their food.

"You and Hawthorn scout the back trail. See if there's anything or anyone we need to plan for. Turk and I will trail the slaves. Once we find out where they are keeping them, we'll need to come up with a plan to free them and get them out Father's back door. Once you find out what's back there, come join us. Oh—and Eldan, remember—they don't know we're here, so let's keep it that way."

"Why, Bubsy!" Eldan began with a hurt expression on his face. "How could you say such a thing? It's me you're talkin' to, the King of Stealth. You know you can count on me."

"Just get going, Eldan!"

"Tobs, have I ever let you down? I mean, besides that time at the creek."

"Eldan!"

"We're going, Tobs, we're going! Don't bust your britches! Come on, Chummy," Eldan called to Hawthorn. "Let's make tracks before Bubsy bites our heads off."

A low growl began to emanate from deep inside the bush of curly red hair surrounding Tobin's head.

Eldan led the way back down the path with a slow trot as Hawthorn followed. He paused frequently to listen for sounds and look for torches. They eventually came to a fork in the path. Eldan studied the sandy trail and saw clearly that most of the traffic followed the path on the right side of the fork, where the tracks went down and behind a large boulder. They followed the left, lesser-used path, moving quickly, looking for signs of the enemy. Eventually they heard a distant, roaring sound.

"What's that noise?" Hawthorn asked.

"Sounds like a river," Eldan returned.

"A river?! Down here?!"

"You don't get out much, do ya, Chummy?"

"What?! Yes, I get out!"

"Calm yourself, Chums. It's just a figure of speech. Rivers do go underground sometimes. Take this one, for example."

They eventually came to a large opening on their right. The river noise was coming from this dark opening. Eldan stood in the opening for a few moments. "It's another huge cavern, Chummy. The river must run through the bottom of it."

"So do we explore it?" Hawthorn asked.

"No, let's go back and see where the other path goes."

Retracing their steps, they returned to the fork and took the right path this time. They followed the winding trail as it descended deeper into the mountain.

278

After awhile they began to hear the roar of the river again. Soon they came to another large opening.

"This must be the same cavern," Hawthorn speculated.

"Good guess, Chums. The mines they work the slaves in must be down in this huge room too. They marched 'em all out through this way. Let's head back; Tobs will be wondering what became of us."

The trot back up the path wasn't as easy as the trot down. Hawthorn was winded, and they were both sweating hard when they got back to the fork.

"How about we stop and rest, Eldan?"

"Sorry, Chums, but we need to keep moving. You'll have to rest on your feet."

"But my feet want me to rest on something else."

"You can rest on whatever you want," Eldan chuckled, "as long as you keep moving."

Eldan kept them walking at a steady pace for several minutes. "Let's try to pick it up now, Chummy. But keep it quiet. A little noise travels a long way in a cave." Increasing their pace to a long-distance trot, they continued along the sandy path back the way they had come.

Hawthorn was starting to feel his chest tightening up from the exertion of the run when his companion came to a stop. Lifting his light stick a little higher, Eldan searched the right side of the path. "Here it is, Chums." Eldan was pointing at three stones set up like a pyramid just off the path. "This is where we came down." Eldan took a long pull from his water pouch, then handed it to his friend. Hawthorn looked at the three stones and then raised his head, looking up into the darkness above.

"So that's the way out of here!" he said, lifting the pouch to his mouth.

"Don't forget where it is, Chummy. You may have to find it."

Hawthorn firmly seated the wooden stopper in the water pouch and replaced it in the pack on Eldan's back.

"Thanks, friend," Eldan spoke, acknowledging Hawthorn's courtesy of replacing the pouch for him. "Now let's do the traveler's dance and find our partners."

The long distance trot began again, but this time at a much more cautious pace. They were definitely moving toward enemies, and they weren't sure what to expect. Not more than ten minutes had passed when Eldan stopped them. He quickly crouched down and motioned Hawthorn to do the same. Hawthorn knew Eldan had seen or heard something that warned him of danger. Hawthorn could see nothing but blackness beyond the greenish glow of their light sticks. Listening intently, he thought he caught the faraway sound of voices. Keeping close to the ground, they moved forward again. They continued their cautious progress for several more minutes. The path they followed made a sharp turn to the right around a large boulder. As they made the turn, a flickering yellow light could be seen in the distance. Eldan stopped and placed his mouth right next to Hawthorn's ear.

"This is it, Chums," Eldan whispered. "We've got to be absolutely quiet from now on. If you have to say anything, get next to the person's ear and speak as I'm talking to you now. Got it?" Hawthorn nodded in agreement. "Okay," Eldan whispered again, "let's move closer and see if we can find Tobs and Turkey. Oh, and whatever you do, don't sneeze!"

Hawthorn looked at his friend and saw him grinning from ear to ear. They tucked their light sticks inside their tunics so that they wouldn't be seen and moved toward the torches. As they got closer, they could see that the torch light was shining through a window in a heavy wooden door that was built into the rock wall. They stopped just outside the glow of the light. A movement on the right caught their attention. The bulky form of Tobin eased out from behind the shadow of a large rock. Seeing their leader, they moved over to join him. Crawling further back behind the boulder, they drew very close to talk.

"Anything back that way we need to worry about?" Tobin whispered.

"No signs of any guard," Eldan whispered back.

"Turk's scouting up and around to the left side of the path."

"Is that door where they keep the slaves?" Hawthorn asked.

"Yes. They marched them up to the door and searched each one before they took them in. They were still searching them when we came up. The door hasn't been closed for very long, but when they shut it, it sounded like they bolted it on the inside."

"That's gonna make gettin' in there tougher," Eldan said.

"We'll just have to use our heads," Tobin said, looking at Hawthorn. Hawthorn couldn't see his mouth behind his thick, red beard, but he could tell by his eyes that Tobin was smiling at him. A feeling of confidence and peace settled over Hawthorn as he looked into his friend's smiling eyes. He was constantly amazed at the resourcefulness of these Makerians.

"Did you find anything, Turk?" Tobin asked. Hawthorn jumped when he realized that Turk had suddenly appeared right beside him without making a sound.

"Nothing to the left. It's solid rock and boulders all the way up the slope on that side," Turk reported.

"Eldan and I will scout up the right side," Tobin said. "When you've had a few minutes to rest, you and Hawthorn slip up to the door and let our Larkin friend steal a look through the window to see if he recognizes anyone.

"Hawthorn," Tobin spoke again, "when you look in there, you will be in the greatest danger of being spotted. If you make a sound, or if you let them see you, all will be lost."

"But if I see Poke or one of the others, shouldn't I try to get their attention to let them know we're here?"

"No!" all three of his companions said in unison.

"They won't be able to help us, 'cause they're all locked up in cells," Turk spoke. "Tobin and I have already looked in there. Besides, if we let them know what's happening now, one of them might get excited and give us away before the time comes."

"From what you told me, Chums," Eldan spoke up, "your friend thinks you're dead. If he sees your ugly face in that window, he's liable to scream, and then where would we be?"

"Best you don't let them see you, young one," Tobin said.

"I understand."

Eldan and Tobin moved silently up the rocky slope to the right of the path, staying well back in the shadows. Hawthorn and Turk watched them until they were lost in the darkness.

"Well, I'm ready if you are," Turk smiled. Turk led the way along the left edge of the sandy path, staying as much as possible in the dark shadows. As they approached the door, they heard more yelling and moaning. Moving quickly up to the rock wall, they stood with their backs flat against it to the left of the door. Turk gave Hawthorn a nod, and the young Larkin silently moved up close to the barred window in the heavy wooden door. The light from the torches made him squint. Looking into the room at an angle, he could see the cells on the opposite side of the room from where he was. There were maybe twenty or thirty very dirty people behind the wooden bars. Most of them were either sitting or lying down on the dirt floor of the cell. The majority of them had very ragged clothes, and all of them were caked with dirt. They were the most tired, forlorn, and hopeless-looking people he had ever seen.

The guards had a basket with pieces of bread in it. They were trying to get some of the slaves to beg for the biggest piece. Some of the slaves were actually doing it. Eventually the guards tired of this torment and began throwing the bread into the cells. Most of it landed in the dirt.

Hawthorn pulled back from the window, heartsick at what he had seen. Turk took his place and spent several minutes studying the door. Then being careful not to show himself, he peered through the window and studied the room and its inhabitants. There was more commotion in the room. Apparently all the slaves were secured and fed, and now most of the guards were leaving. Turk watched them file through a door directly across from the one where he was. One guard remained in the room with the slaves. When all the rest of the guards had left, the other door was shut and bolted on the outside by another guard who was stationed just outside of the door.

Turk slowly withdrew his eye from the window. He looked at Hawthorn and touched his index finger to his lips. Hawthorn didn't need to be reminded of the necessity of being quiet. Turk cautiously moved away from the wall and silently led the way back to the shadows behind the large rock. "Did you see your friend?" Turk whispered.

"I couldn't tell if he was in there or not. They were all covered with dirt."

"Yeah," Turk said in agreement. "They all looked pretty rough."

"Turk, it makes me sick to my stomach to see what they're doing to those poor people in there!"

"S-s-s-h-h-h! Keep your voice down!"

"Okay! Okay!" Hawthorn whispered. "But that's horrible. I hate those Renegades. I hope we kill a bunch of them when we come back down here for the rescue."

"Listen to what you're saying," Turk said sternly. "You sound like a Renegade yourself when you talk like that. Thorn, that's all they understand. They don't know any better."

"Are you defending them?" Hawthorn had a look of disgust on his face.

"No, I'm not. They're a cruel people, and they live a very cruel life. I'm not defending them, but I understand them. Six years ago I was one of them."

"You were a Renegade?!" Hawthorn was shocked.

Turk nodded. "I was just like they are, but the Father in heaven poured out His mercy on me. I was out with a raiding party, and I fell and broke my leg. Nobody wanted to have to deal with me, so they left me to die."

"You mean you don't hate them for that?" Hawthorn asked.

"No, I don't hate them. If they had carried me back, I would never have heard about Jehesus. I would never have become a child of the Maker. My leg probably wouldn't have healed, because Renegades don't know anything about caring for injuries like that. I would probably still be here, dragging myself around, hating everybody. When they left me behind, it was the best thing that ever happened to me, though I didn't know it at the time. Some Makerian Rangers found me and carried me back to Stillwaters. They healed my leg, and Jehesus healed my soul.

"Any of them that we kill will be condemned to an eternity of fiery torment. They'll never have a chance to hear about the love that Jehesus has for them. They'll never have an opportunity to trust in Jehesus' death to pay for their evil deeds. They'll never know the peace, joy, and freedom that come to you when you're a child of the Maker.

"Thorn, the Maker takes no pleasure in the death of anyone. When a bad person dies, they're lost, and that means Satan, the evil one, won the battle for their soul. The Maker is never happy about that. What gives the Maker real pleasure is when He can change bad people into good people as they come to trust in Jehesus.

"None of the rest of us wants to kill them, Thorn. We want to save them."

Just at that moment, Eldan and Tobin reappeared out of the shadows. "Did you two find anything that would help us?" Turk asked.

"As a matter of fact, we did," answered Eldan smugly.

"Is that right?!" Hawthorn asked, looking at Tobin.

Tobin nodded his head, "Yep, I think we found just what we need to get them out."

The moon had long since set, and the night seemed especially dark. Most of the camp was sleeping soundly, except for the guards and a small group of Makerians sitting in a tight circle under the overhanging rock of the bluff. They had their cloaks wrapped tightly around them in an attempt to fend off the chilly breeze blowing through the camp from the north. The greenish glow of a light stick illuminated the center of the group. Sitting in the circle were Hawthorn, Turk, Eldan, Tobin, Charlock, and Graceson.

It had taken Hawthorn and his companions well into the third watch of the night to climb out of the secret entrance to the Lair and drag themselves wearily into camp. Charlock had left orders with the guards to wake him and Graceson as soon as the scouts returned. He was now getting a report of what they had found.

Tobin had been drawing a map in the sand with a sharp stick. Information was occasionally added by Turk and Eldan. Hawthorn spent most of his time taking long swallows from a mug of warm, sweet nectar and trying not to fall asleep. Charlock and Graceson both had many questions about every part of the expedition in and out of the Lair. "You're positive it's there?" asked Graceson.

"Yep," was Tobin's answer.

"We looked straight down into it with our own beady eyes," Eldan added.

"And it drops straight down into the guard room where the slaves are?" Graceson asked again.

"Yep," Tobin returned.

"We watched the guard walking around as he made sure the cells were locked," Eldan said with a little frustration beginning to show in his tone of voice.

"But is it wide enough?"

"Yep."

"Graceson, Graceson, Graceson!" Eldan burst forth. "Brother Tobs is a Makerian of few words, but there's a wealth of meaning in them. Allow me to interpret for you. 'Yep' means that the crevasse that we found in the rocks above the slave cells is perfect for what we need. It is a straight drop directly into the room where the guard is, and it's plenty wide enough for one of us to be lowered into it."

"Is that really what 'Yep' means, Tobin?" Graceson asked with a half smile.

"Yep."

"The plan is a good one," announced Charlock. "But we need to work on a diversion."

"I've been thinking about that," Turk spoke up. "I think I've just about got it worked out."

"We will let everyone sleep late tomorrow to get extra rest," said Charlock. "At noon, we will eat a hearty meal and then get everything ready to go. As soon as we are packed up, we will march for the secret entrance. We will leave Costal, Jonel, and Kordilon here to have hot food and medical supplies ready for us when we return with the slaves. Any questions?" he asked, glancing at each of them. "All right then; go get some rest."

"Oh, Turk," Charlock added, "before you wander off, tell me your idea for a diversion."

CHAPTER NINETEEN

DELIVERANCE

Rush had been busy. His main goal had been to secretly gather as much food and as many weapons as he could to work out his escape plan. But since the appearance of the Wompus Rat, Rush had found new enthusiasm for his work. Sightings of the monster were becoming the terrifying topic of conversation among the Renegades.

A work detail had been attacked by the creature as they repaired a storeroom door. The demon had dropped down on them from a dark ledge above, slashing at them with its terrible claws. The way they told it, they barely escaped with their lives.

As the cooks were preparing the morning meal for the Renegade leaders and captains, the horrible creature came charging out from behind some grain sacks. They all ran screaming for the door, overturning tables and shattering pots and jars. Before the last one could make it out of the room, he had the seat of his pants ripped completely out.

Later some grunts were moving clay boxes of dried meat in another store room when suddenly the door flew open. There stood a tall, cloaked figure with a rat skull for a face. Long, fierce-looking, boney claws reached out for them from under the cloak. With a hideous gurgling howl, the rotting creature charged the Renegade workers. Terrified, the five grunts screamed and ran into each other in their frantic attempt to flee. A running fight then broke out among them as they elbowed and slugged their way to be first to escape the slashing claws of the Wompus Rat. As they were chased around the storeroom, the grunts in the rear beat and clawed the ones in front, mercilessly trying to pass them. By the time they made it out of the storeroom door, they were all bruised and bleeding from many places. Most of the injuries that were suffered they had done to themselves.

All everyone could talk about was the terrible demon rat and where the latest attack had occurred. Rush was having the absolute time of his life. "I'm sure gonna miss this place and all the good times," Rush chuckled to himself as he hid his Wompus Rat disguise. "Maybe I'll come back to this booger town for a vacation someday."

He had acquired quite a collection of weapons. Rush knew that it probably wasn't enough, but he also knew that it was only a matter of time before he made a mistake and the Renegades caught him.

"Tonight," he said to himself decisively, "we'll escape tonight."

Once he had made the decision, he felt more at peace than he had since he had come there. For better or for worse, his mind was made up. He would free them or die trying.

He climbed to a dark ledge high on the wall of the little-used passageway he had found. Tucking himself back in the shadows of this shelf of rock, Rush was able to get a few hours sleep. He was awakened twice by Renegades moving through the passage below him. The second time he awoke, he decided it was time to contact the others.

Upon finding his friends in the mines, Rush roughly grabbed Savin and threw him behind a large boulder. Once he was sure the guards could neither see nor hear them, Rush came straight to the point. "It's gonna be tonight, Savin."

"All right!" Savin whispered enthusiastically.

"Tell Syc and Jay, but it might be best to keep Poke in the dark. I'm not sure he could hide his excitement enough not to give us away.

"I'll slip back down to the cells, probably around the third watch, and take out the guards. Then we'll try to make our escape."

"Why wait so late?" Savin wanted to know.

"'Cause some of these varmints don't go to sleep 'til then, with all their gamblin', fightin', and gyratin' around like a bunch of wild heatherns."

"Then I guess we'll just have to wait for you," Savin said.

"I guess you just will," Rush returned.

At that moment a horn sounded in the distance, and they knew it was time for the slaves to march back to the cells.

"You ready to join the others?" Rush asked.

"Yeah," Savin answered, "let's go."

"Okay, let's make this look good," Rush said as he grabbed the neck of Savin's tattered shirt and dragged him around the boulder. As soon as they were out in the open where the guards could see them, Rush hurled Savin forward. Savin helped the act by pretending to trip on a rock, and then fell hard on the gravely path. As Rush walked past Savin's prostrate form, he made sure the guards saw him spit at Savin.

Carrying a torch to light his way, Rush walked out a little ahead of the slow procession of slaves being herded back to the cells. He took his time walking back because his mind was on the escape plan. He went over it again and again, trying to think of ways to improve their chances. As he approached the door to the slave cells, he was completely unaware that he was being watched by fourteen pairs of eyes from the darkness.

<hr>

Hawthorn and the other scouts had been allowed to sleep until late morning. The rest of the camp had been up for some time preparing their equipment and packs. About midday Charlock called them all together. He led them in a prayer of thanksgiving, then they ate a hearty meal of honey cakes, dried meat, and fruit. When the food was finished, several large pouches of different fruit nectars were passed around to drink. Hawthorn tried them all, but the blackberry was his favorite.

"You'd better take two or three more pulls on that nectar before you pass it, young one."

"Thanks, Tobin," Hawthorn smiled. "It is good, but I've had plenty."

"You don't understand," his friend returned. "This isn't dessert. We drink the nectars to give us extra strength, and you're gonna need it today, so drink up."

A little over an hour after they had finished their meal, the camp was set in order, and the call was given to assemble. Forming a large circle, they fell to their knees and spent quite some time in intense prayer for what they were about to do. Hawthorn knelt with the rest of them, listening with fascination at the moving and sometimes passionate words that were spoken to the Maker by people who considered themselves His children. Hawthorn wondered if the Maker actually paid attention to their prayers. He still wasn't sure yet, but he knew one thing: if the Maker did consider these people His children, His father's heart had to be moved by what He was hearing now.

When they finished their prayers, the order was given to sling their packs and line up to march. Quick goodbyes were said all around to Costal, Jonel, and Kordilon, whose jobs were to stay and prepare the camp for their return with the slaves.

"We'll have a hot stew waiting for you when you get back," Costal announced.

"Good," growled Charlock. "We may have to eat and run."

"Keep the prayers up," Graceson called as they marched out.

"You can count on it," Kordillon shouted back.

A twenty minute march up the wooded hill brought them to the secret entrance of the Lair. At this point Charlock called them all together. "I don't need to tell you how important it is that we make the descent into this cave as quietly as possible. Make certain of every foot hold and of every place you put your hand. If we start rocks rolling, the whole mission could be doomed. You each know the plan; let's stick to it."

Charlock took a moment to look around at each one of them. "May the grace and mercy of God our Father and of the Lord Jehesus be poured out on us all this day."

"Amen!" most of the voices responded back.

Charlock nodded at Eldan, who walked over to the hole and climbed in. One by one they followed, descending the rocky chimney into the enemies' stronghold.

Even with so many climbing together, Hawthorn was surprised at how quickly they were able to make the descent this second time. Following the marked path, Eldan led them unerringly into the depths of the Renegade Lair.

When finally they could see the sandy path at the bottom of the cave, they halted. Charlock had them all move back up into the rocks far enough to where they would not give away their presence to the guards and slaves when they returned along the path from the day's work. They lay in the darkness for over an hour listening to the occasional drip of water. When the horn calling the slaves back to their cells did finally sound, the contrast between it and the long silence was startling.

"So what happens now?" Cari whispered in Hawthorn's ear.

"The guards gather all the slaves out of a larger cavern where the mines are and march them back by here," Hawthorn whispered in response. "They move pretty slowly, so it'll take some time before they get to where we are. In a while you'll see torches appearing off to the left. Then the whole procession will move in front of us and disappear around a turn to your right."

After several long minutes Cari put her hand on Hawthorn's arm. "Look!" she whispered. "Here they come."

Hawthorn peaked over the ridge of rocks behind which he had been lying. He saw a point of light appear to his left in the darkness below him.

"Hey!" Cari whispered to her friend, "I only see one torch."

Hawthorn looked carefully. "That's just one of the guards heading back to the cells. The rest of them will be along soon with all the slaves." Hawthorn watched the lone torch moving along the path below him, little realizing that the bearer of that torch was his friend Rush.

It was almost a quarter of an hour more before they saw the torches appear signaling the approach of the procession of slaves. As they moved along the trail below them, Hawthorn could again hear the occasional cracking of whips and the groans of the slaves. "That will end soon enough," he thought to himself as he watched them.

Several minutes after the last torch passed from view around the bend, Eldan and Turk left the rest. They quietly descended to the path and followed the guards and slaves, being careful to stay in the shadows. It seemed to Hawthorn that they had been gone a really long time when finally Turk returned and word was passed to begin the descent to the path. The chances of being detected were now much greater than before, so everyone took extreme care as each climbed down the rocky slope.

When everyone was down, Charlock gave the hand signal for them to move out. They quietly and cautiously moved up the sandy pathway toward the slave cells. Part of the plan included Hawthorn and two others hanging back from the rest. As the main party followed Charlock and Turk toward the cells, Hawthorn and his two companions moved down the trail back toward the mines. Their job was to be sure no straggling guards would come up from behind and spoil the rescue. Hawthorn led them down almost to the great cavern where the mines were. They could hear the roaring of the underground river quite clearly. Satisfied that no one would be coming from that direction, they retraced their steps. By the time they had joined the others, everyone was in position and ready to put the plan into effect.

Charlock had spent the time getting his principal team members into position. Several minutes before he had received the signal that everyone was ready, but he would not give the sign to begin until he was sure that they would not be assaulted from behind.

When Hawthorn and his scouts returned, Charlock looked at them anxiously. Hawthorn gave Charlock the agreed upon signal that it was safe to proceed with the rescue plan. Charlock then held up his fist, which was the sign for all of those near him to get ready. He positioned himself behind one of the large boulders so that his light stick could not be seen from the window in the door to the cells a short distance up the path. He then waved the green glowing stick back and forth. Looking up into the darkness above and to their right, Hawthorn saw a small green light suddenly appear almost a bow shot away and begin waving back and forth. In a few moments the light in the distance went out. Hawthorn knew that this was one of the Rangers who was stationed high enough on the hill to be able to signal Eldan, Tobin, and Marsh. They had climbed up to the crevasse that Eldan and Tobin had found which formed an opening into the roof of the prison chamber where the guard sat. The plan was that, as soon as they saw the signal, Eldan and Tobin were to begin lowering Marsh as quietly as possible into the crevasse. Their returned signal was to let Charlock know that Marsh's descent was beginning.

As expected, the green light reappeared in a few moments. They were committed now! Charlock knew that it was time for Turk's diversion. Still remaining partially hidden by the boulder, he used his light stick to signal again, only this time his signal was directed toward the dark shadows just to the left of the door to the slave cells. Almost immediately a green light flashed back from the shadows.

Charlock turned toward the group of Makerians standing near him and brought his hands together to indicate that each one of them should be praying for what was about to happen.

After seeing Charlock's signal Turk moved out of the shadows toward the door to the cells. He was wearing a tattered and filthy tunic, and he had dirt smeared all over his face and hands. He knew that at that very moment, Eldan and Tobin would be lowering Marsh through the crevasse and down into the cell room. Turk's job was to distract the guard so that Marsh could enter the room from above unnoticed. As Turk drew near to the door, four other Makerians appeared out of the shadows. They took their positions with two on either side of the door. They stood against the rock wall, back and out of the sight of anyone who might look out of the barred window in the door.

Turk stepped up to the door and pressed his dirty face against the bars of the window. He had expected the guard to start yelling at him, but the only sounds were murmurings and moaning from the slaves. Turk took a moment to look around. There were twenty to thirty slaves in each of the two cells located on either side of the room. He looked for the guard and found him rocked back in a chair against the opposite wall taking a long drink out of a wine pouch. They had intentionally waited until all the other guards had left before starting the rescue plan. Turk looked up at the ceiling. He noticed that it sloped upward from both sides of the room to meet the opening of the crevasse. There was no sign of Marsh yet, but he should appear at any moment.

"Hey, boss!" Turk said rather loudly through the window.

The guard jerked up from his comfortable position, and with cheeks bulging from a mouthful of wine, he glared menacingly around the room for the no-good slave who had disturbed his tranquility.

"Over here, boss!" Turk called again.

The guard glanced over at the door and was startled at seeing the filthy face of Turk smiling at him through the barred window. An explosion of wine sprayed out of the guard's mouth. "What do you think you're doin', you dirtball!" the guard screamed at him.

"Well, I kind of got left behind," Turk said, still smiling.

"Left behind!" the guard roared as he stamped angrily across the room, stopping just in front of the door. "You steamin' pile of useless scum! You didn't get left behind. You slipped away from yer work and went to sleep, didn't cha?!"

Turk's answer was the same annoying smile.

"And then," the guard continued to rant, "when you did wake up from yer beauty sleep, you found out everybody was gone! So now you come slinkin' up here like the captain of the guard wantin' yer supper!"

Turk could see Marsh descending slowly out of the hole in the ceiling behind the guard. "Oh, come on, boss," Turk whined. "Have a heart; let me in. I promise I won't do it no more."

"Y're scared, huh?" the guard snarled. "Well, maybe I'll just let you stay out there. What'll you do if the Wompus Rat shows up, huh?! He'd eat you faster'n spit."

By now Marsh was hanging just a short ways above the floor. He could easily drop the remaining distance, but if he did so the guard would surely hear him and turn to attack. Marsh was a good fighter, but the guard might be too. Marsh decided to get the rope swinging, and when it had swung forward to just behind the guard, he would drop on top of his enemy.

As the guard yelled at him, Turk saw Marsh swinging himself. Marsh's intentions were clear. Just as Marsh swung backwards with a strong swing, Turk heard the rope creak. The guard heard it too. He started to turn toward the sound.

"OH, PLEASE DON'T LEAVE ME OUT HERE!!" Turk screamed loudly. Startled, the guard looked back at Turk just as Marsh came swinging forward.

Whump! Marsh landed his full weight on the guard's back, driving him face first into the door and then into the floor. Marsh jumped up and quickly pulled back the wooden bolt that locked the door and yanked it open. Turk and his four friends rushed inside. Before the dazed guard could recover, they had gagged him and pulled a large sack over his head and chest.

The guard sitting outside the other door had heard some commotion in the cell room, but he didn't think much of it. He knew the other guard enjoyed tormenting the slaves, and the yelling and screaming was commonplace. Besides, he was busy eating his supper.

"Help me! Help me! One's loose!" a voice shouted clearly.

Jumping up, the outer guard looked in through the barred window of his door. He saw the guard in the cell room flat on his back with one of the slaves on top of him apparently trying to kill him. Quickly glancing at both sides of the room, he saw the rest of the slaves securely locked in their cells.

"HEL-L-L-P ME-E-E!" the voice screamed desperately.

Grabbing his war club, the outer guard pulled back the bolt that locked the door and charged to the rescue. Rushing up, he drew back his club, preparing to bash the brains out of the rebellious slave, when suddenly his club was jerked from his hands. Spinning around quickly to see what had happened to his club, he saw four determined-looking warriors with weapons in hand. The closest one had his club in one hand and a long, black, thorn dagger in the other. Ropes were quickly thrown around him, and he was placed on the floor with the other guard. They were secured to the wooden bars of one of the cells.

"Get 'em out of those cells!" Turk ordered.

Quickly the Makerian Rangers began knocking loose the heavy beams that were propped against the cell doors wedging them tightly shut. But as the doors were jerked open, none of the slaves made a move. Their eyes were full of distrust and fear.

"Don't you understand?" Turk said so all could hear. "We're here to rescue you."

"And just who are you?" a voice from the cells said suspiciously.

"We are friends!" Turk answered. "We've come to help you escape from here! But you must trust us."

Still none of the slaves moved out of their cells. By this time Charlock had entered with Hawthorn, Cari, and several more of the Rangers. "Why are they still in the cells?" Charlock asked Turk.

"They won't come out. They don't trust us."

Hawthorn, who was standing behind Charlock, heard this and immediately stepped out into the middle of the room. "Poke! Poke! Where are you?!" he cried loudly, looking from one side to the other. "It's me, Hawthorn!" Hawthorn could see nothing of his friend. In a panic, he ran to the open cell on his left, looking at every face. "Poke! Answer me! You gotta be here!" The young Larkin was almost in tears now.

"Hawthorn?" said a young voice from across the room. Hawthorn turned and saw a thin form, covered in dirt and dried blood, walking towards him from the cells across the room. "You can't be Hawthorn. He's dead."

"Poke? Is that you?" Hawthorn unstrapped his acorn cap helmet and yanked it off. Running over to his friend, he grabbed both of his shoulders. "Poke! It's me!"

Suddenly realization struck Poke. He gasped and threw himself at his friend. Hugging each other tightly, the two friends danced and yelled in the center of the room. Their joyful reunion was interrupted suddenly when two strong arms wrapped around both of them.

"Hawthorn!"

"Father!"

"You're not dead!" they both shouted at each other.

"So it would seem," Poke felt compelled to say.

"Did you get captured too?" Hawthorn asked his father.

"We came to rescue you and Poke, but when we got close, Sycamore and I got captured. What are you doing here?"

"My friends and I came to rescue Poke," Hawthorn answered.

"Well, don't I feel special," Poke said as a large grin spread across his face. Pieces of dried dirt flaked off and fell to the floor. "I can't believe it, Thorn!" Poke said, looking him up and down. "You look great!"

"You don't," Hawthorn returned shaking his head. "You look awful."

Very quickly Sycamore and Jay also joined them with more hugs and rejoicing. As the shock of seeing Hawthorn began to wear off, the questions began to come.

"Hawthorn, how did you get here?" his father asked. "And who are these people?!"

"Father, it would take too long to explain. They saved my life, and now they're here to save yours. You know one of them," Hawthorn said as he turned and pointed toward a large, bearded warrior standing nearby.

"Charlock!" Savin said with surprised recognition of his old friend.

"What's he doing here?" Jay whispered in Hawthorn's ear.

"Listen to me, all of you!" Hawthorn spoke with a tone of urgency. "It would take hours to explain everything that's happened to bring us here, and we don't have the time. We must move quickly if we're all going to get out of here. You must trust these people! They saved my life!"

"But the Shaman said Charlock was a traitor," Poke joined in.

"He's not!" Hawthorn said emphatically. "And he never was. Charlock is the reason we're here. He put this rescue together, and he's in charge of it. Father, Charlock is not a traitor!" Hawthorn said firmly.

Savin stood there in silence looking into the eyes of his old comrade. Finally he said, "I never thought he was." Walking over, he extended his right hand to Charlock. They warmly grasped each other's forearms and clapped each other on the back. The others followed Savin's example. Poke apologized to his old master for calling him a traitor.

"I forgive you, young Poke," Charlock responded. "I know why you said it, but you know me better than that."

"So what do we need to do?" Savin asked.

"See if you can get these poor souls out of those cells," Charlock answered. "We've brought packs full of food. We're gonna feed you and try to get some strength in you, 'cause you got a long climb ahead."

The packs were broken open, and the food was displayed. That and the Larkins' encouragement soon had the suspicious prisoners moving out of their cells and toward the food. Once they tasted it, and reality set in, a party atmosphere broke out. Now the Makerians' problem was to keep the slaves from eating so fast that they made themselves sick.

Sammal was standing by the open door leading up into the Lair. He was leaning on the war club they had taken from the second guard. An older, haggard-looking slave hobbled up to him eating a honey cake.

"Many thanks for your kindness," the slave said to Sammal in a weak voice.

"We're honored to help you," Sammal returned with a smile. "This is a gift to you from the Maker."

"You know, if more Renegades come, we'll have to fight our way out," the slave said with concern.

"Let's pray that it doesn't come to that," Sammal answered.

"I'd feel a little safer if I had something to fight with. Could I carry that club?"

Sammal looked down at the war club he was leaning on, then back at the pitiful captive. "Sure," he said, "if it makes you feel better."

The old slave took the club from Sammal and hefted it, testing its weight. Then without warning, he brought the club down with tremendous force on the back of Sammal's neck. As Sammal crumpled to the floor, the slave leaped through the door, slammed it shut, and bolted it from the outside. Then he ran as quickly as his injured leg would let him up the passage, yelling for help as he ran.

The attack occurred so unexpectedly and so quickly that those who saw it happen were unable to do anything to help.

Marsh was the first one to Sammal's side. Braden, one of the Makerian Rangers, ran straight to the door with bow and arrow in hand, but it was too late to stop the traitor. He was disappearing into the dark passage even as Braden tried to take aim.

"How is he?" Turk asked as he knelt with Marsh beside their fallen comrade.

Marsh looked at Turk with tears filling his eyes. "He was probably in the Maker's arms before he hit the floor."

As realization of his friend's death struck Turk, a prayer broke his lips, "Oh, Jehesus! Must it cost so much to do good?"

"Why?!" Marsh cried out, holding his fallen comrade. "Why would he do this?!"

"It was Wolf," said Poke as he stood with his friends looking toward the fallen Makerian.

"Wolf?!" Hawthorn asked in surprise. "Are you sure?"

Poke nodded silently.

"What was he doing here?"

"They made him a slave for killing you," Poke answered. "Well, they thought he had killed you. I guess he saw this as an opportunity to get back in the good graces of the Renegades."

"You can bet he'll be back here in no time with the whole Renegade army," Turk announced.

Everyone looked at Charlock for direction. After a moment's thought, the old warrior made his decision. "I'm sorry, my friends," he began, "but we have no time for you to rest. Take as much food as you can carry in one hand and eat on the way. The other hand you'll need for climbing.

"Cari!"

"Yes, sir!" said an emotional voice over by Sammal's fallen form.

"You can't help Sammal, Cari," Charlock's voice softened, "but these new friends of ours need you now."

With great composure Cari stood up and turned to face her commander. "What can I do to help, sir?"

"Good lass!" Charlock said with obvious pride. "Quickly check our new friends and find out who among them needs help climbing out of here. Assign one of our people with each one who needs help.

"Turk!"

"Yes, sir."

"I need you to cover our retreat. Pick two warriors and try to hold them off for as long as you can."

Turk noticed the worried look on Charlock's face. "It'd be my pleasure," Turk grinned. "Don't worry 'bout a thing."

Turk walked over to where Hawthorn was standing. Eldan was also nearby. Turk put his hands on a shoulder of each of his two friends and pulled them close to him. "Now where am I gonna find two guys dumb enough to volunteer to help me hold off a whole army of Renegades?"

"Why, Turkey! You ol' muskrat!" Eldan began, his thick red hair flopping back and forth as he shook his head. "Did you lose most of your brains last time you blew your nose? You don't need dumb guys for this. This job's gonna require strategy. You need two fellows with some serious thinkin' power. Right, Thornblossum?"

Hawthorn saw the mischievous wink from Eldan. The young Larkin understood the seriousness of the task for which he was being asked to take part, and he knew that being killed was a very real possibility. But he was there to save the people he loved, and he was willing to do everything in his power to accomplish it. "You're right, Eldan," Hawthorn answered with mock seriousness, "and I don't know of anybody here with more brains than you and me."

"Right you are, Chummy! Right you are!

"Well, there you have it, Turkey. You got the two smartest guys down here," Eldan boasted.

"I don't know about that," Turk responded. "I think I need a second opinion."

"Okay," Eldan shot back, "we're good-lookin' too."

The laughter was cut off by Charlock's voice, "Do you think you should keep the lad, Turk?"

"I want to stay, Charlock," Hawthorn said earnestly. "I have the most to fight for."

"He and Eldan know these tunnels better than any of the rest of our people," Turk added.

Charlock thought for a moment, then nodded his head. "So be it," he said. Turning, Charlock addressed the rest of the party, "All right, let's get them moving. Any of you who have arrows, leave half of them with Turk."

"And rope!" called Eldan.

"Rope?" asked Charlock.

"Uh, yes, sir," said Turk as he saw a big grin spread across Eldan's face. "We need rope."

"Lots of rope!" added Eldan.

"Uh, lots of rope, sir."

"Anyone with extra rope, leave it," ordered Charlock.

By this time the Rangers had the healthier former slaves moving quickly down the path. All who were able pitched in to help the weaker ones. Braden helped Marsh lift Sammal's body up onto his back. "I'm not leaving him down here," Marsh said as he started down the path with the others.

Charlock and Tobin were the last to leave. Charlock looked at the three defenders. His eyes seemed to linger a little longer on Hawthorn. "You each know what we need you to do. Try to hold 'em long enough for us to get these poor souls up to where the enemy can't see or hear us. Then save yourselves!"

"Don't worry about a thing, chief," grinned Eldan. "They've got me with them."

"May the Father of our Lord Jehesus bless and protect each of you!" Tobin spoke in earnest.

"Amen," they all said.

When the three defenders were finally left alone, Turk turned to Eldan with a suspicious look. "So . . . you wanna' explain what all this rope's for?"

A huge grin spread across Eldan's face. "Oh, I just figure we need a little help. Grab all this rope and follow me. We got a whole heap of work to do."

Once Wolf was far enough up the passage to feel safe, he slowed his pace a little to spare his injured leg. When he got to the main door leading up to the Lair, he quickly told the guard what was happening, but the guard thought it was a trick and refused to believe him. Wolf cursed and threatened, but still the guard ignored him. It was only when Wolf described in graphic detail what would be done to the guard when it was discovered that he could have stopped the escape and didn't that he agreed to go get help. Wolf was left at the bolted door screaming at him through the barred window. Wolf was still screaming several minutes later when the guard returned, bringing with him his captain.

Wolf was livid. "You only brought one warrior?! You idiot!"

The captain threw his war club at the bars of the window, and Wolf only had an instant to pull his fingers and face back before the heavy weapon crashed into the door. "What's this all about?" the captain barked at Wolf. "And you better watch yer mouth."

Wolf repeated his story as the guard and the captain eyed him suspiciously. "You say there's Gooders down there tryin' to free the slaves? Well, how'd they get in?" the captain demanded.

"I don't know how they got in, but you can bet they're goin' out the same way, and they're takin' the slaves with 'em."

"Why didn't you go with them?" the captain wanted to know.

"Because I ain't no stinkin' Gooder!" Wolf spat. "I'm a Renegade warrior."

"You WERE a Renegade warrior," the captain reminded Wolf.

"I will be again, Pike, if you listen to me, and we stop this escape."

Captain Pike thought on Wolf's words for several moments. Finally he looked hard into Wolf's eyes. "If you're lyin', you die!" he said.

"I ain't lyin'," Wolf shot back.

"Stay here," Pike ordered the guard. Then he turned and ran back up the passageway.

Within a few moments a deep booming sound began rumbling through the Renegade stronghold. Rush was in a distant corner of the great hall eating some roasted meat he had acquired when the alarm was sounded. Moving close to a crowd of warriors, he heard about the rescue attempt and that a large party of warriors was being sent down into the mines to stop it. As Rush looked across the great hall, he could see a large mass of armed Renegades hurrying into the passage to the mines.

At first Rush thought that his own plans had been discovered and that he had better lie low. But then he thought that, if there really was a rescue going on, they needed all the help they could get. Moving quickly across the huge room, Rush came to the passage leading down to the mines and charged after the Renegade army. As he ran, his mind raced to try to form some kind of a plan, but he needed more information. He had to know what was going on before he could help.

As Rush ran past the crevasse where he had stored his weapons and supplies, a sudden thought hit him. Stopping quickly, he slipped behind the boulder and crawled into the crevasse. He was only in there for a few moments before he was out again and running down the dark passageway. In his arms he carried a bundle, and on his face was a wide grin.

chapter twenty

ESCAPE

"Here they come!" Turk called over his shoulder to his two comrades.

"Go help Turkey," Eldan said to Hawthorn. "I'll finish here and join you."

Hawthorn ran to Turk, who was guarding the bolted cell door. He stole a glance through the barred window in the door but saw nothing. "I don't see anything, Turk."

"They're moving around back in the shadows," Turk returned, "probably gettin' ready to rush the door. Put out all the torches, Thorn. Leave that oil lamp burning over by the guard's table. The one torch burning just outside this door gives us light to see them but makes it hard for them to see us."

Hawthorn quickly darkened the room.

"Hurry, Thorn, and tell Eldan to get in here. They're sending two scouts down to check things out!"

Hawthorn ran to the other door, stuck his head out, and called for his friend.

"Now there you went and woke me up," a familiar voice drifted down from the darkness above the door. "I was having me such a fine nap!"

"Quit your kidding, Eldan. Aren't you about done yet?"

"Patience, Chummy. The artist must be given his time."

"Eldan, there's no time left. They're moving toward the door. Turk said to come now!"

"Right, right. Tell him I'll be there in a flash."

When Hawthorn returned to Turk, he found him with his bow drawn and carefully aiming his arrow through the bars of the window.

"There's one behind that sharp ridge on the right, and the other just crept behind that low boulder on the left. I'll take the one on the left, and you go for the other."

Hawthorn grabbed his bow and notched an arrow. As Hawthorn glanced back up, he saw two dark figures moving cautiously from their place of concealment and creeping toward the cell door.

"Let me shoot first," Turk whispered.

Hawthorn could clearly see his target now. He wore a frightful-looking red mask, carried a war club in his right hand, and covered most of his body with a rectangular-shaped, red shield. Because the Renegade crouched low as he moved forward, Hawthorn was having trouble finding a good spot at which to aim.

"Let me take him, Chummy," said a voice in Hawthorn's left ear.

Turning, Hawthorn saw Eldan standing next to him with his bow fully drawn.

Turk released his shaft, and a split second later Eldan's missile whizzed through the window. Paired screams echoed off the rock walls as both arrows hit their marks. Eldan's victim was trying to hobble back up the passageway with a Makerian shaft sticking through his right ankle. Turk hit his Renegade in the left shoulder.

"Well, they know we're here now," said Hawthorn.

"Yep," Turk answered, "and when they come next time, there'll be no lack of targets."

"They'll have their shields up and their masks on," added Eldan, "so you probably won't get a good body shot. Just aim below their shields and you'll most likely hit a leg. Don't take too much time aiming either."

"Right," voiced Turk. "When they charge, get as many arrows out there as you can. Then when I give the word, everybody head for the back door. Understand?"

There was no time for anyone to answer because at that moment a chorus of nearly a hundred voices filled the cave with bone-chilling screams. A human wave of colored masks and shields came rushing down upon the defenders in a frenzied attack.

Arrows flew from the window in rapid succession. Several Renegades in the front ranks went down, causing those behind to trip over them. This slowed the charge somewhat, allowing the defenders to inflict more damage.

While the number of enemies arrayed against them was formidable, only six or seven Renegades could actually face them at one time because of the narrowness of the passageway. By the fifth volley of arrows, enough of the front ranks of the enemy warriors had gone down that the charge had been stopped.

The Renegade captain, seeing that the wounded had almost all received arrows in their legs, commanded his troops to continue the advance by crawling forward behind their shields.

"Uh-oh, they're getting smarter," said Turk as he saw the slowly advancing shields. They poured their arrows at the edges of the Renegades' shields in the hopes that some of the arrows might strike the leg or shoulder of the crawling warrior behind it. Only occasionally were they successful.

"This isn't working!" cried Hawthorn.

"Let's try something different," said Eldan. "Turkey, that's your heavy bow, isn't it?"

"Yeah, what you got in mind?"

"You see that black shield yonder with the red center? Well, how about you hit that shield solid with all the power you got in that bow. Hit it about a hand-width below the center top edge. Let me tell you when to shoot."

Both Makerians took aim.

"Shoot!" called Eldan, and Turk released his shaft. One half second later, Eldan released his.

Turk's arrow hit his mark solidly and with such force that it knocked the shield back, raising its bottom edge up about three hand-widths. At that instant Eldan's arrow flew underneath the raised shield, striking its holder.

"Ha!" laughed Turk. "Now that's a trick I've never seen before."

"Me either," agreed Eldan.

"Hey! I want to try that!" said Hawthorn enthusiastically. "Shoot for that blue and yellow shield, Turk."

"You call it," said Turk as he drew his bow to full length.

Aiming carefully, Hawthorn gave the word. "Shoot!" he called, then right afterward released his own arrow.

Turk's arrow hit the shield hard, raising it just like before to allow Hawthorn's arrow to pass underneath.

"No! I missed him!"

"You shot too low, Chummy. Aim about a hand width below the center of the shield, like this. Green shield, Turkey, on the right."

"Got it," spoke Turk with drawn bow.

"Shoot!"

Twang! . . . Twang!

Thunk!

"Aieee!"

Slowly the defenders chipped away at the slow advance of the shielded horde. But just as slowly the Renegades worked closer and closer to the door. When the crawling Renegades got within half a stone's throw of the defenders, a voice shouted from behind, and the warriors jumped to their feet and charged the door again. The defenders were able to wound three of them before a Renegade shield slammed against the window, preventing them from shooting any more arrows.

"Let's go!" shouted Hawthorn as he heard the Renegades clawing at the bolt that would unlock the door.

"Not yet," returned Turk calmly. "We can buy our friends a little more time here before we leave."

Turk had slung his bow over his shoulder and had unsheathed his sting. Hawthorn quickly did the same.

By now the bolt had been slid, and frantic hands were pulling on the door, but it would not open. The reason was that four ropes had been tied to each corner of the barred window in the door, and these ropes had been pulled tight and secured to the bars of the slave cells on each side of the room.

"They'll have to move that shield to try to cut the ropes, so be ready," Turk said, positioning himself close to the door on the left. Hawthorn stood close on the right.

There was much shouting and yelling on the other side of the door. After a few moments the shield slid up a little so one of them could look through and see what was keeping them from opening the door. As soon as Hawthorn saw the opening made by the lifted shield, he quickly thrust his sting through the bars and into the space.

There was a frantic shout, and the shield slammed back down on the opening, trapping Hawthorn's sting. He and Eldan both had to pull on the sting to retrieve it.

"Next time don't thrust so far, Chummy."

Suddenly the shield was jerked away and almost immediately the ropes were spotted. Eldan, who had still kept his bow, let fly through the bars, striking a Renegade just on the other side of the window in the forehead of his wooden mask. The mask stopped the arrow, but the force of it drove the Renegade backward, toppling him and three others behind him. Long flint knives began to appear at the corners of the window, trying to saw through the ropes. Out shot the stings of the defenders. Several minutes were spent in this way, with neither side doing much damage to the other.

Finally a shield was slammed over the window once more. The shield was slid to the side just enough to expose one knot at a time. It was held so that the Renegade with the knife was somewhat protected from the thrust of the stings. In a short time the first rope was cut, and the second was being quickly severed.

"I think it's time to retreat," whispered Turk. "You two go on, and I'll set the trigger."

It took Turk only a few moments to pull the trigger rope across the door opening and wedge its knotted end in a notch cut into the door frame about knee height. Then he removed a wooden peg that had been holding the rope, and the line across the door instantly snapped tight.

Turk looked up at the door and saw the knife working on the last knot. "Sorry, guys," he said smiling, and he turned and quickly ran to the other door.

As soon as he passed through the door Eldan stopped him. "Don't move!" was all he said.

Eldan reached back and pulled the door until it was almost closed. He carefully wedged a knotted rope in the door as he shut it. Then he quickly turned and walked past Turk.

"Here's the trigger," he said, pointing down at a rope strung tightly across the path. "Be very careful."

Saying this, he cautiously stepped over the rope. Turk followed.

At that instant the last knot was cut, and the Renegades jerked the door open. With terrible shrieks, they threw themselves into the prison room to get at their foes. The first Renegade through the door tripped the trigger rope, and instantly several beams and a load of large rocks came crashing down on him and the four warriors behind him.

At first there was stunned silence except for the moans of the injured, but when they realized that a trap had been set for them, screaming and vicious swearing exploded from the maddened savages. Ignoring their injured comrades, they ran right over them to be first to kill one of their enemies. Searching the room, they found no one but the tied up guards. Jerking the gags from their mouths, one guard shouted, "They've all run down into the mines!"

On hearing this, the Renegade closest to the door to the mines jerked it open and started through. Suddenly remembering the trap on the first door, he stopped himself. Sure enough, he heard a creaking sound and a swish just outside the door, telling him that, indeed, the door had been booby trapped. Satisfied that he had outsmarted his tricky enemy, he looked up just in time to see the butt end of a large beam flying towards his head out of the darkness in front of him. The beam struck him solidly in the mask, lifting him off his feet and hurling him with great force into the Renegades behind him.

This time the furious screams and howls from the enraged Renegades were deafening. Those who had escaped injury picked themselves up and, in a frenzied rush, charged past the suspended beam, through the door, and down the path.

When the third trigger rope was tripped, it jerked free several support poles that had been placed on each side of the path, releasing a cascade of beams and rocks that had been suspended above. The first twelve Renegades were pounded by the raining debris.

"I can't believe it!" Hawthorn cheered as he watched the events with his friends. "All of the traps worked!"

"Why, I'm offended, Chums," said Eldan in a hurt tone. "My traps are a work of art. They always work."

"It's a shame you didn't have time to set more," thought Turk out loud, "because they'll be up and at us again in a moment. Come on!" Off he ran down the sandy path toward their way of escape. Using their light sticks to see by, the three friends sprinted down the trail.

After several minutes Turk stopped them. All three of them spotted the three stones marking the place where they were to climb up the steep, rocky side of the cavern.

"I don't see them," said Hawthorn, staring up into the blackness looking for his retreating friends. "Do you think we bought them enough time?"

Before Turk could answer, a small cascade of stones came tumbling down the steep slope above them. "Does that answer your question?" responded Turk. "They're only a short ways up."

At that moment shrieks and screams could be heard from the direction they had come. Torch light could be seen flashing off the rocks in the distance. "They'll be here any moment!" Hawthorn cried anxiously as he watched the approaching lights and heard the shouts grow increasingly louder.

"You two climb on up and warn the others to be quiet," Eldan said commandingly. "I'll lead those screamin' heathens on a wild Eldan chase."

"Wait a minute," growled Turk. "I'm the leader of this detail, so I'm the one who stays."

"But you don't know where the tunnels go down there; I do. So I'm gonna run down the path aways, and when those savages reach this spot, I'll distract 'em so they'll chase me. They won't even notice where the rest of you went."

"But what about you?" Hawthorn asked with concern.

"Oh, don't worry about me, Chummy," Eldan said smiling. "I got me a plan. Now you two scoot on up there and warn the others to be quiet until the

Renegades pass." Eldan then turned and sprinted down the path away from the oncoming enemies.

Turk and Hawthorn watched him run away and then looked at each other. "I can't let him do this alone," Turk said. "You go up and warn the others to be quiet till the Renegades pass." Then Turk ran after Eldan.

Hawthorn watched his two friends for a moment and then turned to look at the approaching torch lights of the Renegades. "Be quiet till the Renegades pass!" he shouted up into the darkness; then Hawthorn sprinted down the path after his comrades.

As Rush approached the slave cells, he suddenly stopped and scanned the scene before him. Scattered along the floor of the passageway between him and the door were eighteen Renegades, all with arrows protruding mostly from shoulders and legs. Picking his way through the groaning wounded, he came to the open door. Here under a pile of debris were five more. Hearing other groans to his right, he saw the injured bodies of four other Renegades lying near the trussed-up guards. Ignoring the pleas of the guards, Rush walked over to the door with the suspended beam extending through it. Looking down the passageway, he saw the path before him literally covered with injured and unconscious Renegades.

"Thunderation!" Rush said to himself. "Whoever these rescuers are, they know how to take out Renegades. If I do manage to catch up to 'em, I'd better watch my step."

Grabbing a torch, Rush picked his way through the injured and the fallen beams and rocks. Then he raced down the path as fast as he could run.

"Not so fast, guys," Eldan puffed as he, Turk, and Hawthorn ran down the sandy path of the cavern. "We don't want to lose 'em—at least, not yet."

About a bow shot behind them charged the howling, bloodthirsty mass of Renegades. So far the plan was working great. They had lured the frenzied savages right past where the Rangers were climbing out with the slaves.

305

"Okay!" announced Eldan. "There's the fork in the path just ahead. Let's slow down and catch our breath. I want 'em close enough to see for sure which way we're going."

"I think they see us, Eldan," said Turk as he heard some of the shrieks grow sharper and saw some of the leaders pointing towards them.

"Hold up your light sticks so they can see them," said Eldan. "All right, follow me!"

Eldan took off down the right fork. He kept looking back as they ran. He didn't feel satisfied until he heard the screams of their pursuers echoing down from behind and saw the torch light flashing on the narrow walls and low ceiling of the tunnel through which they were now running.

"Great!" Eldan exclaimed. "They're following us."

"Great," huffed Hawthorn unenthusiastically.

"Fellas, it's time to pull on your runnin' shoes. Give it all you got, and let's lose those screamin' beauties."

Eldan burst into an all-out sprint. It was all Hawthorn could do to keep up with him as they raced down the twisting, turning passageway. After a few minutes it was clear that the pursuing Renegades were being left behind. Suddenly they burst out into a gigantic, open cavern. The roaring sound of a rushing river drowned out any sounds of pursuit.

They charged down the path into the heart of the cavern without slackening their pace. The further they went, the louder the river noise grew until the roar was deafening. Suddenly the path stopped, and they found themselves standing at the edge of the swift-moving water. Looking back, they saw a line of small, flickering lights emerging from the darkness far behind them.

"Here they come," announced Turk.

Looking around, Eldan saw a wooden dock in front of them with a large, raft-like ferry moored to it. To the right a sandy path led along the riverbank into the darkness. To the left another path sloped upward.

"To the left!" Eldan commanded, charging up the selected path.

"Does he know where he's going?" huffed Turk as he ran next to Hawthorn.

"Well . . . sort of," Hawthorn puffed back. "There's an opening somewhere above us that leads back to the main trail. This path does go in the right direction."

Eldan stopped abruptly.

"Oh, no! Those sneakin' . . ."

"What? What is it?"

"Look!" spat Eldan, pointing up into the darkness ahead of them.

Tiny dots of flickering light began to appear out of the darkness and slowly began to spread out, moving down to meet them.

"Those guys aren't as dumb as they look, are they?"

"They've cut us off, Eldan!" cried Hawthorn. "What are we gonna do?"

"Something different!" he answered, looking behind them. "Come on!"

Down the path he charged, leading his friends back the way they had come. Looking up they could see the line of torches spilling down the sloping path to their right. Trying to judge the distance, Hawthorn guessed that the three of them would get to the point where the paths joined before the Renegades did, but it would be close.

"We'll make a stand at the dock!" Eldan called. "Unsling your bows!"

When they reached the dock, the charging Renegades were only half a bow shot away and coming hard. Arrows began to fly rapidly from the bows of the three defenders. Caught by surprise by the sudden attack, several Renegades in front went down as the arrows found their mark. Those behind began to trip over the fallen wounded. As more arrows poured into their ranks, the charge faltered.

"Chummy," Eldan called, "slip behind us and untie the ferry while we hold 'em off!"

Rush, having thrown away his torch, cautiously approached the pinned-down Renegades from the rear. Looking past the Renegades, Rush could see three dimly lit figures in the flickering light of the Renegades' torches. They were obviously trying to climb onto the ferry while holding off their enemies.

Sizing up the situation, Rush didn't like what he saw. Being trapped on that ferry raft wasn't his idea of a good, defensible position, but it did provide a way to put some distance between them and their enemies. Rush noticed that some of the Renegades were preparing to use bows and arrows against the three. "Those guys are done for if they don't get some help," Rush thought, and he began to unwrap his bundle.

Rush took the contents and quickly stepped behind a large boulder. In just a few moments a large, hulking figure with a hideous, rotting, rat-like face under a hooded cloak stepped out from behind the rock. Carrying a Renegade war club on the right and fierce claws on the left, the creature approached the Renegades from behind.

As one of the Renegades jumped up with his bow drawn, the creature leaped forward and dropped the archer with a powerful swing of his club. Hearing the moan as their comrade went down, several of the Renegades turned to see what had happened. A blood-curdling scream burst from the chest of the huge demon-like creature, announcing to all those near him that their worst nightmare had joined them. With claws and club swinging at victims on both sides of the path, the Wompus Rat waded into the midst of the panic-stricken Renegades. Losing all interest in the three rescuers, the Renegades now fought each other to escape the terrible wrath of the Wompus Rat.

Hawthorn and his friends could not tell what was happening. To them it looked as if the Renegades had suddenly turned on themselves. They quickly cut the line holding the ferry and leaped on. Using the rope running through the ferry to both sides of the river, the three friends began pulling the ferry toward the other bank.

By this time Rush had fought his way down the path, clubbing and clawing furiously at every Renegade he could reach. Seeing the three rescuers moving the ferry away from the dock, Rush decided it was time to join them. Slashing at a nearby Renegade and throwing his club at another, he turned and charged for the dock. Running full speed to the edge of the wooden pier, Rush launched himself toward the upstream side of the ferry.

Hawthorn looked up in time to see a large, demon-faced creature fling itself into the river toward them. Turning loose of the rope, Hawthorn ran to the edge of the raft just in time to see the rotted rat face appear above the side wall. Hawthorn threw a powerful kick at the creature's face and was amazed to see the hideous-looking head tear loose from its body and go flying off into the river.

"Eeyow!" screamed a familiar voice. "Easy, fellers! I'm a good guy!"

"Rush?!" shouted Hawthorn as he recognized the voice. "Is that you?"

"Well, o' course it's me," he growled back, his neck still hurting where the thong holding the Wompus Rat head had torn loose. As he started to climb up onto the raft, he looked up and saw the face of Hawthorn surrounded by the eerie green glow of the light stick. His mouth dropped open, and he was speechless.

"Rush, it's me! Hawthorn!"

"Hawth . . . Hawth . . . Hawth . . ." Rush stammered. Looking over he saw two other faces, each lit up with the same unearthly glow.

"SPIRITS!!" he finally shouted, his eyes wide. "Mercy on me! Mercy on me!"

"Rush!" Hawthorn said, grabbing his friend's shoulder to keep him from falling back into the river. "It's really me! We aren't spirits."

"You mean you ain't kilt?!" Rush exclaimed, still not convinced.

"No, I'm not killed," Hawthorn answered as he helped pull his friend into the ferry, "at least, not yet."

By this time the Renegades began to regroup to renew the attack. Two arrows flew past Hawthorn. One of them tore through his tunic. Dropping to his knees to make a smaller target, he grabbed the rope and began pulling with Eldan and Turk.

Rush, who had more fallen into the raft than climbed in, lifted himself up and looked at Hawthorn and his two friends. "So . . . who are these guys, and how'd you get here?"

"Long story!" Hawthorn shot back. "Pull!"

Arrows began to hit the raft at regular intervals. Most of them hit the side walls, but a few struck dangerously close to Hawthorn and the other defenders. Pulling with all their strength, they were able to rapidly increase the distance between them and the Renegade archers on the shore.

"So what's the plan?" Rush finally asked as they continued to pull the raft across the rushing river.

"We'll cross to the other side of the river," Turk answered over his shoulder. "Then we'll scout upriver and see if we can find a way to cross back over without being seen and climb out the way we came in."

As Rush took in this information, he looked up at the dark bank of the side of the river to which they were pulling. As he looked, he saw a growing number of small flickering lights begin to appear out of the darkness, moving rapidly toward the spot where they would land the raft.

"You got another plan?" Rush asked.

"Oh, no!" shouted Hawthorn, as they all spotted the approaching enemies. "They've cut us off!"

"Stop pulling! Stop pulling!" Turk ordered.

The raft came to rest in the center of the swift river. Soon arrows began to hit the raft from both banks. With nothing else to do but press against the side walls of the raft for cover, Hawthorn introduced his friends to one another.

"Ah got a whole passel of questions I'm 'bout to bust a gut to get answered," Rush announced as an arrow slammed into the side of the raft near his head, "but I don't suppose this is the time to be askin' 'em."

More arrows hit the ferry. One stuck in the deck between Hawthorn's legs, slicing the flesh on the inside of his right thigh.

"This ain't workin', guys," Rush said as he examined Hawthorn's cut leg. "We've got to make some decisions. Who's the 'daddy roach' of this outfit?"

"Turk's officially in charge," Hawthorn answered his friend, "but Eldan's been leading since he knew more about the cave."

"We're hurtin' fer a plan, fellers! Any idears?" Rush addressed them all. No one spoke.

"How about you, Elmwood?" Rush asked, looking at Eldan.

"Now there you go! There you go!" Eldan answered with his usual enthusiasm. "Just like I figured. You're a fellow who likes to get right to the point. No beatin' around the bush for you. No, sirree! I saw it in your face when I first laid eyes on you. I said to myself, 'Self, now there's a fellow who doesn't mince words. He says what he means and gets right to it!' You know, Roof, old boy, you and I have a lot in common. People are always coming up to me and saying, 'Eldan, you really know how to get to the point.'"

"Eldan!" Turk barked. "Would you just get to the point!"

"Yes, Eldan," Hawthorn added anxiously. "Do you have a plan for getting us out of this?"

"Well, the truth is, I do have an idea, but I don't like it."

"We're runnin' short on options," Turk said as an arrow struck dangerously close to his head. "What's your idea?"

"Cut the rope."

"What!?" Hawthorn almost shouted when he heard Eldan's suggestion.

"Cut the rope?!" Turk was stunned.

"Eldan, that's crazy!" Hawthorn argued excitedly. "We have no idea what's down there!" He pointed toward the blackness downriver for emphasis.

"He's right, though," Rush said calmly. "We can't go back, and we can't go forward. We can't go upriver, and we shore can't stay where we are. The way ah see it, we only got one direction left to us, and that's downriver."

"But look at how fast the water's moving! There's probably some huge waterfall it all goes over. We could be killed!?"

"You're right as rain, Chummy," Eldan said encouragingly. "But if we stay here, we'll certainly be killed."

"Here they come to do it," Turk spoke up.

Renegades from both banks had begun climbing out onto the rope that was holding the raft in the center of the river. Slowly they inched their way toward the raft from both sides.

"It's now or never, fellers," Rush shouted as he pulled out his knife and began sawing on the large rope.

"Eldan, you and Thorn use your bows and try to keep those Renegade archers off our backs while we cut this rope," Turk ordered, and he immediately jumped to help Rush.

310

Hawthorn and Eldan quickly grabbed their bows and began launching arrows rapidly at any movement they saw on the shore. With their knives, Rush and Turk cut fiercely at the rope, one on one side, one on the other.

As realization of what they were doing struck the Renegades, there was much shouting and screaming from both sides of the river. In response to this, more arrows came flying in from both sides.

With a painful grunt, Turk staggered back from the rope and collapsed with a Renegade arrow protruding from his chest.

Eldan and Hawthorn quickly dropped to their friend's side. The location of the arrow told them both the agonizing truth that there was nothing they could do for Turk.

Coughing twice, Turk reached a feeble hand up to Eldan.

"It's bad, Turkey," Eldan said gravely as he held his friend's hand.

"I . . . know," Turk nodded. "I'm glad . . . we did this," Turk spoke weakly. "It . . . was . . . good, good . . . to do."

"You did well, Turkey," Eldan said gently. "We've bought our friends enough time to get the slaves out."

"You . . . think so?"

"I'm certain of it."

"Good . . . good," Turk breathed.

"Eldan . . ." Turk spoke with a little energy. "I . . . just thought of . . . I . . . I'm gonna see Him. I'm finally . . . gonna . . . see . . . Jehesus. In just . . . few minutes . . . see 'im."

"I envy you that, Brother," Eldan said with tears running down his cheeks.

Eldan was startled by loud shrieks close by. Looking up, he saw Rush fighting with two Renegades who had thrown themselves on top of him.

Jumping up, he rushed over and threw himself, shoulder first, into the nearest enemy, launching him over the side of the ferry and into the swiftly moving waters. Rush was now free to deal with the second Renegade. Twisting, Rush drove his elbow deep into his attacker's side, causing him to double over in pain. Rush then grabbed him, picked him up, and threw him across the deck into another Renegade just climbing over the rail, knocking them both into the river.

"My knife!" Rush yelled, scanning the deck. "Where's my knife?!"

At that same moment another Renegade leaped onto Rush's back from the other side of the ferry. Eldan jumped and grabbed the Renegade's knife hand as Rush drove his elbow up into his ribs.

Rush could see more Renegades were clambering over the sides of the raft. "Cut the rope!" he yelled at Eldan. Then, using his attacker as a shield, he drove the other Renegades off the raft.

Jerking out his knife, Eldan slashed hard at the frayed rope.

Hawthorn, consumed with grief for his dying friend, was oblivious to the desperate fight going on behind him.

"Thor . . . Thor . . ."

"I'm right here, Turk," Hawthorn said, grasping his friend's hand.

"'Portant . . . 'portant you know . . . He Lor . . . Jehesus . . . is Lor . . ."

Hawthorn started to respond, but Turk was gone.

Suddenly the raft began to turn and sway. Looking behind him, he saw that the raft was rapidly leaving the docks behind, while several Renegades were desperately trying to hold onto the cut rope in the fierce current. He also saw three Renegades locked in a desperate battle with Eldan and Rush. Running over to help Eldan, Hawthorn drove his foot hard into the ribcage of one Renegade, then leaped upon the head of the other one. The second Renegade saw Hawthorn coming. With a duck and a push he sent Hawthorn over his head. The young Larkin landed hard on the deck. Shaking his head to clear the stars he saw, Hawthorn looked up just in time to see the Renegade lunging for him. Hawthorn drew up both feet and kicked hard. There was a solid "whack" as he drove his heels full force into the Renegade's mask. The Renegade went limp and crumpled to the floor next to him.

Looking around, he saw Eldan was just heaving his attacker overboard, but Rush was having a tougher time of it. His left arm hung limply at his side with blood running down the sleeve. He was doing his best to stay away from the knife of his attacker, but he was definitely in trouble.

Hawthorn ran to his friend's aid, but the Renegade saw him coming and quickly slashed his knife at him, causing the young Larkin to jump back quickly. At the same moment Rush connected with a sweeping blow from his right fist that sent the Renegade sprawling across the side wall of the raft. Hawthorn grabbed his feet and flipped the enemy over the side.

By this time they had left the torches of the Renegades far behind. The deck of the raft was dimly illuminated by the green glow of the light sticks, but beyond the short sides of the raft, all was pitch black.

"Rush, are you okay?" Hawthorn asked with concern as he looked at Rush's blood-soaked left sleeve.

"Well, he sliced me pretty good," Rush said, examining his wound. "But I reckon I've had worse.

"Me and ol' El . . . uh . . . El . . . Elrod here . . ."

"Dan," Eldan corrected.

"What? Oh, yeah, sorry. Me and ol' Danrod here were havin' a tough time of it 'til you jumped in."

"Maybe we should try to bandage that wound, Rash," Eldan suggested.

"No time now!" Rush said. The raft was beginning to buck and twist wildly as it was pushed along at terrific speed down the dark, underground river. "Grab anything you can and hold on for dear life! We're in for a ride, fellers!"

Rush and Eldan found handholds on one side of the raft. Hawthorn did the same thing on the other.

"Hey, uh . . . uh . . ." Rush was trying to get Eldan's attention. "Hey, you with the floppy hair, I've only got one good arm, so if I start slippin', how about grabbin' me?"

"You can count on me, Rag, ol' buddy."

The roar from the river around them became deafening. Suddenly they were falling. Then, with a crashing jolt, they hit and water poured all over them. They twisted violently to the right and fell again. There was another hard crash, and what was left of the raft took a spiraling dive into the wet blackness.

CHAPTER TWENTY-ONE

FLOPPY AND WRETCH

Sweating and breathing hard, Charlock pulled himself out of the secret opening that led out of the cave. He could tell by the position of the stars that it was well into the third watch of the night. Stretched out on the ground all around him were the former Renegade slaves in various stages of exhaustion. Most of the Makerians were either assisting the weaker slaves or standing guard. Tobin, who had led the group in the climb out of the cave, had already sent Carineda and Braden ahead to the camp to get things ready for their arrival and to send back help.

Tobin looked past Charlock to the cave entrance, then back at Charlock. Charlock saw his friend's questioning look. "I left Graceson and Blesstis behind with some weapons and supplies for the others if they make it out." Tobin nodded his wordless response.

After a few minutes' rest, the Makerians began to move among the former slaves, giving them water and distributing the last few pieces of honey cakes to the weakest ones.

It was not quite half an hour later when Costal, Kordillon, Jonel, and Braden came trudging up the hill, each carrying several heavy pouches of sweet nectar. Every one of the former slaves was encouraged to take more than a few long drinks of nectar, which they eagerly did after tasting the deliciously sweet liquid.

Soon after this the weary army was stirred to its feet, and the slow, stumbling journey to the camp was begun. Even though it was all downhill, and the way was lit by Makerian light sticks, it took almost an hour to get the last of the former slaves into camp.

They were each given a blanket or a cloak in which to wrap up and a bowl of hot stew to eat. Plenty of sweet nectar and honey cakes were also available. Most of them were so exhausted that, after finishing their meal, they curled up right where they were and dropped off to sleep. The weaker ones were helped to a lean-to shelter constructed against the face of the bluff.

Just as the sky was starting to lighten Graceson and Blesstis arrived in camp. As ordered, they immediately reported to Charlock, who was sleeping near the bluff. Charlock woke Tobin, who was sleeping nearby, so that he could hear Graceson's report also.

The two Makerian scouts had remained hidden in the darkness above the path in the Lair for quite some time, waiting for Turk's group to return. When they did not, Graceson decided to slip back down closer to the trail to see what information he could gather from the conversation of the Renegades as they passed by. He was eventually able to hear enough to figure out that Turk's group had been unable to slip past the pursuing Renegades and had tried to escape down the underground river. Since they would probably not be climbing out through the hidden entrance, Graceson and Blesstis climbed out, leaving some food and water behind on the secret path just in case.

Charlock asked a few more questions, then thanked his scouts and sent them off to get some food and rest. After several moments of silent thought Charlock spoke, "Well, we've lost Sammal."

"And maybe Turk, Hawthorn, and my brother," added Tobin. Charlock nodded in agreement.

"We need to plan as if they will be of no help to us, and Tobin," Charlock said firmly, "we can't go back for them—at least, not right now."

"I know," Tobin said grimly. "Our first responsibility is to these folks we've rescued. They're in pretty bad shape, you know."

"Yes," growled Charlock. "It's going take some work to get these people strong enough to march back to Stillwaters."

"Even when they're strong enough to march, we won't be able to move very quickly with them," Tobin agreed.

"As hard as we pushed them climbing out of the cave, most of them won't be able to move at all for the next twenty-four hours."

"There are three or four of them," Tobin added, "who would need a week to recover enough to start a march like that."

After a moment of thought Charlock spoke again. "The weakest ones you'll need to take back on Chatter. The rest of us will hole up here for a day or two to get them rested up to travel."

Tobin thought about that for a moment. "It's a good, defensible position," he said finally. "I don't know of a better place around here to hide nearly a hundred people."

They spent the next twenty minutes making plans. By then there was enough morning light by which to see, and the two Makerian leaders set to work putting their plans into effect.

"Hoowee, Chummy! How much water have you got in there?!"

Hawthorn was suspended head down from a large rock. Rush was sitting on his legs on top of the rock while the upper half of Hawthorn's body was hanging over the edge. Eldan was kneeling on the ground close to Hawthorn's head, pounding him on his back to encourage him to cough out more water. It seemed to be working, because between gasps for air Hawthorn would cough and wretch out large quantities of river water.

Finally Eldan heard Hawthorn's weak voice say, "Pull me up."

Hawthorn could see relief in both of his friend's faces as they lifted him up and laid him down on the large, flat rock. He was shivering badly from being so long in the cold water. Rush wrapped some dry moss around Hawthorn to warm him.

"You'd a been a gonner fer sure if ol' Floppy Hair hadn't a gone back after you," Rush said.

"Oh, go on, Wretch. You're turnin' my head."

"What happened?" Hawthorn asked Rush.

"The raft broke all to pieces coming down the cataracts in the cave, and me and Floppy came shootin' out of that opening over yonder and into this river." With his eyes Hawthorn followed Rush's good arm as he pointed across the river to the face of a rock wall on the other side. By the light of the moon, Hawthorn could see a roaring cascade of water foaming out of a large opening at the base of the rocky bluff. "We swam to safety and started looking fer you. I figured you was drowned fer sure but Floppy here just wouldn't give up. He swam back over to the opening looking fer sign. He found part of the raft caught against the rocks and figured that the rest of it was hung further up in the cave, so he just climbed up in there."

"I found the rest of the raft a short ways up in the cave," Eldan said, taking up the tale. "It was jammed between two large rocks in the middle of the waterfall. One of the broken beams had snagged your belt and had held you there with the water pouring over you. Sorry about your belt, Chummy, but I had to cut it to free you."

"Eldan, thank you," Hawthorn said earnestly. "You saved my life again."

"Snatched you from the jaws of death, I did. But what are friends for, I say? It's all over and done with, and I don't want you to think any more about it—but that's three you owe me, Chummy."

"Where are we?" Hawthorn asked as he pulled himself up into a sitting position, rubbing his cold arms to increase the circulation in them.

"I ain't got no idear," Rush answered proudly. "All I know is, we're out o' that skunk-hole them wild heatherns call home, and that's all I care about."

"Do you know where we are, Eldan?" Hawthorn asked, turning to his redheaded friend.

"No worries, Chummy! I got it all figured out."

"Now you're not just kiddin', are you, Eldan?" Hawthorn spoke seriously. "Do you really know?"

"Chums! It's me! Calm your fretful self. You and Wretch are in good hands."

Hawthorn turned a questioning look toward Rush. "Wretch?" Rush just shrugged his shoulders and smiled.

"At this very moment," Eldan continued, "the three of us are sitting on the shore of a large, black water creek that flows around the southwest end of the tree-covered ridge which contains the Renegade Lair. Our people are camped high up on the west side of that hill." As he spoke, Eldan pointed across the creek to the large bluff on the opposite shore. "I suggest that we follow the base of the hill around to the west until we cross the trail of our friends, and then we'll join up with 'em."

"That sounds simple enough," Rush mused.

"Well, I can just about guarantee you that it WON'T be," Hawthorn said confidently. "Rush, you don't know Eldan. He does not understand *simple*. This guy is an adventure waiting to happen."

"I do make life interesting, don't I, Chummy?"

"I like him already!" Rush said with a grin.

Seeing that Hawthorn was doing fine, Eldan turned his attention to Rush. "All right, Wretch, let's see that arm of yours."

With a great deal of bantering back and forth, Eldan finally managed to get Rush to take off his leather hunting shirt so he could examine his wound.

"Oh, me!" Eldan exclaimed as he studied the large gash. "The inside of your arm and the whole side of your chest is split open. Looks like your ribs kept the blade from going deep enough to kill you. This mess is gonna take some work."

Eldan searched through his pack and pulled out a small, brown pouch. Pulling the stopper, he squeezed some yellowish paste into his water pouch. After shaking it vigorously to mix it, he began to bathe the wounds with the solution. After thoroughly cleansing the wound, Eldan reached into his pack again and came out with a small wrapped bundle. Opening the package, he held up a sharp, brown object.

"What's that?" Hawthorn asked.

"That's a thorn from an aralia bush." Wrapping it back up in the cloth, he dipped the whole thing in the creek water and began pounding it with a rock. As he did so, a frothy juice began to squish through the cloth. Squeezing the fabric, Eldan began to trickle the juice into Rush's wounds. After several minutes, Eldan began to probe the wounds. When he was satisfied that the injured tissues were completely numb, he pulled a sharp needle made of carved bone out of a small leather case and threaded it with some thin, dried sinew. Carefully and methodically he began to join cut muscles back together again, working by the green glow of his light stick hanging from his neck. Whenever he would notice Rush starting to flinch, Eldan would stop his work and bathe the wounds in more of the numbing juice. It took well over an hour for Eldan to sew the muscles and the skin back together on both wounds. Then Eldan smeared the area with some of the greenish Makerian wound balm. Finally he bandaged Rush's left arm against his chest so that Rush would not be able to move the upper portion of his arm very much. Eldan was concerned that too much movement would pull the stitches open.

Rush was very appreciative for all the work that Eldan had done to care for him, but he was also full of questions. He wanted to know about the numbing juice, the wound balm, and the light stick. The more Eldan explained to him, the more questions Rush had.

By now the sky was beginning to lighten as dawn approached. At that moment Eldan and Rush's conversation was cut short by a huge splash. As they looked, they saw Hawthorn thrashing in the shallow water a short distance below the large rock on which they sat. In a moment Hawthorn rose to his feet, standing in the thigh-deep water. His arms were wrapped tightly around the body of a fish that was almost as long as he was. With a wild look in his eyes, he looked up at his two astonished friends and announced, "We eat!"

Suddenly the fish gave a violent thrash with his tail, and Hawthorn flipped over backwards back into the black water.

"Hold him, Chummy! Don't let him get away!" Eldan quickly leaped into the water to help his friend save breakfast.

All three of them were ravenously hungry. Rush was for eating the fish raw, but Eldan and Hawthorn out-voted him. Eldan quickly gathered the makings for a fire while Hawthorn and Rush skinned the fish and cut the meat into thick strips. Eldan pulled out his fire stone and flint and, striking a spark, quickly had a fire going. Using short sticks, they hung the fish over the flames to roast.

Rush was no longer thinking about breakfast. He was completely fascinated by Eldan's fire stone and had him demonstrate again and again how it worked. Then he had Eldan teach him how to use it. Soon Rush was starting fires all over the place. When he'd find a little bit of dried moss or dry, frayed grass, he'd strike a spark in it. As soon as it caught and a small flame appeared, he would roar with laughter and then stomp it out.

"Wretch! Have you lost your mind!?"

"You're gonna' burn the whole forest down, Rush!"

Rush looked up at his two friends with an expression of excited delight. "This is great!! Hey, Floppy, you've got to help me find one of these fire-startin' rocks! Please!"

"Well . . ." Eldan said, "I'll tell you what, Wretch, I'll see what I can do."

"Let's eat, guys!" Hawthorn called out, lifting a toasted strip of fish. There was plenty, so they stuffed themselves. Finally Eldan stood up and wiped his hands. "While you fellows are finishing up, I'm going to scout around a little. I'll be back before the sun clears those trees over there."

Following the creek Eldan quickly disappeared in the brush and woods to the west. After Eldan had gone, Rush turned to Hawthorn. "Awright, Thorn, now what's the deal?" he demanded through a mouthful of fish. "Who are these people? And where did they get all this amazing stuff?"

For the next half hour Hawthorn told Rush everything he knew about the Makerians and tried his best to answer all of Rush's questions. "Well, how 'bout dat?!" Rush finally said in amazement. "A whole society of folks out here in these woods who know a lot more 'bout things than we do, and we've never heard of 'em."

"I guess the Shaman know about them," Hawthorn said, "but they've kept it a big secret."

"Well, you can see why," Rush shot back. "If all that stuff about that Jahuzit character is true, then the Shaman would be out of a job."

"His name is Jehesus, Rush. They say He's the Maker's Son. They worship Him and always use His name when they pray to the Maker."

"Was that what Floppy was doin' before he ate?"

"Yes. The Makerians always pray before they eat to thank the Maker for giving them their food. They pray about everything. Usually they pray out loud, but I guess, since we were here, he decided to pray to himself."

They both sat there in quiet contemplation for several minutes. Finally Rush broke the silence, "So what do you make of it, Thorn?"

"I'm not sure. I really have thought about it a lot. I like the idea of being able to talk to the Maker any time I want." After a pause Hawthorn continued, "I used to think that I was a pretty good person and that the really evil people in this world were the Renegades, but over the last several days, I've seen that there's an awful lot of Renegade in me. The idea of having a savior sounds pretty good."

"Well, if you feel that way, just do whatever you got to do to make Him yer savior," Rush said off-handedly. "It couldn't hurt."

"It's a lot more than that!" Hawthorn responded with feeling. "They've made it clear that you can't make Jehesus your Savior unless you're also willing to make Him your Lord."

"Yer Lord?"

"Yeah, you know. You stop doing what you want, and you start living your life the way Jehesus wants you to live."

"So how do you know what He wants you to do?" Rush wondered aloud.

"It's written down in their sacred books."

"The books that Shaman guy copied from the treasure cave at the Steps?" Rush asked.

"That's right."

There was another period of silence as Rush thought on all this. "Hawthorn," Rush said finally, "do you believe in this Jehesus?"

"Well, they sure do," Hawthorn shot back. "They're always talking about Him, and some of the things . . . no, a lot of the things they do, can only be explained by the fact that the Maker is doing things for them. I mean, they ask Him for stuff, and He does it! That happens all the time."

"Yeah, but do YOU believe in Him?" Rush persisted.

Hawthorn was silent for a while. "I'm not sure yet," was his eventual answer, "but I want to."

It wasn't long after that that they saw Eldan returning.

"You see anything?" Rush asked as their friend walked up.

"No sign of enemies."

"So are we ready to head out?" Hawthorn said, jumping up.

"Not yet, Chummy," Eldan said with a little sadness. "I've got one more chore to do."

"What's that?"

It took Eldan a moment to answer. "I found Turkey's body washed up on the shore. I'm gonna bury him before we leave."

Eldan led the sad little procession in silence to the place where the body of their dead comrade lay. "I found a little rocky island out in the middle of the creek that's just around that bend right there," Eldan said, pointing down the creek. "I want to put him there. Turkey would like it."

It wasn't an easy journey along the creek bank. A lot of brush, fallen logs, and patches of tall grass made the trip especially difficult, but no one complained. Finally they reached a spot on the bank of the creek directly across from the island. Laying their burden down, they sat down to rest beside the slow-moving black water. They had been sitting there in silence for several minutes when Eldan suddenly stood up. Hawthorn saw that Rush was on the alert also. Then he heard it—a soft, scrapping sound from the brush close by.

"Kneel down! Quick!" Eldan ordered as he frantically tried to untie his cloak. "Get close! Hug each other!"

"What is it?" Hawthorn asked as he and Rush grabbed each other and fell to the ground.

"Serpent!" Rush answered.

Eldan jerked his cloak off and plunged it into the creek. He whipped around just in time to see a large, copper-colored snake burst through the brush within easy striking distance of the three friends. Dropping to his knees with his back against his companions, Eldan held his wet cloak in both hands, spreading it out so as to shield himself and his friends from the great serpent.

"That's a brown viper!" Hawthorn whispered. "Those are bad!"

"They're all bad," Rush whispered back.

"What are we doing?" Hawthorn asked desperately.

"Shhh! Just be still. Floppy has a plan."

The huge snake stopped, reared its head, and swayed back and forth, flicking its tongue. The viper was searching for prey, and it obviously knew there was some close by. But for some reason, even though it hovered right in front of the three friends, the snake was unable to locate them. It was persistent. It moved back and forth for several minutes, constantly searching. With every move of its head, Eldan would shift the position of the cloak, keeping it always between the serpent and themselves. Finally the great snake lowered its head and slid off into the woods, following the creek in the direction they had come.

FLOPPY HAS A PLAN

"Whoa!" Hawthorn whispered in relief as the big copperhead disappeared into the brush.

"I ain't never seen anything like that!" Rush said in amazement. "How'd you do that?"

"Oh, it's really not hard, Wretch. You've just got to know how to reason with them."

"You know somethin', Floppy. I've found the same thing to be true about weasels."

"But why didn't he eat us, Eldan?" Hawthorn broke in.

"Because he couldn't find us, Chummy. Serpents don't see very well. They use their tongues to taste the air to get your scent. That's why he stayed so long. He could taste that we were around here, but he couldn't find us. Vipers locate their prey by the warmth that comes from the prey's body. My cloak is lined on the inside with mica thread, and it won't let heat go through. As long as I kept the cold, wet side of the cloak toward him, the viper couldn't find us. Eventually he got tired and gave up."

"Let me see that cloak of yours," Rush said suspiciously. Taking the offered cloak, Rush examined it meticulously. Finally he sat back, and shaking his head in amazement, he said to his redheaded friend, "You've got the neatest toys!"

Eldan stood on the bank of the creek looking out at the island. "Can you help me with Turkey, Chums?"

"Sure, Eldan."

"Wretch needs to stay out of the water as much as he can 'til his wounds heal, so we'll leave him here with our stuff, then you and I will swim Turkey over to the island. You do swim, don't you?"

"Wel-l-l . . . I don't know," Hawthorn answered honestly. "I've never had to swim before."

"Chummy, Chummy, you've lived such a sheltered life. But no worries; I'll show you a little trick to get you across." Eldan had Hawthorn take off his leather hunting pants, then he showed him how to make a float out of them by tying the leg holes and the waist closed after trapping them full of air. "Hang on to that float, Chums, and it will keep you above water. Just kick with your legs to make yourself go forward. Now help me carry Turkey out into the water."

Because the current of the creek was fairly slow at this point, they were able to make the crossing easily. The island was really just an oblong, rocky hill. After scouting it, Eldan decided to bury his friend at a flat spot on top. It took a bit of work to carry Turk's body to the crest and lay him on the selected spot. Eldan took his knife and carefully cut a lock of Turk's hair and placed it in a pouch around his own neck. Then he began to carefully build a tomb around his friend with the many rocks covering the ground. Once the tomb was made, he and Hawthorn continued piling on rocks until the mound was chest high. Finally they sat down to rest, leaning back against the mound of rocks, looking up into the sky.

"Jehesus promised that He would come back," Eldan said, still looking up. "He said He would just appear in the sky one day to get those who love Him and take them to live with Him and His father, the Maker, forever. Chummy, He said that those of His followers who died before He comes back would be raised from the dead, then they would rise up into the air to meet Him. This is where Turkey will see Him, probably right there," Eldan said, pointing above them, "between those two trees. What a beautiful place to meet the Lord."

Getting up onto his knees, Eldan began to pray out loud, thanking God for the privilege of knowing Turk and remembering special qualities that he had shown in his life that had encouraged Eldan. He asked the Maker to honor his friend's name, because he had given his life to save many others. When he finished his prayer, Eldan rose to his feet. He picked up a small stone from Turk's grave and placed this in the pouch around his neck. He then slowly started back down the hill.

Hawthorn had not said anything the whole time, but he was deeply moved by Eldan's words.

It was a short swim back to where Rush was waiting for them. Gathering their things, Eldan led them along the bank to the west.

"We got a runner coming in!" Blesstis called out from his post among the rocks surrounding the camp.

"Who is it?" Charlock called back from the middle of the camp where he, Tobin, and Graceson were discussing their plans.

"Looks like Kordilon!" Blesstis answered.

"He was with Goodclaw and Braden," Graceson spoke up. "They were scouting west, the way we came."

Several minutes later the young Ranger topped the wall of rocks and trotted across the sandy clearing to where the leaders were.

"Sit down, Kord, and catch your breath," Graceson said.

Kordilon obeyed, and after several deep breaths, he was able to make his report. "Renegade war parties are all over the place."

"The scouts we sent to the north are reporting the same thing," put in Tobin.

"We saw four separate groups of warriors as we made our way west, sir," continued Kordilon. "One of the groups found our whirlers."

"That's not good," thought Tobin out loud.

"If they found our whirlers, they should be able to track us right to this spot," Graceson said what they all thought.

"Sir," Kordilon continued, "Goodclaw and Braden are laying down some false trials to try to lead them away from our camp."

"Good thinking," said Graceson.

"The false trails are a good idea," said Charlock, "but even if they work, they will only buy us a little more time. Eventually the Renegades will find us."

"Our early discovery by the enemy, as well as the slaves being too weak to travel quickly, have put us in a tight spot. We need to make some decisions. What options do we have?"

"We could try to escape to the south," said Graceson.

"The slave crowd is too weak to travel very far or fast," Tobin responded. "If the Renegades catch us out in the open, we won't have much of a chance."

"We could take everybody back into the cave and hide in there," said Kordilon. "If they find us, they could only send in one or two at a time to attack us."

"They won't have to attack us," said Graceson. "We'd be trapped in there. All they'd have to do is wait a few days, and we'd be too weak to fight."

"The only other option is to stay right here and defend this position if we're found," Charlock said.

"How long do you think we could hold out?" Graceson asked.

"Hopefully long enough for Tobin to get to Stillwaters and bring back help."

"When do you want me to leave?" Tobin asked.

"The sooner you leave, the sooner you get back."

"Graceson, get the five weakest of the former slaves ready to travel," Tobin ordered. "I'll get Chatter."

In twenty minutes five very reluctant former slaves were strapped into the seats on Chatter's back, and Tobin was climbing up to take his place. Tobin and Charlock had spent the last several minutes talking about every possibility and what they should do. Then with a wave, Tobin gave the word, and the huge squirrel raced away.

"Graceson!" barked Charlock.

"Here, sir."

"Set a guard of three Rangers along the wall of rocks, then bring everybody else in here."

"Slaves, too, sir?"

"Yes, slaves, too. Bring 'em all in. It's time we had a meeting."

When everyone had gathered around Charlock, he began to explain their situation. "Our plan was to take all of you to our home at Stillwaters. It's a safe place that's too strong for the Renegades to attack, but the trail to get there is long. There are many enemy war parties all around us in these woods. So far they haven't found us, but eventually they will. Most of you former slaves aren't strong enough to travel as far and as fast as we need to in order to get out of here, and we aren't going to leave you behind. So the only reasonable plan left is to prepare as strong a defense of this camp as we can and, if we're found, to hold it against the enemy until Tobin returns with help."

"How long do you figure that will be?" Savin asked.

"When Tobin has help coming, our plan is for him to return here as quickly as possible to let us know what's happening. He could return as soon as tonight, but more likely it will be tomorrow. A large party of Rangers could come marching in here three or four days after that if they don't run into trouble. Between now and then, we need to prepare for anything."

"Stoke!" Charlock called out.

"Here, sir."

"Open up all the packs. Let's see what we've got to fight with."

All of the extra weapons were handed out to the slaves. A few got bows and a small handful of arrows. A few more got slings. Some extra knives were passed out to several of the others. Then the whole company was sent out to collect as much as they could for the making of arrows, bows, clubs, fighting sticks, and lances.

There was plenty of rope available, so one of the ropes was untwined for cordage to make bowstrings and slings and to attach arrowheads and fletching to the arrow shafts. With a little bit of organization, quite an efficient manufacturing operation was begun. Charlock and Graceson worked out the strategy for their defense, then supervised the moving and levering of stones on the rocky wall surrounding the camp to create a more formidable defensive position.

Later in the afternoon, Jay was carrying a bundle of newly fletched arrows to where they were being stored along the wall when he suddenly stopped. He was staring at the coils of rope laid out near the packs when an idea struck him. Jay chuckled to himself as he thought about it. "Rush would love this," he muttered to himself. Looking around for someone to help him, he spotted Poke nearby talking with a young Makerian. "Hey, fellas," he said, walking up to Poke and his new friend, "I've got an idea for keepin' the Renegades from getting' over that wall, but I need some help puttin' it together. Could I get you two to help me?"

"Sure, Jay!" Poke answered. "This is Kordilon."

After greeting the young Ranger, Jay led them into the woods to help him gather some long branches. It didn't take much time to find what he needed, but the actual fabrication of his project took three tries and over an hour.

"So," said Graceson as he came walking up to them, "what is this new weapon that Kordilon says I've got to see?"

"This is it right here, sir," Jay said, gently patting his creation.

Graceson saw a long, stout oak limb that had one end jammed tightly into the ground between two boulders near the wall surrounding the camp. The limb had been bent backwards until its free end almost touched the ground. This end of the limb was a forked branch, and rope had been woven between the forks to form a net. Six rocks, each one about the size of a fist, were lying in the net. The tightly bent limb was held in place by an L-shaped piece of wood that hooked onto the bent limb. The L-shaped hook was attached to a rope which was tied to a peg driven deeply into the ground.

"What is it?" Graceson asked suspiciously.

"Well," drawled Jay, sounding very much like Rush at that moment, "I call it my *whoosh-smack*."

"A whoosh-smack?" Graceson questioned with his eyebrows raised. "What does it do?"

"Well, Mr. Graceson, sir, if you'll just look over the edge of the rock wall over there, you'll see some pieces of bark that we've set up down the hill to represent some attacking enemies."

Stepping over to the wall and climbing up so he could look over, Graceson could see four large slabs of bark a little less than a bowshot away. They were wedged upright among some of the rocks, and funny faces were painted on them with mud. "I see them," Graceson said, grinning at Jay.

"Well, sir, what you do is this: when the enemy comes charging up the hill, some one gives the command, and you yank this cord like this." Jay held a cord in his hand that was tied to the L-shaped hook. Giving a quick pull on the cord released the limb, which sprang forward with startling rapidity. "WHOOSH!!!" The rocks were hurtled down the hill with tremendous velocity. There was a loud "SMACK" as they hit the targets. Wood splinters and fragments of rock scattered over the ground. Graceson's mouth dropped open as he viewed what was left of the bark faces.

"What do you think, sir?" Jay asked, smiling.

"I, uh . . . I think we need about fifteen of these things just as fast as you can build them."

"If it's all the same to you, sir, I'm gonna let Kordilon here show your people how to put these things together and shoot 'em. I've got another idea I'd like to work on, with your permission."

"Uh, sure. Go ahead. If it's anything like this idea, it ought to be a doozie."

"Thanks, sir!" Jay said enthusiastically. Then turning to his companion, he said, "Come on, Poke. We've got more work to do."

"What'cha gonna build now, Jay?" Poke asked curiously.

"Just wait and see!" Jay said with a chuckle as they walked off. "My creative juices are flowing!"

"That guy is dangerous!" Graceson said after Jay and Poke had left.

"Yep," Kordilon agreed. "It's a good thing he's on our side."

CHAPTER TWENTY-TWO

THE THREE BATTLES

"Shouldn't we be getting ready to shoot the whooshers?" Poke whispered to Jay as they lay side by side behind the wall of rocks in the grey light of the breaking dawn.

"No," Jay whispered back. "We don't want to give away too many secrets 'til we have to. Our scouts said that they thought this was a single Renegade war party of about thirty warriors."

It had been a long night. The moon had illuminated the forest, and the enemy scouts had been active. Five times the camp had been called to arm themselves and maintain absolute silence as Renegades had been spotted moving through the woods nearby. Twice during the night captured enemy scouts had been brought into camp after the Makerian Rangers had caught them snooping around close by. About two hours before daybreak the discouraging report came in that, as one of the Rangers was attempting to capture a third Renegade scout, the enemy overpowered his would-be captor and managed to get away—carrying with him the location of the Makerian camp.

Again the camp had been called to arms. For the past two hours they had stood vigilantly behind the wall of rocks surrounding the camp, prepared to defend against the attack they all knew was coming.

"There's the signal, Poke! Get ready!"

As they looked to the left toward the center of the wall, they could see Graceson standing a short distance back from the wall so all the defenders could see him. He held his right arm straight up over his head in the *"ready"* signal.

He was watching Charlock, who stood in the center of the wall peering over the top at the approaching enemies. Charlock looked back at Graceson and said something. With his right arm still raised, Graceson began rotating his left arm in a circle.

"They want slingers only," whispered Jay. "That's you, Poke."

Swallowing hard, Poke, with his sling loaded and at the ready, moved up closer to the top of the wall with the others who were armed with slings.

Suddenly Graceson's right arm shot straight forward.

"Go, Poke!" urged Jay. "Make it count!"

Jumping up onto the wall of rocks with the other slingers, Poke looked anxiously for a target. A little less than a stone's throw away, he could see numerous shapes moving toward them in the shadows of the grey dawn. A crouching figure cautiously moved out from behind some brush in Poke's line of sight. Quick as lightning, Poke whirled his sling once and released his stone. The missile whizzed through the air, striking the Renegade a glancing blow on his right shoulder, making him spin. It was enough to get a howl out of the enemy warrior. Maddened with pain and rage, the Renegade whipped around again to face his young attacker. Screaming his war cry, the Renegade raised his club and charged for Poke. By this time Poke had placed another stone in his sling. He stood unmoving on the wall as the shrieking enemy charged him. Poke thought of all the beatings, all the insults, all the abuse and torment he had endured from these people. When the Renegade was less than five paces away, Poke whipped his sling around viciously. The stone struck the Renegade's mask squarely between the eyeholes, sinking deeply into the wood, snapping his head back so hard that his feet flew out from under him, silencing his war cry instantly.

The stones were flying from the slingers on the wall with telling effect. Within a few moments the attack was over. The enemy, dragging their injured with them, melted back into the shadows and the brush.

Taking his place behind the wall with the others, Poke waited for the next attack, knowing as they all did that it would be much more serious.

"Why don't they come!" demanded Poke impatiently. "It's been over two hours since they attacked."

Jay corrected him. "It's been almost three hours," he said, looking up at the sun. "Keep your pants on; they'll come. They're probably waiting for reinforcements."

After a while Blesstis came by gathering fighters. Following orders from Graceson, he was picking out every fourth fighter to form a reserve group to stand ready to rush to the place of greatest need when the next attack came. Jay was pulled out to join this group. Gathering his small reserve force together on the sandy plain behind the center of the wall, Graceson explained the plan.

"That first attack was merely to test our strength," he began. "They'll hit us much harder next time. They may try a mass assault along the whole length of the wall, or they may try to attack our flanks. Once we see where they plan to attack, we can send some or all of you to that area to strengthen our defenses."

In the distance a chorus of shrieking screams began to rise up out of the shadowy forest. The noise grew louder and louder. Suddenly, like a stampede, a large crowd of brightly painted Renegades burst through the brush directly in front of the defenders. With deafening screams they sprinted fearlessly toward the center of the wall of rocks. This time slingers and archers were called to the top of the wall. Stones and arrows flew furiously into the ranks of the charging Renegades. Though the front ranks of the enemy fell, those behind simply leaped over the fallen and kept coming.

"Cut them down!" Charlock urged his fighters. The arrows and stones poured forth more fiercely. More of the enemy dropped, but still they came. Defenders from both ends of the wall began to move toward the center to help.

"Do you need us?!" Graceson shouted at Charlock.

"Not yet!" Charlock shouted back. "Watch the flanks!"

Obediently Graceson quickly scanned the right end of their defenses. All seemed quiet there. Looking to the left end, his eyes grew wide. There was a lot of activity on that end of the wall. The slingers and archers were launching their missiles furiously. Graceson saw one of the slingers turn toward him and begin waving his arms frantically. Dividing his reserves in half, Graceson ordered Jay's group to reinforce the defenders on the left flank.

"Costal!" Graceson shouted. "You lead them! Once you see what it looks like, wave if you need the rest of us."

"Right!" the Ranger returned. "Let's go, warriors!" With a shout he led the band in a dead run across the sand.

Jay quickly out-distanced his companions as he sprinted to the aid of their friends. His heart dropped as he saw the defenders retreating from the top of the wall. Just as Jay drew near, he saw five hideously painted masks appearing over the top of their defenses as Renegades scaled the other side. "It's too late," he thought as he approached the wall. "They'll be over before we can get there." Just in front of him was a mounted whoosh-smack that was drawn, loaded, and ready to launch. Without hesitation Jay grabbed the trigger cord and yanked hard.

RENEGADE ATTACK

"WHOOSH . . . SMACK!!"

Looking up, Jay was excited. Not a single Renegade was left standing. The wall had been swept clean by the salvo of rocks. "She works!" Jay yelled, leaping into the air.

"Come on!" Jay encouraged the retreating defenders, and he charged up the rock wall, bow in hand. As he topped the wall, his eyes grew wide at the number of enemies climbing up on the other side. There was no lack of targets, so he started to work with his bow, launching arrows as fast as he could notch and draw them. He had stopped three of the attackers when Costal and the others drew near. Seeing his friends approaching from behind, Jay waved them forward.

Just then a Renegade reached the top of the wall near Jay. Standing below the Larkin, the Renegade swung his war club hard at Jay's knees. Jay turned around just in time to see the club coming at him. Leaping high and pulling up his feet, the club swished underneath him. The momentum of the missed swing spun the Renegade in a half turn, exposing the back of his head. Jay saw his opportunity and brought his bow down hard on the back of the Renegade's skull. There was a howl of pain as the blow drove him head first into the rocks.

Looking down, Jay kicked a large piece of a broken mask out of the way and picked up a wicked-looking war club that had been dropped by a fallen Renegade. It was a strong piece of oak with a leather-wrapped handle on one end. A large, rounded rock was tied firmly to the business end. Jay tested its weight. Choking up a little on the handle, Jay made a huge, arching swing at the masked head of another Renegade as he cleared the top of the wall.

The red and black mask broke in half as the Renegade went tumbling away. Suddenly Jay felt himself falling backwards off the wall of rocks as a Renegade club cut his legs out from under him. He hit hard on the sand and rocks. Looking up from the ground, he blinked hard to get the sweat and dirt out of his eyes and saw a large number of Renegades swarming over the top of the wall. Jay knew that he and his friends were done for, but he was determined to fight to the end. He attempted to get to his feet, but a pair of strong hands grabbed his shoulders and held him down. He struggled hard against his captor as he saw more and more of the enemy gaining the top of the wall.

"Stay down, Jay!" he heard Costal's voice shout in his ear. At that same instant he heard "WHOOSH! WHOOSH! WHOOSH!!!" Immediately there was a crash and much screaming as the stone launchers swept the enemy from the walls.

"Keep it up, Rangers!" Jay heard Costal shout to those working the rock throwers. "Are you hurt badly, Jay?"

"I'm all right," the Larkin returned. "Help me up."

Along most of the wall Jay could see the defenders loading and launching the whooshers as rapidly as possible. The Renegades' shields and masks could not protect them against the powerfully thrown clusters of stones, and the attack was broken. Again the defeated Renegades withdrew into the shadows of the surrounding forest.

With this break in the fighting, the wounded and injured were moved across the camp to Carineda's aid station under the bluff. She had recruited three of the former slaves to assist her, and all were busy tending to the hurts of their comrades. Considering the fierceness of the last attack, their list of casualties was fairly small. Three defenders had been killed and six injured. All of the killings and most of the injuries had occurred in the flank attack. Cari expected three of the injured defenders to be able to return to duty. The other three were more serious. Spar, a former slave, was delirious from a blow to the head. Gilly had a broken leg, and Sycamore had a concussion and a broken shoulder. Helping one of the wounded defenders to the aid station, Jay looked up and saw Poke and Savin kneeling over the prostrate form of Sycamore.

"Is he gonna be okay, Lady?!" Poke asked for the fifth time as he knelt over his father. Cari looked up from where she was readjusting the splint on Gilly's swollen leg. A look of impatience crossed her face as she blew a string of hair away that had fallen in front of her eyes. "He's my papa," Poke added as tears began to streak his dirty face.

A wave of compassion swept over Carineda as she looked at this young Larkin and thought of all that he had endured. She gave Poke a big smile. "Your papa should be fine if the Maker's willing," she said reassuringly, "but he needs to rest now so that his head injury can heal. I've given him some herbs to drink to help him sleep."

It was now well past noon. Some of the supplies were opened, and dried meat and fruit were passed out for a meal. After eating, the exhausted defenders lay down where they were to rest. Jay, Poke, and Savin stayed with Sycamore. They took turns taking naps and caring for Poke's father.

"Rangers! To the wall!" a voice boomed across the camp nearly three hours later.

"Well, I guess they're comin' back for more," Savin said gamely.

"Looks like it," Jay answered, springing to his feet. "Come on; let's go give it to 'em!" The three friends sprinted across the sand to their stations next to the wall.

"They've advanced within bow shot!" Charlock announced. "Use the whooshers!" The signal was given, and the teams of defenders assigned to this task quickly had the stone throwers hurling large numbers of stones over the wall.

"That's enough, Graceson," Charlock's voice boomed. "Tell them not to waste any more stones. They're crawling forward this time with their shields up. The stones are just flying over their heads. Call up the slingers and archers."

The order was shouted, and all along the wall the defenders rose up to launch their stones and arrows at the oncoming enemy. Almost immediately arrows poured down upon the unsuspecting defenders from Renegade archers hidden in the brush, shrubs, and trees. Before they could regain the protective cover of the rock wall, several of the defenders were wounded. With the enemy shooting at anyone who showed his head above the wall, the slings were useless. The Makerians were forced to take quick shots with their bows from behind the rocks while dodging the arrows of the enemy. The crawling Renegade warriors continued to slowly advance, effectively covering themselves with their shields.

"Jay! Jay! Where is Jay?!"

The young Larkin released his arrow and quickly ducked behind a large rock. Turning, he looked down to see who was calling him. He saw Graceson anxiously scanning the faces of the defenders. "Graceson! Here!" Jay responded and leaped down next to his captain.

"We can't stop them like this, Jay. Charlock wants you and Kordilon to get your crews together and see if you can slow them down with those swinging things you built."

"All right!" Jay shouted enthusiastically. "It's as good as done."

"Savin! Poke!" Jay called up to his two friends. "They want us to use the swing shooters! Get the rest of our team together and meet me there as quickly as you can. I'm going to tell Kordilon."

Savin and Poke sprang to their task as Jay sprinted to the south end of the wall to find Kordillon.

The swing shooter was the other of Jay's ideas. It consisted of a platform made of bark, having walls of sticks and thick grass on all four sides. Several large slits had been cut into the walls through which to shoot arrows. This box-like structure was suspended by a long rope attached to a tree limb high above the rock wall. The hanging platform had been pulled back and was now tied high in the branches of a stout bush that was growing on top of the bluff. Three archers were to climb inside and release the rope holding the platform. This would allow the suspended structure to swing down past the wall and out over the advancing Renegades, giving those inside the box an opportunity to shoot their arrows straight down at the enemy. Two of these swing shooters had been built. One was suspended over the north portion of the wall, and the other was over the south portion.

Kordilon had enthusiastically supported Jay's plan, but it had taken both of them some doing to find four more intrepid souls with enough intestinal fortitude to join them.

After informing Kordilon, Jay raced across the camp to the north end of the bluff and followed his companions as they climbed rapidly to the top. Hand and foot holds had been cut into the trunk and branches of the bush to allow them to ascend quickly to the place where the platform was tethered. Jay climbed inside and was joined by Marsh and Jonel.

"I was hoping we wouldn't have to use this thing," Marsh growled.

"I think we'd better tie ourselves in," Jay suggested.

The inside of the box-like structure was just large enough for the three of them to use their bows without getting in each other's way. Three quivers full of arrows were attached low on the wall in front of where each one of them would stand.

Having tied themselves securely in their positions, Jay stuck his head through the hole in front of him. "We're all set, Savin. When I give you the signal, cut us loose, then climb down the bush and join the other guys on the edge of the bluff. When we lose enough of our swing to where we're just making it back to the edge of the bluff, that's when you catch us with the hooks. Got it?!"

"We'll do our best, Jay. I just hope you fellas don't break your necks."

"Just cut the rope, Mr. Cheerful," Jay grinned at his friend. "And be ready with those hooks!"

"Okay, here we go!" Savin called to them as he sawed through the rope.

Suddenly the walled platform dropped free, leaving Savin to hold on for dear life as the branch whipped back and forth. Jay and his two companions felt their hearts leap into their throats. The first two seconds felt like a free fall, but then the rope by which they were suspended caught and pulled them into a long, swinging arc. Looking down, Jay saw the sandy plateau of the camp passing quickly underneath them as they swung rapidly toward the wall. Jay also saw that the ground appeared to be coming up to meet them awfully fast. "Get ready!" he shouted, his teeth clenched against the thrill of the rapid descent. "We're passing the wall."

Steadying themselves, they each drew their bows and waited for an enemy to appear in front of them. The platform reached the bottom of its arc just as they passed over the wall. The downward force against them caused their knees to bend. As they passed the wall, the swing shooter began to climb upward, completing the back swing of its arc. This caused the walled platform to tip, allowing the three archers inside to look straight down on the crawling Renegades.

"Oh, yes!" said Jonel with satisfaction as he saw before him all the targets he could ever want.

"Give it to 'em!" shouted Jay.

Arrows began to fly from the holes in the platform walls in rapid succession. A chorus of howls and yells echoed across the battlefield as the arrows hit their marks.

Jay was impressed with how rapidly Jonel and Marsh were able to draw and shoot their arrows. "How do you fellas do that?" he asked as they completed their swing back across the wall. "You shoot two arrows before I can shoot one."

"Practice," they both answered in unison.

By now Kordillon and his crew had the second swing shooter in action over the southern portion of the rock wall. Again the screams and howls of the Renegades evidenced the effectiveness of their arrows.

As Jay's platform reached the top of its arc, he saw Savin, Poke, and the large former slave named Beetle standing a short distance below them on top of the bluff. "Catch us next time!" was all Jay had time to shout before their swinging fortress again dropped toward the enemy.

The Renegades were ready for them this time, and many rolled over onto their backs to use their shields to protect them from the arrows from above. As the Renegades did this, it temporarily exposed them to the archers on the wall, and many more of their numbers were struck by the shafts of the defenders.

When Jay's platform had completed its second pass back and forth above the enemy and had swung back to the top of the bluff, Savin, Poke, and Beetle were all ready with the wooden hooks they had made. The hooks were tied to ropes, while the other end of the ropes were securely tied to a nearby bush. When the platform had reached its nearest point to the bluff, all three whirled their hooks and flung them toward the box-like structure. Beetle's hook caught in one of the openings while the other two bounced off. There was a sharp jerk as the rope snapped taunt, holding the platform fast.

"Good job!" Jay called to his friends. "Savin! You and Beetle pull us in as close as you can, and Poke, throw me your hook."

This was quickly accomplished, then Jay had more orders. "Poke, I've secured your hook in the window. Now you can untie it on your end and haul the rope to that bush about twenty paces to your right. Anchor it there."

It took only a few minutes for Poke to obey. Once he had his rope securely fastened to the new anchor point, he gave Jay a signal, and Jay called back to Savin, "I'm going to release Beetle's hook. Once I do, you two join Poke and pull us in as close to that new bush as you can. Then we'll release the hook. That will swing us at a different angle and let us pass over the wall closer to the center."

Savin and Beetle quickly ran to Poke, and the three of them, pulling with all their strength, managed to draw the platform quite close to the new anchor point.

"Perfect!" Jay called again.

Now Marsh and Jonel grabbed the anchor rope and pulled with all their strength. By so doing, they were able to create enough slack for Jay to release the hook. Down the swing shooter dropped again, but at a little different angle.

By changing the swinging angles, the two crews were able to cover most of the wall. The aerial assault was more than the Renegades could stand, and after taking many casualties, most began to retreat. A furious group of Renegades on the right flank jumped up and, out of sheer frustration, made a screaming charge at the wall. But the efficient use of the whooshers stopped that charge as quickly as it had started.

As the sun set, this long afternoon battle finally came to an end. After the wounded were taken care of, more food and drink was distributed to refresh the weary defenders.

Fearing a night attack, Charlock gave orders to implement plans to illuminate the area in front of the wall. Large pieces of pine resin were mounted on long poles. As darkness approached the resin was lit, and the poles were lifted into position behind the wall. Several of these tall torches were raised along the length of the rock wall. This not only lit up the area from which the enemy would come, but also forced the Renegades to look into the bright light of the torches in order to attack.

Guards were placed at intervals along the wall. The rest of the camp was divided into two groups. One group tried to get some sleep while the other group worked on making arrows and gathering stones for slings and the whooshers.

Poke had been assigned to the group gathering stones. Jay and Savin were put in the group to rest first. To ease Poke's mind, they told him that they would check on his father before they lay down. As they approached the aid station, they saw that Sycamore was awake, and one of Carineda's assistants was feeding him a soup made of medicinal herbs.

Looking around, Jay and Savin could see that the number of injured had grown considerably since the last battle. Jay counted ten new casualties, all of them with arrow wounds. Four of them appeared to be wounds of lesser severity, requiring not much more than bandaging the injuries. Six of the wounded were in more serious condition, having arrows protruding from their bodies.

Carineda had examined each one carefully as he came in and had made decisions on what each one needed. She had identified the greatest threat of each wound and what steps could be taken to help. Then she had decided which injured person had the most urgent need, which one had the second most urgent need, and so on. She had assigned tasks to each of those who were assisting her to begin caring for those with the less urgent needs, while she and Stoke worked on the most severely injured person. Jay was shocked to discover that the person she was working on so diligently was a Renegade. There were actually two Renegades who had been brought in by the Makerian Rangers.

The Renegades usually dragged their wounded away with them, but these two had fallen near the wall and had been left for dead. When the Rangers brought the wounded enemies to the aid station, some of the former slaves who were assisting Carineda refused to help them. Cari directed them to help some of the other wounded. When she asked some of the Rangers to help her with the wounded Renegades, they did so willingly.

"Don't get me wrong," Jay spoke quietly in Savin's ear. "I'm grateful for these people, and I have great respect for them. But I don't understand 'em at all. She's over there working as hard to save that cutthroat's life as she would for one of her own people."

"They all seem to feel the same way about it," Savin whispered back. After a moment's thought Savin continued, "It's not like they're being foolish. There seems to be a goodness to them that goes beyond anything I've ever seen."

Kneeling down beside Sycamore, Savin reached out for the bowl of soup the assistant was feeding to the injured Larkin. "I can do this," Savin said to the assistant. "I'm sure they could use your help with the newly wounded."

Toward the end of the first watch, some scratching and thrashing of leaves was heard in the trees far overhead. At this the whole camp was aroused to arms. Suddenly out of the darkness above them a shrill whistle sounded, and all of the Rangers showed relief at the sound.

"What's going on?" Jay asked Kordillon, who was standing near him.

"Tobin!" the Makerian smiled. "He's come back!"

Letting his eyes follow the noise in the darkness above, Jay saw a dark shape descending the shadowy trunk of a large tree near the camp. When the big squirrel got within a few feet of the ground, he leaped from the trunk of the tree, sailed over the rock wall, and landed lightly on the sandy plateau of the Makerian camp.

As the red-bearded Tobin slid from Chatter's back, a large crowd of Makerians and former slaves crowded around him. Questions flew at Tobin the Flyer from several mouths at once.

"You made it to Stillwaters, didn't you?"

"Is help coming?"

"When will they get here?"

Tobin held up both hands to quiet them. "Where's Sir Charlock?" Tobin asked loudly over the quieting crowd.

"I'm here!" a deep voice boomed from a short distance away. Charlock was seated on a large rock at the base of the wall. "Welcome back!" Charlock continued. "Some of us were starting to get worried about you." A low chuckle broke out among several in the crowd.

"Sir Tobin," Charlock continued, "we all have an intense interest in the news you've brought us. Please share it with us." It was clear from Charlock's remarks that whether good or bad, he was not going to hide any information from the rest of his command.

Tobin gathered everyone around him, and using a low voice that would not carry past the rock wall, he warned them not to betray by word or action to the Renegade spies what he was about to tell them. "Help is coming," Tobin began, "but it's going to take two days to arrive, maybe longer if they have trouble."

"Can we hold out for two more days?" a voice from the small crowd of defenders interrupted.

"We'll have to," Charlock's voice cut off any more discussion. "Go on, Sir Tobin."

"I have more bad news. As I was coming in through the trees, I saw the Renegade camp, so I stayed for a while on a limb above them and observed their activity unnoticed. Shortly after sunset I saw large numbers of reinforcements arriving in their camp."

"How many Renegades do you think there are?" another voice asked.

"I figure around three hundred or better," was Tobin's calm answer.

"Their number really doesn't matter," Charlock stood up. "Our task is the same whether there are three hundred or six hundred. We can't run from them, and there's too many of us to hide from them. All that's left is for us to fight them—unless some of you want to go back to being slaves."

With Charlock's last statement Jay noticed that the defenders around him seemed to grip their weapons a little tighter. A couple of the former slaves spat on the ground. It was clear slavery was not an option to any of them.

"They'll be back at us by daylight if not before," Charlock continued. "We need to be ready for them."

"I figured you fellas could use all the help you could get, so I brought some weapons back with me. How about four of you helping me unload the bundles from Chatter's back?" Tobin quickly climbed up on his squirrel's back and began to untie the load.

"What'd you bring us?" Charlock asked cheerfully.

"Let's see . . ." Tobin said thoughtfully. "I've got thirty of our strong bows, plenty of bow strings, ten bundles of arrows with one hundred arrows in each bundle, thirty stings, and thirty shields."

"That'll help a lot!" Charlock returned. "Good work!

" Stoke!"

"Here, sir!"

"Take charge of these weapons. Those strong bows will shoot twice as far as the bows the slaves have made. Make sure our best archers have one, then distribute the regular bows to everyone else. Put good bow strings on all the bows we made. Between the arrows we've made and the ones Tobin has brought us, we should have plenty."

"Do you want the ones who have been making arrows to get some rest?" Stoke asked.

"No," Charlock answered. "We've got a lot of work to do before they attack us with all those reinforcements. Where's Jay?"

"Uh, here! I'm over here!" Jay answered, making his way over to Charlock.

"How many people does it take to work each of those swinging things of yours?"

"The swing shooters? It takes six to work one of them—three inside and three out."

"Six," Charlock said to himself as he pulled on his thick, grey beard. "We should be able to supply the crew for a third swing shooter and still be able to defend the wall. Jay, take whoever you need and build another one. Hang it so that it swings over the center of the wall."

"Yes, sir!" returned Jay enthusiastically. He immediately began gathering the people he needed.

"Graceson!" Charlock called. The Ranger captain quickly stepped up to his commander. "If we lose many more fighters, we're not going to be able to keep the enemy on the other side of that wall," Charlock observed.

"I've been thinking about that," Graceson responded.

"Graceson, get everybody who's not working on one of these other projects and build us a fortress to fall back into if the enemy breaches the wall."

"I think a good spot would be back where we have the aid station," Graceson suggested.

"I think so, too. You can take some of the rocks from the back side of the wall to construct it. Maybe Tobin here might be persuaded to use his squirrel friend to haul some of the rocks and timbers for it."

"Chatter and I would be happy to oblige."

"That'll help a lot," Graceson said gratefully. "I'll get a few folks to put together a sled and harness for him."

Graceson quickly set to work organizing the rest of the defenders into a construction work force to design and build a fortress up against the bluff as quickly as possible.

Tobin started to leave with Graceson, but Charlock called him back, speaking in a quiet voice so no one else could hear Charlock address his friend. "You know it's likely we'll be overrun by the enemy before help can get to us."

"I think just about all of us know that," Tobin answered.

"Well, if they do, I want you to grab Carineda, put her on Chatter, and get out with her."

"I can't leave all of you like that!" Tobin protested.

"Listen to me. I know how you feel, and I know I'm asking a lot of you, but it's our duty to save her if we can."

The truth of the old warrior's words cut off any further protest. Tobin knew he was right. It was their duty to save Cari if they possibly could. Chatter was her only chance of escape, and Tobin knew that he was the only one Chatter would obey. With a sigh Tobin hung his head. The faintest nod of his bushy head showed his agreement. "You know she won't go," Tobin said.

"No, she probably won't go—voluntarily," Charlock agreed, "so we won't tell her. Keep Chatter tethered at the aid station. If the Renegades threaten to break through our defenses at the wall, you are to grab Carineda, place her on the squirrel, and get her safely away. Will you do this?"

"You have my word on it," Tobin said resolutely and extended his hand.

Charlock grasped his hand firmly with the absolute assurance that Tobin would accomplish the task or die in the attempt. With this weight lifted from his shoulders, Charlock joined the others to prepare for their last stand.

CHAPTER TWENTY-THREE

THE LAST FIGHT

"We sure don't seem to be making much progress, Eldan," Hawthorn observed as he pulled himself up from where he had been hiding under a piece of rotted bark. "Between the thick brush and all the creatures we seem to be constantly running into, we're getting nowhere."

"I'm afraid I'm in agreement with young Thorn here, Floppy," Rush spoke up. "The brush on the other bank doesn't seem to be nearly as thick as it is on this side of the creek."

"We gotta cross the creek sometime, Eldan," Hawthorn added. "Why not now?"

"Well, I guess you're both right," said Eldan, picking a piece of twig out of his great mop of red, curly hair. "I was hoping to find an easier place to cross."

"It's not so far across right here," Hawthorn said encouragingly. "We could swim it."

"You and I could, Chummy, but if ol' Wretch here soaks his stitches in this black water, his wounds could foul."

"So what do we do?"

"We'll build a raft and float him across."

"That's gonna take some time," voiced Rush.

"Not as much time as you'd think," said Eldan, looking around at the available materials.

A large sycamore tree grew close to the creek, and a number of the gigantic green leaves had been blown off the limbs and lay nearby. Eldan selected the two largest of these broad leaves and dragged them to the bank of the creek. He also pulled out two of the dry grass reeds that lay all around them and plugged both ends of the hollow reeds with the white clay that was exposed along the creek bank. Cutting multiple slits perpendicularly to the edge along the side of one of the leaves, he pushed one of the reeds through the slits, weaving it along the length of the leaf. He then repeated the process on the other side of the leaf, creating makeshift pontoons. Next he positioned the second leaf on top of the first so that any water seeping in through the slits would not get Rush or their packs wet as they rode on top.

"There you go, Chummy!" Eldan said with satisfaction as they laid the top leaf in place. "We put Wretch and the rest of our stuff on top of here, then you and I will hang on to the sides and swim the whole thing across. Nothing to it!"

"I think I'd rather take my chances swimming," said Rush as he looked skeptically at the flimsy raft.

"No worries, Wretch ol' boy. You'll be as safe as in your mummy's arms. Now help me drag it to the creek."

Rush was pleasantly surprised at how well it floated, and with no more argument, he helped load their packs and weapons and climbed on. Placing themselves on either side of the raft and holding onto the pontoons, Eldan and Hawthorn swam the raft out into the slow-moving current of the black water creek.

"Don't wear yourself out, Chummy," Eldan shouted to Hawthorn. "The current is taking us in the direction we need to go. Just kick easily toward the other shore. Is everything all right up there, Wretch?"

"Well, you know, this here's one tough job I've got, but I reckon I'm Larkin enough to handle it." This statement was followed by a deep, satisfied chuckle. "You know somethin', fellers?" Rush continued. "I almost feel guilty sittin' up here, baskin' in the sun on a nice day, enjoying the breeze, and watching the beauty of the Maker's creation drifting by, while you two poor ol' mud puppies are down there sloggin' away. Yes, siree, I almost do feel guilty."

In this way they continued slowly drifting downstream for almost half an hour, all the while inching closer and closer to the opposite bank. Suddenly Rush's voice broke the quietness. "Uh-oh, fellers! Things are about to get interestin'."

"What is it, Rush?" came Hawthorn's muffled voice from underneath the right side of the raft.

"I just seen a big ol' snapper slide off that log over yonder, and he's aheaded this way. He ain't far off, neither. You two better climb on up here right now!" Rush helped pull Eldan up first since he was on the side closest to the approaching turtle. Then they both dragged Hawthorn up.

"How big is he, Rush?!" Hawthorn asked breathlessly.

"Big enough to eat all three of us and still be hungry."

"No worries, Chums," Eldan said with a relaxed grin on his face. "The fact is, snappers aren't very smart. He won't guess we're even here. From underwater, he'll just think we're a big ol' leaf."

"Don't those things eat leaves?" Hawthorn expressed with concern.

At that moment a huge, dark green head broke the surface right next to them, its large, beak-like mouth gaping open. The raft jerked violently, and the turtle's head disappeared below the water. A large, jagged section of their leaf raft was missing.

"I ain't feelin' too secure right now, Floppy," Rush said as they picked themselves up and examined the damage.

"He bit clean through the floater reed on that side," Hawthorn said, leaning over the torn section. "Maybe he won't like the taste, and he'll leave us alone."

Once more the huge head surfaced, and Hawthorn found to his horror that he was falling forward into the snapper's gaping jaws. Suddenly Hawthorn was jerked backwards just clear of the cavernous mouth as it snapped shut and tore away almost a third of their raft.

"Thanks for pulling me back, guys! I was done for!"

"You may still be if we can't keep that critter from eatin' the rest of our raft!" Rush said as he jumped up from where they had fallen on top of each other. Quickly kneeling by the large tear in their leaf raft, Rush grabbed what was left of one end of the reed with his good arm and pulled it free.

Again the head of the large turtle burst from the water. As the huge snapper started to take another bite, Rush placed the far end of the reed against the turtle's head and pushed. This caused the raft to move away from the snapper just as he bit down.

"Good thinking, Rush!" Hawthorn shouted.

"Help me with this!" Rush called over his shoulder. "Ol' Lumpyhead's comin' back up, and I can't control this thing with one arm!"

Hawthorn jumped to Rush's side at the same time the turtle surfaced for another bite. The damaged raft was again pushed away from the big snapper as he tried to bite into it.

"All right!" Hawthorn exclaimed. "It's working!"

"We're keeping him from eatin' the raft, but we're gettin' further and further away from where we need to go," Rush observed.

"Hold him off a little longer, Chums!" Eldan called from behind them. "I've got an idea."

Again and again the turtle attacked, and each time they pushed away before his powerful jaws could rip through more of the raft.

"Hurry, Eldan!"

"Okay, I think I'm ready!"

Once more the snapper rose to claim his meal. As they pushed away from him, Rush and Hawthorn saw a large piece of sycamore leaf affixed to the end of the other piece of the broken reed being shoved into the face of the hungry turtle. Drawing his head back, the turtle took a moment to look at this new obstacle to his lunch. Eldan waved the piece of leaf in front of his nose.

"Hey!" said Rush. "Is that part of our raft?"

"Calm yourself, Wretch Ol' Boy. I just needed some bait."

After a moment's hesitation the hungry snapper reached out to take the offered morsel. Just as he grabbed for it, Eldan moved the piece of leaf out of his reach. With his head above water, the huge turtle began to follow the leaf on Eldan's reed. As the turtle moved along the side of the raft, the top of his shell passed next to Hawthorn and Rush.

"All right, Chummy, grab the edge of his shell right behind his head, and we'll let him tow us to shore."

"Eldan! Are you crazy?!"

"Hurry, Chummy! Don't let him get by you!"

"Oh, no!" Hawthorn said through clenched teeth as he threw himself flat on the leaf raft and grabbed the edge of the turtle's shell as it moved past. Rush grabbed Hawthorn's legs and hooked his own feet in the torn edge of the damaged raft.

The turtle continued to swim for the piece of leaf which Eldan always kept just out of his reach. Waving the leaf back and forth in front of his nose, Eldan steered the swimming snapper toward their destination.

"Ugh! This thing is slimy," Hawthorn said in disgust, "and it stinks!"

"You're doing a marvelous job, Chummy. Just hold on a little longer."

What seemed like an incredibly long time to Hawthorn was in reality no more than three minutes for the turtle-powered craft to bump into the shore. Actually, it was the turtle who bumped into the shore, with the raft lying along his opposite side.

"Here we are, mates," said Eldan pleasantly. "It's time to disembark."

348

"And just how are we going to do that?!" Hawthorn shouted back, still hanging onto the turtle's shell. "The snapper is between us and the shore!"

"You've got about as much imagination as our friend here, Chummy. Just turn loose and follow me." Eldan shoved the leaf on his reed into the turtle's waiting jaws. Then he quickly leapt up on the top of the turtle's shell. Turning, he addressed his friends, "Toss me a pack, Wretch! You guys better shake a leg before he finishes eating that leaf."

Catching the tossed pack, Eldan bounded onto the shore and scurried up the bank. Pulling Hawthorn to his feet, Rush encouraged his young friend along, "Get a move on, lad! Snappers wait for no Larkin!"

Quickly they both grabbed their packs and sprang up on the back of the terrible creature. As Rush landed on the spiny, slime-covered shell, his feet slid a little. Hawthorn turned to steady his friend, and as he did so, his own feet slipped out from under him. He fell face first onto the nasty shell. Grabbing him by the collar, Rush pulled him up, and they both jumped to the shore and ran up the bank. Eldan was waiting for them with a huge grin on his face.

"Oh, Chummy, you should have seen it. You and the noble Wretch leaping gallantly over the fearsome snapper! It was downright majestic. Just the thought of it brings tears to my eyes."

"Eldan," Hawthorn growled, "I'm not in the mood for this."

"Whew, Chums!" Eldan said, curling up his nose. "You stink!"

Moving along the bank of the creek a respectable distance from the feeding snapper, they gave Hawthorn plenty of time to wash himself and his clothes.

Once Eldan spotted the western slope of the great hill, he led his party away from the creek, traversing the lower face of the western slope.

The forest here was very old, and the brush and undergrowth was sparse due to the thick canopy of leaves above. This allowed the three friends to travel more quickly. Stopping only for brief rests and to eat some smoked fish, they were able to get across the major portion of the thickly wooded hill by late afternoon.

"Do you think we'll cross the trail before dark, Floppy?"

"I expect so," was Eldan's answer. "We really should be getting close." After several more minutes of walking Eldan stopped them. "Look!" Eldan said suddenly as he pointed off into the distance. Following Eldan's extended arm and pointing finger, Hawthorn could see a dark spot moving along some tree limbs in the distance.

"What is it?" Hawthorn asked.

"It's a squirrel," observed Rush.

"No! It's Bubbsy!"

"What's he talking about?" Rush looked at Hawthorn.

"He means that's his brother."

"His brother's a squirrel?"

Hawthorn started laughing. "You know, Rush, that's funny, 'cause the first time I saw his brother, I thought he was a bird."

"What's this guy look like?" Rush asked with a strange look on his face.

"He doesn't look like a bird or a squirrel," Hawthorn said, still laughing. "He sometimes rides on a bird or a squirrel."

"He rides on 'em?!" Rush was incredulous.

"How can you tell that's Tobin and not just some other squirrel?" Hawthorn asked Eldan.

"Because this one was carrying something on its back, and as far as I've seen, Bubbsy's squirrel is the only one that does that. He was headed up the hill," Eldan continued, "but it looks like he stopped on one of those limbs for some reason."

"Can you call him with that thing of yours?"

"I left it in camp when we went into the Renegade Lair. I didn't think I'd need it in there. If ol' Tobs will stay put long enough, maybe we can catch up to him. Come on!"

Eldan picked up the pace and led them through the woods toward the place where he had seen Chatter come to rest. The sun was setting as they drew near where Tobin was perched.

"Is he still there, Eldan?"

"Yes," Eldan returned. "I wonder what's captured his interest so."

"Maybe he's seen us," Rush suggested.

"If he had, he would have come to us," Eldan answered over his shoulder. "No, Tobs is watching something."

"Watch out!" cried Hawthorn.

As they topped a small rise, they found themselves running right into a red ant mound. Stopping suddenly, they began backing off the large, sandy mound, moving very cautiously.

"What do we do?" Hawthorn asked with concern.

"Why don't we get Floppy here to just walk out there an' ask permission to pass through," Rush chuckled.

"He can do that," Hawthorn said with all seriousness.

"Why does that not surprise me?" Rush returned, shaking his head.

"Let's backtrack aways, and then we'll swing to the east and stay wide of the nest," Eldan suggested.

The daylight was waning when they finally cleared the large ant nest. "Come on!" Eldan encouraged them. "We're really close now!"

Almost as soon as Eldan picked up their pace, he stopped again. Hawthorn started to ask what was wrong, but before he could form the words, he heard them. Drums! Moving cautiously ahead, they came to a long, low depression in the slope of the wooded hill in which were hundreds of screaming Renegades.

"So that's what Tobin was watching for so long," Hawthorn spoke his thoughts. "Is he still there?" he asked Eldan,

"Um . . . no," Eldan finally answered after searching the tree limbs above the camp carefully. "Looks like he's gone."

"Do you think they've found our friends yet?" Hawthorn asked.

"I don't know," Eldan answered. "That's one of several questions we need to answer before we plan our next move."

"That sounds like a job fer me," said Rush as he began pulling his old Renegade garb out of his pack. "I'll pull on this here heathern suit and stroll in there like I own the place. Once I find out what's goin' on, I'll slip back out and meet up with you two to decide what to do."

"All right," agreed Eldan after a moment's thought. "While you're doing that, I'll scout to the west up the slope of the hill where our people should be and see what I can learn.

"Chummy, you stay here, and we'll both meet back here with you in, say, an hour."

"Or there about," added Rush as he pulled on the nasty tunic and bent down to pick up the frightful-looking mask. "I wish I hadn't lost that war club. But if they've put guards out, I should be able to get another one.

"I'll see you birds back here in about an hour," Rush said as he strolled purposefully through the brush toward the enemy camp.

"Just stay put, Chummy. We'll both be back soon." With that, Eldan disappeared up the dark, wooded slope of the hill.

"They found your friends all right," Rush began when they reunited a while later. "They've been a fightin' 'em all day. Our guys must have whupped 'em purdy good, 'cause these cutthroats are madder'n hornets."

"Did you find out where our people are?" asked Hawthorn.

"Yes, I did," responded Eldan. "Our camp is up the slope a short distance through the woods above the camp of the Renegades."

"Did you let 'em know we're here?" Rush asked.

"I couldn't. They had the thing lit up so brightly that I couldn't get close without being spotted by the Renegade scouts. Did you learn any of the enemies' plans, Wretch?"

"Oh, shore, that weren't hard. All they're talking about is the big attack they're gonna make at dawn, now that they've got all their reinforcements here. It don't look good fer our side, fellers. There's a whole heap of heathern down there workin' themselves up to a froth. There's a lot more of 'em than our guys can handle, I'm figuring."

"So what do we do?" asked Hawthorn.

"Well, we could try to slip into your friends' camp before daylight," mused Rush, "and help 'em when them cutthroats attack. Does that sound like a plan to you, Floppy?"

"Now, let's not be too hasty, Chums. You two sit tight for a little bit. I need to go get some advice."

"Some advice?!" said Rush with a strange look on his face. "From who?"

"From the Maker," Eldan said over his shoulder as he walked off into the darkness.

It was almost an hour later when Eldan suddenly reappeared.

"Did you catch up on your beauty sleep, Chummy?"

"Sleep! Are you kidding? With all those screaming murderers so nearby?"

"Well, that's too bad," said Eldan, "'cause you're not likely to get another chance the rest of the night. We've got a lot of work to do."

"Did the Maker give you a plan, Eldan?"

"I believe He did," answered Eldan with a big grin on his face. "I believe He did, and let me tell you, this is some more plan!"

"What 'chu gonna do, Floppy?"

"Wretch, ol' boy, we're gonna recruit ourselves an army. But the first thing we gotta do is find where those red ants pile their dead."

"Oh, no, Floppy! You ain't gonna mess with them things, are you?"

"No worries, Wretch. If we run into any of 'em, just let me do the talking."

The moon was now beginning to rise, and by its light they were able to find the ant nest. Once it was found, Eldan led his friends a safe distance away and had them wait while he looked for the ant graveyard. It seemed to Hawthorn that Eldan had been gone an awfully long time when he was startled to hear his friend's voice right next to him.

"Did you miss me, Chummy?"

"Don't do that, Eldan! You scared me spitless, creeping up like that!"

"Calm your sweet self, Chummy. All is well."

"Did you find your pile of dead ants?" Rush asked with a hint of skepticism.

"Indeed I did, Wretch, ol' boy, and a fine pile it is, too, I might add. Just wait 'til you see. Come on, let's go!"

"I can hardly wait," growled Rush as he and Hawthorn followed Eldan through the shadowy, moonlit woods.

As the first hint of a new day began to approach, the dawning skies over the Makerian camp found the defenders tensely alert and ready for the battle that they all knew was just moments away. Carineda's aid station was now surrounded by a formidable stone wall that was almost two Makerians high. A stone and wood platform had been constructed on the back side of the fortress wall to allow its defenders to stand and shoot their arrows down upon the attacking enemy. Two openings had been built into this wall to allow the defenders to enter quickly. Once all the defenders had retreated into the fortress, doors carved from thick sheets of bark could be positioned to block the openings. They were held in place by strong poles wedged against them from behind. Three workers were frantically trying to finish the second door.

"Here they come!" announced Charlock as he peered over the top of the wall. "They're crawling forward again. Signal the crews of the swing shooters to get ready to drop on my signal."

Graceson waved his signals to the three crews on the top of the bluff, who immediately began preparing to release their swinging platforms. The rest of the defenders on the wall began to move into position with arrows at the ready.

"There's Graceson's signal to drop, Jay," Savin yelled up to his friend. "Are you fellas ready?"

Leaning out the window and looking to his right, Jay saw first one and then the other swing shooter drop to the attack. "Cut us loose!"

After a few quick strokes of Savin's flint knife, Jay and his two friends plunged to attack the approaching enemy. As they swung past the wall, they looked down on the advancing Renegades.

"They're gonna make it harder for us!" Jay shouted to his two companions as he released his first arrow. The crawling Renegades had covered their backs with sheets of bark to protect them from the arrows shot at them from above.

"Try to aim for their legs!" Marsh called out.

Back at the wall Charlock gave the command, and the defenders jumped up to launch their arrows at the slowly-advancing enemy. Almost immediately a wave of Renegade arrows flew back at them from enemy archers hidden in the branches of the brush and shrubs.

Jay and his crew had just swung back to the bluff and were starting to drop again when he heard voices screaming at them. Looking down at his companions on the edge of the bluff, he saw Savin and Poke frantically pointing back toward the wall and yelling. Beetle was trying to fling his hook at them, but it was too late. They had already dropped too far for him to reach them.

Sticking his head out of the window and leaning as far out as he could, Jay looked to his right to see the wall. At first his view was blocked by the corner of the swing shooter, but as they swung back toward the wall, he was able to see the whole battle.

Suddenly a flaming ball appeared off in the distance and seemed to pass over the south end of the wall heading toward the bluff. Jay's confused mind tried to deal with this curiosity when something caught his eye back toward the wall. Small balls of fire were streaking up into the sky from the dark shadows behind the crawling Renegades. Suddenly the terrible truth dawned on him. "Fire arrows!" Jay yelled, his eyes riveted to the scene of the fiery attack on the second swing shooter.

Jay pulled his head back in. "They've set the other two on fire!" Jay announced anxiously.

"Well, you can bet we're next," Jonel answered.

"There's nothin' for it," Marsh said resolutely. "Make every shot count."

At that moment they swung past the wall. As the crawling Renegades came into view, the three archers launched their arrows with great rapidity. When they approached the peak of their back swing, fire arrows streaked past their windows.

"Here they come!" Jonel exclaimed.

"Never mind 'em!" Marsh shouted as he released another arrow. "Do yer duty!"

Jay could hear crackling behind him. He also heard the faint roar of a wind-fanned flame as their walled platform sped back toward the rock wall, and Jay knew that the fire arrows had done their job.

"We gotta' get out'a this thing, or we'll be cooked!" Jonel said excitedly.

"Right!" agreed Jay. "They'll try to catch us with the hooks. Be ready to jump."

They each grabbed for their knives and began slashing through the cords with which they had tied themselves in. Smoke was quickly filling the small, grass-walled box, choking them and burning their eyes. They were all three leaning as far out of the window as they could when they reached the top of the bluff. Three hooks flew toward their fiery prison. Savin's hook caught in the burning grass on the side; Beetle's hit just below the window and bounced off; and Poke's hook fell just short, but Jonel managed to stretch out and grab it. Just at that instant Savin's hook pulled out of the burning grass. As the platform dropped again, Jonel, who was holding Poke's hook, was jerked from the window and was left hanging from the rope. Savin watched in horror as he saw the swing shooter now completely engulfed in flames dropping away, carrying Jay and Marsh to certain doom.

"Help me!" Poke called out as he tried to pull Jonel to the top of the cliff. Savin and Beetle quickly grabbed the rope, and in a moment they had their friend safely in their midst.

Standing there in silence, they watched the small ball of flame that was the fire-engulfed swing shooter climbing up into the sky in the distance as it reached the top of its arc. It was just starting back again when the brightly burning platform broke free of the rope and crashed into the ground, sending up an explosion of sparks.

"They're climbing up the wall!" a voice shouted from Charlock's left. "Should we attack?!"

"No!" Charlock shouted back. "Their archers will cut us to pieces if we rush over the top of this wall! Let 'em come to us! Everyone move back and prepare to fire the whooshers!"

The order was quickly passed down the line. The defenders jumped down from the wall and ran to form a new defensive line behind their rock throwers. By now the crews from the destroyed swing shooters were hurriedly descending the bluff to join their companions.

"Wait 'til they top the wall, then let 'em have it with the whooshers!" ordered Charlock. "The rest of you use your bows!"

All along the wall masked heads began to appear. On seeing the defenders lined up a short distance away, the fierce Renegade warriors let out fiendish screams and charged over the wall.

"Whoo-whoo-whoosh!" The windy roar split the air as most of the rock throwers were fired at the same time. Arrows flew rapidly from Makerian bows.

Many of the war cries of the attacking Renegades were instantly silenced, and most of the rest turned into howls of pain as stones and arrows found their marks.

The charge was broken, and the enemy quickly retreated over the top of the wall, leaving their dead and wounded scattered along the Makerian side of the wall. The arms of the whooshers were pulled back into throwing position and loaded with stones, ready for the next charge.

They could hear much cursing and shouting from the other side of the wall of rocks, but after several minutes, when the next attack still hadn't come, the defenders began to get nervous.

"I don't like this, sir," Graceson said as he stood near Charlock. "They should have done somethin' by now."

"Yes," Charlock growled. "Something's amiss, and when these rascals start thinking, they get dangerous.

"Tobin!"

Tobin, who was commanding a group of defenders to Charlock's left, quickly trotted over to his friend.

"What do you think?" Charlock asked his friend without taking his eyes off the wall.

"It's not good," Tobin said thoughtfully. "They're cookin' something up for us. With all of us out here in the open and them behind the wall, my bet is that they're bringing their archers up."

"Yes, I think you're right," Charlock agreed. "It's just taking them some time to get them down out of the trees to up behind the wall."

"They should be getting there any time now," Tobin speculated.

"Shields!" Charlock yelled. "Those with shields get 'em up and stand in front! The rest of you get behind the shield bearers with your bows ready! Crews, stay close to the whooshers."

"It's time, Tobin," Charlock said to his friend. "If they bring archers, we'll have to retreat."

Tobin nodded his bushy head in agreement.

"Go get Cari and get her out of here now."

Tobin looked deeply into the grey eyes of the old warrior. "The Maker be with you."

"And with you," Charlock returned.

Tobin turned and sprinted for the fortress. He hadn't run fifteen strides when black arrows began to pour into ranks of the defenders. Even though the shields stopped many of the shafts, several of those behind them were wounded.

356

"Graceson! Take half of the fighters with you and run to the fortress. We'll cover you."

"What about you?"

"If we all run, they'll slaughter us. We'll come after you're in."

When the order had been passed down the line, Graceson signaled Charlock.

With a roar, a storm of rocks was flung at the top of the wall. At the same instant Graceson led his group in a dead run to the fortress.

"Disable the whooshers, then let's retreat!" Charlock ordered. Quickly the crews cut the launching cords and the rope netting that held the rocks. This would keep the Renegades from using the whooshers against them.

"Shield bearers! Start backing toward the fortress. The rest of you stay behind the shields and keep your arrows flyin' at the top of that wall!"

Charlock looked back to check on Graceson and was just in time to see Chatter bound off carrying Tobin and Carineda. A wave of relief swept over the old warrior as he saw the big gray squirrel leap onto the trunk of a tree near the wall and race up into its branches.

By this time the defenders had moved back away from the wall far enough that the Renegade archers were losing their accuracy.

Suddenly a deafening chorus of shrieks and howls rose from the Renegade army. Vast numbers of the masked savages climbed up onto the wall, brandishing their weapons and screaming their war cries.

"Look how many of them there are!" a voice spoke on Charlock's left.

"Enough of that!" Charlock shouted. "They're workin' themselves up for a charge. When they come, take good aim, shoot your arrow, then run for the fortress!"

"The fortress is too far away! We'll never make it!" one of the former slaves yelled at him.

"That will be for the Maker to decide," Charlock answered back. "Get ready! They'll be at us any moment now!"

Just as the frenzied Renegades seemed ready to charge them, Charlock noticed something happening on the far left end of the wall. The enemy warriors had turned their backs on the Makerians and seemed upset about something happening behind them. All along the wall more and more of the screaming savages stopped their war dances to look at what was happening in their rear. Suddenly mortal terror struck all of the enemy warriors, and with screams of panic they threw themselves back down the wall the way they had come. Some actually clubbed other Renegades nearby in order to be first off the wall.

"What's going on?" Savin asked.

"Let's find out," Charlock answered him, turning to the shield bearer in front of him.

"Let me borrow your shield. Savin! Goodclaw! You two bring your bows and come with me. Blesstis! Take the rest of our fighters and retreat to the fortress."

"Yes, sir," Blesstis returned, and with a wave of his hand he led the others in an easy trot to the fortress.

"Let's go see what can scare a Renegade army," Charlock said to his two companions as he led the way back to the wall.

When they poked their heads over the top of the rock wall, they were amazed at what they saw. An army of red ants was marching single file parallel to the wall and not quite a stone's throw away. The long line of fierce creatures had almost marched the entire length of the wall, and the last of the Renegades were retreating from the ants. They did not want to be cut off from their camp by the advancing insect army.

"Look at that!" Goodclaw exclaimed. "These ants have completely cut the Renegades off from us!"

"It's lucky they came when they did!" added Savin.

"Luck had nothing to do with it," Charlock announced. "Look over there." Charlock was pointing off to the left. Savin turned and saw two figures approaching out of the woods between the wall and the line of red ants. "Look who's come back from the dead . . . again," Charlock chuckled.

"Hey, everybody," Eldan waved, his grin spreading from ear to ear. "Did you miss us?!"

Hawthorn, walking beside him, waved to his father. Savin jumped down from the wall, ran to his son, and gripped him in a huge bear hug that lifted the young Larkin off the ground.

"I thought I'd lost you again, Thorn!" Savin said with emotion.

"I have so much to tell you, Father. But first we must finish with these Renegades."

"Are these ants your doing?" Savin asked.

"No, this is Eldan's plan," Hawthorn answered. "He actually talks to them with two sticks, and they know what he says. The ants have this sack inside them that produces a scent. When you put it on you, the ants think you're one of them, and if you pour it along the ground, they will all follow the trail."

"So is that how you got all these ants to march across the battlefield?" Savin asked turning to Eldan.

"Oh, it was nothing," Eldan said with a shy smile. "I really didn't do that much."

"Come on, Eldan," Goodclaw chided. "Don't be so modest."

"Oh, he's not," Hawthorn remarked cheerfully. "He made Rush do all the work."

"Chummy!" Eldan exclaimed with a hurt look on his face. "I liked it better when you were bragging on me."

"Is Rush here, too?" asked Savin.

"Yep. He made it out with us. Eldan had him slip across in front of the wall last night and lay a trail for the ants to follow. There he is now, just coming out of the brush."

They all turned to the right and saw the distant figure of their burly friend. He was standing on the north end of the battlefield between the marching column of ants and the rock wall. He waved at them, then began to whirl something around his head.

Hawthorn turned to his father and handed him a small, flesh-colored pouch with a wooden stopper. "This is some of the friendly ant scent. Rub some of it on you and pass it around to the rest—just in case our insect army gets out of control."

"It looks like the ants are where we want them, Chummy. Why don't you do the honors and give those painted savages our ultimatum?" As he said this, Eldan moved several paces off to the left. Then he pulled a large, brown pouch out from under his cloak. The pouch was secured to a long cord with a loop tied in the end. Grabbing the loop, Eldan began whirling the weighted pouch around and around his head.

Hawthorn stepped forward to face their enemies, who because of their mortal fear of stirring up the ants had become very quiet.

"All of you Renegades!" Hawthorn shouted to them. "Leave this place immediately and go back to your home, or else at the count of ten my friends will release pouches containing a scent that will cause these ants to turn on you and tear you to pieces! Now go! One! . . . Two! . . . Three! . . ."

Hawthorn definitely had their attention. There was a great deal of animated discussion among the Renegades. They seemed particularly interested in Rush and Eldan as they whirled the large pouches around their heads. By the time Hawthorn got to seven, one of the Renegade captains, standing as close to the line of marching ants as he dared, called out, "You win this time, Gooder!" He spat, shaking his clenched fist. "We're leaving—but you stole our slaves, and we'll get even!"

The Renegade captain turned and ordered the warriors to return to camp. Most were eager to obey and get as far away from the red ants as possible.

"Look!" shouted Hawthorn. "They're leaving! Eldan, you're a genius!"

"Oh, go on, Chummy," Eldan said shyly. "You're makin' me turn all red."

"Eldan!"

"Yes, sir, Sir Charlock, sir," Eldan said as he quickly presented himself before his commander.

"Where's Turk? And what happened in the cave?"

At the mention of their dead friend's name both Eldan and Hawthorn lowered their heads. Sadly Eldan began to relate the events surrounding their friend's death.

As the Renegade captain was sullenly moving his troops toward the brush in the direction of their camp, he was suddenly confronted with a very angry Renegade archer. "What are you doing?! You can't let them get away!"

"Do you see those ants, Wolf?" the Renegade captain called Greatfighter snarled back. "There's nothing we can do about them. Now get back to camp before I make you a slave again!"

Wolf was seething with fury as he watched Greatfighter turn and walk away. "Someday I'll get you," Wolf murmured under his breath as he stared at the back of the Renegade captain.

Turning his attention to the real object of his hatred, Wolf looked across the line of marching ants and stared at the Gooders with fiery eyes. As he recognized the face of Hawthorn, his fierce hatred exploded within him into an uncontrollable, demonic rage. Waving his bow and screaming his war cry, he charged forward. With his good leg he leapt onto the back of the ant moving across in front of him and sprang off the other side, running to the attack, oblivious to the pain in his injured leg.

Although the small group of defenders were at that moment unaware of Wolf's attack, Rush could quite clearly see Wolf's leap over the line of ants and his charge up the slope to attack Rush's unsuspecting friends. Rush also saw the startled ant Wolf stepped on go into a frenzy, triggering a spreading frenzy among the rest of the fierce red ants. Dropping his scent pouch, Rush began running toward his friends, yelling a warning, and waving his arms.

"Now what's ol' Wretch bellerin' about?" Eldan wondered out loud as he looked in the distance and saw Rush's frantic efforts to get their attention.

Just then a rumbling, crashing sound mixed with many screams pulled their attention back toward the ants. What they saw was a fierce-looking Renegade not six paces away, his face twisted in hate, drawing his bow and aiming straight at Hawthorn. Behind him the army of red ants, in a massive frenzy, were rushing in every direction, destroying everything and everyone in their path.

"Look out!" Savin screamed and leaped for his son.

Goodclaw, who was holding Eldan's pouch, threw it at Wolf, striking him in the face just as he released the arrow. As the pouch burst in Wolf's face, he howled in pain. Dropping his bow, he clawed desperately at his face as the liquid ant scent seared his eyes.

Savin leaped upon his son, knocking him to the side just as the arrow arrived. The deadly missile sliced Savin's back, cutting his tunic and opening a deep, red gash from one shoulder to the other.

Goodclaw drew his knife and started after Wolf, who by now had fallen to the ground and was still clawing painfully at his eyes. Goodclaw was stopped as Eldan reached out and grabbed his arm. "No time for him, Goodie. We've got bigger problems!"

"He's right!" Charlock barked. "Those crazed ants will be on us in a moment! Grab our people, and let's get over the wall!"

Hawthorn and his father were yanked to their feet—Savin painfully so—and were almost carried up the steep, rocky slope of the wall. Rush arrived just in time to help Eldan and Goodclaw lift Savin over the top of the wall. Looking back, Rush saw the huge wave of berserk red ants roll over the thrashing form of Wolf.

"Humph!" Rush said with a satisfied nod. "Good riddance!"

"Is he gonna be okay?" Hawthorn asked with concern. He was nervously watching as Blesstis worked on the large wound across his father's back. Savin was lying face down on a large, flat rock inside the Makerian's fortress against the bluff.

"Well," began Blesstis with some hesitation, "it's a pretty deep wound . . . and it goes clear across his back . . . but nothing important seems to be injured."

"Nothing important?!" squawked Savin. "My back is important to me!"

"You tell 'em, Savin," chuckled Rush, who was standing behind Hawthorn. "A minor wound is a wound somebody else has."

"Thanks for saving my life, Father," Hawthorn said with feeling.

"I had to, Son. Your mother would skin me if I brought you back home with an arrow hole in you." After a moment's pause Savin continued more seriously, "Thanks to you and to all of your friends for getting us out of that Renegade slave pit."

"Yes, sir!"

"That's right!"

"Thank you!" a chorus of voices from the former slaves standing nearby added.

"Goodclaw's coming back!" a voice shouted down from the top of the fortress wall. A few minutes later the Makerian scout appeared through the open door of the fortress.

"What's the news of our enemies, Goodclaw?" Charlock asked.

For a moment Goodclaw just stood there and shook his head. "Those ants of Eldan's did a pretty thorough job," he finally said. "There's not enough of that bunch of Renegades left to cause us any worry."

"May the Maker have mercy on them," Charlock said softly.

"Amen," Goodclaw agreed.

Hawthorn looked across the cave-like room and saw Poke kneeling beside his injured father. "Well," Hawthorn said, "at least we're all back together again."

"Not all of us, Thorn," Savin said sadly. "We lost Jay in the battle."

Savin spent the next several minutes relating to Hawthorn and Rush what had happened after their escape from the Lair, how the Renegades had found their camp, and the three battles that had taken all of yesterday to fight. He told them how Jay had saved the day with his inventions.

"This morning when the battle began, Jay, Marsh, and Jonel were in one of the swing shooters when the Renegades set them on fire using flaming arrows. Jonel escaped, but Jay and Marsh were unable to get out."

There was a long period of mournful silence after Savin finished.

"Where's Carineda?" Hawthorn finally asked.

"The young lady?" his father asked.

Hawthorn nodded.

"The enemy hit us really hard in this last battle. When it looked like we were about to be overrun, Charlock had that Tobin fellow get her out of here on his squirrel. If you guys hadn't of gotten those ants here when you did, we would have been in real trouble."

"All right, friend," Blesstis announced when he finished bandaging Savin's back, "that should help for the time being."

Hawthorn was helping his father pull his tunic back on when they heard one of the guards call out, "Tobin's coming back!" Hawthorn, Rush, and Savin joined many of the others outside the fortress to welcome their friend.

The big squirrel jumped off the tree trunk he was descending and bounded quickly across the sandy plateau, sliding to a stop directly in front of the fortress. On his back were Tobin, Cari, and two other unrecognizable individuals who wore blackish-gray clothes and who had blackish gray skin.

"Who you got there, Tobin?" someone called out.

"When Cari and I got up into the top of that tree yonder, we found us a couple of roasted Rangers sittin' up there on a limb. I thought about leaving them up there, but Cari wouldn't have it, so we brought them back with us."

"Hi, guys," one of the black figures said with a wave. "Sorry we missed the fight, but once we climbed up on that limb, we couldn't figure out how to get back down."

"It's Jay and Marsh!" a chorus of voices rang out. The two slid off Chatter's back and into the crowd of excited friends. Clouds of ash rose from them as many hands slapped their backs in welcome. For the next thirty minutes Marsh and Jay entertained everyone with the story of their escape.

"The truth be known, fellas," Jay was saying, "when I saw us falling away from the bluff, I figured we were goners for sure. But not ol' Marsh here. He wouldn't give up. Tell 'em what you did, Marsh."

Marsh was busy trying to wash the soot off his face. "There's not much to tell," Marsh said in his low, monotone voice. "The Maker made a way for us to get out, and we did."

"Come on, Marsh, there's more to it than that!" a voice called out.

"Yeah, you tell it, Jay!" another voice demanded.

"Okay, okay, I'll tell ya," Jay said, taking up the tale again. "Marsh here just don't wanna take any credit for hisself. But I'm here to tell you fellas, he's my hero.

"Like I said, when the hook holding us came loose and we started swinging back toward the wall, the flames just covered us up. At that point I gave up, but Marsh started hollerin' at me to tear a hole in the roof. It didn't take us no time at all to make a couple of holes big enough for us to crawl through, so up we went. Marsh shoved me up the rope ahead of him and yelled, 'Climb!' So I became a climbing fool."

"It must have been hard to climb up that rope with all that downward pull from the swinging platform," Kordillon said, who was standing nearby.

"You're right," Jay admitted. "But you'd be surprised how well you can climb a swinging rope when your pants are on fire."

"Your leggings were on fire?!" asked Hawthorn.

"Yeah, but just for a while," Jay said matter of factly. "Marsh beat 'em out for me."

363

Jay continued his narrative, "So we both started up the rope, but we hadn't gone very far when Marsh started hollerin' again. It seems that the rope below us had caught on fire, and the flames were running up after us. So Marsh pulled himself up right under me and grabbed my knife out of my boot, then hanging on with one hand, he cut the rope below him, sending the burning swing shooter crashing into the ground.

"Hey!" Jay turned to Marsh. "You never did give me back my knife."

"I dropped it."

"You dropped my knife?!"

"I didn't need it any more."

"Well, anyway," Jay continued, "we climbed up to that limb way up yonder and sat there like two knots—'til company finally arrived."

There were more questions for them, then Jay and Marsh wanted to know about the battle.

"So what do we do now, Sir Charlock?" asked someone when there was a lull in the story telling.

"It sounds like we've got nothing to fear from the Renegades, but we'll keep guards posted and continue sending out our scouts. We've got enough work taking care of the wounded to keep us busy 'til the relief patrol gets here. Then as soon as we can, we'll march for Stillwaters. All you former slaves will be safe there until you recover fully. But the first thing we're going to do is kneel right here and thank the Maker for our deliverance."

CHAPTER TWENTY-FOUR

LOOSE ENDS

There was a soft knock on the ornately carved cypress door. Slowly it opened, and Hawthorn's smiling face popped around its edge. "Hey," he said softly. "Is it all right to come in?"

"Sure, Thorn," Poke answered. "come on in."

Poke was sitting in a chair next to his father's bed. Light was streaming warmly through a large, round window in the wall to Hawthorn's left.

"Is he sleeping?" Hawthorn asked quietly as he approached the bed.

"More or less," said Poke. "His head was hurting this morning, so they gave him some kind of herbal drink that made him really drowsy. He comes and goes."

"Looks like he's gone right now," chuckled Hawthorn. "So how is your father, Poke?"

"Well, that healer guy seems to think he's doing very well," Poke returned. "Papa can move his arm some now, and his shoulder doesn't hurt him at all, but it's his head injury that worries me. He doesn't have any dizzy spells anymore and only an occasional headache, but he can't remember anything."

"He doesn't know who he is?" Hawthorn asked.

"Oh, he knows all that stuff. He knows me, and I'm sure he knows you, but he doesn't remember anything about what's happened to us. He keeps asking me where we are and what happened to him, then a half an hour after I've explained it all to him, he'll ask me again. He doesn't remember any of the things I just told him. It's very frustrating, 'cause I keep having to answer the same questions over and over again."

"Well, look at it this way, Poke. At least you never run out of things to talk about."

"It's not funny, Thorn! I'm worried about him!"

"Have you asked Taumis the Gentle about that?" Hawthorn asked in a more serious tone.

"You mean that healer guy? Yeah, I asked him. He said that there's a good chance that Papa's thinking will clear with time."

"Well, that's encouraging," Hawthorn said cheerfully.

"But what if his thinking doesn't clear, Thorn?! What if he's always like this?!"

"You've got to think positively, Poke."

"That's easy enough for you! It's not your papa lying here talking crazy!"

"Poke, I know you're worried about your father, but Taumis the Gentle and his people are really good at what they do. You need to trust them."

"Trust them?! Thorn, do you know where these people come from? They were banished from the First Clan—that means they're Renegades!"

"Poke, how can you say that? If it weren't for the Makerians, I'd be dead, and you and your father would still be slaves."

"Okay!" Poke snapped back. "So they do good sometimes. Maybe they're nicer than the other kind, but they're still Renegades! And they're arrogant, too. Several of 'em came marching in here this morning wanting to pray for my father. They act like they think they can talk to the Maker anytime they want!"

"You let them pray, didn't you?"

"No, I didn't! Thorn, I'm surprised at you. You know that only the Shaman can pray to the Maker."

"Haven't you listened to any of the things the Makerians have said?" Hawthorn argued. "What about the stories of Jehesus?"

"They made all that stuff up," Poke responded confidently. "If there really was such a person as Jehesus, the Shaman would have told us. You know that."

At that moment there was another knock at the door. When it opened, Taumis the Gentle entered, followed by his daughter Carineda. "Greetings, friends," he said cheerfully.

"Hello, Sir Taumis. Hello, Cari," Hawthorn greeted his friends with a smile. Poke averted his eyes and said nothing.

"I wanted to come back and see if your father was getting any relief from his headache," Taumis said to Poke.

"I guess it must have worked," muttered Poke. "He's been sleeping off and on since he drank that stuff you gave him."

Poke changed the subject. "So when do you think my father will be well enough to go home?" he wanted to know.

"His mental confusion should improve slowly over time, but that won't keep him from traveling. I would say that in just a few more days he will be physically up to a trip like that, providing you take your time."

"Are you anxious to leave us?" Taumis asked, half teasing.

"We just want to get home," Poke answered, not meeting Taumis's gaze.

"Uh, excuse me," said a voice from behind them. Turning, they saw the head and shoulders of a bearded Makerian leaning around the edge of the open door.

"Hello, Podomon," said Taumis as he spotted the familiar face of his assistant.

"I'm sorry to interrupt," Podomon continued, "but, Miss Carineda, your Renegade patient is awake, and he's rather upset."

"Thank you," Cari responded. Turning to her father, she said, "Excuse me, Father. I must try to calm him down before he does himself more damage."

"Please be careful, Carineda," Taumis called after his retreating daughter.

Cari paused at the door. "It'll be fine, Father," she smiled. "I have help."

"I don't know, Miss Cari," said her bearded companion as they hurried down the dimly lit passageway. "Taking this rascal off of the sleeping herbs may not have been a good decision."

"Don't start in on me again, Podomon. We had to take him off of those strong herbs eventually. We knew something like this might happen; that's why we put the guards in his room."

They heard lots of yelling and crashing when they were still several doors away. When Cari and Podomon entered the room, they saw the angry Renegade tearing savagely at the remaining bandage material around his head as he stumbled drunkenly around the room. The two guards were standing back near the door, both nursing bites and scratches where they had tried to restrain the maddened patient.

Finally the Renegade managed to rip away the last of the bandages covering his eyes. When he was able to see, he quieted down and began to examine his surroundings. He was standing with his back to Cari as she approached him. "Those bandages were meant to help your eyes to heal," she said in a quiet, soothing voice. "They really weren't ready to come off yet."

At the sound of Cari's voice the Renegade spun around. The face that glared so venomously at her was the face of Wolf. "Where am I, and what have you Gooders done to me?" he snarled.

"You were injured in the last battle. You took a blow to your head when the ants caught up with you, and your eyes were burned with ant scent."

"It was your people who did that!" he shot back.

"Yes, it was one of our Rangers who hit you in the face with the sack of ant scent, and although it did burn your eyes, it was that scent which kept the ants from tearing you apart. We brought you back to our home to take care of you until you're well enough to leave," Cari continued.

"Listen, little girl, y'er not foolin' anyone. I'm a prisoner, and you just kept me alive so those scum hiding behind you can torture me into telling you our secrets."

"You're wrong," Cari said firmly. "You would have gone blind and possibly have died if we had left you on the battlefield. The reason you're here is because our Lord Jehesus loves you, and He wants us to show you His love by caring for your injuries."

There was silence for a moment. Slowly a smile began to spread across Wolf's twisted face. "Heh, heh, heh," Wolf chuckled, "so y'er Lord loves ol' Wolf, huh?"

"Yes, He does," Cari said sincerely. "He loves you more than you can imagine."

"Well, all right," Wolf said, still chuckling. "This is sounding better all the time. So what are you gonna do to show me this love?"

"Well, first of all, I need you to sit on the side of the bed so I can examine your eyes to see if they've healed enough to be without the bandages."

"Go ahead and look," Wolf said, still smiling, as he sat down on the edge of the bed.

Cari walked over to the double doors just to the right of the bed. Opening both of these allowed bright sunlight to stream in from the balcony overlooking the lake. Wolf squinted at the bright light.

"Now open your eyes as wide as you can," Cari said as she drew near to examine him. As she reached up to steady his head, Wolf's right hand shot up. With the speed of a striking serpent, he grabbed one of Cari's wrists in his vice-like grip and quickly spun her around, twisting her arm painfully behind her back. At the same instant his left hand circled her throat.

"You stupid fools!" he spat at the three other Makerians. "Don't try anything, or I'll break her neck 'afore you'd get halfway to me." He glared at them menacingly. "Now if you want this little girl to stay alive, you three scumheads are gonna lead me outta here."

"You don't have to do this," Cari choked out.

"Quiet!" Wolf yelled and clamped his fingers tighter around her throat.

"She's right!" yelled Podomon. "We'll be happy to lead you out. Just let her go!"

"You'll lead me out all right, but I'll keep the little girl with me."

"Hey! You by the door!" Wolf barked. "You've got a knife in yer belt. I want it. Pull it out very slowly, then walk over here and drop it on the bed."

The Ranger cautiously began to move forward with the knife. Wolf was careful to keep the bed between himself and the approaching Ranger. "You try somethin', Muck Breath, and I'll kill her. I swear it! Now drop that knife on the bed and back away from it."

Obediently the Ranger dropped the knife and began to back away. Dragging Cari with him, Wolf edged closer to the bed. With his left hand still gripping her throat, he released her arm with his right hand and reached for the knife.

Cari saw her chance. She raised her right foot and drove her heel into the top of Wolf's foot with all her might. With an agonized howl Wolf released his grip on Cari's throat. Instantly Cari buried her elbow into Wolf's ribcage, and as he doubled over in pain, she leapt away from him. Podomon and the Rangers rushed forward, and Wolf made a staggering retreat to the balcony. A quick look over the edge revealed a long drop to the water, but Wolf didn't take time to think about it. To him it was his only way of escape. He threw himself over the low wall and dropped the six levels into the dark, green water below. Podomon and the others arrived at the edge of the balcony just in time to see Wolf surface and begin swimming toward the shore.

"Did he hurt you, Miss Cari?"

"I'll be all right, Podomon."

Cari continued, "I can't believe he did that. He could easily have broken his neck falling that far."

"That guy's a loon, Miss Cari."

"Look at how he's churning up the water when he swims," one of the Rangers pointed out. "He has no idea of the danger he's in."

Cari let out a sudden gasp as she comprehended the significance of the Ranger's words. "The Gonch!" she cried. "I forgot about it. Oh, Podomon! He doesn't know! We've got to help him."

Podomon turned to the Ranger next to him. "Get word to the crew on the Turtle to paddle over and try to pick him up, and hurry!"

"Right!" the Ranger answered and sprinted from the room.

"And tell them he's dangerous!" Podomon shouted after him.

Cari stood at the edge of the balcony and shouted as loud as she could, trying to get Wolf to stop swimming and to be still. The others joined her.

In spite of the loud splashing of his powerful strokes, Wolf heard them yelling. He stopped and looked up at them waving and screaming at him. So he shook his fist at them and yelled back. He shouted every vile curse and every filthy name he could dredge up from his black heart. Just then a movement in the water below him caught his attention. He looked down in time to see a gigantic, gaping mouth rising rapidly to engulf him. A fear-choked scream escaped his lips an instant before the huge bass broke the water, then Wolf was gone.

Jay pushed back from the table and patted his stomach. "I'm tellin' you the truth," he began earnestly, "this is about the best meal I think I've ever eaten. Lady Morningdove, you are a wonderful cook!"

"Would you care for more, Sir Jay?" returned his hostess, her dark eyes smiling at his compliment.

"Thank you, ma'am, but I couldn't eat another thing. I've already stuffed so much good food in me that if I pulled my tunic off right now, I'd never get it back on! Heh, heh, heh!" Jay noticed that his hostess didn't laugh at his joke. Although she still wore the same polite smile, he noticed a bit more blush in her cheeks. He made a mental note to himself to not talk so much.

Morningdove rose from the table and, picking up her plate and cup, left the room. Jay was starting to think that he might have offended her when she suddenly returned carrying two mugs of hot plum cider. She placed one in front of Jay and the other in front of Marsh, who was just finishing his meal. Then she began to remove the dirty dishes from the table, carrying them into the other room.

"Marsh," Jay said in a soft voice, "does your sister cook like this all the time?"

"Um, well, she fancied it up a bit since we were having company, but Dovey does all right."

"All right! After a meal like that, all you've got to say is, 'She does all right'? Marsh, ol' buddy, she's too good for you."

"You're right enough there, Jay lad," Marsh returned in his expressionless monotone, "but if I wasn't here to eat it, think of all the good food that would go to waste."

"Marsh!" Jay exclaimed at his unsmiling friend, "that was funny!"

"It was?" Marsh responded. "Well, don't hold it against me."

Jay took a sip of his hot cider. "You really amaze me, Marsh."

"A fellow tells a little joke, and you're amazed?" Marsh said as he lowered his own mug. "You don't get out much, do you?"

"I'm not talking about the joke—I'm talking about you. You know, there's nothing really very special about you . . . ."

"Yep," Marsh interrupted, "that's pretty amazing."

"What I was going to say was that there's nothing special about you, and yet you're not like anyone I've ever known. When we were in the burning swing shooter, I just knew we were going to die, and I was paralyzed with fear. But you weren't afraid to die. I could tell that when I looked at your face. The way you made sure I started up the rope first when there were flames all around us made it seem like you were more concerned for me than you were for yourself."

"Don't get me wrong," Marsh began. "I wasn't anxious to get cooked in that contraption of yours. In fact, I'll admit that the thought of burning to death did scare me, but death itself doesn't scare me, if that makes any sense."

"I'm not sure I follow you," Jay answered.

"Thinking about all the pain in burning like that was scary to me, but the moment of death would have been a blessed peace, followed the next instant by great joy. I know where I will be afterward. But I was afraid for you, Jay, because you aren't ready to die. You don't know the Lord Jehesus."

"I've heard some of your people talking about him," Jay offered.

"Well, that's a start, but there's a huge a difference between hearing about Him and actually knowing Him, believing in Him, and following Him as the great chief of your life."

"Okay," Jay acknowledged, "so where do I start?"

A smile spread across Marsh's face. He got up from the table and walked over to a wooden chest. Opening it, he lifted out a large, rectangular object wrapped in a white cloth. Marsh set the object on the table in front of Jay and began to unwrap it. "You start here," he said.

"What is that?" Jay asked.

"It's my copy of some of the Maker's words."

Jay stared in awe at the large, leather-bound book. Marsh reached over and opened it. On the page before him Jay saw row upon row of small, neatly-printed figures of various shapes. Turning the pages, he saw that every one was filled with the same small figures. "What do they say?" Jay asked as he ran his fingers gently across a page.

"They tell of the Maker and His Son, Jehesus. They tell what Jehesus did when He came into this world, what He said, and what He wants."

"Would you read me some of the words?" Jay asked.

"I would love to," Marsh smiled. As Marsh read, Jay sat listening in complete fascination. They continued in this way until it was quite late. At Marsh's suggestion, they met the next morning to read more of the Maker's words. This time as Marsh read, Jay had questions. Many times Marsh would turn a few pages and read the answer to Jay's question directly from the Maker's words.

"Well," Jay began, "what if someone believed in the Lord Jehesus and wanted to know what to do to be His follower?"

"You follow Him," Marsh answered.

"But how do you know what He wants you to do?"

"His word tells us, His nature tells us, and His Spirit in us gives us understanding."

"So what does His word tell me?" Jay wanted to know.

Marsh flipped some pages and found the words for which he was looking, "'Believe on the Lord Jehesus, and thou shalt be saved.'"

"Thou shalt?" questioned Jay.

"Those are just old words," explained Marsh. "It means that if you want to be saved, you must believe on Jehesus: that He is the son of the Maker and that He is Lord of all."

"I do believe in Him," said Jay earnestly. "What else do the words tell me?"

Marsh turned back a few pages. In a moment he found the place. "'Repent ye and be converted, that your sins may be blotted out.'"

"So what does that mean?" Jay asked.

"It means that you must turn away from those things in your life that don't please the Lord Jehesus and run after those things that do."

"I'm willing to do that," Jay said with conviction.

"Then you should go to be bapatized," Marsh said, his eyes smiling.

"What's *bapatized?*"

"It's a ceremony," Marsh explained. "Jehesus talked about it." Marsh turned the pages in his book again. "Jehesus said, 'He that believeth and is bapatized shall be saved, but he that believeth not shall be damned.'"

"But what IS *bapatized?*" Jay asked anxiously.

"It's the time when the person who believes in Jehesus gets buried in water. The ceremony symbolizes that you join with Jehesus in His death, burial, and resurrection. Jehesus dies for your sins: you die to your sins. Jehesus was buried in the ground: you are buried in water. Jehesus rose from the dead and lives a new life: you rise up from the water to live a new life with Jehesus as your Lord and King. Bapatize is where you begin to put your faith into action."

"Hmmm," Jay was thoughtful. "Didn't you tell me Jehesus was buried for three days before He came back to life? When you bapatize someone, you don't keep them under the water for three days, do you?"

"No, we don't," Marsh answered with no expression. "But it might not be a bad idea. You'd get to be with Jehesus a lot faster that way."

"So," Jay said when he finished laughing, "when could I be bapatized?"

"Anytime," Marsh answered. "Whenever you're ready. We could do it now if you want."

"Not right now," Jay said thoughtfully. "I want to talk to somebody first."

Jay found Rush standing at the railing of the watch deck, the top of the Makerian stronghold. Rush was fascinated with how they caught fish, and since they had come to Stillwaters, he had spent hours watching the process.

"So what do you think about it?" Jay asked his friend.

"You mean about this *fish-a-thang* they've built?"

"Not just that," Jay responded, "I mean all of this."

Rush looked down the side of the Refuge to the green water far below. He let his eyes scan the shore. As he looked to the north, he saw the Makerian paddle barge working its way slowly to shore. "I think it's absolutely amazing what the Maker has done for these folks."

"You believe that all this is the Maker's doing?" Jay asked.

"It has to be!" Rush said with conviction. "Look at how much these folks know and what all they can do. Thunderation, Jay! Think about it! Only twenty-five or thirty seasons ago when these folks started out, they didn't know anymore than we do. Our clans were established, but they had to start from scratch. Just look at what they've done compared to us. All this is the Maker's work; there ain't no other explanation."

After a few moments of silence Jay decided that he would probe a little deeper. "What do you think of Jehesus, Rush?"

"Floppy says He's the Maker's son," Rush answered. "It's really quite a story. They say the Maker sent Him into the world to live among the people, to teach them, and to show them what the Maker is like. Some Shaman-type guys hated Him and had Him kilt, but after three days He came back to life."

"Oh, I've heard the story," Jay interrupted, "but I want to know what you think about Him."

"Burn yer hide, Jay! You're gonna' make me answer that, ain't cha?" Rush lowered his head as he gathered his thoughts.

"Well," he finally said, "I guess thar's no way around it." Rush lifted his head and looked his friend straight in the eye. "Jay, I believe in Him." He raised his hand in defense. "Now hear me out 'fore ya jump all over me!

"A couple of days ago," Rush continued, "Floppy and I were talkin' about stuff, an' I asked him some questions about Jehesus. He and his brother got to readin' some of the Maker's words to me. I'm tellin' ya, Jay, it was amazing! When I heard the stories about Jehesus, I just knew it was true. When I saw how Jehesus was working in their lives, I decided that I wanted that too. So . . . uh . . . I got in."

"What do you mean?" Jay asked. "Did you become a Makerian?"

"In a way, I guess I did," Rush said thoughtfully. "Oh, I'm still a Larkin an' all, but I did become one of the Maker's children, and I reckon that's what Makerian means."

"So what did you do?" asked Jay with great interest.

"Well, that's what I asked them. They read some of the Maker's words to me that said that I needed to believe that Jehesus is the son of the Maker and that His death paid the price for all my sins. I told 'em that I already believed that, so then they read me a part of a story from the Maker's book about a feller who wanted to be one of Jehesus's followers. He was told to get up, be bapatized, and wash away his sins, calling on the name of Jehesus.

"At that point, if Jehesus had said for me to stand on my head, I was ready to obey him. So I told 'em that whatever bapatized was, I was ready to do it."

"I feel the same way," said Jay. "Marsh has been reading to me out of the Maker's book. I've been thinking about it for two days now, and I've decided that it's the truth."

"So what have you done about it?" Rush asked.

"Nothing yet. I didn't want to do anything until I had talked to you about it. I guess I wanted to know if you thought I was crazy."

"I reckon you know what I think," Rush smiled.

"I reckon I do," said Jay. "Come with me; let's go find Marsh."

It was almost an hour later when Marsh led Jay and Rush into a circular chamber on one of the lower levels. Light was streaming into the room from a round window high up on the wall. A pool had been cut into the floor near the opposite wall. Narrow slits in the side wall of the pool allowed water from the lake to flow in and out.

"Yep," said Rush, looking around. "I couldn't have found it again, but this here's the place Floppy and his brother brought me."

Several people were already there, standing around the pool. In the pool was a Makerian up to his waist in water. He was slightly bent over, and his arms were in the water. Suddenly the head and chest of a second person came bursting up out of the water. As they came closer, Jay could tell that it was one of the wounded Renegades from the battle that Carineda and Blesstis had worked so hard to help. He had a big grin on his face as he came up the steps from the pool in a dripping wet, white tunic. As he reached the top step, he dropped back his head and let out a terrific yell that echoed down the passageway behind them. Those who were with him laughed and ran up to congratulate him. Jay recognized Kordillon and Blesstis in the happy group.

As the happy, former Renegade stepped away from the pool, a warm blanket was wrapped around him. Immediately Jay saw two other candidates for the watery ceremony step forward. A black robe was fished out of the pool and wrung out. This robe was then placed around the shoulders of the first person.

"Do you believe that Jehesus is the blessed Son of the Maker?" the question was asked by a middle-aged, bearded Makerian who had placed his hand on the shoulder of the person now wearing the black robe.

"Yes, I do," was the response. Jay could clearly hear his answer even though he was standing several paces behind the candidate.

"Do you accept the death of Jehesus as payment for your sins?"

"Yes, I do."

"Do you believe that Jehesus rose from the dead and is alive even now with His father, our Maker?"

"Yes, I do."

"Are you now willing to say before these witnesses that He is your Lord?"

"Yes, I am. I now take Jehesus," the candidate continued, "to be my one and only Lord forever."

"Then because of your confession that Jehesus is Lord," the bearded Makerian replied, "we now bapatize you. As Jehesus died for your sins, you die to your sins. As Jehesus was buried in the ground, you will now be buried in water. As the water washes away dirt from your body, so the blood of Jehesus washes you clean of all sin. As Jehesus rose from the dead and came out of the ground with a new life, so you will rise from the water a new person."

At this point the person wearing the black robe turned and descended the steps into the pool. Jay was stunned when he saw his face. "Rush!" Jay whispered excitedly as he grabbed his friend's arm. "It's Hawthorn!"

"Thunderation!" Rush exclaimed under his breath.

"And look over there!" Jay continued. "There's Savin with one of those white tunics on. I'll bet he's next."

Hawthorn stood before the Makerian who was in the pool. The smiling assistant spoke some words to him. Then placing his hands on Hawthorn's head, he directed him under the water. When Hawthorn surfaced a few seconds later, he wasn't wearing the black robe anymore. A huge smile crossed his face as he walked back up the steps.

"You are now one of the Maker's children," said a voice at the top of the steps.

"Yeyeyeyeyeyeyeyeyeyiiii!!!" another terrific yell burst from the former Renegade in celebration for Hawthorn.

After Savin also completed the watery ceremony, a small crowd surrounded the three with great celebration. As Jay, Rush, and Marsh approached the happy group, Jay was surprised at the number of faces that he recognized. Charlock was there, along with Burdock and his mother and sister. Carineda was also there with her family. Jay saw several of the Makerian warriors he knew from their rescue.

Hawthorn and Savin looked a little sheepish when they saw Jay and Rush standing there, but when they found out that Rush was already a follower of Jehesus and that Jay wanted to be, they were elated. Almost everyone stayed to witness Jay take his first steps of submission to the Lord Jehesus.

"Master Blesstis," the former Renegade said, "you and Master Kordillon have been so good to me, and I am so happy. I don't want to trouble you, but I have a question."

"Your master is the Lord Jehesus, Snarl. Just call me Blesstis. What's your question?"

"I have a new life now, is that right?" Snarl asked thoughtfully.

"Yes, that's true," Blesstis answered reassuringly. "The Lord Jehesus has done away with your old life, and He's given you a new one to live for Him."

"Good!" Snarl answered. "That means I am not a Renegade anymore. Since Jehesus has taken away my Renegade life, can He take away my Renegade name also?"

"Well, sure He can, Snarl. What name would you like to have?"

"I am now a son of the Maker," Snarl said thoughtfully. "Master Jehesus has made me very glad. I think that is the name that I will wear to honor Him. I will be called *Gladson* from this day on."

"*Gladson* it is!" said Blesstis with a big grin. "Come on, Gladson; let me introduce you to all these folks."

CHAPTER TWENTY-FIVE

FAREWELLS

There was a quick series of knocks on the round cypress door. Taumis the Gentle strode purposefully over and opened it. "Hawthorn! Please come in."

"Hello, Sir Taumis. Thank you." Hawthorn stepped into the familiar living quarters, and Taumis closed the door behind him.

"I'm sorry you couldn't make it for supper tonight," Taumis continued. "You would have loved it. The girls outdid themselves this time."

"I'm sorry, too," Hawthorn returned earnestly. "But we had to meet with Charlock and Tobin this afternoon to plan for our return home tomorrow. As it turned out, we had a lot to talk about. We only just now got through."

"That's fine," Taumis said reassuringly. "We're just glad that we get to see you again before you leave. Please come in and sit down. There's someone here I want you to . . . ."

"H-a-a-a-t-o-r-n-n-n!!!" Taumis's youngest son came running across the room and launched himself into Hawthorn's arms.

"Ooof!" blew Hawthorn as he hurriedly grabbed for his little friend. "Robbie! How are you doing?"

"I'm doin'gweat!" Robbie answered with his usual enthusiasm. "Oh, Haatorn guess what?"

"What?" Hawthorn answered, setting the dark-haired little boy down and squatting next to him.

"Waken's here!"

"Who?"

"Waken! You know, my big bwudder. I tol' you about him."

"Oh, Raken!"

"That's what I said," Robbie returned, a little annoyed. "Come on! You gotta' meet him!"

Robbie grabbed Hawthorn's hand and began to drag him into their family room. In one of the high-backed chairs surrounding the big table, Hawthorn saw a dark-haired Makerian maybe two seasons older than himself.

"See, Haatorn, see! I tol' ya Waken was here. Hey, Waken, dis is Haatorn da Larkin. He's da one I tol' ya 'bout."

"Robbie," Taumis's voice was firm but not harsh. His youngest son immediately stopped and turned to face his father.

"Yes, suh."

"Thank you for making Hawthorn feel welcome," Taumis said, a faint smile causing his cheeks to rise. "Now I would like for you to go find your sisters and let them know that our guest has arrived."

"Oh, yes, suh!" Then releasing Hawthorn's hand, he sprinted through a nearby doorway. "Cawiii!!" Robbie's voice trailed away.

"Hawthorn," Taumis continued, still smiling, "I would like for you to meet my oldest son, Raken. He just returned last night from Patrol.

"Raken, this is Hawthorn, a hunter from the . . . uh . . . was it the Third Larkin Clan?"

"You have a good memory, Sir Taumis."

Raken stood to greet their guest. He was half-a-head taller than Hawthorn. He had a tanned face, wavy black hair, and an easy smile that reminded Hawthorn of Carineda's. As Raken approached him, Hawthorn saw that he was injured. There were two deep cuts on Raken's forehead, a dark bruise and a scratch on his left cheek, and his right arm was bandaged and placed in a sling.

"I was hoping that I would get to meet you," Raken said pleasantly. Raken extended his left hand to greet the young Larkin. There was an awkward moment as Hawthorn tried to figure out what to do with Raken's left hand. Finally, he extended his own left hand, clasping Raken's in the typical Makerian way. "My family has told me so much about you and your adventures," Raken continued.

"Well, I guess I have had a few adventures, " Hawthorn responded, a little embarrassed. "But I didn't go looking for them. They just, sort of, found me."

"That's not the way my little brother tells it," Raken said with the same mischievous expression that Hawthorn had seen more than once on Raken's oldest sister.

"Has Robbie been talking about me?" Hawthorn asked with a smile.

"You've made quite an impression on him," Raken returned. "He wants to grow up and be a great warrior like 'Haatorn da Larkin.'"

An involuntary laugh burst from Hawthorn's mouth. "He is so funny!" said Hawthorn, still laughing. "Believe me, Raken, I'm no warrior, and I'm not much of a hunter."

"Well, I just want you to know," the young Makerian said sincerely, "that any hero of Robbie's is a friend of mine."

"Thanks, Raken. I wish that you and I had been able to spend some time together."

As they all sat down at the table, Hawthorn asked, "How did you get hurt?"

"As my patrol was returning yesterday, we tried to kill a mooflon, but I got a little careless."

"Raken," Hawthorn responded, "you and I have a lot in common."

Soon the girls and Robbie entered, bringing mugs of warm, sweet nectar for everyone. As they all settled down around the table, Hawthorn began to tell them the plans for returning home.

"Aw, Haatorn. I was hoping you'd stay wif us."

"That's nice of you to say, Robbie. I'm really going to miss you a lot, but I need to go back to my home. I'm sure my mother is very worried about my father and me."

"Are you all going back?" Taumis asked.

"Yes, sir. I wasn't too sure about Rush and Jay at first. They really love this place, but they both feel a responsibility to get all of us back home safely. Also, I think they feel the same way my father and I do. We believe that the Maker worked all this out so that we could take the good news of Jehesus back to our people—at least to the ones who will listen."

"I don't think your Shaman will appreciate that," Taumis observed.

"We've decided not to declare our faith in Jehesus openly unless we have to. The four of us will form a secret clan of the Maker's children among our people. We will share our belief in the Lord Jehesus to only a select few and slowly build the Lord's clan among us."

"Don't you think Poke or Sycamore will give you away as soon as you get back?" asked Carineda.

"They don't know," Hawthorn answered. "Sycamore is still so confused from his head injury that he doesn't remember anything you tell him or what's happened to him. Poke is so worried about his father that he won't listen to anything I try to tell him about Jehesus."

"Well, maybe he doesn't know that the four of you are followers of Jehesus," Raken began, "but he does know that you've been with us. If he says anything to the Shaman about you being in contact with Makerians, then you'll be banished—or worse."

"I don't think he'll say anything," was Hawthorn's response.

"Why not?" Raken replied.

"That's one of the things Charlock talked to us about this afternoon. He told us that the Shaman are so suspicious of anyone who comes into contact with the Makerians that their response is to immediately banish them. He made sure Poke understood that's what happened to himself and Burdock's family."

"Did Poke listen to him?" Carineda asked.

"Yes. Charlock's story seemed to make a strong impression on him. Burdock was there also, and he assured Poke that his uncle was telling the truth. Charlock warned all of us that if we didn't want to be banished, we'd better not ever mention the Makerians to anyone."

"But what are you going to say when people ask you what happened?" asked ten-year-old Clarea. "You know they will, and then you'll have to tell them about us, unless . . . but you wouldn't lie, would you?"

"There was a time in my life, not very long ago, when I might have lied, but not now. The Lord Jehesus wouldn't want me to. But even though we will tell them the truth, we will not tell them all the facts. We have all agreed that when we are asked what happened, we will tell them that Poke and I were captured by the Renegades and made slaves. While trying to rescue us, my father, Sycamore, and Jay were also captured. Rush dressed up like a Renegade and slipped into the Lair. He spent several days collecting weapons and food for our escape. With his help we were able to get away. When the Renegades discovered that we had escaped, they tried to pursue us. We had to fight some of them, and that's when Sycamore received his head injury."

"All that's true," agreed Carineda.

"Right," Hawthorn smiled, "and not a single Makerian mentioned in the whole thing. We know trouble might come if the Shaman get suspicious and start asking a lot of questions about specific things. If that happens, we've agreed to trust in the Maker and tell the truth."

"We'll all be praying for you, Hawthorn," Taumis assured him.

Carineda and her sisters excused themselves to the kitchen and returned shortly with a huge bowl of plum pudding and a stack of smaller bowls for everyone. For awhile no one spoke as they savored the delicious treat. Raken had seconds; Hawthorn had thirds.

When Hawthorn had scraped every last morsel from his third bowl of pudding, he pushed his chair back. Thanking them profusely for the pudding and their kindness, he declared that he needed to be going. "I really don't want to go, but we're supposed to leave at first light in the morning, and we're trying to get to bed early tonight."

"Before you leave, Hawthorn, we have something that we want you to take with you back to your home." It was Taumis who was speaking. "Robbie, would you go get our gift to Hawthorn?"

"Yes, suh!" the little boy exclaimed and darted into the next room. In a moment, he returned carrying a long, straight stick that resembled a fighting staff.

"Thanks, Robbie!" Hawthorn said sincerely as his little friend handed him the stick. Examining it and feeling its weight, Hawthorn gripped it firmly in both hands. "I'll use this staff to protect myself on the way home," he said to Robbie.

"All of your weapons of Makerian design you'll have to leave here so that none of your people will suspect that you've been among us," Taumis said.

"When we get close to the Keep, we'll have to change back into our old, tattered clothes also," added Hawthorn.

"We wanted you to have a weapon you could carry back with you that didn't look like it came from here," continued Taumis. "But this is a specially made staff."

"It has a secret," smiled Cari. "Let me show you."

She picked up a small table knife and walked over to Hawthorn. Examining the staff close to one end, she pointed out a small, circular spot that looked like a scar where a little branch had been cut off. "You'll have to use a small stick or the point of a knife to work it," she said as she pushed the circular spot with the point of her own knife. This spot was actually a wooden peg embedded in the staff. When it was pushed in, it allowed the upper end of the staff to be twisted off, revealing a hollowed-out chamber. Hawthorn saw that some rolled up sheets of parchment had been placed in the chamber. He pulled the parchments out of their hiding place, and unrolling them, Hawthorn spread the sheets out on the table in front of him. The sheets were covered front and back with small, very neat writing.

"Wead it, Haatorn! Wead it!" cried Robbie, bouncing up and down.

Hawthorn bent close to examine the writing. He studied it intently for several long moments. Suddenly Hawthorn took in an audible gasp and straightened up, looking wide-eyed at first Cari, then Taumis. "These are the

Maker's holy words," he said with astonishment, "and they are written in the Larkin language!"

"We know you'll always remember what Jehesus has done for you," Taumis said, "but we wanted you to carry some of His words with you also."

"This is a priceless treasure!" Hawthorn said, looking with awe at the written words before him. "I can't believe you did this for me."

"Father had one of the scribes translate the Maker's words into writing that you could read," Cari added. "The parchment is so thick that we could only fit five rolled-up sheets into the staff's hiding place. So we had to pick out just the verses we thought you would need the most. By keeping them rolled up and hidden in your staff, no one will know you have them."

"But what if the staff gets wet?" Hawthorn said with concern in his voice. "Then the parchments will be ruined!"

"The hidden compartment fits together so tightly that no water can get in," Taumis smiled.

After rolling up the sheets, replacing them in their hiding place, and reattaching the end on the staff, Hawthorn looked up to face his dear friends. "This is such a wonderful gift. I owe your family so much. Thank you, thank you all! I will never forget you."

"You'd better not," said Cari with her sly smile, "or I'll have to come see how good you are with that staff."

"Oh, yeah?!" said Robbie, jumping to his feet. "He's Haatorn da Laawkin, Cawi, and he'll fight 'chu anytime! Right, Haatorn?!"

"Robbie, there is no way I'm getting into a staff fight with your sister."

"Oh, come on, Haatorn! You can take her!"

"Are you kidding? Have you seen what she can do with a staff? She'd clobber me!"

"Well . . . ," said the little boy thoughtfully, "maybe you could sneak up on her."

"It was sure hard saying goodbye to Burdock and his family," Jay said as he stood on the shore of Stillwaters, adjusting the backpack he had just retrieved from the Makerian paddle barge. The air was crisp and cool. Streaks of morning light were just beginning to crease the dark blue sky above the cypress trees on the eastern shore of the lake.

"It was hard to say goodbye to a lot of people there," Hawthorn said sadly as he gazed across the water to the dark outline of the Makerian Refuge.

"The sooner we're away from all this and back home, the better I'll like it," grumbled Poke as he grabbed his and Sycamore's packs. The others watched as the young Larkin carried the two packs a short distance away to where his father was sitting on a patch of moss with a confused look on his face.

"Try not to let him get to you, Son," Savin said, softly placing his hand on Hawthorn's shoulder. "He's confused and worried about his father. Once we're back home, and Sycamore is better, Poke will think differently about all this."

"Yeah, Hawthorn," Jay agreed encouragingly. "He'll come around."

"Well, lookie what I found!" exclaimed an approaching voice. "It appears our shore is overrun with an infestation of Larkin!"

"Eldan!" cried Hawthorn happily as he saw his approaching friend. "I wasn't sure I was going to get to see you before we left. They told us that you and Tobin had left the refuge in the middle of the night on some mission."

"The truth is, Chummy, Bubsy's the one on the mission. He just asked me to help him get the big saddle on his squirrel. He's supposed to be meeting one of our Ranger troops at sunup over across the meadow where you fellas hid your whirlers."

"I wondered how they were going to get those things back here," Hawthorn said.

"Well, being the fine, upstanding Bubsy that he is, he agreed to haul 'em back on his squirrel."

"I'm sorry we're not going to get to say goodbye to him," Hawthorn said sadly.

"Oh, it's just as well, Chums. Tobs is just a sentimental ol' fuzzy head. If he was here and you fellas were to start saying a bunch of nice stuff about him, why, he'd probably break down and start blubberin' like a baby.

"Oh, I just remembered. Tobs gave me a little speech for you." Eldan cleared his throat two or three times, stood as tall and straight as he could, and made a very serious, almost scowling face. "'My good friends,'" Eldan began as he attempted to impersonate his older brother, "'I'm sorry I could not see you off. I pray the Maker's blessings on each of you, and may you arrive home safely. Farewell, and may the Lord Jehesus be with you all.'

"Hee, hee, hee," Eldan giggled as he finished. "Now isn't that just classic Tobs? The boy has a good heart, but he has no imagination."

"You tell him *goodbye* for each of us and that we're going to miss him. We're going to miss you too, Eldan," Hawthorn said.

"Now don't get all mushy on me, Chummy. Besides, Bubsy and I will be around. I taught Wretch some of the caller signals Tobs and I use to call each other."

"He shor' did," Rush added. "Floppy also showed me how to make one of them caller things he uses."

"See, Chummy? You can call us whenever you need us."

"Say, Floppy," Rush said. "You said you were gonna see about getting me one of those fire startin' rocks."

"You mean like this one?" Eldan pulled one of the dark grey stones out of his pouch.

"I knew you wouldn't let me down," Rush said with a big grin. "Hand it here."

"Now wait a minute, Wretch," cautioned Eldan as he pulled back the rock. "If I give you this and someone asks where you got it, you'd be in trouble. So you're gonna' have to find your own."

"Now where am I supposed to find one of those?!" Rush growled.

Eldan tossed the fire stone under a nearby oak leaf. "Try looking under that leaf."

"Are you coming with us, Eldan?" Hawthorn asked.

"I'd love to, Chums, I sure would. But I've got big things goin' on. I'm supposed to appear before the Ranger Council tomorrow. I think Tobs has about convinced 'em to promote me to a lieutenant . . . again."

"Again?" Hawthorn questioned.

"This will be the third time," Eldan admitted sheepishly. "But now, that last demotion wasn't totally my fault. I had no idea that stinkbug was gonna get excited in the middle of the counsel meeting."

"So," said Hawthorn, trying not to laugh, "do you think you'll make lieutenant again?"

"Tobs says that if I let him do the talking, I'll probably make it, but with a probation period."

"So are you gonna' let yer brother do the talkin'?" Rush asked.

"Probably not," Eldan grinned. "Besides, I've been a second-season Ranger off and on for four seasons now, and I kind of like it."

"Sling packs, Rangers!" a voice shouted in the distance.

"Ah reckon it's time fer us to be a goin'," Rush said. He extended his hand to Eldan in the Makerian fashion. Eldan gripped his friend's hand firmly and shook it with feeling. Then releasing Rush's hand, Eldan reached up and grasped Rush's forearm in the Larkin manner.

Rush smiled at his good-natured friend. "You'll see me again, Floppy. Me and Jay have already decided—some day we're comin' back."

Rush jerked up his pack and slung it across his shoulders, "Come on, fellers," Rush barked. "Our troop's aheadin' home."

"Thanks for everything, Eldan!" Jay said, shaking Eldan's hand.

"I guess this is goodbye, Eldan. I'll never be able to thank you for all you've done!" Hawthorn said as he gripped Eldan's hand and looked warmly at his friend.

Eldan opened his mouth to say something, but nothing came out.

Savin also stepped up and put a hand on Eldan's shoulder. "Eldan," Savin began with feeling, "there was a time when I thought I'd never see my son again. But the Maker raised you up to save his life for his mother and me. I am deeply grateful for what you've done."

Eldan's face and ears were now a deep, red color. His lower lip began to quiver, and large tears began to form in the corners of his eyes. "Oh . . . Sir Savin, sir!" was all he could get out.

As he saw his friends marching away, he tried to control himself enough to speak his parting words. "Farewell!" Eldan squeaked. "And may the Lord Jehesus be with you!"

-THE END-